Clairvoyant
Mike Nelson

Writing has been a driving force in my life since I was young. Among other things, I fancy myself a dreamer and a storyteller. Writing is what I do when I find a little time in my life. While my family was young, I didn't find a lot of that. Now that I have retired and have an empty nest, I have finally found a little time to daydream. I often retire to the quiet recesses of my home, where I work to finish the stories that have often haunted me for years.

I would like to dedicate this, my third published novel, to my wife, Donnell. She has supported me and allowed me the time and the personal space I need to do what I do. She is the love of my life, my best friend, my confidant, my mentor, and my most loyal fan. Without her, I would be nothing.

Preface

Every story I write has some of me in it. *Clairvoyant* is no different. Ever since I can remember, I have been a dreamer, both in my conscious moments and while I'm sleeping.

The dreams I have while I'm conscious could best be described as those I create during my mental free time. They could be called daydreams, wild imaginings, whatever—and they always occur during my waking hours when I can control their content, subject, and outcome.

The other dreams I have come to me while I'm asleep, and generally involve three basic types of dreams. The first are what I call nonsensical dreams. These are dreams that often invade my sleep and, if I awake to remember them, leave me confused—sometimes disturbed—but absolutely convinced that what just occurred in my mind made absolutely no sense whatsoever.

The next are those everybody has: nightmares. These are the dreams that sometimes bring you out of a deep sleep screaming because someone or something in your dream has either done something awful to you or is about to. Hopefully, we wake up before that happens, but the mental effect can often dog you for hours or days afterward.

The final type I want to talk about is dreams that actually come true.

For as long as I can remember, I've have had these types of dreams, although none of them have been life changing or especially noteworthy. Most often, I wake in the morning knowing that I have dreamed one of "those" dreams, but I can't remember much of anything that took place. Then days, weeks, or even months later, I'll suddenly "know" that I've seen something that is about to happen.

I believe the term for what happens next is referred to by some as déjà vu. For a few brief seconds or even minutes, I know exactly what is going to happen. I recognize people, places, things, even actions I know could have never happened before—and yet I've seen what is about to transpire. If I could freeze-frame the situation, I could point out exactly who is going to be involved and what is going to happen.

One of the most memorable of these experiences happened when I was twenty years old. I had enlisted in the United States Air Force and was assigned to a communications intelligence base in northwestern Turkey. A couple of months prior to reporting to my new duty station, I woke up one night, having had one of "those" dreams. I couldn't remember a thing about it, only that when I woke up, I felt uncomfortable—even a little disturbed. But I had no real recollection why.

Now fast-forward two months. My flight landed at Istanbul International Airport. From there, I was to take a military transport bus to my new base. Part of that journey involved a ferryboat ride across the Bosphorus, a narrow stretch of water separating the Asian and European sides of Istanbul. All of us piled out of the bus and climbed to the top deck of the ferryboat to take in the sights as we sailed across.

The second I turned to look back at the Asian side of Istanbul, the recollection hit me like a ton of bricks. Even though there was no way I could have ever seen the Istanbul skyline before, I knew instantly that I had. Not even a photograph or a series of panoramic photographs could have done justice to the magnificence of what lay there before me in living technicolor!

The "living vision" lasted for several minutes as I turned my head from side to side and took in everything that lay there before me. Several magnificent mosques, with their domed architecture, literally glowed in the sunlight amongst the sprawling city that stretched from the vivid blue of the strait to the cluttered tops of several surrounding hilltops. The sight took my breath away, and yet felt all so very familiar, because I'd seen it before. It wasn't until that moment that I realized why I'd felt uncomfortable or disturbed the morning after my dream. Quite simply, what I was seeing was totally foreign, completely beyond anything I had ever experienced before. And yet, in its own rite, it was utterly awe inspiring.

What, you ask, does this have to do with *Clairvoyant*? As you read the story, you'll learn that my main character has experienced the same phenomena—but as the result of a horrific accident, he has suddenly had that mental ability enhanced a thousand-fold.

A little of the premise of this story is based on actual happenings. There have been recorded instances where clairvoyance in some form or other has actually occurred in the aftermath of a horrific incident, usually involving a severe electrical shock. The rest of the story is a figment of my imagination. Here is where I follow the theory of clairvoyance into ordinary life. What, for instance, would your significant other do if you could suddenly hear his or her thoughts and feel their emotions? What could you do to aid police work? How would criminals react to what you can do?

Most of us believe that reading thought is only something God can do (if of course, you believe there is a God). I believe that if we live with any dishonesty in our lives, the premise of mind reading would be totally unacceptable and frightening. But if, on the other hand, we could be totally honest in our interpersonal relationships, where there could be no misunderstandings in our communications, what would life be like? Would verbal communication even be necessary? Could our society survive, or would we destroy each other? Given the mortal state of man, I unfortunately believe that the latter would be the case.

Chapter 1
The Accident

Scott reached for consciousness. There was no intelligent thought, only existence and pain. He was aware of his own breathing—at least it seemed to be his. He felt like little more than a tiny point of light smothered under tons of flesh he knew must be his own body.

A blinding flash of light filled his mind. It seared him but brought no pain. Then it vanished as suddenly as it had come. He waited. It came again, this time from another direction, but with less intensity. A muffled cacophony of sounds passed around him like a soft summer breeze. He strained, listening intently for something he could understand. Nothing made sense.

The sounds slowly ceased. Blackness smothered him.

He dreamed. A young woman's face stared at him from the shining surface of a mirror. It was as if he were seeing through her eyes. He watched as a slender hand appeared in the mirror and gently dabbed a washcloth against the ugly purple bruise that darkened her right eye. The flesh was split open above her eyebrow. Blood oozed from the wound's tattered edges. He could feel her fear.

In spite of the ugly wound, she was beautiful.

The young woman turned, and the mirror suddenly swung away, out of sight. Fear paralyzed her. It choked Scott, too, as if it were his own. A man strode quickly toward her. He held a knife high over his head. She screamed and raised her arm in a futile attempt to block the blow. The man knocked her arm away with a huge left hand and plunged the knife into her chest. He stabbed her again and again. Bright-red blood sprayed across the man's light-blue shirt. Her emotions faded. The vision darkened and went black.

Waves of panic swept over Scott. He tried to cry out but couldn't. Then, faintly, through all the horror, he recognized Mary's voice. She was speaking, but he couldn't understand what she was saying.

He tried to relax. He felt pressure around his wrists and ankles. He was bound. He opened his eyes but saw nothing. He tried to fight the restraints. Mary's voice came again, louder this time, and now he understood what she was saying.

"Easy, Scott. You're okay."

He tried to speak. A tube clogged his throat. He tried to jerk an arm upward to tear it away, but the restraint around his wrist held his arm fast.

"Leave it alone, Scott," Mary ordered. "You're okay. Don't try to talk. You're on a ventilator."

Scott's mind raced. His senses began returning, a dozen at a time. He hurt in a million places all at once. Some hurts screamed for relief. Others merely throbbed. A huge moan formed in his chest. The tube in his throat refused to give it utterance.

Mary sensed his struggle and began talking quickly, quietly in his ear.

"You were in a bad accident," she said. "You broke some ribs, and your lungs collapsed. You have a chest tube to draw fluid away from your lungs, and they put a tube down your throat so you can breathe. Don't fight it. You'll be okay."

He relaxed as much as the pain would allow and waited for the rest of the explanation he knew would follow.

"Your eyes will be okay," Mary said calmly. "They had to take out a bunch of glass slivers. They put patches over your eyes so you won't try to look around."

She hesitated before she went on.

"You're okay," she told him again. "You took a nasty blow to the head, and for a while they thought you'd have some brain damage. But your vitals have been really good the last couple of days, so they think you'll fully recover."

Her words hung in his mind.

The last couple of days? How long had he been here?

"Calm down, Scott," Mary ordered again. "Just relax. Don't fight."

He could feel her cool fingers on his cheek. Her other hand held the fingers of his right hand firmly against the bed.

A huge sigh of relief formed inside him, only to be refused utterance again by the lousy tube. *Good old Mary,* he thought fondly. *It's as if she knows what I'm thinking.*

Thoughts of her wafted through his conscious mind. She'd been good for him. Their eighteen years together had been the happiest years of his life. He tried to smile. He'd been twenty-two when they met, and was still twenty-two when they married. Their courtship had hardly been a courtship at all. Barely five weeks had slipped by between their introduction and their marriage. Sure, there'd been

11

challenges, but . . .

"The other driver's car insurance will probably cover most of the bills," Mary said, interrupting his thoughts. "They tell me you're really lucky to be alive."

Scott had never felt so much like talking. Frustration colored his cheeks. He could feel the soft flutter of Mary's long hair against his face as she leaned in close.

"I love you, Scott," she whispered. "I don't know what I'd ever do without you."

He sensed her emotions as if they were his own. They welled up inside of him. Tears flowed out from under his eye patches and ran down his cheeks.

"Are you hurting?" she asked, dabbing at his tears with a soft tissue. "Try to relax. I'll get the nurse."

Seconds later, an intercom crackled.

"Yes, Mrs. Corbridge, how can I help you?"

"My husband is conscious," Mary said, "but I think he's in a lot of pain. Could he have some medication?"

"I believe so," the voice answered. "I'll check his chart, and we'll bring him something. I'll call his doctor and let him know he's conscious."

Scott winced at the thought of needles; he hated them. He knew it would have to be a needle. His mouth was full of plastic. He couldn't possibly swallow a pill.

"Jess and John are staying with my mother," Mary said as she sensed his increasing tension. "Trish has to work three nights this week, so I let her stay home alone. She promised me she wouldn't let Brandon come around while I was gone. I know that may not mean much, but I think that under the circumstances, she'll keep her word."

Scott relaxed as he heard her talk about their children. Their first child, Patricia Lynn, (Trish for short) had been a handful from the time she was born. First came colic, then the terrible twos. Then, after what seemed too short a reprieve, came her teens . . . and boyfriends. Trish had attracted boys from the time she was ten. She was beautiful, like her mother. Scott had never been comfortable around her friends, especially her male friends. He naturally assumed that every boy came to his home with one purpose in mind, and it wasn't to do homework or any of the other lame things Trish could dream up. As a result, his relationship with her had been testy at its best.

His two boys, Jess and John, were different. They had been a godsend. They were only a year apart, and early on they had pretty much entertained each other. As a result, they didn't need to be coddled, and they didn't get into much trouble. Neither were teenagers yet, though, so the jury was still out on them.

Scott became aware of another presence in the room even before he caught a whiff of her perfume. Her clothes rustled as she approached. She said nothing. There was no needle stick, but the medication burned as it entered his arm.

There must be an IV, he thought.

As the drug eased his pain, his body relaxed. A few moments later, he drifted back into a sleepy stupor.

When he awoke, the throat tube was gone, and so was Mary. Even without being able to see, he knew she wasn't in the room. His mouth and throat were parched, and although he could taste a salve of some sort on his lips, they were cracked and swollen. He tried to lift an arm to touch his face, only to find it still attached firmly to the side of the bed.

He lay still for a long time, listening to the sounds around him. There didn't seem to be anyone else in the room. What sounds did reach him were muffled and soft.

The door to the hallway must be closed.

He wondered where Mary was, and the thought of her brought a dawning realization.

I didn't just hear her talk, he thought. *I could feel her emotions. And I knew it was her standing beside the bed, even before I heard her voice.*

Something inside of him had changed. Even without the ability to see, he knew there was no one else in the room with him. He lay still, concentrating on every small sound, listening carefully for anything that might indicate the time of day by the traffic in the hallway,

The dream flashed through his mind again—the dream of the woman in the mirror. Was it a dream? It almost seemed too real. He was fully conscious. He knew it because he could hear the sound of his fingernails scraping against the sheet as he clenched his fists and felt its texture beneath his fingertips.

The scenes of the dream played out in his mind, unrestrained, the same as before. Every detail of the woman's face burned deep into his memory. He knew exactly what she would see as she spun away from the mirror. He knew the face of her assailant as well as he knew the face of his own father.

Scott tried to drive the apparition away but it continued. Only this time, there was more. This time, he saw her body, but not through the reflection in the mirror. This time, it was as if he was seeing it through the eyes of someone standing above the woman's body. Blood was everywhere. The killer worked feverishly, wrapping the body in a flowered sheet. Perspiration hung on his brow and dripped from his chin as he worked.

Scott tried to look away but couldn't. The element of time fled. The horrific event continued to play on, seeming to merge with his consciousness as if he were witnessing it in person. Each event became a separate entity, like paintings hung from a museum wall. At a glance, he could see them in sequence: her face in the mirror, the assailant, the murder, the car's trunk as her body was stuffed inside, a shallow grave where she was buried.

Just before the vision faded, Scott focused on an old stone well. He saw it for only a brief instant, and yet he knew there was something significant about it. Then the images faded.

He lay still for a long time, terrorized by what he had seen. This was real. It was no dream. He'd had dreams since he was a child. This was more like a vision—an event in time seen through someone else's eyes. Could this horrible event have actually happened?

He searched his mind for a similar event he might have seen in a movie or read in a book. There was nothing. Nothing except for the memory of a documentary he'd seen years ago about clairvoyants.

He remembered two cases in particular—both of them men. One had been struck by lightning; the other had been accidentally electrocuted. Both had been normal before. Both had survived. And afterward, inexplicably, both had been able to see and know things beyond explanation.

One part of Scott wanted to see the vision again. He wanted more details: a name, a place, something concrete. Another part of him wanted nothing more to do with it. It was one thing to watch it happen, like watching a scene in a movie. The real horror came in actually feeling the woman's emotions as it was happening. He could still feel her terror and her sense of loss and hopelessness as she watched her own body being buried in the dark, damp earth.

Scott forced himself to think of other dreams he'd had. They were not the same.

He remembered Mary's words. He'd suffered a blow to the head. How bad a blow was it? Could a smack on the head have caused him to experience strange visions? Or was it all the result of a drug-induced nightmare? As he latched onto that thought, he slept again.

The next time he awoke, there was noise all around him. He was aware of three people in the room, one of whom was Mary. His eyes were still bandaged, yet he knew she was there. Thirst ravaged his mouth and throat. He opened his mouth to speak but no sound came. He tried to swallow, only to feel the parched tissues in his throat stick together. He parted his lips and thrust his thick tongue between them.

"Scott?" Mary asked in a low voice. "Are you awake?"

He nodded his head.

"Are you hurting?" she asked, concern coloring her question.

He remembered losing consciousness shortly after his last dose of medication. As bad as he was hurting, he didn't want that again—not until he had some answers. He slowly shook his head from side to side. He thrust his tongue out again.

"You're thirsty," Mary said matter-of-factly. "The doctor said you can only have ice chips until your bowels start working again and you're strong enough to sit up so you won't choke."

Ice had never sounded so good. Scott nodded and tried to smile. He felt his upper lip split and burn.

He heard Mary pull a lid off a nearby container. The promising clatter of ice tantalized his senses. Moments later, a welcome cold sting burned his swollen lips. He lay still and relished the sensation as the ice melted and wonderfully cold water trickled slowly over his thick, dry tongue.

He became aware of another indignity. He'd never had a catheter before. Embarrassed, he wondered who had put it in. His head throbbed, as did his chest, and particularly his right knee.

"The doctor said it would be a day or two before you could talk," Mary said, seeming anxious to answer his unasked questions. "The ventilator bruised you a little." She paused, searching for a place to continue. "They moved you out of intensive care last night. You're doing a lot better than anyone expected."

Scott struggled briefly against the bonds that held his arms down.

"I'll undo the straps if you promise to be a good boy," Mary said.

Scott heard the sharp rasp of Velcro as she freed his right hand. He reached out for her. She took his hand in hers and touched it to her lips.

"It's so good to know you're going to be okay," she said as she drew the knuckles of his hand across her soft, warm lips.

He tried to raise his right leg.

"Oh, yes," she said as if it were no big deal, "your knee took out part of the dashboard, and, well, it sort of took off your kneecap. The surgeon said he did the best he could, but you'll need some more surgery and a lot of physical therapy."

Scott sighed. He wondered what else she hadn't told him.

Mary picked up on his frustrated sigh. "The best news is the swelling in your brain has gone down, and there's apparently no permanent damage."

She brushed his forehead softly with her fingertips.

"You really messed up the car, I might add." A light chuckle hid just beneath her understatement. They'd had several frank discussions over one another's respective driving habits, and Scott found it ironic that it was he who'd been first to crack up the car.

He had no memory of the accident. He strained to remember. As he concentrated, he felt her frustration. Her emotions again became his. It was almost as if he had stepped into her soul. It scared him. He quickly moved the fingers of his left hand and concentrated on the sensations that tingled through his own fingertips. The diversion worked, and their emotions parted.

"Jess really misses you," Mary said. "He insists I tell him everything."

Scott wondered again how long he'd been this way. She spoke of the days as if there had been several. He worried. They didn't have much of a health care plan.

He thought back to when he'd still worked for Rogers Architecture. The health care had been great, but his freedom had been worth much more. The past year, the first out on his own, had been tough. There was a lot to be said for having a steady paycheck and a cushy benefits package. His co-workers had wished him well, but he knew most of them thought he was crazy to start a business of his own. The way Scott figured it, he still had nearly twenty-five good years until he was sixty-five, and he was sick of marching to the beat of someone else's drum.

"Trish and I had quite a talk a couple of nights ago," Mary said after a short pause. "We really talked for the first time in months. She actually apologized for being such a pain in the butt. Can you imagine that?"

Scott could feel her emotions—the joy of finally being allowed to be part of Trish's life.

"I think she's finally becoming human again," Mary said.

Scott's eyes watered as her emotions flowed through him.

"I'm afraid to ask why she's changed," she said after a long pause. "I think she may be having sex. She and Brandon have been spending a lot of time together."

A flash of rage streaked through Scott. Brandon wasn't exactly what he wanted in a son-in-law. He was three years older than Trish, but at twenty, hardly old enough to be considering marriage. The thoughts of Brandon doing the wild thing with his daughter were intolerable, even if it did mellow out Trish's behavior.

"I don't know whether or not to get her on the pill," Mary said. "I'm afraid if they're not having sex, it might encourage her. You know, sort of tell her that I approve of what she's doing. On the other hand, the last thing I want is for her to get pregnant. They're both way too young."

She paused.

"This is really hard, Scott. I wish you could answer me. I wish I could see your eyes. I can always tell if you're upset when I look in your eyes."

A long silence passed between them. Scott's emotions settled a little, and as he set his rage aside, he could feel Mary's concern. She needed his reassurance. He could feel the warmth of her fingers in his. He gently squeezed her hand.

"Thank you," she whispered. "I hope you're not mad. After all, I wasn't an angel myself when I was her age, and I turned out okay."

Her confession struck him hard. Their courtship had been short, passionate, and intimate. He'd never met anyone so uninhibited, so giving, and so easy to love. He'd wondered many times if there'd been others before him, but the subject had never come up in their eighteen years together. He wasn't particularly jealous, but then she'd never given him reason to be.

"I was about Trish's age my first time," she said. "I thought I was in love. I thought he was, too. I was wrong. I was lucky. I thank God I didn't have a baby when I met you. My life would be nothing without you."

She caressed his cheek with her fingertips.

Scott searched her emotions. He felt her love for him. Suddenly, what she may have done and who she may have been before they met no longer mattered. He drew a deep, slow, cleansing breath and tried to relax.

Mary spoke to him for a while, then grew quiet. He could tell she was exhausted. He reached for her chin, a gesture he often used to convey what he couldn't say in words. She leaned forward to lay her chin in his open palm. He cradled her chin between his fingers for a few seconds, then pulled his hand away and waved goodbye to her.

"Are you sure you don't want me to stay with you tonight?" she asked softly.

He waved again, then sought her hand. She squeezed his fingers gently and leaned down to kiss him on the cheek.

"Thank you," she sighed softly. "I'm exhausted. Can I call the nurse for you before I leave?"

Scott shook his head slowly.

"Well, I'm going to pin your call button to your sheet so you can reach it," she said. "Don't be a hero. They'll give you all the medication you want."

Long after Mary had gone, Scott lay thinking about their life together. The good thoughts helped drive his physical pain back to a tolerable level. Then he became aware of another person in the room with him. The soft rhythm of a ventilator echoed across the room. Scott listened and concentrated, searching for the other person's emotions, but other than knowing there was someone there, he felt nothing.

Depression began to close in around him. He'd seen places like this before. This was the head trauma unit—the place they often put people who'd been turned into vegetables in one way or another. As he wondered what his silent roommate's prognosis was, he turned his thoughts to himself.

How much mental capacity had he lost in the crash? He needed his motor skills. He needed to be able to work. He wished he could talk. If he could hear himself talk, he'd know if there was any obvious damage.

At that moment, another presence entered the room and moved toward him. Scott raised his hand in gesture. He had to show them that he was coherent.

"Ah, Scott," a male voice greeted him. "I see that you're feeling better this evening."

Scott recognized the voice of his family physician, Dr. Gilbert, and mouthed a word to respond. His vocal chords refused to cooperate.

"No, don't try to talk," Dr. Gilbert said good-naturedly. "After two weeks with a tube down your throat, that's got to be a painful if not impossible."

Scott mulled over the doctor's words. Although Mary had never said so, he had evidently been in a coma for two weeks. At first, he worried about how much of his memory he'd lost and then relaxed as he realized he still was capable of intelligent thought. He wished he could remember the accident—then decided he was glad he couldn't.

"Let's have a peak at those eyes," Dr. Gilbert said.

Scott felt him lift the bandages. He closed his eyes tightly, fearing the worst.

"Come, now," the doctor said, "I can't see anything with your eyes slammed shut like that."

Scott cautiously opened one eye. Even the dim light in the room caused the tears to flow.

The doctor held Scott's eyelids open. A blinding stab of light pierced his eye, and a dim memory came back to him. He'd seen that stabbing light before. The sensations he felt after first becoming conscious now made sense.

"Now the other one," Dr. Gilbert said.

The penlight stabbed deep into his right eye.

"They're both coming along nicely," the doctor said as he pulled his fingers away. "There's going to be a little scarring on the left lens, but I'll refer you to a specialist I know. With a little laser work, I think we can completely eliminate that. I want you to wear the eye patches for another day or so, just the same. I don't want you to look around a lot. It aggravates your eyes and impedes healing. We'll take another look at your ribs and your skull in the morning, but from what I can see from your vitals, you're healing nicely."

Scott wished he could ask about his knee. He lay still while the doctor slipped the eye patches back in place.

"I also want you to leave your restraints in place for another day or so," Dr. Gilbert said as he pulled the Velcro straps back over Scott's free hand. "With a head wound like that, sometimes we see a few seizures. You really don't want to fall out of bed."

Scott's back and backside ached, not from injuries as much as from having been in one position for so long.

"I'll have the nurse bring you a little something to help you sleep, and I'll see you tomorrow morning," Dr. Gilbert said before he left.

Scott felt the doctor leave. A few moments later, someone else entered. He sensed the person was male, but without his sight and without a hint of perfume or cologne to give them away, he could only guess. Scott felt the burn in his arm as the man injected the medication into the IV. Then he left without saying a word.

Scott wished he could tell the man he wasn't the usual head case. Somehow, considering the person lying in the bed across the room from him, that mattered. A few thoughts later, consciousness left him again.

Two nurses—one male, the other female—descended on him. It seemed only a few moments had passed, but from the sounds around him, Scott figured it had to be morning. They stripped him, washed him from head to toe, and rolled him onto a gurney while they changed his bed linens. Then, without re-dressing him, they draped a sheet over him and wheeled him out of the room. He tried to keep track of how many turns they made but soon lost count. His trip ended in what he presumed to be the X-ray lab. There was someone already in the room when he arrived.

"Slide him off on the table," a female voice said. "Does he need to be restrained?"

"Don't know," a male voice answered. "He was tied down in his room, but there's no mention of it on his charts."

Scott raised his right wrist and waved his hand back and forth.

"Hi, Scott," the woman said. "I see you're awake today. That's good. The last time I saw you, you were really a mess. Can you talk?"

Scott opened his dry mouth and tried. A few croaks were all he could manage.

"I see they've still got you hooked up to an IV," she continued, "so I doubt they've given you anything to eat or drink yet. Your voice should come back as soon as they do that."

Scott had never wanted to eat so badly in his life. He responded as well as he could to each of her commands as she set him up for each X-ray. In a few short minutes, he was done.

"I'm really glad to see you're doing so well," the woman said as she helped another person slide him back onto the gurney. "The first time I saw you, I didn't think you had a chance."

Her words, and the words he'd heard spoken indirectly to him, settled over him as they wheeled him back to his room. He felt pain, but until then he hadn't really considered how badly he must have been hurt. Even though he couldn't remember a thing about the accident, he felt lucky.

Long after they left him alone with the silent person in the next bed, thought after thought rambled through his mind. Mostly, he thought about his family. Feelings of guilt crept over him as he realized how often he'd taken Mary for granted. He had never cheated on her, but he hadn't done much to keep their love fresh and alive, either.

He thought about his children. For the most part, he realized he'd mostly ignored them. That was easy to do now that they were older. After all, they didn't need diaper changes or spoon-feeding anymore, and they didn't often throw temper tantrums. In fact, now that he thought about it, there wasn't much they needed him for. Mary had mostly raised them from the time they were little. He had always been too busy doing the *man* thing.

He thought about Trish. He barely knew her. She was slim, attractive like her mother, and quick-witted. Despite the multiple ear piercings, pink hair, and wild clothes, she was a good kid. She ran with friends that looked as bad as or worse than she did, but she had never brought home anything less than a B on her report cards, and he'd never had reason to suspect her of being tangled up with drugs.

He worried over her relationship with Brandon. The kid had opted to go to work after he graduated from high school rather than go to trade school or college. Scott knew it would only be natural for Brandon to be pressing Trish for marriage. Scott hated the idea. Trish was way too young. He recalled Mary's words from the night before. The thought of someone touching his daughter enraged him.

John crossed his mind next. He pictured his impossible cowlick and infectious smile. The boy wanted to be doing all the exciting things twelve-year-olds do. He'd asked Scott if he would go to Boy Scout summer camp with him, but Scott had never been much of a camper. He remembered how well John had hidden his disappointment when Scott was unable to go. It was only later that Mary told him how disappointed the boy had been.

And then there was Jess, a strapping lad of eleven, big-boned and larger than his older brother, but infinitely more tender hearted. Scott suddenly hurt inside from the realization that although he had two sons, he didn't really know either of them.

"Are you awake?" he heard Mary say.

Scott nodded his head.

"Let me undo those blasted restraints," she said as she hurried around the side of his bed. She lifted the sheets and laughed. "Why, Mr. Corbridge! I see you're naked beneath your sheets. Have you no shame, or have you been fooling around with the nurses behind my back?"

Scott smiled. It felt good to have her there. He so wished he could talk.

"I see your gown is right here by the bed. If you'll help me a little, I think I can manage to make you decent."

Scott did what little he could to lift this part or that as Mary carefully slipped the cool fabric of the hospital gown over his body.

"Your bruises have all turned yellow and green," she said. "I think that's a good sign. You wouldn't want to fool around, would you?"

Her words slammed into his mind. In their eighteen years together, she'd quite often said those words. He instantly forgot his injuries. He longed to see her face. He was sure she was mocking him. He caught her arm as she worked over him. She showed no resistance as he pulled her close. She kissed him softly on the lips. In comparison to the ever-present pain, the sensation was heavenly.

"The doctor caught me in the hall," Mary said as she gently pulled away and tugged the last of his hospital gown in place around his battered right leg. "He tells me your recovery has been nothing less than miraculous. You get your first real meal today. Of course, you won't like it much. I believe it's a little beef broth and some green Jell-O."

Scott winced. He hated both.

Mary chortled, teasing him again. "Really, though," she said, "I can feed you all the ice you can handle and a little warm tea if you feel up to it."

Scott nodded his agreement.

"Your lips look terrible. Let me get you some ChapStick."

The touch of the ointment against his parched lips soothed him in a miraculous way. He had no idea that such a simple thing could feel so great.

Mary held ice cube after ice cube for him while she recited the events since his accident. Their insurance company had recovered a nice sum from the other driver's insurance. It would be enough to not only replace their car but would also be enough to cover most of the medical bills.

Next, she rehashed what a police officer had told her about the accident, but strangely, even though he wanted to know the particulars, he barely heard her words. He had merged with her emotions again. When she spoke of what the car had looked like, he felt her fear. When she spoke of his injuries, he felt her concern. When she paused, searching for words, he felt her uncertainty. Through it all, Scott felt an unstoppable flood of love coming from her. A love he had only suspected before.

The time between them passed too quickly. Soon, an orderly brought lunch. Scott could smell soup and tea. Mary fed him slowly at first, then as his dried throat and mouth rehydrated and he swallowed more easily, she stepped up the tempo. He smiled. A thought came to him, and he remembered her feeding the boys. First one and then the other—both in high chairs at the table, both clamoring for another bite. He considered this bond between Mary and him and prayed it would never leave. He had never felt so loved, so accepted. She was willing to do whatever it took to please him.

"I love you," he whispered.

"Thank God!" Mary answered back excitedly. "You can't imagine how good it feels to be able to hear you talk."

Scott did know. He just didn't know how to tell her.

Mary spent the afternoon first talking, then listening to his hoarse responses. Scott searched her emotions for the words she wanted to hear. The peculiar sensation of being able to *feel* her emotions remained, and try as he might, he could not shake the idea that somehow, in some way, the accident had changed something within him.

Dr. Gilbert showed up a few minutes after Mary left. This time, after the doctor examined Scott's eyes, he didn't replace the eye patches. Having his eyesight back was a glorious bonus to the rest of his obviously enhanced sensory perceptions. He did notice, though, as he looked around the room that the vision in his left eye was still a little blurry.

For the first time, he was able to see the patient in the bed across the room. The boy was a pitiful sight. His head was covered by heavy gauze bandages. Tubes and wires of all sorts were either attached to or inserted into his body. The only movement coming from his bed was a constantly moving accordion-type contraption attached to the large tube that ran down his throat.

* * * * *

Mary brought Jess with her in the morning. Scott instantly realized something else had changed, because from the moment the boy entered the room, Scott could feel his thoughts. Each time the conversation lagged, Scott knew what his son was thinking and asked him questions that would launch the boy off into another run of verbal thought. Mary seemed to note their communication link and kept discreetly quiet in the background while they talked. By the time they brought in his lunch, Scott felt he knew more about his eleven-year-old than he ever had before.

Scott's first solid food came in the form of a lunch of thinly sliced roast beef, fake potatoes, green peas, and a small green salad. Jess insisted on feeding Scott every morsel. When it was gone, the boy resisted when his mother insisted it was time for them to go get a lunch of their own. Jess wasn't much to turn down food, though, so Mary won out in the end, and the two left Scott alone.

Dr. Gilbert came in only minutes after they left.

"Your X-rays look really good," he said. "Your ribs are knitting nicely. The nurse tells me she heard you talking to your family. That's good. Is there anything I should know?"

The question seemed dumb at first, but then Scott sensed what Dr. Gilbert really wanted to know, and answered him.

"I'm not feeling any weird pains other than in my leg and head, if that's what you mean. I do wish I could see better out of my left eye, though."

"Well, let's have another look."

Light pierced his eye as the doctor searched.

"Well," Dr. Gilbert said cautiously after a few long moments of looking, "everything looks good inside the eye, but your iris is really slow to respond to light. That indicates there may be some damage to the optic nerve, or perhaps to the brain itself."

Scott instantly knew from the doctor's thoughts that the man was concerned.

"Will I be blind in that eye?" Scott asked, fighting to maintain control. He'd grown up near a boy who'd lost his eyesight to diabetes. Since then, he'd lived with a horrible fear of blindness.

"I don't think so," Dr. Gilbert said. "My main concern is that you may have suffered some brain damage that we haven't detected, or it might be as simple as a small bone fragment."

"Were there a lot of those?" Scott asked dumbly.

"Hasn't your wife told you?"

"Told me what?"

"You suffered a severe skull fracture in the accident. A neurosurgeon removed a good share of the right side of your skull and replaced it with a metal plate. The bone was too fragmented to chance leaving any of it in place."

"What does that mean?" Scott said, not fully understanding.

"You don't have to worry much about the plate, but you'll have

24

to be careful not to get hit in the head." He smiled. "And you're probably going to drive the airport metal detectors nuts."

"What about my left eye?" Scott asked.

"There may have been a little trauma to the optic nerve. Nerves don't like to be messed with. It may be something as simple as some lingering inflammation. It may take a month or more before we'll know for sure."

Shortly after Dr. Gilbert left, a nurse came in and pulled back the curtains around the other bed. Scott watched as the nurse checked the young man's vitals. He wondered how long he had been there. Scott hadn't noticed any visitors. He strained his one good eye to focus on what little he could see of the boy's face. Then a thought entered his mind.

Instantly, Scott was carried away into another dream. He saw a motorcycle careen out of control, jump a guardrail, and plunge down an embankment. The young man's naked head slammed against a rock with a tremendous thud. Then, as suddenly as it had come, the dream vanished.

Scott's upper lip felt cool as beads of perspiration formed on the skin. He lay still, eyes open wide. He looked away and focused on the hole pattern in the ceiling. He concentrated on his flexing fists. He didn't want to see any more.

The nurse closed the curtains and left.

Mary and Jess were nearly at his bedside before he noticed them. "Are you okay?" she asked.

"Yes, why?"

"You're as pale as a ghost, and you're all sweaty."

Scott relaxed and forced a smile. "I'm okay," he lied. "How was lunch?"

"You know Jess," she said with a smile. "It has to be McDonald's or nothing."

"Oh!" Scott said, giving Mary a knowing glance. It wasn't that they didn't like McDonald's food. It was just that Jess would hardly eat anywhere else. The trips to the fast food joint had become a little tedious.

"Are you sure you're okay?" she asked. "You look like you're upset."

"I'm fine. Will you do me a favor? Find out what happened to that boy over there." He nodded to the curtains separating him from his roommate.

"How do you know he's a boy?" Mary asked. "And why do you

want to know?"

"Never mind that," Scott said. "Just go ask."

She stared at him. He could sense a stubborn surge within her. He saw her thoughts; she refused to be ordered around.

Scott smiled. "Please. It's really important. I'll tell you why when you come back."

Mary softened. "Okay," she agreed.

Scott sensed her hesitancy and turned to his son. "Jess," he said with a smile, "would you go ask for me? Your mom is a little nervous."

The boy beamed at having been given a grown-up assignment, and before Mary could object, he was gone.

"Why is this suddenly so important?" Mary asked sternly.

Scott looked deep in her eyes. "If I'm right, something's happened to me. I see things." He paused and looked toward the shaded windows. "I saw a motorcycle crash," he continued haltingly, searching the memory of what he'd seen only moments before. "I saw a young man on a motorcycle go over an embankment and slam his head on a rock. He wasn't wearing a helmet. I think it was him."

Mary stared at Scott. She was uncomfortable. Before she could say anything, Jess hurried back into the room, face aglow with the information he was begging to share.

"Well?" Scott prodded.

"He was in a bad motorcycle crash," Jess said. "He wasn't wearing a helmet. He went over a cliff and smashed his head on a rock. He's been here for two months."

Scott looked up at the ceiling. He couldn't look at Mary. He knew she was shocked. He could feel the confusion rising in her. He could see her thoughts. She was wondering what it all meant.

"I don't know what it means," Scott answered before she asked.

Suddenly, realizing what he'd done, he looked at her. She was staring at him, dumbfounded.

"And I suppose you knew what I was thinking?" Mary asked.

"Huh?" Scott said, feigning ignorance.

"I was just thinking that very thing, and you answered my question before I even asked it."

"Coincidence," Scott said. He knew she didn't believe him. "Maybe I heard someone talking about his case when I was unconscious."

"You've only been in this room a couple of days," Mary said.

"They brought you in here from intensive care. I haven't heard anybody talk about him. If he's been here two months already, there's probably nothing more to say."

Scott changed the subject.

The rest of the afternoon was fun. The diversion of actually being able to talk and carry on a conversation masked many of Scott's nagging aches and pains. Dr. Gilbert came back to check in before going home for the night.

"They can't do a CT scan until Monday," the doctor said. "Have you told your wife why I want to do another one?"

"Not really," Scott said, "but maybe you should tell us both again what you think is going on."

Dr. Gilbert explained in his usual, jovial bedside manner what he suspected and why he'd ordered the tests. Then, without much of a goodbye, he was gone.

Mary's eyes watered as she stood looking down at Scott.

"Knock it off," Scott said. "I'm alive and can carry on a relatively sane conversation. You said yourself that nobody can believe how fast I'm recovering. That's news to be happy over, isn't it?"

He felt her concern. It wasn't fear. It wasn't pity. It was worry over how Scott would handle the possibility of losing an eye.

"I'm fine with this," he said in a low, careful voice as he grasped her hand. "I just thank God that I'm alive and can hold you again."

He knew what she wanted him to say. His words were right. She teared up and smiled.

"I love you so very much," she whispered as she leaned forward to kiss him. She smiled down at him as she pulled away. "We need to be going. I'll come back in the morning after church."

"Bring me the Sunday paper," he said as she turned to leave. "You know how I love the funnies." Scott sensed Jess was feeling left out. He held up his arms. "Come give me a careful squeeze."

Jess grinned and gingerly bent to hold him. Scott squeezed as hard as his broken ribs would let him. When he released, there were tears in the corners of Jess's eyes.

"Go on, now," Scott said, "and don't forget my paper."

Chapter 2
Sunday's Paper

Scott lay awake for a long time after Mary and Jess left, trying to process his feelings. He thought about the two men he'd heard about—those who'd become clairvoyant after some sort of electrical shock. He wondered if he had the same abilities they did. There was no doubt in his mind that something strange had happened to him. The ability to feel the emotions and see some of the thoughts of those around him offered increased evidence of that now.

Ever since waking up in the hospital, he had known when Mary was in the room without hearing her voice and had been able to sense her questions before she asked them. Was that a form of mind reading? If so, how deep could he reach?

He thought about the young man behind the curtains in his room and reached out to him with his mind, as he'd done before. At first, he felt nothing. Then, all at once, Scott felt the man's confusion and panic. It had to be coming from his subconscious mind. There was absolutely no indication that he was the least bit physically active. The only sound came from the patient's respirator as it drummed on and on in the semi-dark room.

Scott probed deeper, wondering if he could send thoughts as well as receive them. He tried to project all of the calm he could muster across the few feet that separated them—then suddenly wished he hadn't. A hail of panic slammed through him. He could see the loose gravel on the curve in the highway. He could see the guardrail. He could sense he was losing control of the bike.

Time stood nearly still; everything happened in slow motion. Scott could hear the hiss of the loose gravel beneath the tires as the motorcycle slid ever nearer to the guardrail. He could smell the dust in the air. He felt the jarring impact as the bike slammed head-on into the thick metal barrier, and blind panic as he catapulted headfirst through the air.

The jumbled rocks below raced up at him. He held out his arms. *Dear God*, the words formed in his mind, *please don't let me die!* Then came a brief, blinding surge of pain followed by blackness.

There was nothing more.

Sweat poured down Scott's face. It was as if he'd been the one flung off the speeding motorcycle. The young man's panic had stirred the adrenaline in him, and his heart raced. He clicked his fingers and took a few deep, cleansing breaths. Eventually, his heart calmed.

A thought came to him. If the young man had been able to unconsciously transfer his thoughts, why were they locked on those last terrifying moments? Scott longed to know more. Who was the young man? Who were his parents? Did he have a girlfriend? Was he in school? If he could calm the boy's terrible thoughts, would his mind heal?

Scott lay still for a long time. He wanted to know more, but if he couldn't get past those last horrific thoughts, he didn't want to go there again.

Eventually, curiosity got the best of him. He finally decided to try again. This time, instead of reaching out—simply probing for a response—he thrust out with a question of his own: "Do you have a girlfriend?"

He waited for a response. Nothing.

He asked again, this time concentrating hard on the young man. In a flash, he saw the accident again. He tried in vain to interrupt the thoughts as they poured from the boy's mind. Unwilling to follow the rider over the edge again, Scott threw his eyes open and snapped his fingers. The vision disappeared. It was as if the boy's mind was stuck in a rut, reliving those last hellish seconds over and over again. His mind was obviously broken. Scott felt bad for the boy. He was literally trapped in his own private hell.

Scott turned his head away. He didn't understand what was happening, but he didn't like it. He hoped his probing wasn't what had stimulated the young man's thoughts. He had meant him no harm.

All of his life, Scott had had *special* dreams—the sort that came true. He would wake up in the morning, knowing he'd had a dream and that it was somehow different from the typical nightmares that occasionally stalked his mind. The difference was that a few days later, or sometimes even months later, that dream would come true. For a few brief seconds, he would relive the dream, knowing exactly what was going to happen. It was as if he was seeing a film clip of his forgotten dream played out in real life.

Most of the events had no real significance, but they happened nonetheless. He had always wondered what purpose they served. Was every act in his life predestined? Was he powerless to change the outcome? He struggled with the thoughts. It was impossible for those dreams to be mere coincidences because in every scene he relived, there had to be hundreds, perhaps thousands of tiny details in his life and in the world around him that would have had to fall sequentially into place for those things to happen as they had.

He'd read biblical stories where this or that prophet had been carried away in spirit to the top of a high mountain and shown by God all the doings of mankind, often from the beginning of the world to its end. How was that possible? Was mankind just an experiment, like a rat in a maze searching for the cheese at the end? Were they free to jump out of the maze before they found the cheese? What was the purpose of the maze? Did they have to find every wrong turn, recognize their mistakes, and then backtrack and go on until they eventually found the cheese? Could they die in the maze without ever finding the cheese? Did everyone have their own personal maze to navigate, or were they all tossed into the same one? How did God know the outcome so he could show it to the prophets?

Scott's mind swam with the implications. Was it possible the dream he'd had of the woman in the mirror was not one of *those* dreams, but simply a nightmare? Something told him it was more. In all of his other dreams, he'd seen things that hadn't yet happened, and usually, he wasn't able to remember the details until he saw them played out before his eyes in waking life. But this dream was different. He had the distinct impression that what he'd seen had already occurred.

He could still remember every detail: her features; her pain; her fear; her attacker's face; her burial site; and the old rock well at the gravesite. He didn't want to think about what it might mean, but as his mind folded in on itself and he slept, he somehow knew he hadn't seen the last of it.

* * * * *

A nurse interrupted his fitful sleep just after four a.m. He was irritated but realized it was probably necessary for her to probe and poke to be sure he wasn't dying. All he wanted was to sleep.

He played possum for a few moments as the nurse scurried around the room, checking his vitals and typing the results into the computer that sat on a stand against the wall. Then he felt her emotions. She was distraught. He concentrated, and he suddenly knew she was divorced. Bills were due. The child support was late . . . again. Her two kids were staying with her mother while she worked. Scott felt the nurse's frustration and hatred for a man he assumed to be her ex-husband. She was exhausted. The twelve-hour shifts were killing her, but if she worked three days straight, she'd get paid for forty hours and could stay home with the kids the other four days of the week.

Scott couldn't resist opening his good eye. The room was semi-dark, but there was enough light that he could see the nurse's features. He knew she had cut her hair short so it wouldn't take so long to get ready for work. His good eye confirmed that her dark hair was, indeed, cut short—but the rest of the details had come from her.

He pulled back. What he was experiencing was almost an invasion of the woman's privacy. That wasn't him. Or at least it hadn't been before. Now he wondered.

The nurse moved to his roommate's bedside. Scott felt her pain as she touched the young man. She wanted to do more but knew she couldn't. He'd been there for weeks, and there had been no change in him. He didn't get visitors anymore. They'd given up on him.

Scott mouthed the words, but then he held back. There was nothing he could say—and besides, if she knew he was invading her thoughts, she'd probably freak out.

He tried to sleep after the nurse left, but there was a hole in his memory—one he was trying desperately to fill. What exactly had happened to him? Mary told him he'd been in a car crash. She'd mentioned the other driver's insurance. Evidently, it hadn't been Scott's fault. But why couldn't he remember a thing about the wreck or what had led up to it? Why, if he could almost read the minds of others, couldn't he probe his own memory?

An orderly brought him breakfast a while later. Scott tried to concentrate on the food tray as the orderly raised the head of the bed so he could reach the food, but before he could control it, the man's thoughts flooded his mind.

He only had an hour left on his shift. He should sleep, but Stephanie (whoever that was) wanted him to go to church with her. He didn't really want to go, but she expected him to be there, and at dinner with her parents afterward.

Suddenly, Mary's presence thrust the orderly's thoughts aside.

Scott smiled as she swept into the room.

"Hey, lover," she said, "how did you sleep?"

"Great!" he lied. "You're in a good mood."

"And why shouldn't I be? I just talked to your doctor in the hallway. He'll be here in a few minutes. He told me you might get to go home at the end of the week." She moved alongside him and kissed him lightly on the lips. "I brought you the paper. Would you like some help with breakfast?"

Scott handed her his fork. "That would be great. I can't sit straight up in the bed. I'm afraid I'll dribble food all over myself."

He listened to her thoughts as she fed him. He could also feel her emotions. She was trying to be upbeat on the surface, but inside she was worried about his eye. She was worried about his business. She was worried about the medical bills. She was worried about their only good car; it wouldn't start. The neighbor had given her a ride to the hospital, bless his heart.

Scott knew he had to be careful. It was good to know what was really on Mary's mind, but he didn't want to frighten her. He decided to start with the car. That would be a natural question.

"We never talked about it," he began cautiously, "but I suppose I totaled our car?"

"You did."

"What happened? I don't remember a thing."

"The other driver apparently passed out at the wheel. He was dead drunk. You'd been in Lincoln on a job all week and were driving home for the weekend. The other car crossed the median and hit you nearly head-on. They told me if it weren't for the air bags, you wouldn't have survived. The other driver didn't make it."

"What job?" Scott asked.

"You designed a big building in Lincoln. You were there working with the general contractor."

"I don't remember."

"The building, or the crash?"

"Neither one."

He felt a surge of concern from her as she collected her thoughts.

"It's a good thing Alan was able to pick up where you left off," Mary said, referring to Scott's business partner. "Apparently, the contractor had been cutting some corners. You called Alan before you left to come home and told him what was going on. You didn't make any brownie points with the contractor, but I hear they're back on track now."

Scott dug deep, trying to recall what had happened. He couldn't remember a thing.

"You need to just let it go for now," Mary said. "There's nothing you can do about it. The doctors told me that temporary amnesia is common with head trauma."

"I remember our firm," Scott said. "I remember Alan. I remember a few things, but I don't remember the wreck."

"You just need to take it one day at a time. It might all come back."

"And if it doesn't?"

"Then it probably doesn't matter."

He squeezed her hand, demanding her attention. "Mary!"

Her thoughts fled as she looked down at him.

"This is all going to work out," he said quietly.

She looked away quickly to hide her tears. It took a few seconds, but then she remembered the Sunday paper. She fished it out of a bulging cloth bag. "I told the boys I'd be home in time to take them to church. I need to go, but we'll all come and see you after. Pay attention to what the doctor tells you. Is there anything you need before I go?"

"Just a kiss."

"That's a given," she said, bending over him.

"Is the neighbor waiting for you?" he asked, and nearly panicked when he realized he'd slipped up.

She stared at him. "How did you know that?"

"You told me."

"I did not!" she said urgently. "You're scaring me, Scott. What else do you know?"

He turned his head.

"Oh, no you don't!" she demanded. "Tell me."

He turned back and looked into her frightened hazel eyes. He hesitated for a few seconds before answering. "I know our other car wouldn't start and that you got a ride from the neighbor."

She stood upright, stunned. Her mind raced.

"Mary," he said kindly, "don't be afraid of me. I'm not a weirdo."

"What else can you see?"

"A lot," Scott said humbly. "Something happened to me when I was in that crash. I don't know how or why, but when I came out of my coma, I realized that I can *feel* your emotions. Sometimes, I know what you're thinking."

"Just me, or can you pick the brains of every little candy-striper who trots in here?"

He didn't answer.

Tears trickled down her cheeks. "I've never really come to grips with the other stories you've told me. You know, about thinking you'd seen things happen before they really happened."

Scott reached for her hand, but she pulled away. "I know you had a hard time believing me before, but this is different—way different. When people walk in here, I know who it is before I even open my eyes. If there's something on their minds that's really bugging them, I know what they're thinking. I think it has something to do with high emotion. Take you, for instance. I could sense that you were freaked out about the car. That's all I saw—"

"I've got to go," she interrupted. "I don't know if I can deal with this. Even in a good marriage, there has to be some secrecy. Now you're telling me that I have none."

"It'll probably go away," Scott said. "I've read that a whack on the head can sometimes do strange things to people."

Mary turned and hurried through the door without responding. The thoughts and emotions that trailed in her wake swirled through his mind for a long time after. Why had he been so stupid? He knew there might be trouble if he told her the truth. He put himself in her shoes and knew he would have a hard time being with someone who could read his every thought. He should have kept his mouth shut, but he'd never really lied to her before. Somehow, honesty in marriage seemed so important—until now.

After a while, he noticed the Sunday paper lying on his breakfast tray. He needed something to help calm his mind. He fanned out the weekend advertisements and tossed them on the foot of the bed. He was tempted to start with the comics, but he knew it would be a while before he had visitors again, so he dutifully picked up the front section and scanned over the articles. One headline stood out.

Lincoln Woman Still Missing.

When he saw the photo of the missing woman, his heart froze. It was the woman in his dream.

Chapter 3
Trying to Help

Scott read the newspaper article half a dozen times before he set the paper down and closed his eyes. The victim in his dreams now had a name and an age. She was Nancy Bennion, a twenty-four-year-old resident of Lincoln, Nebraska. According to the article, even though the police hadn't yet found a body, they had found enough blood in her apartment to treat her disappearance as a homicide. Every time he read over the story, Scott relived the horrific vision of her stabbing death. The problem was, even though he'd seen her murder there was little he could do about it. Nobody would believe him.

He weighed his options. If he described her attacker to the police, would they find him? If they couldn't, would Scott himself be implicated? The safest thing he could do was absolutely nothing.

Were his dreams a gift, or a curse? Who or what was giving him these visions?

Dr. Gilbert interrupted his thoughts.

"You don't look well," he said as he touched Scott's forehead. "What's wrong? Are you in pain?"

Scott took a deep breath. He wanted to blurt out all the mental things that had happened over the past two days, but he was afraid he'd end up in the looney bin. He doubted doctors had a very high tolerance for the supernatural—if that's what this was.

"I haven't been sleeping well," Scott said. "I just think I'm exhausted."

"Pain can do that. I'll get you some medication," Dr. Gilbert said, folding back some pages on his clipboard.

"No, please don't. I hate the way the drugs make me feel. I'd rather be in pain and conscious than all doped up."

Dr. Gilbert put the clipboard down on the roll-around table and ran through the normal sequence of tests: blood pressure, pulse, temperature. Last, he checked Scott's left eye. Then he paused.

"What's bothering you?" Dr. Gilbert asked. "I'm not seeing anything out of the ordinary, and yet you appear to be on the verge of a breakdown."

"I'm just a little freaked out mentally," Scott said. "I'm having a hard time wrapping my mind around the crash, the two-week coma, and the memory loss. I feel like I need to go run a mile just to work off the stress."

"If it wasn't for your knee, you could walk. That would help. But your orthopedist doesn't want you to put any pressure on that knee for a while. He's got you in a soft cast so the injuries will heal, but it doesn't give your knee any support."

"I thought I might be able to go home at the end of the week."

"Oh, you can go home," Dr. Gilbert said, "but you'll be staying in bed for at least another two weeks. Your surgeon doesn't want you using crutches or even walking with a cane."

"How do I get up to go . . ."

"You'll have to have a catheter, and your dear wife—or a home health care nurse—will be getting you on and off of a bedpan."

"That sounds like hospital stuff to me."

"Ten years ago, it would have been, but today's insurance companies won't pay for the extended stay, so the hospital doesn't have a choice. You can only stay as long as you're incapacitated. Once you're ambulatory, they toss you out!"

"I don't remember a thing about the accident or what was going on in my life for a while before that."

"I wouldn't worry about that. It's not uncommon. You may never recover those memories. We think that's the brain's way of dealing with trauma. You're probably better off not remembering."

"I'm having nightmares."

"That's probably just a byproduct of your head injury. I can't talk to that for sure. Would you like me to see if your neurosurgeon would drop by? I'm sure he can answer those questions better than I can. He sees the aftermath of head trauma almost every day. That's his line of work."

Scott considered the doctor's offer. He wanted to hear the head doctor's professional opinion, but he wasn't sure he could talk about his nightmare. Or vision, or whatever it was. His thoughts rushed to his roommate. Even though the young man was seemingly unconscious, there was still some mental activity going on. That might explain how Scott knew about Nancy Bennion's murder. Maybe somebody had been talking about the story and his subconscious had dreamed up a perpetrator and—

Scott knew what he was thinking was all wrong. He had *seen* her in a vision. How else would he have recognized the picture in the newspaper?

"Well?" Dr. Gilbert said.

"I suppose that might be good. Doesn't he have to see me again anyway?"

"Generally not. He's a surgeon. He's done his best. The rest—the healing—is up to you. Unless you develop complications."

"I guess that's your call," Scott said. "I'd like to talk to someone. I guess it doesn't have to be my neurosurgeon, but I need to have someone with credentials tell me that all of this horror I'm feeling is normal."

"I know a psychologist who's on call here at the hospital. I'll send him up to see you. He generally deals with the psych ward patients, but he's good. I think he might be able to put your mind at ease."

"I suppose I need something. I just don't want it to come out of a needle."

* * * * *

The name on the gold-colored tag read *Dr. Frank Talbot.*

"Hey," Dr. Talbot began as he sat down on the side of Scott's bed, "I hear you've had quite an ordeal."

Scott instantly found the man's thoughts. Dr. Talbot been dealing with a suicidal teenager most of the afternoon. He and his office partner, a psychiatrist named Dr. Franklin, had been treating the girl for over a year. Talbot was doing her counseling. Franklin was prescribing her medication. She had overdosed on a month's worth of medication and had been rushed to the hospital, unconscious.

Talbot was interested in Scott's predicament, but a little annoyed. He'd only dropped in to see Scott as a favor to Dr. Gilbert. He doubted there was much he could do. Knocks on the head were physical things that often brought on nightmares or delusions, but most of the time, as the body healed, they went away. On the other hand, what he'd just left on the fifth floor wasn't nearly as treatable.

Scott took a chance. "How's your patient on the fifth floor doing? I believe her name is Susan?"

Dr. Talbot gaped at him. Scott now had his full attention. "Who told you about my patient?"

"You did."

"That's impossible. We just met. I haven't told you a thing."

37

Scott managed a faint smile. A quick plan flashed through his mind. If he could convince this shrink that his mental gift—or ability—was real, maybe the good doctor would believe his story about Nancy and convince the police he was sane. Then somebody could go look for her and the man who had murdered her.

"I woke up from a car crash with some sort of strange ability to read people's emotions," Scott said. "Even some of their thoughts. I know that probably sounds crazy. Maybe I am. All I can tell you is I've already scared the hell out of my wife. She left. She couldn't deal with me being able to answer her questions before she asked them."

"So what exactly am I thinking now?" Dr. Talbot challenged.

"You're wondering how I know about Susan. You're wondering what kind of freak I am. You're wondering if what I have is temporary or permanent. You're wondering if you should have me sedated so my brain will have time to heal."

A slight smile curled the corners of Talbot's mouth. "I've seen a lot of things in my career," he said, "but this is a first. So, how do you suggest we proceed? I don't suppose I can ask you a question if you already know what I'm thinking. That might be a waste of time. Maybe I should just think the question, and you can answer it. Tell me. What exactly would you like to know?"

"I have something to tell you," Scott said, "but first I'd like to perform a little experiment, if you don't mind, so you'll know I'm for real. I think we can both agree that we've never met before. Think of a few things I couldn't possibly know about you."

Scott instantly sensed the doctor's hostility.

"Look, I didn't mean to piss you off," Scott said. "It's not my intent to invade your privacy. Anything I see stays between us. Call it doctor-client privilege or whatever. I don't really care about your personal life. I just need to demonstrate what I can do before I tell you the rest of my story."

Talbot smiled, but Scott knew he was uncomfortable.

"Okay," Scott continued after a brief pause. "Let's start with the easy stuff. Your wife's name is Margie. You've been married twenty-eight years. You have two children, both girls, both in college. Neither are married, but your oldest, Clarice, is living with her boyfriend, Jason. You drive a dark-black Audi that you bought this spring."

"Stop!" Talbot said, holding up his hand. "Where exactly is all this leading?"

"I need you to believe I'm not delusional before I tell you the rest."

Talbot didn't answer.

"Okay," Scott said, "I can tell you're not convinced. You've seen Susan before. She's a patient. You got the call about her suicide attempt just after five this afternoon. You were annoyed because you had a dinner date with your wife at six thirty. Your partner, Dr. Franklin, prescribed the standard post-overdose drugs. You had her restrained until the effects of the drugs are out of her system."

Talbot was no longer smiling. "Okay," he said, "maybe I'm convinced. What exactly do you want from me?"

"Validation," Scott said simply. "Hand me that newspaper." He pointed to the newspaper, which an orderly had tossed on a chair just out of reach. "Let me begin by telling you a quick life's history. All my life, I've had dreams. I've seen things happen before they did. Then, I'll see a real-life flashback of that dream and know exactly what's going to happen. It's never been anything significant . . . until now."

He took the newspaper from the doctor and opened it to the appropriate page.

"Like I just told you, I was in a car wreck a little over two weeks ago. I got my head caved in. They tell me they had to put a metal plate in my head, that my brain was bruised, and that I was in a coma for a couple of weeks. It seems that whatever this gift—or curse, if that's what it is—I've had all my life has suddenly intensified. I woke up being able to know who was in the room without opening my eyes. At first, I could only sense emotions. Now it's gone way beyond that."

He paused and briefly sought out the doctor's thoughts. Talbot was still skeptical, but he'd read about a couple of cases of clairvoyance—if this was what this man had. He wanted to hear more before he said anything.

"I had one of my dreams just after I came out of a coma, but this time it was way more than a dream. It was more of a vision. I witnessed a murder."

Scott held up the paper and pointed to Nancy's picture.

"I know this girl was stabbed to death. I saw her assailant through her eyes. I even watched as he buried her. The problem is obvious. I would love to help the cops catch this man. I'd love to help them find her body so her family will have closure. The issue is, I'm sure nobody will believe me. People don't believe in soothsayers or clairvoyants, or whatever you want to call them."

Talbot's eyes narrowed. Scott could hardly believe the thoughts screaming around in the doctor's mind. In a millisecond, Scott knew he'd made a terrible mistake. Talbot was already wondering who he should call. The man was convinced Scott was not the observer, as he claimed to be, but the actual doer of the deed. Talbot was afraid. He needed to distance himself before this battered freak could glean anything else from his mind.

"I've got to go," Talbot said as he quickly got to his feet and headed for the door.

Suddenly, Scott understood why. The man knew Scott's abilities were real. He had to get away before he found out anything more about Susan. A brief thought flashed through Talbot's mind as he closed the door behind him: Susan was pregnant, and it was Talbot's baby. She was only fifteen.

Chapter 4
The Cops

The clock read quarter past seven when two uniformed officers walked into Scott's room. Neither of them was smiling.

"Are you Scott Corbridge?" one of them asked.

Scott instantly knew why they were here. Talbot had called the cops. They were convinced they were looking at Nancy Bennion's murderer.

"I am," Scott said. "Did you come here to read me my Miranda rights?"

The two officers exchanged glances.

"We will if it'll make you feel better," the first officer said as he approached Scott's bed. "But I hardly think that's necessary at this point."

Scott quickly searched the man's thoughts. He didn't like what he saw.

"You're here to get me to talk about a murder," Scott said. "You must have talked to Dr. Talbot. He doesn't believe what I told him. He thinks I'm involved. I hardly think I could be. I've been lying here in a coma for the last couple of weeks."

"That girl disappeared two weeks ago, Mr. Corbridge, and we've been doing a little checking. Your car wreck and her disappearance both happened the same day. You told Dr. Talbot that you saw her murder in your dreams. He thinks you may have just *thought* you were dreaming."

Scott shifted uncomfortably in his bed. He knew he had to be very careful with what he said. He was afraid this would happen. He decided to try to shift the attention away from himself.

"You know, before you start asking me questions about that, maybe we should have Dr. Talbot come back in here and tell you *everything* I told him. I talked to him because he's a psychologist. I've got some mental things going on that I needed to talk about. He's afraid of me because I know about his connection to a young female patient of his who just attempted suicide. What, may I ask, did he tell you about the girl in the newspaper?"

The officers looked at each other nervously.

"I don't see why we would need Dr. Talbot here," one of the officers said.

Scott couldn't see their name tags clearly in the room's dim light, so he reached out to them mentally. "Okay," he said, "we'll talk. But before we do, I'd like to offer you a little demonstration. Let me begin by explaining to you why you're here."

"I don't think that will be necessary," the officer nearest his bed answered snottily. "We're very aware of why we're here."

"Actually, Officer Jones," Scott said, "I think it is necessary. Should I call you by your last name, or should I just call you Derek? Derek is your first name, isn't it? Are you married, Derek? How long have you been on the police force?"

The look on Officer Jones' face softened from contempt to apprehension. The mention of his wife brought on the thoughts Scott had been looking for.

He looked at the officer for a moment before he began. "Your wife's name is Janice. You've been married eleven years. You've been on the metro police force six years, and you were recently promoted to detective. Am I right?"

Before Jones could answer, Scott glanced at the other officer and saw similar thoughts rattling around in his mind. "And you, Officer Roger Privit, are a ten-year veteran of the force, and you're also a detective. Your wife's name is Patty, and you've been married fifteen years."

Neither of the officers responded, but the looks on their faces were priceless.

"Now, having said that," Scott continued, "I need to tell you the rest of the story Dr. Talbot clearly didn't pass along when he called you. It's pretty obvious that you two came here ready to arrest me as a prime suspect in Nancy Bennion's murder, so if you'll allow me to, I'll tell you how my discussion with Dr. Talbot went. Then, I think, from the way our conversation has started out, that I should have a lawyer present before I say anything more about the girl in the newspaper."

Neither responded.

"Should I just call an attorney now, or shall we continue?"

"I'm sorry," Officer Jones said. "I don't know what kind of parlor tricks you're up to, but actually, that was pretty impressive."

"I can tell that neither one of you are convinced," Scott said. "You're thinking I'm a freak of some sort. Maybe I am. But what I can tell you right now is that I know what you're both thinking, and if you come back here with an attorney and a sketch artist, I'll give you a description of the guy who murdered Nancy Bennion. I might even be able to tell you where she's buried."

The officers shifted their weight from one foot to the other uncomfortably. They obviously had no answer to his question, so he went on.

"Like I tried to tell Dr. Talbot before he raced out of here, I've had this gift—in some form or other—for a lot of years. I can see things before they happen. I just survived a car wreck where I got a severe smack on the head. Evidently, whatever gift I had has now been enhanced to where I can pretty much tell what people around me are feeling, and even some of the things they're thinking."

"And I suppose you expect us to believe all that?" Jones laughed.

Scott simply stared at the officer for a few seconds. "I can see we're not getting anywhere. I apologize for wasting your time. If you want to know anything else, you're going to have to ask my lawyer."

"We'll do that," Officer Privit said, pulling a small notepad from his shirt pocket. "Who is he?"

"I don't have one yet. Until you two showed up, I didn't think I needed one. I was just trying to help you guys catch her killer and get her family a little closure. Our conversation is over."

"We can make your life pretty miserable if you don't cooperate," Jones said.

"Look at me," Scott said with a sneer. "I think I'm about as miserable right now as a person can be. You don't scare me. If I hadn't told Talbot my story, you two wouldn't be standing here at all. And frankly, without my help, you may never solve her case."

"I'm sure we'll be talking to you again real soon," Jones grumbled.

"Maybe while you're waiting for me to get some legal representation you ought to ask Dr. Talbot if his fifteen-year-old patient who just attempted suicide is pregnant, and who the father is. He's obviously trying to screw me over. I think it's time I returned the favor."

Scott rang for the nurse as the officers were leaving.

"I need a telephone," he said when the woman came through the door.

She glanced around the room. "I'm sorry," she said, "I don't think the phone cord is long enough to bring it to your bed."

"Then would you please call my wife and ask her to come down here? It's really important that I talk to her right away."

Scott's mind ran rampant after the nurse left the room. He hated his "gift." He should never have told anybody about Nancy. He shouldn't have said a thing to Mary, either. The human mind, it seemed, was the last great bastion of privacy. He wondered how many others had his gift. How had they managed to deal with its power? He was intrigued and excited, yet he had realized—perhaps too late—that such a gift had to be carefully hidden away from others. As much as he wanted—no, as much as he *needed*—to share his gift, from that time on, he simply couldn't.

Mary walked into his room around eight. She exuded fear as she approached his bed.

"Hey," he said simply.

"What's so important that it couldn't wait until tomorrow?" she asked.

"I'm so sorry. I didn't mean to scare you this morning."

"I'm not afraid," she said, and yet he could instantly tell she was. Now, though, was no time for honesty. "What did you need?"

"I need an attorney," Scott said. "I had a little conversation with a shrink this afternoon after you left. I tried to explain what I'd seen in a vision about that girl in today's newspaper. He couldn't handle it. He called the police, and now they think I'm somehow involved."

"What are you talking about?"

He reached for the newspaper, found Nancy's picture, and held it up for Mary to see. "I know what happened to this girl. I had one of my dreams just before I regained consciousness. I saw her murder. I saw the guy who did it. I know where she's buried."

Fear surged through Mary. She was thinking the same thing as the cops.

"I tried to tell them about what I'd seen," he said. "All I wanted them to do was bring in a police sketch artist so I could show them who murdered her. Of course, they think it was me."

"Are you sure it wasn't?"

Scott stared into Mary's eyes as he read her thoughts and emotions. She was terrified.

"I honestly don't know," he finally answered. "I don't remember anything about my life for the last two months. But I'm not a killer, Mary. I know that much for sure. I didn't know that girl. I don't know a thing about her."

Mary took the paper from him and read the article. "It says she's from Lincoln, Scott. You were in Lincoln. In fact, you spent a lot of time in Lincoln this summer. Were you having an affair with her?"

He felt her pain—her anger. How could he convince her he wasn't involved?

"No," Scott said. "I'm not cheating on you. Before the dream, I had never laid eyes on her. In the dream, all I saw was her reflection in a mirror."

Mary wanted to believe him—but he'd spent so much time in Lincoln the past few months. When he came home on the weekends, he'd been distant. But he'd been that way before. They'd been married a long time. Had he gotten bored and reached out to someone else? Who was she? From her photo, the girl looked young and beautiful. Did he work with her? If not, how did they meet? What did the girl know—or what had she done—to make Scott mad enough to kill her? Was she pregnant? Had she threatened to expose him?

Scott fought for restraint. He *wanted* to answer Mary's every question, but she hadn't asked them yet. Talking about what she was thinking would only make her more afraid than she already was. He waited.

"Why do you need an attorney?" she finally asked.

"Because the cops are convinced I'm involved in her death," Scott said. "I told the shrink that I saw her murder, and they're convinced what I saw was real and not a dream. I told them I wouldn't say another thing about the case without an attorney. I'm worried. I should have kept my mouth shut. People don't deal well with things they don't understand."

"Are you talking about them, or me?"

"Both, I suppose. You can't put me in prison. They can."

"Well, if you can tell what I'm thinking, then you already know I'm scared to death."

"I can control it," Scott said. "I can't tell what you're thinking unless I really concentrate. I'm trying to stay away from that. The last thing I want is to do or say something that will drive you away. Mary, you're my life! Please don't be afraid of me."

"I can't help it!" she exclaimed. "This is just too weird. I can't stand the idea that you know my innermost thoughts."

"I wish you could read mine. Then you'd know I'm not lying. You'd know how much I love you. I'd never cheat on you."

She stared at him for a few seconds. He avoided her thoughts.

"I'll call Alan," Mary said. "I don't know anything about attorneys—who's good or bad."

At the mention of his partner's name, Scott instantly pictured Alan Stiver's face in Mary's thoughts. He thought it a little strange but didn't dwell on it.

"Did you tell the kids?" he asked after a pause.

"Tell them what? That their dad woke up from a car crash and can suddenly read minds? That would go over really well."

Scott forced a smile. "At least we'll know what Trish and Brandon are up to."

"That's sick. Maybe I don't want to know. Some things are better left unknown."

"It's not like I can see what they've been doing."

"Why not? Isn't that what happened when you had your *dream* about that woman?"

"No. That was different. That was like the dreams I've had all my life. Except this time, I remembered all the details when I woke up. This time, what I saw wasn't something that was going to happen in the future. This time, I saw something that has already happened."

"You're not making any sense. You tell me you can see what people are thinking. Why was that any different?"

"Because she wasn't here. I wasn't reading her mind. I wasn't feeling her emotions. What I saw was like—" He stopped. He could tell he was just confusing her. "Mary, I don't know what more I can tell you. I wish I hadn't said anything. I don't want this to come between us."

"It already has."

She opened her purse, pulled out her cell phone, dialed Alan's number, and handed Scott the phone.

"Hi, Mary," Alan answered.

"Hello, this is Scott."

"Oh, hi Scott!" Alan quickly recovered. "It's really good to hear your voice. How are you doing?"

"I'm awake. They tell me I'm doing well."

"I'm glad to hear it. Do you know how long it'll be before you can come back to work?"

"Not yet. I just came out of a coma a couple of days ago."

"Get well soon. I could really use your help. I've hired a temp— well, he's doing some drafting for us. He's pretty good. I think we should keep him on."

"I can't get my mind around that right now. Hey, Alan, I need an attorney."

"Mary told me the wreck wasn't your fault."

"It's not about the wreck. It's hard to explain over the phone. I need a criminal lawyer. The cops are trying to accuse me in a murder case. Do you know anyone?"

"A murder case! What the—"

"If you'll come by the hospital, I'll explain everything to you. I really don't want to do that over the phone."

Alan hesitated. "I'll call our business lawyer. I'm sure he can suggest somebody. I don't personally know anybody. Did you have anyone in mind?"

"No. I've never had the need for one before. I don't think I do now, but . . . well . . . it's complicated. Like I said, we should talk face to face."

"Okay. It's pretty late tonight, but I'll see what I can do first thing in the morning. Should I call Mary's phone, or do you have your own phone?"

"I have no idea where my cell phone is. I suppose it's still in my wrecked car. I haven't thought to ask. I'd have you call the hospital phone, but I can't reach the phone on the wall."

"Okay, I'll call Mary, then, and she can let you know. Sorry, man. I can tell I need to come see you. My head is spinning."

"I have that effect on people lately," Scott said. He disconnected the call and handed the phone back to Mary.

Suddenly, the events of the last few seconds swept over him. Mary had dialed Alan's number without doing a lookup. Alan had assumed he was talking to Mary when he answered. Scott fought off the thoughts. Mary must have been talking to Alan a lot since the crash. Alan and he were business partners. She would have had to keep him informed.

Then another thought crossed Scott's mind. Is that why Mary was so afraid about him being able to know what she was thinking? He needed to know, but he didn't want to. He began to reach out to her, then stopped. *No*, he told himself. He didn't want to know. At least not like this.

Then, in a millisecond, he felt her emotions; he saw her thoughts. His heart shattered. He wanted to die. He couldn't breathe. He looked away. He couldn't bear to look at her.

"Scott?" Mary asked. "Are you okay?"

"I don't think so," he said. "I suddenly hurt all over."

Mary snatched up the nurse call button attached to his pillow and punched it.

Scott writhed in his emotions as Mary stepped away and let the nurse do her thing. He nodded dumbly or shook his head in response to the nurse's questions, but he barely heard what she was saying. Instead, he was listening to Mary, and he really didn't want to hear what she was thinking.

The church thing, the doting mother thing, lately was little more than a big fat lie. Thoughts of Alan filled her mind. Anger surged through Scott. He was about to lose everything. His partnerships in both his business and his marriage were bound to dissolve. And if the cops could come up with enough circumstantial evidence, he could even lose his freedom.

He silently cursed his so-called gift. That little "thing" that had been with him all of his life and had given him an element of comfort until now had suddenly turned vile. He wanted nothing more to do with it.

He slammed his eyes tightly shut and tried to drive Mary's thoughts out of his mind. They wouldn't leave. He wanted to scream at her, to tell her that he could see the two of them together, and send her running from the room. Then he felt the sting in his arm as the nurse injected the medication into his IV. The warming feeling began to flow through his body. Slowly, gratefully, he slipped into unconsciousness.

Chapter 5
Legal Counsel

Scott was alone in his room when he woke up. The lights were low. No light shone through the window blinds. The room was quiet except for the soft cadence of his roommate's respirator.

His first conscious thoughts brought only anguish. He wondered how long Mary had been sneaking around behind his back. He suddenly hated Alan. Their partnership was over—even if Scott didn't wind up in prison for a crime he hadn't committed.

He could barely stand the thought of Mary being with another man, but especially not Alan! Scott was confused. Only yesterday, he'd felt her love pour over him. Now the dual betrayal of trust was simply more than he could stand. He wondered if Alan's wife, Val, knew what was going on.

Both his marriage and his partnership seemed irretrievably broken. His partnership with Alan was barely solvent as it was. If Scott walked away, it would go bankrupt, and along with it would come personal ruin. He and Alan had mortgaged their homes to raise the capital to get the business up and running. The thought of ruining Alan financially was the only bright spot in his otherwise dark and dismal room.

Then thoughts of the girl in the newspaper pushed everything else aside. In spite of the fact that telling his story might land him in prison, Scott knew he wouldn't be able to rest until the cops found her body. They would undoubtedly put him first on their list of persons of interest until they found the man responsible. He concentrated on the killer's face. He needed to remember every tiny detail when they had him talk to a sketch artist.

He began to have second thoughts. What if he couldn't give a police artist enough to go on? If they couldn't find the man, it left only one person—him—knowing anything about Nancy's disappearance and murder. Memories of the old TV show *The Fugitive* flitted through his brain. He didn't know if that story had been based on fact or on fiction, but now he knew firsthand that something like that could really happen to him.

Nebraska was no longer a death penalty state. That took some of the sting out of what he was thinking about doing. If they found him guilty, he'd probably lose his wife to Alan and his home and business to the banks. There wasn't much else. He'd seen the aftermath of bitter divorces before. At best, the kids would be torn. His family would probably believe he was guilty, too. Without family, he had nothing.

Then he felt ashamed. If family was so important, why had he spent so much time away from them? Why hadn't he seized the opportunity to go to summer camp with John? Why had he spent so much time in Lincoln?

He wondered if his marriage was really broken. If Mary believed he could read her every thought, it probably was. Could he hide his gift from her? Could he forgive her and move on? People could recover from affairs. It required love and forgiveness. He had the first: love. But he worried about the second. When he considered her motive, he realized he was probably to blame. He hadn't done anything to keep the romance alive. Realizing that, he believed he could forgive her.

Maybe, if he was careful, he might be able to lead Mary to believe his ability to read thought was just a temporary thing. She already knew about his dreams; they'd often talked about them. He could probably do whatever it took to get past this latest episode. If she didn't see any further demonstrations, things might be able to return to normal. His feelings for her really hadn't changed. He was crushed by what she'd done, but he wanted her in spite of that.

With his gift, he could really listen to Mary when they talked. It had been easy with Jess. He could work hard to win her back. She could never know he knew about her affair. If the subject came up, the confession had to come from her. He'd have to show shock and sorrow, but she could never know he'd already known about it by reading her mind. Otherwise, he'd be guilty of manipulation of the worst kind.

He thought about Dr. Talbot, about the cops, about what he'd already told Mary. He'd been so anxious to prove to everyone around him that he did, in fact, have this miraculous new gift that he'd been very foolish with it.

From that point on, he couldn't let anyone know about it—except for the dream. The dream was different. When he told people about the dream, he wouldn't be standing there reading back to them their most intimate thoughts. They had to know they could work with him without being afraid of him.

If the tables were turned, he would run away from anyone who could tell what he was thinking. Thinking thoughts and acting on them were two very different things. You couldn't get your face slapped for a random thought about the size of a woman's breasts; telling her what you were thinking, though, was a very different matter. Scott decided the next few days, months, or even years would have to be a judiciously controlled exercise in careful thought and discretion.

The drugs they gave him earlier left him groggy. At first, he refused to lapse back into slumber. He had so much to think about. He had to decide what to do before he saw Mary again, but he was exhausted. He still hurt in a hundred places. He needed to give his body some time to heal.

He took a deep breath. Instead of letting thoughts fill his mind, he concentrated on his body. He found his toes first and considered each one of them. Then he moved to his feet, and then further up his body. Finally, he dozed.

In what seemed like only seconds, it was morning. An aide woke him when he replaced his IV bottle and took his vitals. Shortly after, Scott got another gurney ride to the radiology lab for a CT scan of his head. He'd barely finished breakfast when a tall man in a business suit knocked on his open doorframe.

"Good morning," the man said. "I assume you're Scott Corbridge? My name is Paul Rodriguez. I'm a criminal law attorney. Your partner, Alan Stiver, asked me to come by and talk to you."

Scott motioned him to his bedside.

"The details I got from your partner were pretty sketchy, Scott. Is it okay if I call you Scott?"

Scott nodded.

"Rather than waste a lot of time, why don't you tell me why you think you might need legal representation?"

Scott hesitated. If he told the man everything, he doubted he'd stay. Instead, he reached out to the man's thoughts. Paul didn't really know much, so Scott began by telling him about his dream. Then he pointed to the article in Sunday's paper. He finished up by recounting his brief but fairly hostile encounter with the two police officers. He wanted to mention Talbot, too, but didn't think that was germane to their current conversation.

"Okay," Paul interrupted before Scott could finish telling him about the officers' visit. "Correct me if I'm wrong, but as I understand it, you cracked up your car the same day this girl"—he pointed to the paper—"disappeared. You claim you saw her murder and burial in a dream, and they're thinking you're the guy who killed her. Is that about it?"

"Yes."

"Did you do it?" Paul asked flatly.

"I honestly don't know," Scott said. "I don't remember much of anything that happened less than a month or so ago. They tell me I was working a job in Lincoln at the time. My wife overreacted. She thinks I was having an affair with the woman and that I may have killed her to shut her up. I have to admit, that all sounds pretty incriminating. But if I did it, why do I remember that other guy? I saw him stab her to death. I watched him bury her. If I were an artist, I could draw you a picture of him."

Scott tuned in on Paul's thoughts. He could barely keep up with what the man was thinking.

"Okay," Paul said. "I can certainly see why you need an attorney. I'm going to need you to tell me everything you can remember. Then, I need to have my people do some investigative footwork. We need to establish an alibi for you. If we can do that, anything else you tell the cops should do nothing more than aid in their investigation to find the real killer."

Paul reached into his pocket, took out a small recording device, spoke into it, and rewound it to verify it was working.

"Tell me again about your . . . dream," Paul said. "Don't leave anything out. Be as descriptive as you can."

Scott carefully relived the vision for the recording device. When he was finished, he could tell Paul was skeptical. Not that he could blame him.

"I'm sure the cops are going to be back today," Scott interjected as Paul finished off the recording. "What do I tell them?"

"My visceral reaction is to tell them nothing. You can give them my card and tell them to refer their questions to me. I can tell that you want to help them find that girl, but make them do their job. If they can find any evidence that might link you to her disappearance, we'll evaluate how much you can tell them at that time. Meanwhile, let me do some footwork. I hope I can find something that will completely distance you from her. But if I can't, I think you can see what the cops are implying could have some merit."

Paul paused before he continued. "You can't remember anything that happened to you for over a month. This eventually might go to a jury. Can you imagine what the prosecution will be telling those people? If the prosecution can put you anywhere near the murder scene, I doubt the jury will buy your *dream* theory. In fact, if I were the prosecuting attorney, I'd go find some head doctor who would explain your dream away. Frankly, with the knock on the head you got, I could easily see how you might just *think* you had a dream."

"What about the other guy?"

"Did you have an accomplice?" Paul asked, then immediately added, "Oh, that's right, you don't remember."

Paul's thoughts were dark. He was convinced Scott was guilty. He wondered about taking the case at all. Would it help or hurt his and his firm's reputation? If he got Scott off in the face of incredible odds, he'd get more business than he could handle. But what if he lost? Both sides of any case needed legal representation. The media would have a field day, especially if Scott could lead them to a body. A lawyer couldn't get better publicity. He certainly couldn't be faulted for losing against such odds. Paul wondered how much Scott was worth. Could he afford the investigative work it was going to take to do due diligence?

"I run an architectural consulting partnership," Scott said, interrupting Paul's thoughts. "We've only been in business a little over a year. We don't have much. Our building is leased. Both of our homes are mortgaged to the hilt. If I go to jail, I can't promise you'll ever get paid. Maybe you should just back away and let the courts assign me a public defender."

Paul considered what Scott had just told him. Financially, it would be a bust, regardless of how the case turned out. But then he reconsidered. You could find a lawyer on any street corner, and most of them were hungry. He wasn't that hungry. He and his firm were doing well, but he needed to talk to his partners. It might not take many resources to briefly review the case and make an appearance in court. On the other hand, the case had the potential of being a barn burner. It might even make national news.

"I'll be honest with you," Paul said. "This could be a hard case to defend—depending, of course, on what we find when we try to recreate the last month or so of your life. Let me go talk to my partners. You can buy anything for money, but where you don't appear to have any, this could be a hard decision for us to make."

"What do I tell the cops in the meantime?" Scott asked. "I'm sure they'll be back this morning."

"Give them my card. They don't have to know whether or not

we've accepted you as a client. In the meantime, don't answer any of their questions about the case. Don't let them intimidate you, but don't be hostile. Play dumb. Tell them you think you were hallucinating or something. I'll bet head trauma patients often do that. You'll know they're dead serious if they read you your Miranda rights. They'll use anything you tell them from that point on against you. When it comes right down to them interrogating you, assume you're a prisoner of war. Offer name, rank, and serial number. Nothing more."

He paused.

"You might placate them for a while by simply telling them that what you remembered might simply be a figment of your imagination. Something you dreamed up after seeing that newspaper article. Unfortunately, where you've already opened your mouth, they have a place to start. I'll bet what you told them is a lot more than what they had before they walked in here, and they will follow it as far as it leads. They work for somebody. They have to show some progress in the case. They're going to do everything they can to place you at or near the scene of the crime. Even if you don't tell them anything else, that might be enough to get you arrested. It's amazing what they can do with circumstantial evidence today—if that, in fact, is what they find."

Paul's thoughts literally flew from his mind. He was convinced Scott was lying, but he'd successfully defended guilty clients before. The real decision would rest with the partners. Would they be willing to take the chance, nearly gratis? And if they did, what could they expect to gain in return?

Scott bit his tongue. He felt like speaking aloud every one of Paul's thoughts, but that hadn't gone well with anyone yet. Even Mary, who he thought would understand, was afraid. No, he told himself as Paul gathered up his briefcase and turned to go. He'd already done far more damage than he might be able to repair. From that time on, he would do like Paul suggested. He had to play dumb. Nobody knew what he was thinking. He had to learn to use his gift and yet keep it hidden so nobody would suspect the truth.

After Paul left, thoughts of his conversation with Dr. Talbot the day before grated across the smooth surface of his resolve. Scott knew the doctor had to protect himself. How far was he willing to go to do that?

An implication in an underage client's pregnancy was a career buster, or worse—especially where he was a psychologist, someone in a position of trust. Was the good doctor willing to do something bordering on insanity to protect himself? After all, Scott was strapped to a gurney in a head case ward. He still had all manner of tubes running into him. He was sure Talbot knew enough chemistry to know what it would take to silence Scott before he could ruin his career.

Scott's blood ran cold. How long could he stay awake? He needed to write down what he knew and give it to someone, like Mary, so that if something did happen to him, Talbot couldn't simply walk away.

He looked around the room for paper and a pen but found none. Before he could reach for the nurse call button, three officers entered the room. He didn't recognize them. Evidently, he had intimidated detectives Privit and Jones, because they hadn't returned. He figured that was a good thing. He could start with a clean slate so far as these officers were concerned.

Chapter 6
The Artist

The three officers waited in the doorway of Scott's hospital room until they could tell he was awake, and then the tallest of the trio reached over and turned up the lights.

"I'm Detective Pat Ableman," the man said as he strode to Scott's bedside, "but from what I've heard from the officers who came to see you yesterday, you probably already know that."

Scott was instantly on edge. He didn't answer. There was something about Detective Ableman that he didn't like. For one thing, Scott could sense his arrogance, and he'd never liked snotty people. The man's thoughts were all about himself. From that, Scott knew his name, his rank, and the fact he worked for Homicide—but Scott wasn't going to play that card yet. He knew he had to be very careful about what he told anybody from now on.

"How can I help you gentlemen?" he asked as he quickly scanned the thoughts of the other two.

"Let me introduce our sketch artist," Ableman said, pointing to a slightly built man with a full head of wavy dark-brown hair. "This is Jonathan Fleming. He's really good at what he does."

Scott lifted his unencumbered right hand toward the artist. The man stepped forward and shook it.

"Pleased to meet you, Jonathan," Scott said warmly. "Do you go by John or Jonathan?"

"I prefer my given name," Jonathan said without any visible emotion.

"I've never done anything like this before. I mean I haven't ever tried to describe anybody," Scott said. "I assume you've done this a time or two. Do I just start out, or do you lead me a little?"

"It used to be a lot harder than it is now," Jonathan said. "We have computer software that really helps."

"Do you guys need to read me my rights or anything before we start?" Scott asked. "My attorney was here earlier this morning, and he told me not to talk to you unless he was in the room."

The three exchanged glances.

"I believe his card is on my table," Scott added.

Ableman's thoughts turned hostile. He needed information and didn't have time to play games. The Chief had talked to the Lincoln Police Department after Scott had terrorized his first two officers. Because of that conversation, now the Omaha Metro Police Department was involved, and this weird case had been dropped in his lap. He'd already briefed the two officers with him, and between the three of them they were convinced Scott was the killer. This thing with the sketch artist was just a ruse. What Ableman really wanted was any information he could use to tie this weirdo to the murder. Then he could step away and let the courts deal with the rest.

"Tell you what," Scott said, "I think we all know why you're here. I know how this looks. My lawyer tells me I need to protect myself, but in the spirit of cooperation, I'll do my best to describe the guy I saw in my dream. I can't see any harm in that. If you want to ask me anything besides that, I'm going to have to decline."

Ableman's temper subsided. "Aren't you going to tell us all about ourselves like you did the two officers who came to see you yesterday?"

"Sorry," Scott answered carefully. "My gift . . . if you want to call it that . . . comes and goes. I'm not feeling any of that right now. They tell me I took a real hard blow to the head. I think some of my wiring might have been short-circuited or something. I don't know anything more about you three than what you just told me. I believe your name is Pat, and you're a detective of some sort, and the artist here is Jonathan." Scott nodded at the third man. "I don't know your name."

"James," the third man said, nodding his head slightly.

Scott could sense an immediate sense of relief from all three men. He had learned a valuable lesson. From that point on, he couldn't afford to offer any information that wasn't specifically asked for.

Scott looked at Jonathan. "How do we do this? I've got a pretty vivid memory of what the killer looks like, but I'm going to have to rely on your expertise to draw it out of me."

Jonathan opened a laptop computer, set it on Scott's roll-around table, and clicked a few keys. "We'll start with the basics. I'm going to show you a series of features. We'll start with head shape, hair, that sort of thing. Then, with the help of the computer and this touch wand," he said, holding up a pencil-shaped object connected to the laptop, "we'll flesh him out. You know, eye and hair color, that sort of thing."

"I'll do my best," Scott said.

Jonathan positioned the table over Scott's midsection so he could see the computer screen. As Scott nodded or gestured, he began adding detail after detail to the personage that began to take shape on his computer screen. Scott was amazed at how Jonathan was able to draw the details out of the vision that lay locked in his mind. As the drawing took on more and more form, he remembered a small dark mole at the corner of the killer's right eyebrow. He remembered the slight crook in the bridge of his nose; the prominent chin, the muscular jaw.

Then the vision came forward in Scott's mind, and when it did, he was able to flesh out the sunken eye sockets, the hard glare in the eyes, the scowl of fury on the killer's face, the wavy twist in his dark hair. The killer had no prominent facial hair, but he was unshaven like he hadn't used a razor in a couple of days. The slight sag in the skin under the man's chin spoke of either age or recent weight loss, or both. The Adam's apple was broad and thick; the neck, muscular and wide.

Scott raised his hand and pushed the table away a few inches. "His right ear was pierced," he said. "He was wearing a stone earring. It was smooth and round, not faceted like a diamond. It seemed to be sort of translucent—maybe like an opal or something."

Jonathan guided Scott through a series of ear shapes and sizes until Scott identified the right pair. Then Jonathan prompted him through the placement and size of the ear stud and waited.

Scott compared the computer rendering glaring at him from the laptop screen against the dark memory burned into his mind. It mostly fit, but there was something missing.

"Can you remember anything else?" Jonathan said.

"I'm struggling. It looks close, but something's not quite right. The cheekbones and the forehead were different."

Jonathan clicked a few keys and began adding features. Then, suddenly, it fit. Scott recognized the high, sharp cheekbones and nodded. He suggested the three weathered lines that squinted outward from the corners of the eyes and the four pronounced lines in the furrowed brow. He had Jonathan narrow and thicken the eyebrows. At that point, the vision in his head and the face on the computer screen seemed to be a perfect match. Then Scott remembered the acne scars. There weren't a lot of them, and they weren't grossly obvious, but they were there. As he tried to describe them, Jonathan expertly filled in a few examples until Scott raised his hand.

"That's him," he said quietly. "I don't remember much of anything else."

"You've done very well," Jonathan said. "It's not often I come up with the degree of emotion in a sketch like you've done with this one. If I didn't know better, I'd think you were describing an artist's painting, not a man."

Scott closed his eyes for a few seconds, trying to remember the man's hands. There was something about the hands. He could clearly see the knife, but the hands—

"Are you feeling okay?" Jonathan said.

"I'm trying to remember his hands. I can remember the knife he used, but I know there's something about the hands. I'm struggling a little."

"We usually don't worry about hands unless they've got a tattoo or some other identifying marks," Jonathan said, "so let's start with the knife. Was it a folding knife, or a fixed blade?"

"Fixed."

"Single or dual cutting edges?"

"Dual. I don't remember the handle, but there were stops where the blade and the handle came together. Sort of like a hunting knife. You know, so you don't slip down over the blade when you're thrusting or skinning."

Jonathan pulled up a blank screen and quickly punched away on the keyboard. A few seconds later, an entire page of knives popped up on the screen. Scott scanned the first page and shook his head. Jonathan clicked the mouse and another page popped up. All of the knives on the page were hunting knives with slightly curved blades.

"The blade was straight," Scott said, shaking his head.

Jonathan clicked some more keys. This time, the knives that appeared all had straight blades with cutting edges on both sides.

"That looks more like it, except . . ."

Jonathan slowly clicked through several more pages. The second knife on the third page was a match. Scott instantly recognized it and pointed.

"That's it!" he said quickly.

"That's a switchblade," Ableman said. "The blade comes straight out of the handle. It's illegal, of course. If you're right, you may have significantly narrowed down our search for the murder weapon. I've only seen one like it before. I believe it's Italian, and it's old. Pretty rare, actually."

Then it hit Scott. "I remember his hand!" he exclaimed. "His fingers were short and hairy, really thick, like he was overweight, but his face was gaunt."

"He's probably a gym freak," Ableman said.

"And his index finger has a long scar that goes from knuckle to knuckle on the back of his hand. There was no hair growing on the scar."

"Right hand or left?" Jonathan asked as he clicked away on the laptop keys.

"Right," Scott said. "He came up behind her. She saw him in the mirror and whirled around. He stuck her in the chest first. She tried to ward him off, but he kept stabbing her. There was blood everywhere."

Scott closed his eyes tight against the vision and stopped talking. A silence fell over the room.

"Did he stab straight in?" Ableman finally said.

Scott opened his eyes. "No, he was holding the knife over his head. He stabbed down at her. He was probably a foot taller than she was."

"Scott," Jonathan said, "could you look at these?"

The laptop screen was filled with hands. Each example showed a palm shot and one of the back of each hand. Jonathan patiently clicked through page after page of examples, but nothing fit. When he finally ran out of examples, he glanced up at the detective.

"You've been very helpful," Jonathan said. "Do you have any questions, Pat?"

"Let me ask you a question," Ableman said. "Are your dreams always this vivid?"

Scott sensed the intent of the detective's question. Ableman had recognized the man in the sketch, and he'd seen the knife before. It was as good as a photograph. He needed to quickly turn the brunt of the investigation against Scott. If he was careful, he could hang the murder on him and protect Vince.

"Yes," Scott lied.

"Don't they haunt you?" Ableman asked.

Scott looked away. "Yes, they do," he said, speaking only of his latest dream. Then he turned back to face Ableman. "That's why when I saw that poor girl's picture in the paper, I knew I had to do something, or I'll never have any peace."

A slight smile curled the corners of Ableman's mouth. Scott had said exactly what he wanted him to say. Now he had two witnesses. If he was careful, he could tell the jury he'd heard the confessions of a guilty man. Now all he had to do was come up with a little physical evidence to place Scott at the scene. In the meantime, he had to warn Vince.

Scott felt the blood drain out of his face. Ableman had almost everything he needed to frame him. Then he thought about what he'd seen. It was more than a dream. It was a vision. There was a man and a woman. There was a bloody murder scene. There was a car trunk and a bedsheet. There was a lonely road. There was an old rock well. There was a shallow grave. Who but the murderer could know all of that detail? If it hadn't been for the face Scott saw in the mirror, he might have believed he'd killed the woman himself. Now that he'd heard the detective's thoughts, he was worried. If his attorney couldn't establish an alibi for him, he was screwed.

Scott could barely breathe. Where had he been before or during the murder? The damnable part of the whole mess was that he simply couldn't remember. He had lost a month—maybe more—of his life, and without those memories to help defend himself, he couldn't do a thing to help Paul establish his innocence.

"I can see that you're struggling," Ableman said, nodding to the other two. "We'll let you rest. We'll probably be back, but next time, we'll be sure to bring your attorney with us."

With that, the three men turned and filed out of the room. Ableman's thoughts rang out loud and clear behind him as he walked away. The first thing he needed to do was discredit the drawing. He needed to have a shrink listen to Scott's crazy story. He was sure he could build a case based on the wild imaginings of a lunatic. Without the drawing, the rest was child's play. It should be easy enough to find some way of putting Scott at the scene.

Chapter 7
The Psychologist

Dr. Frank Talbot glanced impatiently at his watch. It was already five twenty. He'd agreed to see this last patient after business hours because she couldn't get away from work any earlier. His patient droned on and on. He still had another ten minutes before he could put an end to another fruitless session. He'd heard the woman's story at least a dozen times: her husband had ruined her life; he had left her with nothing; her kids had sided with him; they all thought she was nuts—but she wasn't! Okay, so maybe she obsessed a little over some things, but it wasn't like that made her a bad person. She liked order in her life. Was that a bad thing? Why couldn't they just meet her halfway? If they picked up after themselves, if they helped out with the chores, things would be different. Was that too much to ask?

She glanced up at the doctor, looking for validation. He nodded his head without saying anything that might reveal his true thoughts. Clinically, she was a textbook example of what it meant to be obsessive-compulsive. Talbot had used all of the skills he'd been taught to try to lead her thoughts, hoping she might catch a small glimpse of what he was trying to tell her—but she wasn't ready to accept any of the blame.

The high emotions from the divorce and the loss of the children to her ex-husband were blocking any reasonable thought. From a clinical standpoint, there was nothing dangerously wrong with the way she was. But only if she lived by herself. She was functional. She held down a job, but it had quickly become obvious in their sessions why nobody could stand to live with her.

Maybe if he had his partner medicate her so she could deal better with the anger, it might help. He hated doing that, though, unless it was absolutely necessary. Too many of his patients were already drug dependent.

That thought led to another, and a shiver ran down his spine. He wondered if the blood tests they'd given his fifteen-year-old female patient had gone beyond what was required to determine what drugs she'd overdosed on. He hoped the lab tests didn't indicate she was with child. She'd called to tell him she was pregnant just hours before she took the drugs. If she ever regained consciousness and confessed who the father of her baby was, he would be ruined.

That thought only brought with it another. How the hell did that head case he'd seen the day before know the truth about what was going on in the psych ward? Dr. Gilbert said the guy had been in a coma for weeks. Talbot didn't really believe in clairvoyance, but he couldn't discount it, either. He'd never seen the man before and yet in seconds, the guy seemed to know everything about him.

Suddenly, he was aware his patient had stopped talking and was watching him.

"Am I boring you?" she asked angrily.

"No, no," he lied. "I'll be perfectly honest with you, though. We've been meeting for weeks now, and we're just not getting anywhere. I've read the court testimony. I've talked to your ex-husband and to your children. I've talked to several of your co-workers. And, well, I'm going to be very blunt with you right now. You may think you're not the problem, but you are. You have a classic psychological disorder that is treatable, but only if you're willing to step up and meet me part way. I—"

"I think our session is over," she interrupted. "I'm going to seek counseling elsewhere."

"That's certainly your choice," he said. "But before you do, you may want to take a week and reconsider. You have an anger problem. Not that I blame you, of course. But your anger is blocking any chance we have of making progress. If you can see past that anger, I think we can work through your other issues."

She jumped to her feet and stormed to the door. "I don't have anger issues!" she bellowed.

He smiled. "Of course you don't. That's why you're standing in my doorway, screaming at the only person who may be able to help you. Call me next week if you want to come back."

She slammed the door violently behind her as she left.

"That was real professional," he muttered under his breath. He'd crossed the line again. But damn, it felt good.

Talbot got to his feet and went to the office's locked drug cabinet. All he needed for his first problem was a small syringe and an injectable variant of the same prescription drug the silly girl had ingested when she found out she was pregnant. A simple boost would close the door on that problem. She was delicate enough already from the massive overdose she'd taken that her death wouldn't be unexpected.

His other problem was more daunting. He had no idea what that guy in the trauma center was being given for pain, so anything like that was out. He had to assume he was on some sort of an anti-convulsive medication. Most head trauma patients were.

His partner, Dr. Franklin, only worked out of their office once a week. Their secretary left at five. Dr. Franklin never locked his office. They often collaborated over the phone on a patient, and Franklin left the key to the cabinet in his desk so Talbot could administer drugs when he needed to without the psychiatrist being present. Talbot took the key and rummaged through the cabinet until he found something that would mimic an overdose.

The biggest issue at the hospital was one of concealment. If he could slip in and out of the man's room without being seen, his death could be blamed on a hospital error. At night, the room lights would either be off or dim. He'd wear blue coveralls, something like the orderlies wore when they were emptying garbage or bedpans.

The psych ward was going to be much more difficult. It was always well lit and often over-manned, especially if it was a busy night. He wasn't a regular there, but if any of the normal staff were on call, they would probably recognize him, even in disguise.

He stopped to lock his office door behind him and pressed his head against the wall. What was he thinking? Was he ready to throw away thirty years of practice? Worse yet, was he ready to kill? Then the other thoughts rained down on him. He really had no other choice. The little affair from five years ago had already driven a deep wedge between him and his wife. He'd had to come clean. There was no way he could have hidden the disappearance of that much money from their savings accounts. Thankfully, the word hadn't gone beyond his wife and the other woman.

His marriage was still intact, if only in name. His wife hadn't threatened him, but he knew he had to walk a fine line. As long as he still brought home the money, she would stay. The hush money he'd paid the other woman had nearly ruined him financially, and an ugly divorce would finish him—especially if the true cause of their marital problems was revealed. The other woman had been one of his patients too, but at least she'd been of legal age. In return for the money, she had agreed to keep quiet and save his professional career.

This new situation was exponentially worse. If the teenager

pulled through and fingered him as her baby's father, he'd be convicted of child rape. He'd go to prison.

He would have offered her an abortion, but he hadn't had time to talk to her about that before she took the pills. Getting an abortion would have been a logistical nightmare, but it would have been doable. Just losing the baby was not an option. Her parents would have known and asked damning questions. She was living at home and was so young that offering her money would have no impact. There was really only one option—and the girl, bless her heart, had already started down that road on her own.

Getting rid of her was Talbot's first priority, but he knew he couldn't ignore the psychic guy. If any public accusations were made, Talbot could try arguing that the man was insane. But if any of it got the attention of the authorities, it was over. All someone would have to do was order a quick examination of the dead girl's body. They'd find the fetus. He simply couldn't let that happen. They both had to be silenced, and it had to happen tonight.

He called his wife and told her he'd been called to the hospital to treat a patient and would probably be late. He stopped at a thrift store on the way downtown and bought an outfit that included rough clothes and a floppy-brimmed hat to replace his suit and tie. Then he parked his black Audi a block from the hospital and waited until dark.

He tried to listen to a talk show to help soak up some of the excess time, but after a while, he switched to a classical music station. His mind was too full of his own preparations to listen to anyone else's drivel.

Just before ten, he changed clothes and walked the long way around to the service entrance of the hospital to avoid the parking lot surveillance cameras. There were four dumpsters sitting in a row alongside a retaining wall. He slipped between them and waited.

He looked for cameras over the back door. There didn't appear to be any. He checked around the nearby light fixtures as well, with similar results. Every exterior door used key cards for access. He had one, but he couldn't afford to use it. The computer kept records of every access. Nobody could know he had been here. He was hoping the janitorial crew would come to his rescue.

At about a quarter after ten, the double entry doors swung open. A man in blue coveralls propped the doors open so he could pull a short train of wheeled garbage carts to the dumpster. When the man moved past him, Frank stepped out from between the dumpsters and walked through the open doors. The janitor either didn't spot him or was too busy with the garbage to care.

Talbot had never been in the deep bowels of the hospital before, but it didn't take him long to find a cart full of blue coveralls waiting to be picked up by the laundry service. He pulled the cart through a nearby door labeled *Electrical Room*. The coveralls he tried were a little large, but they covered his new wardrobe nicely. Not wanting to draw undue attention to himself, he wadded up the floppy hat and stuffed it into the pocket of the coveralls.

He waited until he heard the double doors slam shut, and then he counted off a couple of minutes, giving the janitor time to clear the hallway before opening the door. The corridor was empty. He grabbed an empty garbage cart to complete his disguise and hurried to the elevator.

When he got to the fifth floor, Talbot could see that the psych ward wasn't overly busy. Evidently, weeknights weren't in high demand for recreational drug overdoses. He spotted only one nurse. Knowing exactly where he had to go, he made a quick left turn out of the elevator and headed down the hallway toward room 503. He left the cart outside the door and slipped inside. His young patient was wearing an oxygen mask and had an IV in her left arm. She was either unconscious or asleep. He didn't care either way.

He walked quickly to her bedside and switched off the heart and oxygen monitors so no alarms would sound. Then, without another thought or wasted step, he inserted the needle into her IV line and pressed the plunger.

He wiped the spent syringe on a bedsheet to get rid of any fingerprints and dropped it in a locked disposal container hanging on the wall. He stopped at the door only long enough to make sure nobody was watching, then he walked the garbage cart to the elevator. Step one of his two-step plan was complete.

* * * * *

After the officers left, Scott couldn't control his thoughts. Was he really in Lincoln the day Nancy Bennion was murdered? He was sure he'd never seen her before his dream—or before he saw her picture in the newspaper—but why was this dream so different from any of the others he'd had?

Mary dropped by just after lunch. At first, she was quiet and guarded. He took his time answering her questions so that he wouldn't mess up again. Using what he could see in her thoughts, he guided their conversation around what she was thinking. After a half hour or so, she began to relax. They talked about bills and insurance claims. He asked about the business. Then he asked about Alan—fighting hard to control his emotions when Mary's thoughts of the two of them raced through her mind. Scott had to ask about Trish to pull her thoughts away.

While Mary talked about Trish and her boyfriend, Scott fought to calm the anger that boiled inside him over the Alan thing. Did he hate Alan enough to kill him over what he'd done? Was he capable of doing that? If he was, maybe it was also possible that what Detective Ableman had accused him of was true.

They chatted until his dinner came at six, then Mary made an excuse and left. He saw right through her. She'd told the kids she'd be home around eight. If she left now, she still had time to see Alan before going home.

As she leaned over him and gave him a kiss on the forehead, Scott didn't feel any of the fear in her he'd felt the day before. In spite of her obvious feelings for Alan, he still felt her love. Maybe their marriage was salvageable. Scott hoped the thing with Alan was simple lust. He had to believe that. It was all he had.

The orthopedic surgeon checked in on him after Mary left. The man's thoughts and words were totally divergent. He gave Scott verbal encouragement, but his thoughts said he was looking at a total knee replacement if he ever wanted to walk again. Scott didn't want to think about that. Pain still burned in a couple of dozen other places. He couldn't bring himself to think about heaping even more pain upon himself.

Afterward, he closed his eyes and tried to rest, but his mind wouldn't slow down. He wished he'd never seen the Sunday paper. He wished he'd kept his new "gift" to himself. But it was too late for all that now.

Feeling his thoughts spinning out of control, Scott concentrated on his roommate. He didn't want to go there either, but he needed a break from his own collapsing world. He reached out to the young man again and again, but there was nothing there. The curtains between them were open slightly. He could see him lying there, surrounded by a tangled mass of tubes and monitors, but there was no consciousness. Scott wondered if the young man was sleeping, or if he'd slipped even further into that mental abyss from which he would probably never return.

Scott pulled his thoughts away. He tried to busy his mind thinking about his business, but doing so only brought him close to panic. They told him he'd lost his short-term memory in the crash, but this seemed to be something more. It was as if he had a cancer that was slowly destroying his mind.

Then he remembered his wedding to Mary. That memory was clear. He moved forward, remembering the births of each of their children. Scott knew he had attended school before their marriage, but strangely, he couldn't remember much about it.

Suddenly, his thoughts were pulled back to the dream. This time, he saw the old rock well first. He felt Nancy's presence; watched through her eyes as the killer pulled her body from the car trunk and dropped it in the dirt.

Her body was still wrapped in a sheet. The killer grabbed one corner of the sheet and dragged it through a tangle of grass and weeds around the well and across a small clearing. There was a grave there. The man had cut the sod and laid it aside so that he could cover the scar in the earth when he was done.

As Scott watched, the killer dropped the body, still wrapped in a bloody sheet, into the grave. Then dirt began to rain down into the hole.

Scott felt Nancy's anguish as the killer's car drove away. How long would she stay by her body? Would she be doomed to wander that hillside alone until someone found her?

Scott could barely breathe. He knew he should try to bring the poor woman some peace, even if everything he told the police would be used to further their case against him. But was he willing to give up his own freedom to do that?

He remembered the ugly image he'd helped the police sketch artist build: the thick, hairy fingers; the knife.

Ableman had known the killer's name: Vince. The man in the drawing looked Italian. The name fit. Scott had to tell his attorney what he knew and wondered how long it would be before Paul came back to see him. He wanted to call him, but he couldn't reach the phone.

Even before the door to his room opened, Scott felt Talbot's presence. From the doctor's thoughts, Scott instantly knew why he was here, and he knew how Talbot planned to accomplish his deed.

If I die now, Scott thought, *she will never be free.*

He thought about screaming but knew he shouldn't. Talbot was a big man. He could easily overpower him. If he injected the drug directly instead of putting it in his IV, there would be no recourse.

Scott tried to move his arms. They were restrained at his sides. He felt for the nurse call button but couldn't reach it. His legs were restrained at the ankles. The only thing unrestrained was his upper torso. He wondered if he could head-butt Talbot. Then he thought about the metal plate in his head. He would probably kill himself if he did that.

He lay perfectly still, listening to Talbot's thoughts. The doctor only hesitated long enough to be sure Scott wasn't awake and that there was nobody else in the room, then he quickly walked to Scott's bedside and switched off the monitors.

Scott kept his eyes closed as Talbot found the IV tube and inserted the needle. Before Scott could even begin to feel the sting of whatever drug he'd been given, Talbot was gone.

In a sudden violent movement, Scott lunged upward against the restraints, thrashing his body from side to side. The bed moved. He heard the IV stand crash to the floor and felt a sting in his arm as the tube pulled free. Then he heard a voice. It wasn't Talbot's.

"Can I help you?" It was the nurse, speaking to him through the receiver on his call button.

"I've been poisoned!" Scott yelled. "Help me, please!"

Seconds later, the lights in his room flashed on and two nurses hurried to his bedside.

"You've pulled out your IV," one of them said.

"Talbot was here!" Scott shouted. "He stuck something in my IV. He's trying to kill me!"

"You're bleeding all over the place," the other nurse said, and Scott knew that was a good thing. Maybe his blood would flush out any of the drug the doctor had injected into him.

He relaxed as the nurses worked around him. How would he explain this? They'd probably think he was having a psychotic episode. They'd probably sedate him. If Talbot knew that, he might come back to finish what he'd begun.

"I'm going to tell you something," Scott began as calmly as his wild emotions would allow. "You need to believe me and act quickly, or somebody's going to die."

He had their full attention.

"Dr. Frank Talbot was just in my room. He turned off my monitors and injected something into my IV. Time is of the essence. He has a young patient in the psych ward on the fifth floor who is pregnant with his child. He just injected her with something to shut her up. I saw his thoughts. He knows I know what he did, and he came here to kill me, too."

"I think you're having an episode," one of the nurses said, trying to calm him. "Please, just try to relax. I'll call someone."

"Before you do," Scott insisted, "call the psych ward. Send them to room 503. Tell them that he's turned off her monitors and injected her with a drug she already overdosed on. If they don't hurry, she'll die."

The nurses seemed stunned, but neither moved.

"Do it now!" Scott bellowed. "Or her death will be on your heads!"

The nurses looked at each other, confused.

"Okay," Scott said, looking at the shorter of the two nurses. "I can see you don't believe me. Cindy, you're the nurse on call. You're married to Tom. You have two children. You live in a small home an hour's commute from here. You have a dog you call Brad, and you're two months pregnant with your third child. Now humor me and call the psych ward!"

Cindy lunged for the phone hanging on the wall as the other nurse ripped the tape from the stub protruding from his arm, pulled the IV catheter free, and put pressure on the wound to stop the bleeding. Both were speaking at the same time. Cindy was shrieking into the telephone. The other nurse, whose name Scott now knew was Judy, was asking him if he knew what Talbot had injected him with.

"I think he used an anti-seizure drug of some kind," Scott said. "He turned off the monitors before he did."

Judy looked at the monitors. "You're restrained. You couldn't have reached those on your own, and they're both turned off."

"Now do you believe me?" Scott asked.

Chapter 8
<u>Homicide</u>

Detective Ableman was standing at Scott's bedside at eight the next morning. "From what they tell me, you had quite a night," he said as Scott opened his eyes.

"Good morning, Detective," Scott said, trying to clear his groggy mind.

"I just talked to the two nurses who were on call last night."

"You mean Judy and Cindy?"

Ableman glanced at his note pad. "Yes. I didn't know you knew them."

"I didn't until last night."

"They had a pretty interesting story to tell."

"Did they save that girl in the psych ward?"

"Aren't you going to tell me her name too?" Ableman asked sourly.

"Her name was Susan, if that makes any difference."

"Cindy tells me she didn't tell you her name, but you knew it—and it seems that you knew a lot more about her, as well."

"What do you want me to say?"

"You told me yesterday that you wouldn't answer any more questions without your attorney being present. Are you still holding firm on that?"

Scott searched the detective's thoughts before he answered. "I don't think it would matter much at this point what I told you. You've already made up your mind that I killed Nancy Bennion."

"You don't know that!"

"Don't I? You've already called the county shrink to come analyze me. You're hoping for a 'crazy' verdict."

Ableman stared at him without saying a word.

"I told you everything I know yesterday," Scott said. "You have the perp's picture. You have a cause of death. You even know what kind of weapon you're looking for. Your problem is you've already convicted me. You're convinced the only way I could have known all of those details is if I was the killer."

"I didn't come here to talk about yesterday," Ableman said. "I apparently have another possible homicide on my plate now. Unfortunately, it looks like I have to deal with you on that one, too."

Scott looked away. "I was so hoping she'd make it," he said. He struggled to maintain his composure. He was still groggy from the sedatives they'd given him the night before. He turned back to face Ableman. "Now I suppose you're here to see if you can connect me to her murder, too."

"We don't know for sure if she was murdered. They tell me she apparently died from an overdose she took a couple of days ago."

"And I'm telling you that you better check her blood. I know for a fact that Talbot injected her last night with another lethal dose of the same drug she overdosed on."

"You can't possibly know that."

"Okay," Scott said, "I can see how this is going to go. No, I wasn't there. I can't possibly know that he drugged her up, but if you want to solve this, you'll order blood work. I'm sure you'll find that the drug level in her blood is higher now than it was when she was admitted to the hospital. How do you suppose that might have happened? Oh, and while you're at it, you might want to check to see if she was pregnant. I'm sure you'll find out she was. Then you should check her dead child's DNA. I think you'll find it's a perfect match to Dr. Frank Talbot."

"How do you know all that? Who told you?"

Scott stared at Ableman. "I could tell you, but of course you'll just blow me off. I've said all I'm going to say."

Ableman's anger surged.

"You're dangerous," Scott said. "Right now, you've got tunnel vision. All you can think about is my case. You don't give a shit about that teenager's death. You recognized the guy in that drawing I made yesterday. His name is Vince, and you're trying to protect him. You're trying to find something that will connect me to that murder scene in Lincoln. If you're going to convict me of something I didn't do, you're going to have to do your own police work. I'm not telling you another damn thing."

"I guess we'll see you on the witness stand, then," Ableman said, sneering as he snapped his notebook shut.

"You're so convinced I'm full of shit that you're not even going to check that girl's body, are you?"

"What I do or don't do is frankly none of your business," Ableman said as he turned on his heel and strode out the door.

The thoughts Scott saw as the detective left were frightening. Ableman was not only enraged, but he was also afraid. He couldn't afford to be linked to Vince. Somehow, he had to make this thing with Scott go away.

Scott was able to reach the nurse's call button this time. When the nurse appeared at his bedside, he asked her to call his attorney. He couldn't let that girl's body leave the hospital without a thorough examination, and he had no power to do that. He hoped he could convince Paul to do it.

Mary showed up before Paul did. She wasn't as guarded as she had been the day before until Scott started to tell her what had happened during the night. He tried to tone down what he told her, but the second he mentioned his encounter with Ableman, fear flooded her mind. She fidgeted, worrying he knew what she was thinking. He pretended not to notice and changed the subject to the boys. Then he asked about Trish. He didn't want Mary to leave. They'd only spent a half hour together when Paul showed up.

The moment Paul strode hurriedly through the door, Scott knew he had a significant problem. He wanted to tell him every detail about the night before and what he'd gleaned from Talbot's mind, but to do so would break any trust he'd rebuilt with Mary. Now it was his turn to fidget.

"I talked to the cops this morning," Paul said. "They tell me you helped them build a composite drawing. I thought we talked about that."

"I didn't think there'd be any harm in giving them somebody to look for besides me."

"The problem is, they're thinking your story is all a big ruse. You went a little further than just the composite drawing. They tell me you described the murder weapon. That's more than they had. They're convinced you made that guy up. I thought we'd agreed that you wouldn't talk to them again without me being present."

"I didn't think—"

"No, you didn't think," Paul said angrily. "That's the problem. You need to help *me*, not them, or they're going to hang you. I'll bet ninety percent of what they have in this case so far has come straight from your lips. Do you want to go to prison?"

"No, but I feel like I need to help them catch the killer."

"They think they already have. They're just trying to find a final piece to the puzzle that will put you at the time and place of the murder. They'll use the rest of your story, even though it may be circumstantial, to convince a jury you're their guy. Do you understand what I'm trying to tell you, or am I wasting my time?"

Paul was livid. Scott could tell he was holding it together on the outside, but inside he was seething.

"Mary," Scott said, "could you give me and my lawyer a few minutes alone please?"

She looked shocked. Inside, she was worried he was going to spill his guts to the lawyer—admit to killing that girl—and that he just didn't want her to hear it from his lips. She hesitated. Scott wanted to explain, but knew he couldn't. He waited.

Suddenly, in a huff of emotion, Mary turned and stormed out of the room.

"That wasn't cool," Paul said as the door swung closed.

"I need to tell you the rest of the story," Scott said, "and I don't want her to hear this. She's already scared of me because I can read her thoughts. And, well . . . she's got some things going on that she doesn't want me to know about."

"What are you going to do? Are you going to confess to that girl's murder?"

"No. I almost wish I could. It might be easier. But no, I didn't kill her. You need to know what happened here last night. Somebody's got to do something before it's too late."

"Too late for what?"

"Did they tell you that Dr. Talbot came here to murder me last night?"

"No, but then I feel like there's a lot I don't know about what's going on with this case. Who is Talbot, and why the hell would he risk doing something stupid like that?"

"He's the shrink my doctor sent to see me. I saw something when he was here."

"And of course you couldn't keep your mouth shut," Paul interjected. "What did you tell him to get him all stirred up?"

"I know he knocked up his fifteen-year-old patient and she tried to commit suicide when she found out. She was unconscious in the psych ward upstairs. When he found out I knew, he came up here and tried to stick something in my IV so I couldn't tell anybody. If they'd have sampled the fluids that got dumped on the floor when I ripped my IV out, they'd have found a strong dose of anti-seizure medication that he came here to inject me with. I'm sure he figured the hospital would get the blame."

Paul's eyes narrowed. Scott could sense his skepticism.

"So what do you want me to do?" Paul asked.

"You need to convince somebody to check that girl's blood for the drug she overdosed on. They'll find out there's more of it in her blood than she came in here with. They also need to do a pregnancy test and, if necessary, a post-mortem on her child. They'll find out the DNA matches Talbot's."

"Hell, man," Paul fumed. "I'm an attorney, not a detective. I can't go around ordering all those tests. And for what? Did anybody actually see Talbot in here besides you?"

"I don't know. Probably not. He was dressed in blue coveralls like a janitor or an orderly. He was pushing a trash bin."

"You're out of your mind!" Paul growled.

"No, actually, I'm not. But if you don't do something, Dr. Talbot's going to walk away, and I'll have to worry for the rest of the time I'm here that he's going to come back to finish what he started."

Paul quietly considered what Scott told him. When he replied, it wasn't what Scott wanted to hear. "My job right now is to keep you out of prison. I'll see what I can do about this other mess. Maybe I can pull a few strings—put a few ideas in the right places. But I can't promise anything."

"Well, if you expect Detective Ableman to do *his* job, you're sadly mistaken. I saw his thoughts. He recognized the guy the sketch artist drew. He's trying to protect him by framing me as the killer. He doesn't want to get wrapped up in that other case right now. It's going to be real easy for him to just step away and let the hospital tell everybody she died of complications from the overdose. Nobody's going to know why she overdosed, not even her parents. Nobody knows she was pregnant. She was already messed up mentally. That's why she was seeing Talbot. She was only fifteen. He seduced her. The way the law sees it, that's child rape. He's guilty."

"And unfortunately, that is none of your business," Paul answered matter-of-factly. "I know you don't want to hear that, but it's true. Neither the rape nor the alleged murder of that girl is any of your business. You're trying to make both of these cases your business because you somehow feel morally obligated. But when you go off spouting facts that only the real killer would know, you're pounding nails in your own coffin. Am I making myself understood?"

Scott brooded silently before he answered. He knew Paul really wanted to help. He wanted to win his case. He was even beginning to believe that Scott could actually read other people's thoughts. The problem was that people, in general, refused to believe anybody besides God Himself had the ability to know what another person was thinking.

"Yes," Scott finally answered. "You've made yourself perfectly clear. But if that was my daughter lying out there in the dirt, I'd want to know where she was so I could bring her home."

Paul's thoughts sprang to life. "If you say one word about knowing where the body is, I won't represent you. Do you understand me?" His eyes had turned dark; the threat was real. Scott had pushed him as far as he could.

"Okay," Scott said quietly. "Where do we go from here?"

"You lay there in that bed and get better," Paul said, "and you keep your trap shut. You don't answer another question. I don't care if they threaten to take away your birthday. They know who your attorney is. Don't push me, though. I'm dead serious when I tell you I'll drop your case in a heartbeat if you say one more word. Your case is damned near unwinnable as it is." He straightened the lapels of his suit coat. "I'm going to go see what I can do, if anything, about that mess upstairs. If I can't, you need to let it go. I'll see to it that Dr. Talbot gets the word I know what he did, and that I'll find some way to ruin him if anything happens to you. Do we understand one another?"

"Yes," Scott said. "Perfectly."

Paul turned and walked urgently to the door. "I'll send your wife in," he said. "If I were you, I'd try to mend those fences. You're going to need all the support you can get."

Chapter 9
Home

Mary walked hesitantly into Scott's hospital room after Paul left. She stopped a few feet from the foot of the bed. Scott offered his best smile in an attempt to disarm what he feared was going to be nothing less than an inquisition.

"What was so secret between you and your attorney that you made me leave the room?"

"I needed to talk to him about what a certain homicide detective told me this morning. I didn't want to worry you."

"*Should* I be worried?"

Scott quickly searched her thoughts before he answered.

"Maybe," he said. "Paul—that's my attorney—was furious I helped the police artist put together a composite drawing of the killer. He's afraid anything I give them will be used against me."

"And will it?"

"I thought if I gave them that drawing it would turn their focus away from me."

"You didn't *have* to tell anybody. If what you saw was really just a dream, and you didn't have a relationship with that woman in Lincoln, nobody could have ever connected you two. Now every time you open your mouth you're giving them more brick and mortar for their case. I could tell Paul wasn't happy when he left."

"I guess I thought I could help them find the real murderer."

"Why is that so important? Are you ready to sacrifice everything? To do what, exactly?"

"Think about it," Scott said. "If something like that happened to Trish . . . if somebody murdered her and hid her body in a shallow grave somewhere . . . wouldn't you give anything to find her, even if you knew she was dead?"

"Probably, but that's not the point. Maybe you're just mixed up. Maybe this is some sort of a psychological need to come clean without actually admitting guilt."

"Is that what you think?" Scott asked, already knowing her answer before she spoke the words.

"I don't know what to think," Mary said. Tears filled her eyes. "I went to the library and read all the newspaper articles about her disappearance. Scott, you were in Lincoln when she went missing. In fact, you wrecked the car the same day she disappeared. Now you want me to believe that this so-called dream you had—which, by the way, is totally different than any of your other dreams—is some sort of a gift? Were you having an affair? Was she pregnant?"

Scott stared at Mary for a few seconds. Now her cheeks were wet with tears. She wanted to scream accusations. The only reason she didn't was because just behind her rage stood a mountain of her own guilt. She was afraid. She still vividly remembered their earlier conversation; the talk they'd had when he first came out of the coma. Could he really read her thoughts? Did he know about Alan?

Scott held out his hand. "You need to trust me, Mary. Until the dream, I'd never seen her. I wasn't having an affair. I didn't kill her. How do you explain that man I saw with the knife—the one I described for the sketch artist?"

Mary stood her ground. "You're not yourself. If they put me on the witness stand right now, I would have to tell them that you've changed. You're different. I don't know what changed you. Maybe it was the knock on the head. Maybe it was something else. I don't know if I even know who you are anymore."

"Mary, don't."

"Be honest with me," she demanded. "Do you really know what I'm thinking?"

"I can feel your emotions," he said, side-stepping the question. "I told you that when I first came out of the coma. I can't read your thoughts. Nobody can do that. But I can tell that you're upset. I can feel your anger. I can feel your mistrust. I suppose if I were standing in your shoes, I'd feel the same way. Please don't walk away. You're all I've got right now."

She took a step backwards. "I need some time, Scott. I can't be here right now. I need to work this out on my own."

"And I need to know that I can trust you."

Her countenance broke. Her thoughts were screaming the words she couldn't say: *You can't trust me, Scott. That's the point. We can't trust each other.*

"I need some time," she sobbed. "Just give me some time."

With that, she turned and was gone.

Scott stared at the ceiling for a long time. He tried to organize his thoughts. He tried to remember those lost hours—those lost days—

but there was nothing there. He so wished he could give Paul something to go on, some inkling of where he'd been and what he'd been doing before his wreck.

He knew the dreams he'd had over the years were real. He'd watched them play out before his very eyes. This "dream" was different, but somehow it had to be part of what he'd always been. What had changed from then to now? Why could he suddenly read people's thoughts? Did he need that ability in order to know what had happened to Nancy?

"Mr. Corbridge?" an orderly said, wheeling a food cart into the room. "Would you like some lunch?"

Scott searched his physical needs. "Yes," he said, "I believe I could eat."

The orderly lifted the head of the hospital bed, positioned the portable table over Scott's midsection, and transferred a few Styrofoam boxes from the food cart to the table.

"It's baked chicken," the orderly said as he began opening the boxes. "It smelled really good when I was loading it up in the kitchen. I think you'll like it."

"I'm sure I will, Randy," Scott answered without thinking.

The young man looked puzzled.

"Oh, I'm sorry," Scott said. "That's not your name, is it?"

"It is, actually. But how did you know that? This is my first day on this wing."

"Lucky guess," Scott tried to bluff. "Maybe you look like a Randy. I have a cousin named Randy, and you look a lot like him. You'll need to excuse me. I'm not thinking straight these days. I was in a car crash and took a nasty blow to the head."

"They told me you could do that."

"Do what?"

"Read my thoughts."

"Who told you that?"

"The nurses. They're actually a little afraid of you."

"Which nurses?"

"Cindy and Judy."

"Weren't they here last night?"

"Uh huh. They work twelve-hour shifts. They were just getting off when I came in."

"What else did they tell you?"

The orderly looked uncomfortable. "That you think somebody tried to kill you last night."

"I suppose they didn't believe me?"

"They told me you were out of control, raving about some guy wanting to kill a girl in the psych ward. They said you went nuts and ripped out your IV and they had to sedate you."

"Now that's really unfortunate," Scott said. "I suppose they didn't do what I asked them to do?"

"I don't know what you asked them to do."

"Did a girl die last night on the fifth-floor psych ward or not?"

"I heard they had a fatality, but they said she'd come in on a bad overdose, and they couldn't do anything to turn it around."

"I'm really sorry to hear that, Randy. By the way, you don't need to be afraid of me. I can't tell a thing you're thinking—unless, of course, you're thinking I really am nuts after last night."

"No, I don't think you're nuts. But they tell me that head trauma patients can sometimes do really strange things."

Scott motioned to his roommate's bed. "Tell me, Randy. Is he getting any better?"

"I really don't know. Like I told you, this is my first day on this wing. They told me he's being fed intravenously, so I don't have to worry about feeding him."

"When I first got here, I thought I heard him stir from time to time. I haven't heard anything for over a day now."

"They told me he was in a bad motorcycle crash. I don't think they give him much hope. His parents are trying to decide whether or not to keep him on life support. Cindy told me she thinks they're getting ready to unplug him and donate his organs."

"That really sucks," Scott said.

"Yeah, it does. He's a year younger than I am."

"Do you ride a bike?"

"A pedal bike," Randy said. "I'm still in school. I can't afford a real bike."

"Do you wear a helmet?"

"Yup. I don't want to end up like him. Hey, I've got a couple more meals to deliver. I'll be back in about twenty minutes. If you need anything, ring your call button."

"Thanks," Scott said.

"You're not going to tell me about myself, then?" Randy asked, only half teasing.

"Sorry. I must have broken my antennae last night with all that thrashing around."

* * * * *

Dr. Gilbert bustled in just before five.

"I've been going over all your stats," he said. "Your orthopedic surgeon has decided to cast your leg for now. He'll be in tomorrow morning to do that. He says the surgical wounds have healed, but he's worried there's been so much soft tissue damage that additional surgery may not help you. He's going to immobilize your leg so you can go home until he decides what to do. I know he's thinking about doing a complete knee replacement, and I know he's been talking to the insurance company. That is pretty much the last thing keeping you here. I think we can let you go home as soon as he casts your leg."

After Gilbert left, Scott wanted to call Paul to see if he had done anything about the fifth floor, but he was still restrained to his bed, and the phone was still clear across the room. He felt a deep sadness creep over him. He knew in his heart that Talbot was going to get away with what he'd done, and that poor young girl would go to her grave with her parents thinking she'd successfully committed suicide.

The monitors in his room started shrieking about an hour later. His roommate's bed was instantly surrounded by all sorts of activity. Scott listened as they tried again and again to restart the young man's heart—all to no avail. When a doctor made the final call, they unplugged the tubes and wires and whisked him off to surgery. They had to hurry if they were going to harvest his organs before they died, too.

The room grew deathly quiet after everyone left. He hadn't realized it before, but there had been a lot of white noise coming from his roommate's bedside. Now the only noise in the room was a very subtle beeping from his own heart monitor. Gone was the whoosh and thump of the boy's ventilator. Gone was the chirp of his heart monitor. Gone was the periodic beep of his oxygen monitor. Scott couldn't sleep. In his mind's eye, he could imagine Talbot sneaking back into his room to make another attempt on his life.

They brought breakfast at seven. He was exhausted from lying awake all night, but glad now that other people would be moving around the halls. Talbot wouldn't dare do anything in broad daylight, and if things went well Scott would be in his own bed by nightfall.

True to Dr. Gilbert's word, the knee surgeon showed up at eight, talked to him briefly, and then went to wait for the orderlies to wheel him down to a small operating room. The surgeon made quick work of a rigid fiberglass cast that stretched from crotch to ankle. Then, after warning Scott not to put any weight at all on his leg, he vanished.

Paul showed up at ten. He wasn't smiling. Scott knew why.

"I'm sorry I didn't listen to you," Paul said. "I got to thinking about everything you told me yesterday and, well, I guess I should have believed you."

"What's up?" Scott said quickly. Even though he already knew what had happened, he wanted Paul to have to recite the facts and apologize.

"The girl's parents were so upset and embarrassed about the overdose and everything that they had her body cremated this morning. They don't have a lot of money. They didn't even want a graveside service."

"So now we'll never know if I was right," Scott said solemnly. "And that bastard got away with murder."

"Well, I suppose he did, but at least that lets you off the hook with her psychologist. There's no reason for him to make another attempt on your life now."

"I suppose you think I was just imagining things?"

"I apologize," Paul said. "I got to thinking last night about all of our conversations. I even rewound the tapes I made. I had my own agenda. And, well, you have to agree that what you've been telling me is pretty unbelievable."

"Do you believe me or not?"

"Do I really have to answer that?"

"You already did," Scott said. Paul was finally on his side.

"I hate that!" Paul exclaimed. "Can't I ever have a private thought when I'm around you?"

"No, but let me tell you I get no pleasure at your expense. Actually, I hate this too. It's caused me nothing but heartache. I may even lose my wife over it. She doesn't know how to handle it."

"I can understand that. I don't quite know how to handle it either, and I'm not your wife. I'm thinking a healthy marriage needs a little secrecy."

"Unfortunately, I'm finding out that's true," Scott said. "My challenge is going to be learning how to play like I don't know what she's thinking."

"You mean like you just did when I came in here to tell you about the girl on the fifth floor?"

"You catch on really quick."

"And I think you're beginning to learn how to keep your mouth shut. We need to talk a lot now as we learn more about all this. You're right about that detective. I hear he's getting a court order to have you undergo a psychological evaluation."

"He probably wants to have somebody with credentials tell the court I'm nuts. So how do I handle that?"

"I'm not really sure. On the one hand, you could really bend that psychologist's mind when he starts asking questions. I guess what I'm saying is you need to try to act normal."

"What about the dream?"

"Okay," Paul said, "what about it? I think it's time you and I had a heart-to-heart chat about that. I need to know every detail you remember. I'll get my team on board, and we'll talk about whether or not we might want to give any more information to the cops. I need to tell you something up front, though."

"You've been doing some investigative work and haven't been able to establish an alibi for me," Scott said for him.

"Would you quit that?" Paul said, aggravated. "But yes, I'd be lying if I told you I felt confident about your case."

"All I can ask is for you to do your best."

"We will, but you've got a pit bull snapping at your crotch with that idiot Ableman. The problem is, he's got an excellent record. The city prosecutor loves him. He's no dummy. He knows what it takes to win a case, and I'm afraid you've given him almost everything he needs. If he can get a psychologist to tell the court that you're just trying to cover your guilt by making up a story, we're in trouble."

"I didn't make many brownie points when he was here," Scott said. "He didn't like what I told him. In fact, when he left here, all I could read in his mind were expletives. Did I tell you that he recognized the man in my drawing? He's trying to protect somebody he knows as Vince."

A look of surprise crossed Paul's face. "I think you told me yesterday that he recognized the drawing, but I don't remember you telling me he was trying to protect anyone. Why do you suppose he'd want to do that?"

"I didn't hear the answer to that question," Scott said. "I could come up with a list of guesses, but the first thing that crosses my mind is that Ableman might have had some business dealings with him."

"I brought my tape recorder again. I'd like to get every tiny detail of what you remember about your dream. I've seen that drawing, by the way. I've never seen anything like it. Frankly, that face scares the hell out of me. I felt like I was looking into the face of pure evil."

Paul pulled a small recording device from his inner suit coat pocket, pressed the button, tested it to be sure it was recording, and handed it to Scott. "Rather than me asking you questions, why don't you start with the very first thing you can remember about your dream and walk through from start to finish. That way, I can't be accused of leading your thoughts."

Scott held the small device close to his mouth and began. A half hour later, he finished. Paul had just shut it off and slipped it back into his pocket when Mary knocked on the door.

"Is it okay if I come in?" she said timidly.

"Of course," Scott answered with a smile.

"After yesterday, I didn't know if I should," she said sourly.

"I assume you're here to take me home?"

"I'll leave you two alone," Paul said as he turned to walk away. "I'll let you know what we find out about the detective."

Mary looked at Scott questioningly.

"It's a long story," Scott said. "The homicide detective assigned to my case may be trying to protect the guy I described for the sketch artist. My legal team is going to look into that."

"So now Paul believes you?"

"I think he does. He apologized when he came in. For the first time since all this crap began, I'm feeling a little optimistic."

"You started to tell me about a young girl yesterday before I stormed off. What was all that about?"

"Turns out it's not pertinent to my case," Scott replied. "Besides, her folks cremated her body this morning, so there's no evidence. That fine doctor got away with murder—almost two murders. If I hadn't been awake when he sneaked into my room, he'd have got me, too."

"Isn't there anything you can do?" she asked.

"Nope. It's over."

"Dr. Gilbert called me this morning," Mary said. "He told me what you two talked about. He's got some help coming to pick you up at one o'clock this afternoon. They'll have a van they can put your wheelchair in. I guess once you're home, we'll just have to play it by ear and see what I can do to help you and what I can't."

"Mary," Scott said, searching her face.

"What?"

"I love you so much. Thanks for being patient with me. I'm sure once I get home and settled, and my mind has had some time to heal, things will be better."

"So what am I thinking right now?" she asked hesitantly.

"I feel a little frustration. And some fear."

"Nothing else?"

"No," Scott lied. He didn't want her to know the rest of what he could see.

Chapter 10
<u>Mental Competency</u>

Scott had only been home a day when a police officer knocked on his door. It was just after nine in the morning. Mary peeked through the peephole in the door. Unlike Scott, she didn't know who it was that had come calling without looking. If nothing else, Scott's so-called gift had intensified since his return home. He didn't even have to be in the room with his kids now to know what they were thinking.

"Scott, there are two police officers at the door," Mary said, a flash of fear racing through her mind.

"Open the door. Let's see what they want now."

"Don't they have to have a warrant or something?"

"Not just to ask questions. I've got nothing to hide."

She slipped off the safety chain, clicked back the deadbolt, and opened the door a few inches.

"Mrs. Corbridge?" an officer asked.

"Yes," Mary answered. "What do you want?"

The officer held out a folded piece of paper. "We have a court order to take your husband downtown for a psychological evaluation. Is he home?"

Mary took the paper and quickly read through it. "Of course he is," she said angrily. "He's confined to a wheelchair. Where else would he be? Nobody called us. I'd have thought that would be common courtesy."

"Can we come in?" the officer said, ignoring her objections completely.

"You can, but I'm telling you he's not going anywhere in a cop car. He's in a hard cast with orders not to put any weight on his leg. If you want to take him downtown, you're going to have to either get an ambulance or a van that will accommodate his wheelchair."

The officers exchanged glances. Scott, his extended leg supported by an apparatus on the wheelchair, rolled out of the living room into the entryway where they stood.

Officer Clayton, the one doing the talking, was tall—probably at least six-one or better—and he filled out his uniform nicely. There didn't appear to be an ounce of fat on the man. His companion was of average height and a little paunchy. Clayton spotted Scott in his wheelchair, and his thoughts quickly turned sympathetic.

"Looks like a communication breakdown, if you ask me," Scott said.

"I think we can get him in the back seat," Clayton said. "We can put his chair in the trunk."

"Oh no you won't," Mary said. "They had to put him in a van to bring him here. Besides the obvious cast, he's got broken ribs and a plate in his head. If you want him downtown, you'll have to do better than a squad car. Otherwise, he's not leaving here. Besides, he's nearly naked. If you want to have somebody talk to him, you bring them here."

"Ma'am, we have a court order," Clayton said. He wasn't happy.

"I'll tell your judge what he can do with that court order. This is a bunch of crap! You just wait right here. I'm calling our lawyer."

Scott smiled. Mary was spun up. There were a lot of expletives rolling around in her mind. She was just too ladylike to let them fly.

The cops were a little confused. All they'd been told was to go to this address and bring a man in to meet with the psychologist. Nobody had told them he wasn't ambulatory.

"If I may be so bold," Scott said as Mary hurried from the room to find her cell phone, "maybe you could radio in and explain the situation. I don't want you to think we're being uncooperative. But as you can see, there are some serious medical reasons why I can't just jump in your car and drive downtown."

His suggestion was met with mixed emotions. Clayton's thoughts reminded him a lot of Detective Ableman—belligerent, full of himself. His partner, on the other hand, was willing to compromise.

"Besides that, Officer Clayton," Scott said, "I'm not dressed to go out in public. I'll need some time to get ready, and if you insist on taking me downtown, I think you'd want to get an ambulance and a gurney, or a van like the one they brought me home in. To be sure I don't sustain any further injuries. I'm sure neither you nor your boss would want a lawsuit."

Before Clayton could answer, Mary strode back into the room and thrust her cell phone in Clayton's face. "This is our attorney, Paul Rodriguez. You need to talk to him before this goes any further."

Clayton was livid. He wasn't used to backing down. He angrily took Mary's phone.

Scott couldn't hear what Paul was telling the cop, but he could hear Clayton's verbal and mental responses. What he told Paul over the phone was far from what he was thinking.

Clayton handed the phone back to Mary. "We're going to call this in. You better try to make him presentable. I've got my orders. If it takes an ambulance, then I suppose that's what we'll do, but I'm telling you right now, he's going downtown."

"You didn't tell my attorney that," she said. "I think you get a kick out of bullying people. You'd better think twice. I won't be intimidated by the likes of you. I know my rights. Go make your call, but do it outside. You're not welcome in my home. You'd better not knock on that door again until you have an ambulance sitting in my driveway. Now get out of here!"

Clayton's companion turned and walked outside. "Come on, Max," he said. "We'll make the call from the squad car."

Clayton glared at Scott. Scott could tell he wanted to punch him, or worse. It was probably good that he was sitting in a wheelchair.

Scott smiled. "Hey, we're not trying to be difficult. It's not your fault that your management didn't brief you before you came all the way out here. If they had, this would have been a lot more pleasant. If you'll give me a few minutes to make myself presentable, and you go get me an appropriate ride, I'll be happy to go talk to your shrink."

Clayton's rage quickly subsided. Scott had done well. He could sense the officer's ego. By suggesting it was his management's fault, Scott had quickly defused the situation.

"We'll be out front," Clayton said.

"Don't worry," Scott said wryly, "we won't be going anywhere. And I don't think you'll need the SWAT team when you come back."

Clayton turned and walked outside. Mary closed the door behind him.

"Looks like you'd better slit the side seam out of one of my old Levi's," Scott said, "so I can pull them over my cast. I think my underwear is stretchy enough that I'll be able to get them on."

"This is still wrong," Mary said. "If they want to have you talk to a shrink, why can't they bring him here?"

"Because they probably want me in a sterile environment where someone can videotape and record our conversation. They don't want to have to set all of that up here. Besides, I'll bet the shrink isn't the only one who wants to hear what I have to say. I'll probably have an audience." Scott held out his hand. "Relax, Mary. This shouldn't be a big deal as long as they can get me downtown without knocking me around."

"I'll go get changed. I'm going with you."

"You just want to ride in an ambulance," he teased.

"Not funny! Somebody's got to be with you. I don't like that one guy. I think you called him Officer Clayton. He worries me. If he wanted to knock you around on the way downtown, it would be your word against his."

"They may not let you ride along anyway."

"Then they're going to have to take me into custody before I let them take you out of this house."

Scott smiled.

"What's so damn funny?" Mary remarked. "I don't see anything remotely amusing about any of this!"

"You do get wound up!"

"Oh, shut up! I think I have the right to be. This is serious. I can tell they're going to try to railroad you."

"I have an attorney."

"And you have little more than a fairytale in your own defense. Right now, nobody can establish an alibi for you. Alan called yesterday and told me the cops had been asking him questions about your involvement in Lincoln. He gave them contacts. Names, dates, and places."

"Maybe I should talk to Alan. That's more than I know. I don't remember anything about Lincoln."

"That's convenient!"

Scott just glared at her. She was convinced there was a lot more to Lincoln than anyone was telling her. In fact, she'd already asked Alan to find out if Nancy Bennion had worked for the owner of the building Scott had designed, or for the contractor that was building it. Mary needed to know if he'd been having an affair.

"I'm sorry," Scott said softly, "I know you're struggling with this. I wish I could tell you more. What I can tell you is it just doesn't feel right. I'd never cheat on you, so what other motive would I have had to murder her?"

She turned away. "I've got to go get ready," she said over her shoulder as she stalked off toward the bathroom. Her cell phone rang a few minutes later, just as Scott was pulling on a t-shirt.

"Mary!" he shouted at the closed bathroom door. "Phone!"

She flung open the bathroom door and scrambled to pick it up before it quit ringing. She turned her back to him while she talked. Scott feasted his eyes. She was wearing only a bra and panties. She was an alarmingly lovely woman. She was still very attractive in spite of the toll that three kids and a lot of years had put on her body. A harsh thought crossed his mind. It was no wonder Alan had—

"It's for you," Mary said, holding out the phone, interrupting his thoughts. "It's Paul."

"I talked to the court," Paul said without a hello. "Nobody told the judge that you weren't ambulatory. He didn't apologize. The state needs to establish your mental competency. I can't do much about that. They're going to get you a ride in a handicapped van that has wheelchair access. They claim the shrink you'll be seeing won't ask you any questions about the case, so they won't allow me in the room with you during the interview. They'll give me a copy of the audio, though, so I can determine whether or not they kept that promise. If they ask you anything remotely related to the case, you need to decline. Is that clear?"

"Perfectly," Scott said.

"By the way, we need to talk sometime today after your interview," Paul added. "Would it be okay if I followed you back to your house? You don't mind if your wife hears what I have to say, do you?"

"I'm not keeping any secrets from her. Is there anything you have to tell me that she shouldn't hear?"

"Not really, I suppose. We've put together a few things from Lincoln that you should be aware of."

"Sounds ominous. Do I need to worry?"

"Not yet. I'm hoping that if we can fill in a few of the blanks about your life before the accident, we might be able to jog your memory."

"What about Detective Ableman? Have you turned up anything on him yet?"

"No, we haven't had time, but we're working on it. I'll see you downtown."

Mary bustled out of the bathroom a few minutes later. She was fully dressed this time. Her hair was done, and her face carried the faint glow of freshly applied makeup. She hurried to the living room window and pulled back a corner of the closed curtains. "The cops are still out front. Do they honestly think you're going to try to run away?"

"They may not have anything else to do. They've been given an assignment, and it appears they're pretty intent on making sure they follow through."

Mary looked at the clock on the living room wall. "I wonder how long we're going to be gone? The boys went swimming this morning. I guess I should leave a note."

"Can't you just text them? It seems like everyone in this family has a cell phone except me."

"I can't help it if you lost yours. Until a few days ago, I honestly didn't know if you'd ever need one again. I'll call the phone company and file a claim so we can get it replaced."

"Did anyone think to look in my car for it?"

"They hauled your car to a salvage yard in Lincoln, and frankly, I didn't want to drive eighty miles to dig through it. The photos I saw were bad enough. They'd have to tear the car apart to get into the front seat."

"What about my luggage? You said I'd been staying there. Didn't I have a laptop? If I got hit nearly head-on, the trunk and back seat should have been okay."

"Look!" Mary said angrily. "It was about all I could do to see you lying there in that hospital bed, not knowing from day to day if you were going to live or die. What was or wasn't inside that stupid car was the least of my worries."

Scott could tell by her thoughts that he shouldn't push her any further, but then another thought crossed his mind. Luggage was probably low on the priority list, but his laptop—if he had one—might hold some clues. And his telephone might have Nancy's phone number in it if he'd really been seeing her. On the one hand, he didn't want to know. On the other hand, he realized that if Paul didn't get that stuff first, Detective Ableman probably would. Scott needed to know. He wanted to suggest all of that but held his peace. That was something he'd talk to Paul about the next time he saw him.

"I'm sorry," Scott apologized. "I know this hasn't been easy for you. I'm sure you were doing the best you could. Whatever was in there isn't that important. I just wish I had a cell phone. It's not like I can get up to use the home phone."

"I told you I'd file a claim and get you a stinking phone," she said.

He could scarcely believe the sudden hostility he felt coming from her. Then he saw Alan in her thoughts and understood why. She was torn. Scott changed the subject.

"Have you talked to Trish?"

"About Brandon? Yes, actually," she said, calming down a little.

"We had a good chat the night after you and I talked in the hospital. She was all defensive until I mentioned birth control, and then she calmed down and we had an adult conversation. She admitted they were being intimate but assured me Brandon was 'taking care of that.' I told her that wasn't good enough and that I'd get her a doctor's appointment. I really wanted to scream in her face, but when I put myself in her shoes, I decided to be an adult about it. We've actually been communicating since then."

"Did she ask if I knew?"

"I didn't tell her I'd discussed it with you. I didn't think that'd be a good idea."

"I've really messed up with the kids, haven't I?"

"Jess has been pretty high on you since you talked to him in the hospital. I think that bang on your head may have knocked some sense into you. You seemed to connect with him in a way I've never seen you do before." She paused and then stared at him. "Is that because you knew what he was thinking?"

"I could feel some of his emotions," Scott said, trying to be evasive and yet at the same time not seem so. "I could tell he really wanted to talk. And because of that, I tried to listen to what he had to say. I think that helped."

"It did. You need to try that with the other two."

"I promise I will. That felt good. It's like I saw him as a person for the first time in his life. It makes me sad to think I've been missing out on their lives."

The doorbell rang, and Mary looked through the peephole. "Your van is here. It looks like there are two guys in scrubs along with the cops. Do you think there will be room for me?"

"There should be, but if there isn't, I want you to follow us. I doubt they'll let you sit in the room with me during the evaluation, but I'd like you to hang around anyway. Maybe you and Paul could talk shop or something."

She opened the door, and Officer Clayton stepped in without invitation.

"Come in," Mary said sourly.

"We got a van," Clayton said. "We didn't think an ambulance would be necessary." He turned to Mary. "Does he have any medical devices that need to go with him?"

"No," Mary said.

Clayton turned and nodded to the two men standing behind him. "Load him up."

92

Twenty minutes later, they rolled Scott through the doors of the police station and into an elevator to the second floor. From there, they took him into a bare-walled conference room that contained little more than a stark rectangular metal table bolted to the floor. Surrounding the table stood four unpadded metal-framed chairs. The mirror along the left-hand wall was obviously one-way glass. Scott wondered if Paul was behind it.

They pushed his wheelchair near the table, set the brake, turned, and walked out of the room. The heavy, windowless steel door closed with a dull bang that echoed around the concrete and steel room. Scott listened for any thoughts coming from behind the glass. There were none. He wondered if there was anyone there at all.

Then several things happened almost simultaneously. Four people—three men and a woman—walked into the room behind the mirror and took a seat without talking. There were too many random thoughts flowing through their minds to follow much of what they were thinking. Then the door behind Scott opened and two men strode past him into the room.

One of them, a large man wearing an expensive-looking business suit and white shoes, was obviously the shrink. He took a seat across the table from Scott and dropped a clipboard onto the table. He had a build like a weightlifter; broad shoulders and a thick neck. His larger-than-average head was covered by a thick blob of carefully combed and jelled blonde hair. A bulbous-bellied man wearing a police uniform took the first seat at his right.

"Hello," the shrink said. "I'm Dr. Jeffrey Bracken. I'm a psychologist on retainer to the county. Can I assume you know why I'm here?"

"Officer Clayton told me he had a court order to bring me in for a psychological evaluation," Scott said. "I have to assume you're the shrink who'll be doing that evaluation."

Dr. Bracken bristled. "I'm a licensed doctor of psychology. I can assure you that I'm not a shrink. You'll address me as Doctor, or Dr. Bracken, if you please. The man at your right is a bailiff of the court."

"I doubt we'll need the bailiff," Scott said. "I don't think I'm in any condition to get rowdy."

"I assure you he's here only out of protocol, Mr. . . . ." he glanced at his clipboard ". . . Corbridge. I assure you that I am quite capable of taking care of myself."

In an instant, Scott caught two distinct trains of thought: the bailiff was insulted by Bracken's comment; and from Bracken himself came a series of overwhelming thoughts, mostly concerning his own self-importance.

"Okay," Scott said, "I'll try to restrain myself. I wouldn't want you to have to get your hands dirty. So, what do you want to talk about?"

Bracken's mood darkened.

Where in the hell did they get this guy? Scott thought. *If this is their so-called expert witness, he must not have much of a private practice. He's so stuck on himself there's no way he could work with real people.*

"I have a series of structured questions I intend to ask you," Bracken said. "I assure you I didn't put this questionnaire together. Rather, it's accepted by the courts as a standard to establish mental competency."

"Meaning what, exactly? That if it were up to you, you'd have a whole different set of questions more worthy of your time than the ones the public servants of this fine state have put together?"

Scott smiled inside. He'd used Bracken's own thoughts to ask that question. He felt a slight crack in the good doctor's resolve.

"I'm not here to argue that point," Bracken said. "But you're right. There's never any one set of questions that can be applied to every patient. Unfortunately, the law likes to build objectivity into their system. I'll work with those questions first, and then we'll see where that leads us."

"Well, I'm ready," Scott said, "so ask away. Do I get to embellish my answers, or is this a simple yes/no/true/false questionnaire?"

"As long as you answer the basic question, you're free to embellish to your heart's content."

"And I assume that the more I ramble, the less mentally competent I'll appear. Is that right?"

Bracken's resolve cracked again. Scott has used his exact thoughts again in his remark.

"Let me ask you something up front," Bracken said. "I've heard a little scuttlebutt about your case. Can you read my mind?"

"Now, that's an interesting question, isn't it?" Scott said. "If I answer yes, you'll immediately brand me with some psychological title. Probably something like delusional. If I tell you no, but continue to demonstrate that I know what you're thinking, you'll probably pick up your clipboard and storm out of here, afraid that I might reveal your deepest, darkest secrets."

Bracken's eyes locked on Scott's. Behind his eyes, Bracken's thoughts were running rampant. He'd heard there was a slight possibility that some so-called soothsayers actually had the ability to read thought, but until now he'd dismissed that premise as nonsense. Now he wasn't sure.

"Cat got your tongue?" Scott said, taunting him.

Bracken quickly looked down at his clipboard.

"Let me take the initiative for a moment, if I may," Scott said. "I'm sure it's no secret that I've been accused of murdering a young woman because I've been able to describe her killer and the weapon used in her murder. I can probably tell you a whole lot more. Those wearing a badge assume the only way I could do that is if I, in fact, was the murderer. You've been called here to figure out if I'm totally nuts or if I actually have some sort of gift. Am I right so far?"

"I'm not here to discuss your case," Bracken said. "In fact, I've not been told anything specific about your case. I'm only here to provide a service to the state, and I intend to do that."

"Okay, Jeffrey Boston Bracken," Scott spoke distinctly and firmly so those behind the window would catch every word. "I'm going to play hardball. From your own thoughts, I know that you're forty-two years old. You're divorced. You take a great deal of pride in your body. You work out every day, and you just recently achieved a lifelong goal of bench pressing five hundred fifty pounds. You have twenty-one pairs of white shoes, one for each one of your twenty-one tailored suits. Each one of those suits cost you over five grand. You wear white shoes with every one of your suits because of something that happened to you when you were a boy. Your parents were so poor that they couldn't afford to buy you a pair of white shoes so you could play the part of an angel in your school's Christmas play. Instead, they used white dab-on shoe polish over your rough black shoes. They looked awful. You were so embarrassed that you vowed that—"

Bracken jumped to his feet. "Stop right there!" he demanded in a booming voice bordering on a primal scream. "We're not here to discuss my private life. You'll answer the questions that I ask you and nothing more. Is that understood?"

"Perfectly," Scott said. "I just thought I'd demonstrate the fact that I will know the intent of every question you ask me before you say the words. You're hoping to stuff me into one of two little wooden boxes. One is branded 'mentally competent.' The other is branded 'crazy.' Need I say more?"

Bracken was undone. He spun around and reached the door in three urgent strides. The poor bailiff sat dumbly on his chair, not knowing what to do. The door slammed closed with a resounding boom—not unlike a pistol shot—that echoed around the hardened room.

The bailiff got to his feet. "Ah, let me go see what they want to do with you," he stammered.

The door opened and then closed again, but much more softly this time.

Scott instantly turned his mind to the four people sitting in the room behind the mirror. The woman was not Mary. She was a psychologist assigned to the psych ward where the fifteen-year-old girl had died. She'd been summoned by Ableman's boss, a Captain Roundy, who was one of the four seated behind the glass.

Another man in the room was a court clerk. He was quickly rewinding his recording device to be sure he'd caught every word that had come blaring through the room's speakers. The fourth person behind the glass was one of Detective Ableman's subordinates. It had been his job to go to Lincoln and work with the cops there to find out everything he could about the crime scene. When he went, he'd had an objective in mind—namely, to verify or debunk what Scott had told the police.

"Charlene?" Scott asked loudly, hoping the speakers to their room were still turned on. "If you can hear me, please tap on the back of the mirror. I have something to tell you about the fifteen-year-old girl who died on your floor a couple of days ago."

He waited. Instead of a tap on the glass, a speaker in the room crackled to life.

"This is Charlene," the woman said.

"What I'm going to tell you," Scott said, "I derived the same way I got the information I just told Dr. Bracken, and the same way I know there are four of you sitting there in that room. Like it or not, I have a gift. I'm clairvoyant. Nobody, of course, believes me. Hell, If I were on the receiving end of what I'm saying, I probably wouldn't either. So here it goes. What you do with this information is entirely up to you and the cops. I've tried to tell people before what happened, but nobody would listen to me. Maybe now you people sitting there in that room, will make something happen."

Scott paused, waiting until he had everyone's attention.

"That young girl in your ward was only fifteen years old. Her name was Susan. She was Dr. Frank Talbot's patient. She overdosed after she took an EPT at home and found out she was pregnant with Talbot's child. Talbot was initially sent up by my medical doctor to talk to me about a dream I had when I came out of a coma. I found out about Susan by listening to his thoughts. When I told him what he was thinking, he acted like Dr. Bracken just did. He stormed out of my room. He knew he had to do something about me."

Scott took a deep breath, collected his thoughts, and told them everything that had taken place with Talbot, sparing no details. When he was finished, he paused to let them process what they'd just heard.

"It appears that Dr. Talbot got away with one murder," he finally continued. "Lucky for me, he botched mine or I wouldn't be sitting here today. Unfortunately, because nobody would listen to me before they cremated poor Susan, I doubt there's anything you can do to prove that. You're probably asking yourself why I'm telling you all this. I actually have two motives. First, Dr. Talbot is dangerous. Somebody needs to be watching him. But more importantly, this is a frantic plea from me to you, and to those in there with you, to consider the possibility that I have a gift. One that allowed me to see the murder of another young woman. A woman whose picture I saw in the newspaper. A woman who I saw murdered in a dream along with the man who killed her. I'm sure this all probably sounds like the frantic ravings of a lunatic, but I'm hoping my conversation with Bracken might help to validate my sanity. I'm not just someone trying to save my own hide. I'm trying to use my gift to help you catch Nancy Bennion's killer. I'm sorry if nobody can see the truth, but that's it. I suppose I have nothing else to say. Do you have any questions for me?"

After a few moments, the speaker crackled again. "This is Captain Roundy. Did you tell all this to Detective Ableman when he questioned you in your hospital room?"

"I did," Scott said. "The problem is, Detective Ableman has other priorities on his mind. He recognized the man in my police sketch. He knows that if he can convict me, that takes the pressure off of whoever he's trying to protect. It's obvious he didn't do anything with the information I gave him about Susan, or she wouldn't have been cremated."

"Thank you, Mr. Corbridge," the captain responded. "I believe we have all we need at this time."

"Does that mean you're going to let me go home now?"

"Yes. I believe your wife and your attorney are waiting for you in the lobby. I'll see to it that you get safely home."

* * * * *

Mary and Paul were sitting together in the lobby when the orderly wheeled Scott out of the elevator.

Paul looked surprised. "That didn't take long!" he said.

"It didn't take me long to convince them I wasn't crazy."

"So you're free to go?"

"Yes. Did you and Mary have a good chat?"

"We didn't have much time to talk," Paul said.

"You told me earlier that we needed to talk after my interview. Do you want to do that now, or are you going to drive out to the house with us?"

Paul glanced around. "I doubt there's a room around here where we'd be free to discuss your case without fear of someone eavesdropping. If it's okay, I'll follow Mary out to your house."

A few minutes later, Scott was loaded back into the van. They were just hitting the freeway when one of the orderlies craned his head around and broke the silence.

"I heard you roughed up that psychologist pretty bad," he said.

Scott smiled. "Do you know Dr. Bracken?"

"By reputation only. I've only seen him a couple of times. He's huge!"

"So is his ego. He's probably pretty good at what he does. The problem is, he lives in a glass house. I had something to prove, and unfortunately, I used him to prove my point. I'm afraid I may have broken a few of his windows."

"Shattered is more like it," the orderly said. "They say he stormed out of the station without saying a word to anyone."

"That's a pity, really," Scott said. "The court is still going to want somebody to do a psychological evaluation on me."

"Rumor has it you can read minds. Is that true?"

"What do *you* think, Pete? Is that possible?"

The orderly's eyes narrowed. "I didn't tell you my name."

"Neither did your driver, Larry. Does that answer your question?"

Pete was instantly afraid.

"Relax, Pete," Scott said. "Anything I find out about you stays as our little secret."

"Wow," Larry said. "You should work for the cops. I bet you could make a few dirt bags squirm."

"Maybe, but I doubt the law would allow that. I'm sure that what

I can do would be deemed to be an invasion of privacy. At the end of the day, it really is. Nobody should be able to do what I can do. Just for the record, I didn't ask for this. I don't like it. I don't know why I can do it. I don't know if it's permanent or temporary. Maybe when my brain heals, it'll go away. I hope so."

Chapter 11
Lincoln

Mary and Paul were waiting at the house when the orderlies drove in and carefully unloaded Scott onto his driveway. Jess met them inside and watched while the two men wheeled Scott into the living room and took their leave.

"What's going on?" Jess asked.

Scott could sense his son's concern. "I just had to go to the police station to talk to the shrink. It's no big deal. They had to get a van because I can't ride in a car."

"Oh. I was afraid something was wrong."

"Nope, I'm fit as a fiddle."

"Sure you are," Mary said. "That's why you look like you just got hit by a bus."

"Well," Scott said, "maybe not totally well yet, but I'm feeling a lot better."

"Jess," Mary said, motioning to Paul, "this is Mr. Rodriguez, your dad's attorney. We need to talk for a few minutes. Would you mind going to your room?"

Jess looked at Scott, and Scott winked. "I don't think you'd be interested in all this legal mumbo jumbo anyway. You even have my permission to crank up your music."

Jess grinned. "Thanks, Dad. I'll close my door so it's not so loud."

Mary stared at Scott as Jess bounded up the stairs to his bedroom. "Who are you, and what have you done with my husband?" she said with a smile. "You *hate* his music."

"If he's in his room with all that racket, he won't be listening to us."

"That's pretty smart," Paul said. "I won't take much of your time. I need to tell you what we found in Lincoln. Some of the news I have is good. Some, maybe not so good. I'll talk about the not so good first. My team talked to the salvage yard yesterday afternoon to see if they still had your car. They said the cops seized it and had it towed to a police impound lot. When we called the cops, they told us they won't release any evidence until the pre-trial evidentiary hearing. Do you remember anything that you might have left in your car?"

"No," Scott said, "but Mary and I just talked about that this morning. It only makes sense that my cell phone should be in there somewhere, unless the tow truck driver grabbed it or it got flipped out on the road. I have to assume I might have had a laptop. Other than that, I imagine the only other things that might have been in there would have been my luggage."

"No murder weapons or bloody clothes?" Paul asked. He wasn't smiling.

"I thought we were past all that," Scott said. "I assume this means you still don't believe me?"

"It's not my job to decide whether you're guilty or not. It's my job to defend you in a court of law, and in order to do that I need to know everything you can tell me, whether it might implicate you or not."

"I told you everything about my dream," Scott said angrily. "You recorded it all. That's all I remember."

"Don't get all riled up, Scott. You need to understand where I'm coming from. If the cops had that recording, you'd be in jail right now. I dare say there's not one in a thousand jurors who will buy your 'vision' story. Just the mere fact that you know where she's buried would get you a guilty verdict."

"You didn't tell me you knew where she was buried," Mary said, her voice quivering.

Scott knew her thoughts. She was terrified. She had become one of those jurors Paul had just talked about. Scott knowing where the body was located was simply more than Mary could handle. She, like the jury, believed he was guilty.

Scott looked at Paul. "What else can you tell me about Lincoln?"

"Actually, that's the good part. We sent a team member up there to nose around. He interviewed the people you were working with on that building. The buyer is really impressed with you. He told us the project is ahead of schedule and on budget. He gave you rave reviews for the time you spent with them. He also told us you developed a great rapport with the general contractor. We talked to that guy, too. He told us you were great to work with. You took setbacks in stride and worked with their team on everything to resolve issues. They told us they'd never worked with an architect who took that much interest in a project."

"What about the woman?" Mary said.

A slight smile graced the corners of Paul's mouth. "You'd make a great investigator," he said. "We got her pictures from the newspaper. We even visited her parents and picked up a few more photos from them. We showed them around. Not only to the buyer but also to the general contractor. They knew about the girl's disappearance, but nobody recognized her. We checked the local hotels and found out that Scott had been staying at a Country Inn not far from the job site. The hotel staff recognized Scott from his photo, but none of them had ever seen the girl. We were even able to get a look at their surveillance system videos. He always entered his room alone. We even went so far as to talk to the bartenders and the maid service. None of the bartenders recognized either Scott or the victim, and the housekeepers all said there was no evidence he'd had visitors in his room."

"The bar thing isn't unusual," Scott said. "I don't drink."

"We did learn something interesting, though, when we talked to Nancy's parents. She was a wild child. She ran away from home a couple of times when she was a teenager. They didn't get along well. She dropped out of high school and was always in some sort of trouble. There were times when she'd just disappear. Once, she was gone for over a year. When she did come home, it was usually because she needed money or a place to stay. They told us she started looking rough, like she was doing drugs or something. They hadn't seen her for six months prior to her murder."

"Who reported her missing?" Scott asked.

"I'm getting to that," Paul said. "We got a copy of the police report, complete with lots of photos of the crime scene. The report says she had a roommate. Her roomie works a graveyard shift at a local 7-Eleven. She found the murder scene when she came home around seven in the morning. There were no signs of forced entry. The perp hadn't tried to cover anything up. There was blood everywhere. A couple of bedsheets were missing, but nothing else."

"Was there an oval-shaped mirror on the wall in the bathroom?" Scott asked.

Paul stared at him for a few seconds before he answered. "Yes, just over the bathroom sink. It had blood all over it."

"That's where I first saw the perp's face," Scott said, answering Paul's unspoken question. "It was as if I was seeing the man who attacked her through her eyes. He just suddenly appeared behind her in the mirror. She spun around and tried to fend him off, but he was taller and stronger—and he had a knife."

In his mind's eye, Scott could see the horrific scene unfolding again. He wrung his hands together to drive the vision away. When he regained his composure, Mary and Paul were staring at him.

"Sorry," he said, "I was having a flashback."

"Of her murder?" Paul said.

"Of my dream," Scott answered pointedly. "If it wasn't for the guy I saw standing behind her, I'd swear you could make me believe I was the killer."

"If you tell that story to anyone from now on," Paul warned him, "in spite of whatever alibi we might be able to construct for you, they'll think you're guilty. I realize you might feel some sense of responsibility to her, or to her parents—because for whatever reason, the fates have cursed you with this dream of yours—but you don't owe them anything. Her parents had pretty much written her off anyway. We're talking about your survival here, Scott. Your life! I'm telling you, it's time to shut up! Make the cops do their job! Make them prove your guilt. If you take the stand and spout off every detail of that dream, you're going to go to prison for murder. Can I make myself any clearer?"

Scott looked at Mary. Her eyes were clouded with fear. She was wondering how she could get Scott out of the house—or maybe she should take the kids and go somewhere for a while. Then another thought crossed her mind. If Scott found out about Alan, he might kill her, too. Her panic deepened. What if he could really read her thoughts? If he could, he already knew about Alan. Scott had guns . . .

"Mary," Scott said, trying to interrupt her runaway train of thought. "I didn't do it. I didn't murder anybody. You've got to believe me. I could never hurt anybody. You've known me nearly all my life. Have I ever been physically abusive? I don't even scream obscenities at people on the freeway. *You* do that!"

She calmed a little, but fear still ruled her thoughts.

"You don't have to be afraid of me," Scott pleaded. "Look at me! I can't even stand up on my own. Even if I wanted to, I could never be a threat to you or the kids. If you're that worried, go lock up my guns. We probably should anyway. With all the violence in the schools today, it's only good policy to lock up our firearms so none of the kids or their friends can get to them."

"I have a gun safe," Paul offered. "I could take them until all this is over."

"That would be good," Scott said. "Mary can show you where

they are. I have a handgun, a deer rifle, and a shotgun. They're all in our bedroom closet. The ammunition is on the top shelf."

Scott could sense that Mary was calming down. He had never been abusive or violent. If the guns were gone, that would make a difference.

"Thank you, Scott," Mary said. "That would make me feel better."

"Then do it. I haven't used them in years anyway. I don't hunt anymore, and since I started the business, I haven't even had time to go to the range."

"If I might be so bold as to change the subject," Paul said, "let me tell you the rest of the good news. We have a copy of your hotel bill that last day. You checked out at six forty-five. You got hit less than fifteen minutes later. There was no way you could have murdered anybody in that time. Much less load up her body and haul it away. If you had, it would have still been in your car."

Paul paused to let his words sink in before he went on.

"Better yet, when we talked to the general contractor he told us you'd been on the job site all day. You left around six. The police don't have a body, so they don't have an exact time of death, but the roommate didn't stumble across the crime scene until the morning after your crash. She told the cops Nancy wasn't home when she left for work around seven thirty. By then, you had already been extricated from your vehicle and were in the local hospital's emergency room fighting for your life."

"So there's no way he could have killed her," Mary said.

"Not based on the roommate's testimony and the other testimonial evidence my team has been able to put together. That's why I'm telling you, Scott, you need to keep your mouth shut about your vision, or dream, or whatever it is. Any hard evidence the cops are going to come up with will simply prove your innocence. Then, if you feel the need to go help the cops find her real killer, wait until after they come up empty. Then maybe they'll be more cooperative. Maybe they'll actually go look for that man you described for the sketch artist."

"Not if Ableman has anything to do with it," Scott said. "By the way, I talked to his captain today. He was behind the glass with three other people. After the shrink freaked out, I had a chance to tell him about Ableman. Maybe the captain will take the initiative and have someone else assigned to my case. Let me ask you a question. If Nancy was murdered in Lincoln, why is Ableman even involved? I'd think the case would be under the jurisdiction of the

Lincoln City Police Department, not here in Omaha."

"It is, actually," Paul said, "but it's a little complicated. The murder took place in Lincoln, so the local cops there are technically in charge of the investigation. You crashed outside city limits, so the state highway patrol got involved. Mary had you transferred to the hospital here in Omaha. It was closer to home, and they had a better neurosurgeon in residence here. When you came out of your coma and started spouting off the details of your dream, you got the Omaha cops involved. When they called the boys from Lincoln, those guys officially asked for their help. When it goes to trial, if it ever does, that will happen in Lincoln because that's where the murder occurred. But the great state of Nebraska will probably be the governing entity because of all the crossed jurisdictions."

"Does that mean the people from Lincoln have a copy of the composite drawing I gave the police? Or has Ableman rat-holed that to protect Vince?"

"I haven't thought to ask," Paul said. "I'll check, but nobody's being very cooperative. They'll probably just tell me I'll find out all of that in the pre-trial evidentiary hearing."

"If they don't include the sketch, I'm sort of screwed."

"Not really. The most compelling part of your innocence comes from the girl's roommate. That, and the timing of your wreck, should exclude you completely. But that's why I'm telling you to keep your yap shut. It's bad enough they already have your partial testimony. They had little more than a missing roommate and a bloody crime scene before you decided to talk. They had no idea what kind of weapon was involved. They had no person of interest. They still don't have a body or a motive. Now that they've got you to put under the microscope, they might be able to come up with enough circumstantial and inferred evidence to warrant charges."

"But I thought all the stuff you just told us about his employer, and the hotel, and the timelines would counter any of that," Mary said.

"It will," Paul said, "but keep in mind, that's evidence my team has gathered. The cops may not have had time to put all of that together yet."

"The thing that bothers me," Scott said, "is that Ableman is protecting somebody. He's certainly not passing on everything he knows."

"That's precisely why we're doing our own investigative work," Paul said. "We're lucky to have more than one police agency involved. We actually have three, if you include the county. It's a little hard to frame somebody with that many people looking at a case. I'm thinking when we have the pre-trial and see what evidence the prosecution has, we'll know better how to proceed. It's not common for the defense to tip their hand in a pre-trial, but if the court will allow, I may be able to present what we know and convince the judge to dismiss the case against you before it ever goes to trial."

Paul turned away and looked out the living room window. "I wish I knew what they found in your car." He turned back to Scott. "Let's suppose they found your laptop. Do you think there is anything incriminating on your hard drive?"

"Like what?"

"Pornographic photos of, or letters to, the deceased."

"I've already told you I didn't know the woman. Why would I have anything like that?"

"I'm just grasping at straws. I'm sure you can see where I'm going, but keep in mind you really can't remember anything. I just don't want to be blindsided."

"How long will it be before we know any of that?" Mary asked.

"I don't know," Paul said. "It might be a week. It might be a year. They won't move for a hearing until they feel they've got a case. In the meantime, Scott, mum's the word. Okay?"

Chapter 12
Another Attempt

Scott felt pretty good about his chances after Paul laid everything out for him. Still, two thoughts ravaged his mind. First, of course, was his dream. He felt a driving need to send somebody looking for Nancy's body, but he'd promised Paul he would shut his mouth about that until he was in the clear. The second thought that tormented him night and day was Dr. Talbot's involvement with his fifteen-year-old patient's murder. Was Talbot still dangerous? Scott knew what he'd done, and Talbot knew it. They both knew there was no physical evidence to support Scott's claims, but would that be enough to end it, or did the man still feel threatened by him? He'd already proven he was afraid enough of Scott to attempt his murder—but that was before the girl's body was cremated.

On the one hand, Scott wanted to believe it was over. On the other hand, he had a nagging feeling it wasn't—a feeling that seemed to be coming from somewhere else, almost as urgent and unrelenting as his vision.

Paul had promised to poke around to see if there was anything they could use against Talbot. He'd also said, in no uncertain terms, that the death of Talbot's patient was none of his law firm's business. He reiterated the fact that Scott needed to keep a low profile with the Talbot thing until his own case was settled; that by continuing to yap on about things he "thought had happened," but had no proof of, was tantamount to poking a sleeping grizzly bear with a stick.

Things were better at home. By the third day, Mary had calmed down. The guns were gone, and Scott was being doubly careful not to talk about anything he knew she was thinking. When the kids came in and out, he used what he gleaned from their thoughts to engage them in conversation, but he carefully avoided anything he learned that might make them feel uncomfortable. He watched Mary out of the corner of his eye whenever he talked to them. He knew she was looking for any evidence that he knew what they were thinking.

Paul called on Friday. In order to avoid any obvious connection to the Talbot case, he had used what he called an "independent third party" to snoop around. He didn't have good news. The cops had dropped the issue. There was no evidence to support anything Scott had told them. To make matters worse, Paul found out that Talbot had perjured himself and denied having spoken to Scott on any occasion. It was obvious Talbot was doing everything he could to distance himself from Scott. When Scott suggested that Paul's third party might want to talk to Susan's parents, Paul instantly shut him down.

Scott wasn't sleeping well. Physically, he was still a wreck. His head hurt. His knee hurt. His ribs hurt. And, to add insult to injury, he had begun having seizures.

At first, he didn't really notice them. They weren't the kind that sent his whole body into a series of tight, twisting contortions. Rather, it was as if his mind simply shut down. They were mild enough that at first he thought he'd just had a stupor of thought. After one of those presumed stupors, though, when he regained his mental acuity, Mary was standing over him. She had noticed, and she wasn't happy.

His neurosurgeon put him back in the hospital so they could do some testing and monitor his response to several different anti-seizure medications. Unfortunately, because of the seizures, he was restrained again—not only at night when there was nobody in the room with him, but also during the day when any number of strangers could have access to him. This time there was no IV, and that would make it less convenient for Talbot to finish what he'd begun. But if he stuck Scott with a syringe, there would be no recourse like there had been with the IV tower. Scott hardly dared close his eyes for fear he might wake up to find Talbot standing over him.

His dream about the murder began to invade his thoughts both night and day. It didn't take a sleep episode to bring it on. In fact, all he had to do was think about Nancy, or her killer, or the grave by the well, and the whole scene would begin to play out in his mind again. He was still able to drive it away by clenching his fists and snapping his fingers, but the vision became relentless.

When he was too exhausted or too stupefied by the medications they were giving him to fight it off, he'd simply try to detach himself emotionally as he let the scene play out over and over in his mind. Between that and his growing fear of Talbot, Scott frankly believed he was losing his mind.

His orthopedic surgeon inadvertently came to the rescue. After much discussion with some of his colleagues, the doctor decided to perform a complete knee replacement. The "experts" decided there was simply too much damage to Scott's right knee for any other hope of a cure. He hoped the pain would serve as a distraction.

They took him into surgery on a Thursday morning. It was mostly dark in his room when he finally regained full consciousness. Before that point, he'd had fleeting memories of a recovery room attended by a couple of nurses, but the effects of the drugs they'd used in surgery drove away any hope of cognizant thought.

The searing pain that came with consciousness drove the visions away. Mary was slumped in a nearby chair. He reached out to her with his mind but felt nothing. She was asleep, and if she was dreaming, he evidently had no access to her dreams.

Uncomfortable, he tried to shift his body weight, only to find himself restrained. Thoughts of Talbot, coupled with the residual effects of the knock-out drugs, nearly sent him over the edge. He could imagine the evil man standing in the shadows, waiting for a chance to strike. He began to fight the restraints. He knew he shouldn't, but he couldn't stop. Then suddenly—gratefully—Mary stood at his side.

"You're okay, Scott," she said quietly as she rubbed her soft hand over his bare forearm. "Don't fight it. You'll just skin your wrists."

He did relax. It was heavenly knowing she was standing there, warding off Talbot's attack.

"Sorry," he muttered, "I was dreaming."

"Probably more like a nightmare, from what I saw. Do you want to talk about it? Sometimes, when I have a bad dream, it helps to talk through it."

He almost began to talk about Talbot—about the murder—but then he caught himself. She didn't need to hear that horrific tale again.

"It was crazy, really," he lied. "I was driving. There was a car coming right at me. I couldn't stop."

Mary looked relieved. "Sounds like you may have been remembering your wreck."

"It was awful. Thanks for waking me up."

"Your knee doctor was here an hour ago. He said the surgery went well. He was worried that the bone in your leg had been too badly damaged in the wreck to hold the prosthetic, but he said you'd healed well enough that there shouldn't be any complications. He told me he was pleased about the way it all came together. He said the rest of the tissue had healed well enough that they should be able to get you on your feet in a couple of days. He wanted to put you on a blood thinner to prevent blood clots, but you're so messed up in other places he didn't think that would be prudent. He said you'd be getting a lot of attention in the next few days, whatever that means, so you won't get a blood clot in your leg."

"That's a good thing," Scott said. "I don't like being alone, especially when I'm tied down."

"Are you still worried about that psychologist?"

He quickly scanned her thoughts. She didn't believe a word of his story. Not wanting to argue, he changed the subject. "It's not that. I just hate being tied down. Have you talked to Alan? What about the job I was working in Lincoln?"

She smiled. "Alan told me to tell you to relax. Your out-of-town job was nearly finished. He says it's winding down on its own. He told me he's hired a couple of job shoppers to fill in for you at the firm until you're well enough to work. You're not millionaires, but you're still solvent."

Scott didn't want to know the rest of what she was feeling for Alan. "I think I've had a few really good talks with the kids," he said, changing the subject again. "I can see that I've really been missing out."

"I'm sorry it's taken something like this for you to recognize that."

"What have they told you?"

She laughed. "Trish thinks you died and somebody else came back in your body."

"Ouch!"

"She wanted to know if I'd talked to you about her and Brandon."

"And?"

"I told her we'd talked about it and were in agreement. I did tell her, though, that we didn't like what she was doing. That we just didn't want her to get pregnant before she finished school."

"I hate that," Scott said. "I'll bet ole Brandon has a huge grin on his face."

"You don't give them enough credit. They're in love. I think if we give them both a little time to grow up before they start a family, you may end up being proud of them."

He wanted to argue the morals issue, but under the

circumstances, he didn't want to turn over that stone.

"Could you do me a favor?" Scott asked timidly.

"No, I'm not getting into bed with you," she said with a soft laugh.

"That's not what I was thinking. With this head thing and the seizures, and now this, I hate being alone. Do you think you could get your mom to come and stay with the kids so you could stay here with me for a couple of days?"

The flood of emotion he felt coming from her was almost overwhelming. In spite of her thing with Alan, she still loved him. That was good; that was really good. But right now, Scott needed a bodyguard. He seriously doubted Talbot would try anything himself, but he'd already shown what he was capable of. Scott was vulnerable as long as he was in the hospital. If Mary was there with him, there was little chance anyone would be able to get to him.

"Actually," Mary said, "Mom called this morning and offered. I didn't know how you'd feel about her staying with us, so I told her I'd have to talk to you first."

"I didn't know your mom was uncomfortable around me."

"You really have lost your memory, haven't you?"

"Have I been that mean?"

"Not in so many words, but she doesn't feel welcome."

"I'm going to have to try to change that," he said. "I like your mom."

"You're delusional. But I like it. Don't change your mind. I love my mom."

"So," Scott said, "I'm going to ask you again. Have I really been that big of a dick?"

"Sometimes, yes."

"Would you believe me if I told you I'll try harder?"

She searched his eyes. "Scott, I hope you're not just throwing me a bone here, because we haven't been together on a lot of things for a long time. I really need to believe you."

What he read in her thoughts embarrassed him. It was no wonder she'd reached out to Alan. He made a mental vow to make things better between them. But first, he really needed a bodyguard. If he didn't make it out of the hospital, there was no sense in dreaming about the future.

Mary looked at the clock over his bed. "It's almost six. I'll call Mom. She can be here in an hour. I'll stop at the grocery store on the way home and pick up a few things for her and the kids to eat. I can probably be back by eight thirty or nine. The nurses told me the sofa makes out into a bed and that I was welcome to stay if I wanted to."

"Will you do me a huge favor before you leave?" Scott asked.

She grinned wickedly. "I told you I wasn't getting into bed with you."

"Not that. Not that I wouldn't love to, but I'm tired of being strapped down. Could you undo my restraints? I really hurt when I can't move."

Mary was torn. He was restrained because of the seizures. She empathized with him. She hated lying on her back for any length of time, but she was afraid he might fall.

"Look," Scott said, "just lower my bed as far as it will go. That way, if I do thrash around, I won't fall very far. You don't have to undo the one across my middle. It should keep me in bed. I promise I won't mess with that one. Just free up my hands and feet."

Just then, an orderly entered the room with Scott's dinner.

Mary bent over and kissed Scott on the forehead. "I'll leave you to your dinner. I'll be back about nine."

The orderly removed Scott's hand restraints, raised the head of the bed, and positioned the rolling table over his bed so he could eat. Scott smiled as he looked over his food. He didn't particularly care for pork chops, but the meal came with a shiny steel steak knife. He'd see to it that the knife didn't leave with the food tray. Call him crazy, but there was no telling who might come to visit in the night. Tired and groggy as he might be, he vowed to stay conscious until Mary got back.

The orderly left the food tray for over an hour. Just as the smells of the dirty dishes were beginning to bother Scott, the young man returned to gather up the remains. Scott was grateful the guy was in a hurry; he didn't notice the knife was missing. The orderly took pity on Scott when he pleaded with him not to hook up his arm restraints and agreed to leave them off for a while.

A stranger showed up just before six thirty to work with him on a physical therapy routine that was supposed to help ward off blood clots. A quick scan of the man's thoughts told Scott he was legitimate. Besides that, there were no needles involved, so Scott didn't feel like he had to use the knife on him.

Two more strangers came to answer his nurse's call a few minutes later. It took two of them to get him to the bathroom and back into bed again. They honored his request to leave his hands free. He checked inside his pillowcase after they left. The knife was still there.

A nurse he recognized and somewhat trusted bustled into his room next. She recorded his vitals and offered medication in a small plastic cup. He dumped the meds into his mouth and pretended to swallow them, but the second she turned away he quietly spat them into his hand and slipped them under the small of his back. He knew at least one of the pills had to be a pain med, and the other was probably an anti-seizure pill.

His leg felt like it was on fire. He needed the meds, but he couldn't afford to sleep until after Mary got back. The drug combination would at best make him groggy. At worst, they'd completely knock him out.

He didn't know why, but he became more anxious as each new stranger came and went. It was almost as if an unseen entity was in his room, warning him to beware. Scott carefully searched each stranger's thoughts for any malice. So far, there hadn't been any. He thanked God, or whoever had given him his *gift*, for that ability. He had to be ready if and when the time came.

Able to use the TV remote now that his hands were free, he turned on the set and flipped through the channels, looking for something to help him pass the time. But shortly after he settled on a program, he realized that whenever he lost himself in anything other than his own thoughts, he quickly grew sleepy in spite of the pain in his leg.

He flipped the TV off and concentrated instead on what was going on outside his room. He quickly learned that he could glean thoughts from the people who walked past. To say the least, it was entertaining. As one person drifted out of range, he found himself waiting impatiently for the next to wander by.

He smiled to himself. This was nearly as entertaining as watching a good TV drama. Except in this case, nothing was scripted and the mental scenes that played out just beyond his door were as varied as the people themselves.

As it got later and all of the meals and the meds had been delivered, the hospital grew quiet. Thankfully, a janitor began cleaning the floors in the hallway, but he soon finished and moved away. Scott snapped on the TV again to see what time it was. Mary wasn't due for nearly an hour.

A vivid thought crossed his mind, and he turned the TV off again. He couldn't afford to be distracted. The paranoia drifted back. He felt like he was losing his mind. He wanted to believe that his fears of Talbot were a figment of a tortured mind. But what if they weren't? What if Talbot—

Scott's mind froze on the thought as he became aware of someone walking slowly down the hallway. The man was looking at room numbers. It was late for visiting hours. It probably wasn't a visitor looking for a loved one. It obviously wasn't a staff member; they wouldn't have to look for room numbers. Scott reached into his pillowcase, drew the knife, and held it down by his right leg.

The man in the hallway stopped when he saw Scott's room number. His blood ran cold when he saw the man's thoughts: he was armed with a hypodermic needle. Talbot had given him the syringe, half of the money, told him the room number, and gave him a set of scrubs to wear. The man hesitated. He didn't want to kill anybody, but the money would keep him in drugs for six months. Talbot had assured him he wouldn't get caught.

Scott tensed up. He had the steak knife, but he was also in lousy shape. How could he fend off an able-bodied person? His throat constricted with fear. He gripped the knife and waited.

Then, as the door latch moved, another thought sprang into his mind, and he punched the nurse's call button. He wanted to scream for help, but in the same instant he realized if he began acting irrationally, they'd sedate him and he'd lose the battle. The addict outside the door would just come back when his victim was incapable of fighting back. He needed to buy some time.

"Can I help you?" a female voice crackled over the small speaker.

"Yes, please," Scott answered loudly, "could I get a couple of your big, strong orderlies to come help me into the bathroom?"

The man outside the hospital room door fled.

"We'll be right—" the nurse said, stopping abruptly in mid-sentence.

Several loud voices filled the hallway. An alarm sounded, and thoughts from a dozen or more people shouted their way through Scott's mind. He watched the door, ready to defend himself if it came to that. Eventually, the alarm shut off. Shortly afterwards, his door opened and two men dressed in scrubs walked in.

"They told us you needed some help getting to the bathroom," one of them said as they unhooked the restraints around Scott's legs and middle.

"What's with the alarm?"

"There was some creep on the floor without a badge. He ran when we tried to stop him. We put the facility on lockdown, and security caught him coming out of an elevator down by the laundry room."

"Did he have a syringe full of fentanyl?" Scott asked.

The orderlies stared at him for a few seconds.

"How could you possibly know that?" one of them asked.

"Lucky guess," Scott said. "By the way, in all of the excitement, I've decided I don't need to go after all."

"You pushed your call button, didn't you?"

"I did, and I think that may have saved my life. If you tell the cops to question that guy, I think they'll find out he got his drugs and his orders from a shrink by the name of Dr. Frank Talbot. Frank offered the guy five grand to sneak in here and inject me. Of course, nobody will listen to me. I'm a head case. A freak of nature. You should really be afraid of me."

One of the orderlies held his two-way to his mouth and walked out into the hallway to talk. The other stood dumbly by Scott's bed, not knowing quite what to do.

"Are you sure you don't need to use the bathroom?" he asked.

"I'm sure," Scott said, and the orderly left.

The alarm had stirred up all the patients, and the nursing staff had their hands full answering their calls. Scott kept quiet and waited. Just moments later, Mary showed up. It was fifteen minutes to nine.

"I don't know what's going on," she said as she stepped in carrying a small overnight bag. "I got here fifteen minutes ago. They told me the hospital was on lockdown. They made me wait outside. I couldn't even sit in the lobby."

"I don't know either," Scott lied. "A bunch of alarms went off, and a couple of orderlies told me they were chasing somebody. Hey, I'm so glad to see you."

Mary dropped her bag onto the sofa and walked over to kiss him. "I see they took off your restraints."

"Oh, that's right. A couple of guys came in to help me into the bathroom. They'd just unhooked me when the alarm went off."

"Do you still need to go? I'll go get somebody."

He didn't, but he could tell she wanted to help.

"I think they're all pretty busy right now. I'm sure you can help me. Just get those crutches by the door. If you'll just help me get up and open the bathroom door, I think I can make it on my own."

She wasn't convinced, but she did what he asked. She spotted the steak knife and the pills as he struggled out of bed.

"What's all that?" Mary asked, pointing at the bed.

"I was a little paranoid without you being here. I didn't want to take my meds for fear I'd go to sleep before you got back. And, well, I filched the knife off my dinner tray in case I needed to defend myself."

"Defend yourself from who? Were you afraid some nurse was going to molest you?"

Scott held back a dry laugh. "No, not that, but you've been living with me lately. You know how freaked out I am. I've got way too much time on my hands. I feel a lot better now that you're here. Hold the door for me. When I get back, I promise I'll take my pills like a good little boy."

She was conflicted. She could tell he was lying to her, but she really wasn't ready for the truth, if that was really what it was. She helped him struggle into the bathroom and closed the door quietly behind him.

Scott lowered himself carefully onto the commode, but try as he might, his bowels would not respond. There was too much pain in his leg. He didn't need to worry about his bladder. He was wearing a catheter with a bag taped to one leg. Finally, unable to stand the pain any longer, he stood up, flushed, washed his hands, and opened the door.

Mary was waiting by the door. "A couple of guys in scrubs just came in here looking for you. When I told them I'd helped you to the bathroom, they left."

"They were probably the guys who were helping me when the alarm rang."

"I'd say it's a good thing you could hold it, or they'd be cleaning up a mess."

Mary had just got him situated in his bed when two men in uniform knocked and then walked into the room without waiting for a response.

"Mr. Corbridge?" one of them asked. "Can you tell us how you knew about the guy with the syringe?"

"Huh?" Scott said, feigning ignorance. "What guy?"

"You told two orderlies a big story a few minutes ago. We'd just like you to confirm what you told them."

"I'm sorry," Scott lied. "I really don't know what you're talking about."

One officer looked at Mary and turned to his partner. "We must have the wrong room," he said apologetically.

"Is that why all the alarms went off?" Scott asked.

"Yes. We caught a man without credentials trying to sneak out of the receiving dock. But you don't have to be concerned. He's on his way to jail, and we'll probably arrest his accomplice within the hour."

"Was he stealing drugs from the hospital?" Scott prodded.

The first officer looked at his partner and then back at Scott. "I don't think we should discuss the case with you. If you'll excuse us, we'll be going."

Mary glared at Scott after the two men left. "What the hell was that all about?" she demanded. "They may not have been able to tell, but you were lying your ass off. I think you and I need to have a serious talk, and I want the truth. I don't need you to sugarcoat it. I need to know what I'm up against."

Chapter 13
Marital Trouble

Mary was not going to drop it this time. She stood at the foot of Scott's bed, arms folded across her middle, waiting for an answer.

Scott listened to her thoughts. She was angry. She was afraid. She was guilty. She wanted answers that he didn't want to give her.

"You can't put me off," she said, "not this time. I've seen enough in the last couple of weeks that I think I know what's going on. I can't believe it. No, I don't *want* to believe it. But here we are. Painful as it might be, I need answers."

He steeled himself. "Where do you want me to start?"

"How much do you know?" she asked.

"Pretty much everything."

"No, don't evade me. Be specific. I want to hear it from your lips. Do I have any privacy? Do you really know what I'm thinking?"

"I know you still love me, in spite of your affair with Alan."

Tears sprang to her eyes.

"I also know it's my fault that you turned to him," Scott said. "You were right when you told me that we haven't been together on a lot of things for a long time. I was too blind to see it. It breaks my heart to see how badly I've messed up. I don't want to lose you."

She turned away. "I don't know if I can deal with this," she said as she walked to the couch. She picked up her overnight bag and turned back to face him. "I don't know if anybody can. How would you feel if you knew somebody knew your every thought? That's just wrong in so many ways."

Scott held up his hand and reached out to her. "Please, don't go. Stay a while and talk. I'm not a threat. If anything, this may make me a better person."

"I think I've caught a glimpse of that 'better person,'" she said. "You haven't changed. You just know what to say now to placate me. Take the thing with my mother, for example. You two have never seen eye to eye, and yet now you're ready to let her come and stay, but only if it serves your own purposes. I don't know what went on here tonight while I was gone, but somehow, you knew it was coming. You just wanted me here to help intercept whoever that was."

"He was sent by Dr. Talbot to murder me."

"And I was supposed to do what—stop the guy? He'd have probably killed us both."

"No, he—"

"And the thing with the kids!" she cut him off. "I thought you'd changed. That you were trying to be a better father."

"I have. I am."

"No, you were just telling them what they wanted to hear."

"Isn't that where communication starts? If I know what a person's expectations are and why they feel that way, don't you think it makes it easier for me to talk to them? Think of all the fights people have just because they don't understand where the other is coming from. I wasn't trying to manipulate the kids. I wanted to understand where they were coming from. Take Jess, for instance. Do you remember how happy he was the other day when I told him he could go up to his room and crank up his music? Did it hurt me to let him do that? No, it didn't. For the first time ever, I think I realized I've put a lot of restrictions on him just because I didn't like his music. That was wrong. I can't dictate his likes or dislikes, but if I can understand him, I can act accordingly."

He paused. Mary stood, bag in hand, waiting—not convinced, yet not ready to leave.

"Take this thing with Trish," Scott continued. "I absolutely hate the thought of her and Brandon doing whatever they do when nobody is around. I can't condone what she's doing, but I can't modify her behavior. I see how she feels about the boy. In her mind, she can't get past the emotion, the love. She can't see the consequences of being sexually active at her age. She's not stupid. She knows she could get pregnant. What she doesn't see is how it will affect the rest of her life if she does. We see that. We're older. We've taken off our blinders. We see reality for what it is."

"So what is our reality, Scott? You know about Alan. How can you be so calm about that? If our roles were reversed, I'd be livid! You'd be out on your butt. I wouldn't ever want you to touch me again."

"That was my first reaction. But then I saw the rest of the story. I saw myself through your eyes, and I was ashamed. When we were first married, we lived for each other. I haven't lived for you for a long, long time. I got caught up in the world, in my job, in everything and anything that made *me* happy. It's been a long time since I actually considered *your* happiness. I guess I figured if something was wrong, you'd let me know."

"So what now? How will I know if you're being honest with me or just giving me lip service?"

"I don't have the answers to that. This is all new to me, too. I've found out firsthand that when I need to defend myself, I can use people's thoughts against them. I can be cruel. I can be hateful, but I think the motivation makes the difference. I think you've seen I can also be kind, and loving, and forgiving. That's the person I want to be, and I want to be genuine about it. Take this thing about Alan. At first, I was furious. I wanted to destroy him. I couldn't see our partnership surviving. Then I saw myself through your eyes, and I was ashamed. I felt your love, and I couldn't throw stones. I blame myself, not you. I'll never hold that against you."

"You still haven't answered my question," Mary said. Tears were streaming down her face.

"Communication and trust, I guess," he said. "Now that you know about me, you can talk to me. You can ask me anything."

"And then what—just assume you won't tell me what I want to hear so we won't fight?"

"It's a leap of faith, I suppose."

"And it's all one-sided. I have no idea what you're thinking. After what happened here tonight, I think the only reason you wanted me here was so somebody didn't murder you in your sleep."

"Okay," Scott sighed, "we'll play the honesty game. Yes, that was my initial motivation. I was afraid of being alone. No, actually, it was worse than that. I felt like I was losing my mind. I have no idea why I've had this lousy dream. I have no idea why I can do what I can. It's a curse! I hate it. If it hadn't happened, I would probably be at home now, in my own bed, and I'd no doubt have visions of sugarplums dancing through my head."

He looked down at his hands. "The problem is, that's not reality. Like it or not, I now have a new perception of reality. I know I've been a jerk. I know my wife is having an affair. I know my kids don't even know me. They tolerate me but stop short of love. And everything is my fault."

He looked back up at her. "I can't change what's happened, but maybe I can make things better. I'll know when I'm being unreasonable. I'll know when I've hurt someone. I'll know how to fix things."

"That's my point," Mary interrupted. "You'll modify your behavior just to fix things. What about your true feelings? What about your drives? Are you willing to become a 'yes man' just to survive?"

"No. I can't be that way. I won't be that way. But to every problem, there are a number of solutions. What's wrong with me changing my point of view to make someone else happy, as long as I don't feel like I'm compromising who I really am? I'll use the incident with Jess again as an example. Do I like his music? No, I don't. That will probably never change, but I can be tolerant because that's what makes him happy. Am I less of a person because I gave in? No, I don't think I am."

Mary didn't move, but she turned her head so he couldn't see her tears.

"I've been thinking a lot about John, too," Scott continued. "It's killing me that I didn't go to summer camp with him. I could have rearranged my schedule. The truth of the matter was, it was an inconvenience for me. I don't love camping, but I don't hate it, either. I didn't realize until it was too late how much that would have meant to him, but look at what I lost. Had I known his thoughts at the time, there's no question I'd have gone camping. It may have been an inconvenient thing for me, but so what? I would have survived, and it would have made him happy. Look where my relationship with him might be today if I had."

Mary pulled a couple of Kleenexes from the box on his table and wiped her eyes and nose. "So you plan to live for others from now on. Is that what I'm hearing?"

"I think that's called service. And yes, I could learn to serve others rather than myself. Isn't that sort of Christlike?"

"Oh, please!" she scoffed. "Now you're putting yourself right up there with Christ?"

"Not even close," he countered, "but aren't we supposed to try to be like him? Just because I can read thoughts doesn't make me a moral person. This *gift*, or whatever you want to call it, could be used for good or bad. I've already seen a little of both. I let my emotions get the best of me, and because of it I probably ruined a guy's career."

"Are you talking about that psychologist the cops took you to see last week?"

"Yes. He came at me all pompous and arrogant. I hated his attitude. I could see he thought I was nuts. He was there to destroy me, so I used his thoughts to fight back. That was sick and wrong. He was just trying to do his job. I could have just gone along, and everything would have been fine."

"Why did you do it, then?"

"I suppose I wanted to teach him a lesson. I knew he was there to prove me a fraud."

"No," Mary said, "he was there to attest to your mental stability."

"I can see the difference now. I couldn't then. My problem is, I let twerps like Detective Ableman warp my perspective. If I'd played that differently, he might be an ally now instead of an enemy. Like I said, this is all new to me. I need to learn to school my feelings."

"Where does that leave us?" she asked.

He stopped short. On the one hand, he knew what he wanted to say, and he knew what she was expecting him to say. He decided not to play either hand.

"I still love you, Mary," he said. "I know you don't trust me, but I hope we can get past that. I don't want to lose you, or the kids. Now that I know how much damage I can do, I'll try to stay positive. I think we can fix this. Won't you please just try? I'll try to give you your privacy. I think it would help, though, to talk a lot more."

"You can do that?"

"What—give you your privacy? Yes, I can. Thoughts are like conversation. I can choose to listen, or I can choose to ignore what I'm hearing, and I can't hear anything long distance. Usually, if you're not in the same room, or pretty near, you're out of range and I know nothing. So I suppose if you need your privacy, you could go for a walk or a ride. When we're talking face to face, I'll try to listen to what you're saying, not what you're thinking. We can start by being totally honest with each another. If you ask me what I'm thinking, I'll tell you—no holds barred. You may not like the answer, but you'll know I'm being honest."

"Okay," she said, "you can start by telling me what just happened a few minutes ago when those officers came in here."

Scott answered her without hesitation. He told her every feeling; every thought he'd had.

"Why did you lie to them?" she asked.

"You and I hadn't had this discussion yet. I already knew you were scared to death of me. I thought that would have only made things worse. Furthermore, neither one of those two guys were ready to hear what I could tell them. If I'd told them what they wanted to know, they wouldn't have believed me. Then I'd have felt compelled to tell them something personal about themselves, from their own thoughts, to convince them I was telling the truth. Then they'd have been afraid of me. Fear does strange things to people. Some react by running away. Others react by striking out. I don't need any more cops on my bad side. I figured it was better for them to leave here thinking I was delusional. Besides," he added with a smile, "they already had what they needed. They've got that creep's confession. They've got the syringe as evidence. All without me having to say another word."

"What was in that syringe?"

"Fentanyl."

"Is that the street drug everybody's so worried about?"

"Yes. It's deadly. A tiny dose can be lethal, and he had a lot. I wouldn't have lived through it."

"How did you know it was—"

"I could hear what he was thinking when he was standing outside my door."

"Scott, this is hard for me."

"I know, but you've got to believe me. It's not any easier for me."

"I'll try, but honestly, I can't promise anything."

"I know that, too, but at least you're willing to try. I love you for that."

"I should probably go," she said.

"Please don't. I could lie and tell you I know we'll be able to work through all of this, but I don't know that for sure. Now that we're being perfectly honest with each another, I can tell you there are two reasons I want you to stay. First, I love you, and I feel closer to you right now than I've felt for years."

"And second?"

"I'm afraid to stay alone. I don't want to risk seizing and falling out of bed. And yet I hate being restrained. If you're here, I think I can live with the restraints."

Mary walked to the door and closed it. "I brought my jammies and a blanket. I don't want to sleep in my clothes."

"You can change in the bathroom."

A faint smile lifted the corners of her mouth. "Why should I? We don't have secrets anymore."

Chapter 14
The Roommate

Try as he might, Scott couldn't sleep. He could feel the effect of the meds, but his mind wouldn't let his body relax. The vision kept trying to invade his mind. To avoid it, he listened to every thought Mary had until she eventually dropped off to sleep and that channel of communication stopped. Then he tried to hear anything from outside his room. The hospital had grown quiet. He forced himself to think about other things. He wanted to sleep—he needed to sleep—but he knew as soon as he relaxed, the vision would take over.

At last, he angrily let it in. If this was a tool from the Almighty, or perhaps from Nancy, it was being overused. Why wouldn't it leave him alone? He was going to lose his mind completely, and then what good would his testimony be? Then he had a thought, and he reached out to whatever entity was forcing it upon him.

If you don't leave me alone, I won't help you! he almost screamed in his mind.

Then, strangely he felt calm. He thought maybe he was missing something important—but what? He allowed the vision to come again, this time looking for something he may have missed.

He'd seen the killer. He had helped the police sketch artist create an exact rendition of the man he'd seen in the mirror. He'd seen the victim's face and had felt her anguish as she stood and watched her killer dig her grave. He had seen the well. He could almost count the paces from the well to her grave. He could see the trees—

He stopped. That was something new. Somehow, he knew those details had been there all along. But why hadn't he seen them before? Maybe he was missing something else important.

As much as he hated to, he opened his mind again to the vision, but this time he seized control. Rather than flow with the vision from horror to horror, he forced each scene to slow down so he could look for anything he might have missed. He began to see things he hadn't noticed. He'd been so horrified by the brutality of the murder that he hadn't really looked past the man's face, the knife, Nancy's face in the mirror.

Suddenly, it was as if he was seeing the vision for the first time. He watched as the killer dragged Nancy's limp body out of her bathroom. He watched him rip the sheets off a double bed, using the first sheet like a soft taco shell. Once he'd rolled her body up in it, he wrapped her in the second sheet. There was still blood, but the dark stains weren't spreading through the second sheet like they had the first.

Scott was still seeing through Nancy's eyes. She stood looking down on her cocoon-like body as the man left the room. Although she no longer felt any physical pain, the mental anguish was nearly unbearable. Then the man was back. He picked up her body and slumped it over his right shoulder. He was a big man—a tall man; a strong man. She wasn't tiny; she weighed a hundred twenty-three pounds. But the killer handled her as easily as if she'd been a pillow off her bed.

Nancy followed him down a flight of stairs to a waiting car. The trunk lid was closed but not latched. He lifted the lid and eased her body inside the trunk. When he closed the trunk, Nancy saw the license plate. It was a Nebraska plate. She concentrated on the numbers.

Scott pushed the vision aside and opened his eyes. He could see the license plate as clearly as if he was holding it in his hand. He needed a pen and paper so he could record the numbers before they slipped away. He looked around frantically. There was nothing he could reach—nothing he could use. He thought about waking Mary, then stopped himself. He'd seen the vision dozens of times. This scene would come back again if he needed it to. He closed his eyes and relaxed. Almost as if someone had pushed the play button on a tape recorder, the vision continued.

Nancy was sitting beside her killer in the front seat. He was smoking a cigarette. She looked around at the interior of the car. Then Scott saw the insignia. He recognized it as being a logo, but it wasn't familiar. If it had been a Chevy or a Ford, he would have known what it was, but this was something different. Something more exotic. A rich man's car.

The car turned onto a freeway entrance. Scott slowed the vision down, looking desperately for any road signs. Other than the red, white, and blue I-80 interstate sign that reflected under the car's headlights, there weren't any.

All sense of time fled. He knew they were traveling. He could see the white lines on the road as they flashed by in the dark. Then a larger road sign glowed under the reflected headlights. He saw the numbers 369. It was a freeway exit sign. The car turned off on the exit and turned left. Then he saw another sign—a small sign: *Big Blue River West Fork.*

The car crossed a bridge. A dirt road glowed in the headlights, and alongside the road there were trees—lots of trees. Then there was a disheveled house. And a well. An old stone well. The car turned off the road, and a small meadow came into view between two large trees under the glare of the headlights.

Nancy stood by the car as her killer opened the trunk and took out a short-handled shovel. It had a loop handle like a digging fork. She stayed by her body as the man walked away. Then he was back. He dragged her body out of the trunk and didn't even attempt to catch it. It landed with a dull thud on the grass. He grabbed a corner of the sheet and dragged her away, past the stone well. She could see a short mound of dark earth between the trees in the distance.

She watched as the big man rolled her body into the shallow hole in the ground. The grave wasn't long enough for her body. He stepped in beside her and forced her into a fetal position. Then he shoveled dirt over her. He jumped on the layers of earth as he filled the hole, compacting it tightly around her. Last, he pulled several pieces of sod over the dark earth. There was still dirt left over, so he cast it about with the shovel until only a slightly elevated grass-covered mound remained.

Nancy sat by the mound as the man walked away. Then the car's lights turned away and she was alone. So very alone.

A nurse woke Scott what seemed to be only seconds later.

"Sorry, Mr. Corbridge," she said, "I need to take your vitals."

"What time is it?"

"About four thirty. Sorry I had to wake you."

Mary sat up and watched. When the nurse left, she got up and came to his bedside. "Have you been able to sleep?"

"A little," Scott said.

He knew he'd slept because the nurse had to wake him, but it didn't feel like he'd slept. He hurt. He squirmed in his bed.

"Do you need some meds?" Mary asked. "I think it was past ten when you had your last ones. Should I go get the nurse?"

He handed her the call button, and Mary spoke briefly to the responding nurse. "You were mumbling in your sleep," Mary said, brushing her knuckles softly against his cheek. "More dreams?"

"Not more, just the same one."

"I'm sorry."

"Me too. I think I'm going to lose my mind if it doesn't quit." He paused. "And then what good would I be?" he said, projecting his thoughts to whatever entity had shown him the vision.

"Good for who, for what?" Mary asked.

The nurse interrupted them. Scott swallowed the pills and squeezed Mary's hand.

"Thank you for being here," he said as he closed his eyes. "I think I can sleep now."

Mary held his hand as he relaxed. For the first time in weeks, he felt peace. Somehow, the spirit or whatever it was that had been terrorizing him since he came out of the coma was placated. Now he had everything he needed to help the authorities find Nancy's body. And possibly, her killer.

They brought a breakfast cart at seven. Mary slipped into the bathroom to change back into her clothes while he ate.

Paul arrived a few minutes later. He looked worried. "I got a call from one of my team members last night," he said right away. "We may have trouble."

"Why?" Scott asked.

"He went back to talk to the victim's roommate, and she's gone. He talked to the cops. They made her move out of her apartment. They wouldn't let her take much—told her it was an active crime scene."

"What about her job, did he check there?"

"She quit her job. She told her employer that she couldn't find a place to live. I guess she's got a record. Nancy Bennion had rented the apartment, and her roommate was just living with her. She's a felon, and it's pretty tough for people like that to find a place to rent. So far, we haven't been able to find her. We don't know much about her. We know her name, but little else. We don't have the authority to get her Social Security number from her former employer. The cops will have to do that. If we had that, we might be able to find out where she went—if she's working. Worse yet, the Lincoln cops aren't very motivated to find her. She had an alibi. They know she didn't kill her roomie. Case closed, as far as her involvement is concerned."

"Can't we use the alibi the cops already have? I mean, doesn't that establish a time frame for the murder—a time frame that will prove I couldn't have been there?"

"I'm worried about that," Paul said. "I told you the roommate's got a record. We checked. She's an addict. Before she got a job at that 7-Eleven, she'd been busted several times for possession and was living on the street as a prostitute. I'm assuming that's what she'll fall back on. At best, she's a shaky witness. A prosecuting attorney will have a field day with her in court. If it ever comes to that."

"So what now?"

"That's why I came to see you early, before I went to the office. I think the cops may come to see you today. Without the roomie, all they've got is a grisly murder scene. They don't have a weapon, a body, or a motive. They don't even have a firm time frame for her murder. All they've got is what you told them. I'm sorry, but I'm not liking the odds. This guy, Ableman, if he's like you say he is, he'll probably ignore the hooker's testimony and alibi. That makes it a lot easier to shift everything back to the one constant they have in this case—namely, you and your wild story."

Scott looked Paul in the eyes. "It's about to get a lot wilder," he said. "I remembered some more details last night. I think I know the license plate number on the car the murderer was driving. I may know what kind of car he was driving, and I may know almost exactly where he buried her."

Paul glared at him. "And may I remind you that you need to shut your pie hole about all that? I've worked with you enough to sort of believe you're telling the truth, but nobody on the police force will. If you tell them any more than you already have, they'll throw you in jail."

"I believe Scott," Mary interrupted as she swung the bathroom door open. "I know for a fact that he can do what he says he can."

"That's admirable," Paul said, "but you're little more than a character witness. You're not an expert. Your testimony, if admissible, will never stand up under cross-examination."

"Don't you want the tag number and the description of the car?" Scott asked.

Paul hesitated for a few seconds and then pulled out a notebook.

"Let me borrow that," Scott said. "I'll write down the plate number, but more importantly, I want to draw the logo I saw on the car's horn button. I don't recognize it, so I'm assuming it's an exotic or expensive car of some sort. That might help narrow things down."

Paul took a pen out of the inner pocket of his suit jacket and handed the notebook and pen to Scott. Scott wrote down the plate number and took a few seconds to sketch the logo below the number.

"That's a Nissan Infinity logo," Paul said. "I know, because I drive one. Do you know what color it was?"

"That's a problem," Scott said. "It was dark. I can only guess. It was a light color. Either white, beige, or silver. I think."

"I'll see what I can find out," Paul said, "but I can't promise anything. We don't have access to DMV records. Maybe I can call in a favor." He put the notebook and pen back in his suit jacket and turned to leave. "Remember what I told you about keeping your mouth shut. This is all part of our client-attorney privileged information."

Chapter 15
Trouble

Scott got out of the hospital that Thursday. He was able to walk with his new knee, but he had to use a four-legged walker and somebody had to be with him when he did. They'd put monitors on him in the hospital that recorded seizures. He was having roughly four a day, down from a dozen or more when they first admitted him. They weren't painful, and none of them lasted long. The medication they had given him seemed to be working. His neurosurgeon was encouraged.

Mary attended to his every need, but she often went outside for a walk when she needed her privacy. They talked a lot, but Scott could tell she was uncomfortable. She hadn't told the kids about his new "abilities," and she watched him closely when he talked to them, looking for any sign he was manipulating them. She seemed pleased with the results. All three of the kids were talking to him on a regular basis now. That was different. She liked it.

Paul dropped by the house at noon the following Monday. Mary greeted him at the door and then turned to leave them alone.

"You may want to stick around and hear this," Paul said before she could escape into the kitchen. He wasn't smiling. "I would have called, but I won't discuss anything important over the phone. You never know the lengths this group is willing to go to. For all we know, they may have already convinced a judge to allow a wiretap."

Mary sat down by Scott on the sofa.

"The court informed me this morning that they have set a pre-trial evidentiary hearing for this Friday in Lincoln," Paul said. "When I reminded them that you had never been arraigned or arrested, they claimed the only reason you haven't been is because of your medical condition. They assured me they had my client's best interest in mind when they decided not to arrest you."

"What does that all mean?" Mary asked.

"It means that on Friday, we'll find out what evidence they may or may not have. They have to convince a judge that they have enough evidence to formally bring charges." He looked at Scott. "If the judge decides they have, you'll be arraigned and we can start preparing for your defense."

"Are you worried?" Scott asked.

"It gets worse," Paul said gloomily. "I got a phone call this morning from our team in Lincoln. The cops found Nancy's roomie dead in an alley. Preliminary results indicate she most likely died of a drug overdose. That's really unfortunate because even with her history, her testimony—coupled with that of her employer's testimony and your timeline—would have pretty much let you off the hook. I'm sure the cops are under a lot of pressure to solve this case, and for that reason I find her death very suspicious. Unfortunately, nobody is going to question the untimely death of an active drug addict. I'm sorry to say that without her testimony and her alibi, the prosecution can expand the window of death to wipe out your alibi. Without a body to counter that claim, we don't have a rebuttal."

"Don't the cops have the roommate's sworn testimony and her alibi recorded?"

"I assume they do," Paul said, "but they have no real requirement to present any evidence for your defense, and I can't ask for it to be read into the court record until we go to trial."

"What about her employer's testimony? I thought she told the cops that she left for work about seven thirty."

"That's true. She may have showed up for work, but we can't prove she was even in the apartment that day. The prosecution could claim she may have been 'sleeping over' somewhere and didn't want to reveal that. She probably wasn't making a lot of money working at a 7-Eleven. Certainly not enough to support an active drug habit."

"Where does that leave us?" Scott said.

"I won't lie to you, Scott. This is beginning to look bad. They must be pretty sure of their position or they wouldn't have called for an evidentiary hearing so soon. I've seen other murder cases go months or even years before that happens."

"Have you found anything out about the license plate number I saw in my dream?"

"I didn't dare use my DMV source yet. If Ableman got wind of that and really is trying to protect someone, I'm afraid that car might go missing."

Scott stared at him for a few seconds. "So what you're trying to tell me is that you're afraid somebody got to the roommate, and that same someone might be motivated enough to get rid of any other evidence that might clear me?"

"Like I've already told you, the cops in Lincoln are under a lot of pressure to solve this murder," Paul said. "Worse than that, if Ableman is trying to protect someone, all the judge is going to hear is enough to bind you over for trial. Right now, you're an easy mark. Everything you've told them makes you guilty. I've never talked to this Detective Ableman personally, but after what you told me, I've got a bad feeling about him. I do know that we won't reveal any of the rest of what you've told me about that murder until we can do it in court where your testimony will be recorded. Then, like it or not, the cops will have to follow up. And hopefully, when that happens, it'll be out of Ableman's hands."

"You're just full of good news," Mary said. "Aren't you?"

"I'm sorry," Paul said, "but we don't have a lot to go on. I have to assume that this will go to court. When it does, we'll go in there with sworn testimony from your associates in Lincoln. I'll establish your timeline. Then I'll talk about the roomie's testimony and alibi. They may move to discredit her as a reliable witness. At that point, we may have to talk about the car and the license plate. But that's really all we have."

"What about the sketch artist's drawing?" Scott asked. "Doesn't that count for something?"

"That's an interesting question. If Ableman is really trying to protect the guy, the folks in Lincoln may have never seen the drawing. If they have, I have to assume they've run it against their mug shot data base. If they have, and the guy doesn't have a record, or if nobody else recognizes him, we have nothing."

"What do I need to do to get ready for Friday?" Scott asked.

"Nothing, really. We'll just appear in court and listen to their evidence. If the judge decides they've made their case, they'll hold an arraignment and formally charge you. You'll plead not guilty, and then they'll either bind you over for trial or release you on bail until the trial date. I'll present your medical records and maybe even have your doctors on hand to tell the court that you're in no condition to be placed into custody. I doubt the state will be willing to take responsibility for your medical care, so you'll probably be put on house arrest."

"What do I wear—a suit?"

Paul considered the question for a few seconds. "No, I don't think so. If you go in there with your walker—your head all bandaged up and wearing a pair of sweatpants—it might make it easier to keep you out of jail."

* * * * *

The pre-trial hearing was held in a small courtroom in Lincoln. The room was packed. In spite of the drive from Omaha, they arrived early enough that Paul was able to point out most of the opposition as they came in and took their seats. Besides the prosecuting attorney and his four-man team, there were several men wearing uniforms of various types and colors. Detective Ableman was wearing a suit and tie. He was surrounded by an entourage of people both in and out of uniform. Scott immediately recognized the ones who had visited him at various times while he was in the hospital. None of those he'd talked to would maintain eye contact.

After the judge entered and was seated, the prosecuting attorney, Floyd Carter, took charge.

Scott instantly hated the man. Carter was much like the shrink, Jeffrey Bracken, in that he was full of himself. He was a small man, barely five-and-a-half feet tall, and bald except for a wispy combover probably four inches long that streaked across the top of his shiny scalp. A small mustache thickened his otherwise thin, pale lips. It was much darker than what little hair he had left on his head. Scott assumed he'd darkened it with mascara to make it stand out. Carter's obviously expensive suit fit every contour of his slight frame. His dark-red tie was too large for the smallish button-down collars of his stark-white shirt. He had tied it in a wide double-Windsor knot, making the contrast even that much more obvious.

As he picked up a short stack of paper and began to explain to the judge the nature of the case, Carter's high, tinny voice grated on Scott's nerves. The man reminded him of an IRS auditor he'd had to deal with on business matters the year before. That encounter had not gone well at all.

The putrid little man gestured with his tiny arms as he drew a mental picture for the court of the horrific crime scene. He pointed out the fact that even though they hadn't recovered a body, forensics had concluded there was enough obvious blood loss to conclude the victim had not survived. He included only part of the roommate's testimony—namely, her statements about finding the murder scene and calling 911. Having presented all that, he purposely laid the paperwork aside and picked up another short stack of paper.

"Your Honor," he squeaked on as he picked up a second stack of paper, "we have other evidence from the defendant himself that I'd like to present at this time. Although we have no sworn statements from his counsel, we have the testimony of several people who have interacted with the defendant over the past few weeks. Mr. Corbridge was involved in an automobile accident the day of the alleged murder and received some extensive injuries, including significant head trauma and subsequent memory loss. He was in a coma for a little over two weeks after the accident. He claims he has no recollection of his whereabouts for several weeks prior to his accident. He also claims to have had a dream or a vision—whatever you may want to call it—in which he witnessed the alleged murder."

He paused to glare at Scott for a few seconds before he continued. "He told his story to a psychologist, who then contacted the Omaha Police Department. Mr. Corbridge claims he saw the victim's picture in the newspaper, and he provided a verbal statement to two Omaha police officers. The officers who heard his initial statement informed their immediate supervisors, who turned the case over to Detective Patrick Ableman, a homicide detective with the Omaha Police Department. Detective Ableman subsequently interviewed the defendant."

Carter paused to gather his thoughts.

"During that interview," he continued, "the defendant claimed to have seen the murder weapon—a particularly interesting knife. After having been shown pictures of a number of knives, the defendant was able to identify this knife as being the murder weapon. This knife is a specific type of double-edged Italian switchblade. It's not a common weapon and is actually quite rare. We find that rather peculiar in and of itself. When pressed for more information about his alleged dream, the defendant told our officers he had obtained legal counsel, who told him not to divulge any additional information. Since that time, he has been a hostile witness. It is our opinion that the defendant's dream was little more than a recollection of a murder he committed himself."

Carter laid the second sheaf of papers on the table and picked up a third.

"The state of Nebraska took action to seize Mr. Corbridge's automobile from the impound lot, where it was taken after his accident. It was taken to the Lincoln County police impound lot and processed for evidence. In that vehicle, we found a cell phone registered to the defendant and a laptop computer that has information on it that identifies it as belonging to the defendant."

He then turned to face Scott. "More importantly, we found a suitcase filled with what we have assumed to be the defendant's clothing. In that luggage, we found a pair of shoes. On the toe of the right shoe was a substance identified by our lab as blood. We cross-checked the blood samples that we found on that shoe with blood from the alleged murder scene and found it to be a perfect match to the alleged victim's blood."

Chapter 16
Court

Scott's breath caught in his throat. His head pounded. A dozen thoughts exploded through his mind. The murder scene in his dream had been literally flowing with blood. It should have been everywhere—and if it was, how was it that he only had a small spot on one shoe? Why wouldn't he have simply thrown his shoes away? Why wasn't there any blood on the rest of his clothes?

He focused immediately on Ableman. The man wouldn't look at him, but in spite of the dozens of people in the courtroom, Scott could read his thoughts. Ableman was thinking smugly about the cotton swab he'd used to transplant a smear of coagulated blood from the murder scene to the toe of Scott's shoe. He knew that along with the other details of Scott's so-called dream, all he had to do was place him at the scene. The blood had done that.

Scott angrily turned to Paul. Paul held up his hand for silence. Scott could tell he was thinking the same things.

Scott barely heard the rest of the prosecuting attorney's speech. Echoes of thoughts from a dozen others in the room swirled around his mind as Carter affirmed to the court that the state had proven its case and that Scott should be arraigned and bound over for trial.

The boom of the gavel sounded as the judge proclaimed his concurrence with the findings. The judge was convinced. Scott was to be arraigned, and a trial date set.

Through it all, Paul held his peace.

In order to save the court's time, Carter immediately moved for an arraignment. He was ready with the charges. It was to be murder in the first degree. He wanted bail set at a quarter of a million dollars.

Paul finally got to his feet and addressed the court. "Your Honor," he began, "my client pleads not guilty. There are a number of mitigating circumstances in this case that have not been addressed, and whereas this is only an evidentiary hearing and not a trial, I will hold my comments on that regard until a later date."

Paul paused to stare directly at Detective Ableman for a few seconds, and then he turned back to face the judge. "As to the subject of my client's incarceration and bail, I would like to plead for leniency. As you can see, my client's health is frail at best. He sustained a serious skull fracture in an automobile accident that necessitated the removal of a fairly large portion of his skull and the installation of a titanium plate. Those injuries have not had sufficient time to heal. Any accidental or deliberate"—he paused to stare at Ableman again—"impact to his head could be life threatening."

He turned back to the bench. "In addition, his knee was destroyed in the accident and was just recently surgically replaced with an implant. He suffers from recurring seizures, up to a dozen a day, and is being given a number of medications. Many of those medications are controlled substances that will make his medical care under the state's confinement difficult at best. We instead ask for home confinement, including an ankle bracelet if necessary."

The judge considered the request for a few seconds and then called the opposing attorneys to the bench.

Scott didn't want to know what was going on under the judge's nose. He knew Paul would do his best to keep him out of jail. Instead, he turned his attention to Ableman.

Ableman's thoughts were elsewhere. What Scott heard in his thoughts horrified him and at the same time confirmed what he had already suspected about Nancy's roommate's death. Ableman and a member of his team—someone by the name of Dean—had gone to Lincoln specifically to find the woman. It hadn't taken an inordinate amount of time to find her soliciting near a neighborhood bar. She'd accepted their money for a "twosome" and got in their car. A quick stick of fentanyl in the base of her neck had done the trick.

The judge pronounced his decision. Scott would be allowed to convalesce at his home until the trial date, which would be announced at a later date. A GPS ankle bracelet was to be worn at all times, and the police were given the authority to enter his residence at any time to confirm his presence. With that pronouncement, another boom of the judge's gavel echoed through the courtroom and Paul sat down.

"We need to talk," Scott said earnestly.

"Not here," Paul warned him. "In case you haven't noticed, you have a number of enemies in the courtroom."

Mary's eyes were still wet and swollen as Scott pushed his walker up the aisle. He was horrified when he read her thoughts. She was convinced he was guilty. The blood evidence had been the final straw.

Paul gave them his car keys and sent them to the parking lot while he finished the court's paperwork. Although Mary tried to stay positive on the surface, she was horribly afraid. Scott didn't say much until they got to the car.

"You should ride up front with Paul," he said when she unlocked the car. "I need to stretch out my leg, and I can't do that in the front seat."

Mary opened the rear door and held it for him while he struggled inside and propped his leg up on the seat. Then she closed his door and climbed in the front seat and put the keys in the ignition. "It's hot," she said as she started the car.

Scott knew she didn't want to talk. She knew that he knew what she was thinking, so what was there to say?

"Mary," he said, "I know you think I'm guilty, but there's a lot going on that you don't know about. Will you just promise me that you'll keep an open mind until we've had our say in court?"

"What about the blood?" she said, her reply bordering on hysteria.

"It was planted by Detective Ableman."

"And I suppose you read his mind to figure that out?"

"Yes, but think about it. They said they found blood on a single shoe in my luggage. I wish you could have seen the murder scene. There was blood everywhere. That guy knifed her to death. His shirt was covered with blood. If I'd done that, don't you think I'd have had a lot more blood on my shoes than a single smear?"

"You have more than one pair of shoes. You probably threw the others away."

Scott knew it was hopeless to argue. From that point on, any discussion of his case would have to be done with Paul. From the emotion he felt coming from Mary, he knew she might never be convinced. Right now, he had to work with Paul so they could put together an argument that would put major doubt in a jury's mind. If Mary decided to leave him, that was one thing. If he were convicted and sent to prison, that was another.

Ten minutes later, Paul opened the driver's door and climbed in.

"Sorry for the delay," he said. "They wanted to go to trial in a month. I told them I wouldn't agree to anything less than ninety days on a capital murder charge. We compromised on sixty. Then I demanded written copies of everything they had, which after a preliminary hearing is a pretty standard procedure. But they wanted to play games. I had to threaten to haul their butts back into court to get it released. I'll tell you, that prosecuting attorney—"

"Has a small-man complex," Scott finished for him. "He's a real work of art."

Paul laughed. "That's funny, but don't let his appearance fool you. He's got an amazing track record. I think too many attorneys make the mistake of underestimating him. He's certainly no dummy."

Paul picked his way out of the parking lot. Scott didn't interrupt him again until they were on the freeway headed back to Omaha, then he asked his first question.

"Do you want to know how the blood got on my shoe?" Scott asked.

"Whose mind were you reading to get your information?" Paul asked.

"Ableman's. I caught him thinking about a cotton swab and coagulated blood from the crime scene."

"I only wish I could have offered a rebuttal on the spot," Paul said, "but the defense is not allowed to comment in an evidentiary hearing. We have to wait until it goes to trial. I've seen the photos of the crime scene, though. There's bloody footprints everywhere. Your shoes would have been saturated, and when they said they'd found blood on a single shoe in your luggage, that was almost laughable. It's nice to know about the cotton swab, though. I'm going to insist the forensics lab does an analysis of that blood to see if there are any cotton fibers in it. Also, I'm betting a good analyst will be able to tell how old the blood was when it was either dripped or smeared on your shoe. Tell me, do you know what pair of shoes they're talking about?"

"I'm sorry," Scott said. "I don't remember much about my wardrobe. Maybe Mary can answer that."

Mary looked at Paul. "I only remember him having two pairs. A white pair of Nike tennis shoes he ordinarily used when he walked or went to the gym, and a gray pair of Sketchers. I don't know which pair he was wearing when they pulled him out of the wreck. The first time I saw him in the hospital, he was in a hospital gown. When I asked about his personal effects and his clothes, the hospital claimed they destroyed his clothes because they were covered in blood. So now comes the real question: Whose blood was it, Scott's or that woman's?"

Paul glanced away from the road briefly to meet her stare. "I'm sure we can find that out soon enough," he said as he turned his attention back to the freeway. "If his clothes were all bloody, that means there had to be blood in his car. Any forensics lab worth its salt would have tested and typed that blood. You've got a really good point, though. I'm going to petition the court to have the car and any evidence that may have been taken from it sealed. If Ableman or his accomplices thought to smear a little blood on Scott's shoes, they could have just as easily dripped or dabbed a little on the interior of the car, as well. That car could make or break our case. If we can prove there was any cross-contamination after the crash, any evidence in or on the car will be inadmissible. Thank you, Mary."

Scott sensed a brief flash of relief coming from Mary.

"There's got to be a big difference in whether the blood in the car was dripped or smeared on the interior, isn't there?" Scott asked. "I mean, if I'd got in my car with bloody shoes, wouldn't the floor mats, brake, and gas pedals have smudge marks on them?"

"That's exactly what I'm thinking," Paul said. "I think this is important enough that, with your permission, I'd like to turn around and go back to Lincoln right now and file paperwork to have that car protected. Do you mind?"

"Not at all," Scott said. "Mary?"

"That's fine with me," she said. "Trish promised me she'd stay home with the boys until we got back."

Paul took the next available exit, then pulled off the road to make a phone call. "I'm going to have the team we've had looking for evidence in Lincoln go grease the skids with the judge before we get there," he said.

"While you're at it," Scott insisted, "tell them I know how Nancy's roommate died, and it wasn't from a self-inflicted drug overdose. Ableman and one of his buddies—a guy by the name of Dean something—injected fentanyl in her neck and tossed her body in an alley. Tell them to look for traces of the drug and a stick-mark on the lower left side of her neck just above her clavicle."

Paul turned around in his seat and stared at Scott. "You mean to tell me you got all that from somebody's thoughts in the courtroom today?"

"From Ableman himself."

"Then why the hell didn't you tell me all that before we left town?"

"I didn't think you wanted to talk business where anyone from the prosecution could hear us."

Paul shook his head. "Man, oh man, have we got some fast work to do! The problem is we sort of need to do everything at once. It's been what—four days since they found the roomie's body. They may have already had it cremated! What else do you have to spring on me before I make this call?"

"Nothing, really," Scott said. "There were too many people with too many thoughts for me to make sense of a lot of it. Ableman was different. He wouldn't make eye contact with me. I assumed he was hiding something, so I sort of zoned in on him."

"I'm having a hard time figuring out his motive," Paul said. "This has gone way beyond trying to railroad you. Why would he go to such lengths? I'm thinking there's more to Detective Ableman than meets the eye."

"I already told you," Scott said, "he's trying to protect somebody by the name of Vince. I don't know what hold that guy has on him, but it's got to be pretty serious to risk everything like he is."

Paul turned his attention to his cell phone. He made three quick phone calls, then crossed under the freeway and took an onramp headed back to Lincoln. He didn't pay much attention to the speed limit on the way back.

His phone rang twice before they took an exit and headed downtown. From what Scott could hear in Paul's mind, he had a team of four people on the ground in Lincoln who were pulling out all the stops. The judge, the prosecuting attorney, and a select few members of the prosecution team would be waiting for them in the judge's chambers.

Chapter 17
<u>The Judge</u>

"There'd better be a good reason for me being here," the judge said gruffly as Paul, Scott, and Mary filed into his chambers. Floyd Carter and several members of his team were already there. "May I remind you that this is not a trial? You'll have your day in court to have your say."

"Thank you, Your Honor, for agreeing to see us," Paul said. "I realize this isn't exactly protocol, but I think the court might be interested in hearing what we have to say. Ordinarily, I would have saved the evidence I'm going to present until the trial, but there are mitigating circumstances I'll point out what I think will explain why we have asked for your immediate attention."

"Make it quick," the judge said. "I have another hearing in fifteen minutes, and I haven't had lunch yet."

"If you'll bear with me, I need to do a small demonstration first. I realize that what I'm about to show you will be difficult to believe, but my client can read minds. He collected some thoughts from certain persons in the preliminary hearing today that I think you need to be made aware of in order to protect some vital evidence in this case."

"Stop right there," the judge said angrily. "I don't have time for fairytales."

"If I might be so bold," Scott spoke up, "this is not a fairytale. You, Judge Dawson, are married. Your wife's name is Lilly. You've been married thirty-one years. You have two children—a boy and a girl. Your son, Andrew, is married. And his wife, Linda, just gave birth to your first granddaughter three weeks ago. Your daughter, Brandy, is attending dental school at Creighton University in Omaha. Your favorite color is orange. You have an outstanding coin collection, and you golf for relaxation."

Judge Dawson glared at Scott. "That is common knowledge. Certainly no demonstration of your alleged abilities."

"Pick someone else, then," Scott said. "Until today, I hadn't seen the prosecuting attorney or any of his team. I don't personally know any of them."

He could tell the judge was about ready to dismiss them all.

"Please, Your Honor," Scott said. "What we need to tell you will either make or break my case. Just give me five minutes."

Judge Dawson looked at Carter. "Well, Floyd, do you have any objections?"

"Not at all, Your Honor," Carter replied. "Any evidence the defense is willing to divulge could aid the state's case in court. If they're ready to do that, I'm not opposed to hearing them out."

The judge looked at the clock on the wall and then turned to Paul. "You've got five minutes."

"So you don't think we're doing parlor tricks, I'd like you to pick a person from this group to act as a guinea pig," Scott said.

Dawson glanced quickly at the group and pointed at a member of Carter's team. "I don't know you," he said. "Who do you work for?"

"I'm a forensics scientist, Your Honor," the man answered. "I work for the Lincoln City Police Department."

The judge glanced at Scott. "Will he do?"

"He will," Scott said. "His name is Marvin Lavery. He is married with four children. He's been with the city for eighteen years. He's well respected by his peers, but he's not happy with his supervision. He had a job interview with the Illinois State forensics lab in Chicago two weeks ago. They made him an offer. He's already typed up his letter of resignation. They want him a week from Friday."

"Is that true?" Judge Dawson said, glaring at Marvin.

Marvin was not happy.

"Well?" Dawson asked impatiently.

"Yes, Your Honor, but nobody knows that besides my wife."

"Okay," Dawson answered skeptically, "so where do you plan to lead me from here?"

"In court earlier today," Paul said quickly, "my client discovered some information from an Omaha detective in the same way he got Marvin's personal information. That information has led us to believe the detective has been tampering with evidence. He has been hostile toward my client ever since he recognized the man in a police drawing my client provided when he came to question him in the hospital. We believe the detective is trying to protect someone. That drawing was conspicuously absent from today's proceedings. Detective Ableman planted the blood evidence found on my client's shoe using a cotton swab saturated with coagulated blood he took from the crime scene. I hate to tip my hand, but I'd like to paint a picture for this group. Then, I'd like you to issue a court order to seal my client's automobile as evidence and not allow any further investigation without a team from the defense being present."

"Well, we're waiting," Dawson said. "Paint your picture."

"I've seen photographs of the crime scene," Paul said. "It was a horrific scene. The perpetrator's bloody footprints were everywhere. How do you suppose my client was able to get away with little more than one small blood smear the size of the head of a cotton swab on the toe of his right shoe? I'd think his shoes would have been saturated."

"He could have thrown away the clothes he was wearing during the murder," Carter interjected.

"No doubt, he could have," Paul said, "and I won't waste my time arguing that point any further. My main concern is with the additional blood evidence that should be in my client's car. He was seriously injured in the wreck and lost a significant amount of blood. His blood should be all over the interior of his car. I would like to ask that his car be sealed until all of that evidence can be processed so there is no chance for additional cross-contamination of the victim's blood. If my client was the perpetrator—and I don't believe he was—he would have had blood on the soles of his shoes that would have been transferred to the car's foot petals, floor mats, possibly even the trunk. If he'd handled the victim, he would have had blood on his hands. That blood would have been transferred to the door handles, the steering wheel, and the like."

"He could have been driving another vehicle," Carter countered.

"That's possible," Paul said, "but I already indicated that Detective Ableman is hostile toward my client. It's our contention that he planted the evidence on my client's shoe. Furthermore, my client knows from other thoughts he gleaned from Ableman in court today that Ableman and an accomplice he identified as Dean found the victim's roommate working the street near a local bar. They offered her money for sexual favors and then injected her with a lethal dose of fentanyl and dumped her body in an alley. They did that because her testimony and alibi would have cleared my client."

"You better be very careful, Counselor," Dawson growled. "You're implicating a detective in a homicide, and I understand he has an exemplary record."

"I understand that, Your Honor, but I can tell you that although she was a known addict, you'll find an injection site at the base of her neck. Not in an arm or a leg, as would be the common place for an addict to inject a drug. You'll also find that the amount of fentanyl in her blood would indicate something much more substantial than an accidental overdose."

"What does that have to do with your request to seal your client's vehicle?"

"Detective Ableman may have a stellar reputation, but as I indicated before, my client read his mind when he saw the police sketch. Detective Ableman is trying to protect someone, and he knows the easiest way of doing that is to implicate my client in the murder. Because of the alleged dream my client had, the detective correctly assumed that if he could place my client anywhere near the scene of the crime, any jury would convict him, and the man he is trying to protect would go free."

Paul turned to Carter. "Can you tell me why you didn't present the composite drawing my client gave the detective as evidence in today's hearing?"

"I didn't feel it was pertinent. I wasn't out to prove your client's innocence. That's something I'd expect the defense to offer as evidence when we go to court."

"It's my fear, Your Honor," Paul said, "that Detective Ableman knows who the man in that police sketch is. For that reason, and the others I've discussed here today, I would like my client's car to be sealed. I would also like to request the court to immediately seize the body of the victim's roommate before they cremate or otherwise dispose of her body."

Judge Dawson addressed the prosecuting attorney's team. "Does what the attorney for the defense has to say make any sense to you at all?"

"It does, Your Honor," Marvin answered for the group.

"I would ask you to check out the defense's allegations," Dawson said, addressing Marvin, "but I won't, for two reasons. First, your testimony has now been prejudiced because of what has occurred here. And second, it appears you may not be with us by the time this case goes to trial."

Then he turned to Carter. "If it pleases the prosecution, I'd like to grant the defendant's request. More importantly, because of the rest of what has been alleged here today, I want that woman's body sent to the crime lab here in Lincoln for a full toxicology screen. And if I hear that anyone in this company here today leaks any of this information to anyone outside of this room, I'll not only hold you in contempt of court, but I'll throw out any evidence found in the defendant's automobile or luggage. Do I make myself perfectly clear?"

"Yes, Your Honor," Carter said. "What if we find that the allegations the defendant has made against Detective Ableman are true?"

"At the very least, none of Ableman's testimony will be allowed in court, and more probably, I would expect to hear that the detective and his accomplice have been arrested for murder."

"Thank you, Your Honor," Paul said.

"I'm not finished," Dawson said. "A court of law generally deals with concrete facts and evidence. I'm not stupid enough to think that somehow you may have been able to pull off some sort of parlor trick here today. I know you, Mr. Rodriguez. You've argued cases in my court before. From what I've seen until now, you have an exemplary team and represent an honorable law firm. If I find anything to indicate that this is little more than a ruse to influence the opinion of this court, I'll see to it that you and your partners are all disbarred. Again, do I make myself perfectly clear?"

"Yes, Your Honor," Paul said.

"Then let's go make this happen," Dawson said. "Floyd, I can't prejudice myself with any evidence that might be found in or on the defendant's vehicle. That's a matter for discussion in open court. But I want to know the results of any evidence you may find on the other matter. If we find that Detective Ableman and his alleged accomplice can be implicated in that woman's death, I want him off the case immediately. And whereas that alleged murder would have occurred on the streets of my city, even though he works for Omaha, I want him and his accomplice arrested and bound over here in Lincoln until we can sort this mess out."

Judge Dawson paused to make eye contact with each person in his chambers. Then he turned back to Carter.

"Ordinarily, I wouldn't involve you in something that should be a matter for our homicide detectives here in Lincoln, and I'm not saying you can't involve them in the Ableman case, but due to the sensitivity of this first issue—namely, the protection of the defendant's automobile—I'm going to look to you to take the lead. Don't disappoint me."

"I won't, Your Honor."

Dawson looked up at the clock on his wall. "Well, dammit, it looks like I'll have to forgo lunch today, and when I'm hungry, I have a tendency to be grumpy. I may have to postpone my next case."

"I'm sorry about all this," Paul said. "We really appreciate you taking the time to hear us."

"Apology accepted, but you're not off the hook yet. I'm dead serious. I won't allow anyone to make a mockery of my court or play me for a fool. You'd better not disappoint me. Now get out of here—all of you!"

Chapter 18
Convalescence

Mary was more at ease on the ride home. Nobody said much. Scott sat in the back seat and simply listened to Paul and Mary's thoughts.

The talk about the blood evidence made sense to Mary. *Maybe,* she thought, *he could be telling the truth.*

The judge's threat weighed heavily on Paul's mind. His firm had everything to lose and very little to gain. Winning this case was going to be expensive, and he doubted Scott could pay the bills. His earlier thoughts about the merits of Scott's case and the notoriety it would bring to his firm seemed to pale by comparison.

Paul thought about the rest of Scott's recorded testimony. He weighed their options. On the one hand, if they could discredit Ableman and prove the blood evidence on Scott's shoe had been planted, that would go a long way toward solidifying Scott's alibi. Then, if the prosecution would allow the dead roommate's testimony without trying to discredit her as a prostitute and a drug addict, there was a chance he could convince a jury that Scott couldn't have committed the crime. But if they found any more of the victim's blood in or on Scott's mangled car, they were screwed.

Paul quickly looked in the rearview mirror at Scott. "You've been listening to all that, haven't you?"

"There's not much else to do," Scott said.

"Okay, then. Knowing I can't keep anything from you, what do you think about telling the cops about the rest of your dream?"

"I don't like that idea. I think we should wait to see what they find when they process my car. If they find any more of Nancy's blood in my car, wouldn't that just support their case?"

"Even if they don't, we're still going to have to present a defense."

"Maybe so, but why give them any more ammunition than they already have? Right now, the only thing they've got to go on is what a couple of cops might say about a story I told them while I was on medication in the hospital."

"Did they record any of your testimony?"

"Ableman jotted a few things down in his notebook, but nobody had a tape recorder like you did."

"With any kind of luck, we'll be able to discredit Ableman's testimony," Paul said. "Then, all they'll have is the story you told those two cops that first night and whatever you told the sketch artist when you were describing the perp. If it wasn't for that detailed picture, I could probably argue that the rest of what you told them was a figment of a man's brain-injured imagination— brought on, no doubt, by the photograph of the murder victim you saw in the newspaper."

"So where do we go from here?" Scott asked.

Paul ran a number of options in his head. Rather than try to follow his thought process, Scott gave the man his privacy.

"Did you get all that?" Paul finally asked.

"Nope. I was thinking my own thoughts. I couldn't follow yours."

"Okay, so I'm going to get with my team and do a little strategizing, but here's what I'm thinking. If the cops can't come up with any physical evidence that actually places you at the scene of the crime, I'm going to move to have the charges thrown out."

"What about the drawing? What about Nancy's body?"

"You're getting ahead of me," Paul said. "Once they're convinced they don't have enough evidence to convict, I'll try to do a little horse trading with the prosecution. The state is still on the hook to catch the real killer. The judge might even agree to allow your testimony as state's evidence against the real perp, if and when they actually find him. Then, and only then, will we bring up the license plate number, the car model and description, the burial spot, and the type of shovel the perp used to bury the victim. That will put the state's investigation light years ahead of where it is now."

"What if they won't deal?"

"Then you walk away. You keep your mouth shut, and you go back to being an architect so you can pay my significant bill."

"I don't know if I can do that. I told you how my dream quit harassing me night and day when I finally slowed everything down and told you the rest of the details. You already think I'm nuts, so I don't think it'll do any more harm to tell you that I honestly believe Nancy's ghost is responsible for my dream, or vision, or whatever it is. If I don't follow through with this, I'm afraid she's going to come back."

Mary turned around in her seat. "That's the first sensible thing you've said about any of this," she said. "People believe in ghosts. I believe in ghosts and hauntings. If it wasn't for that other thing, I could honestly believe you."

"You mean the mind reading thing?"

"Bingo," she said.

"Maybe I only have that ability so she could tell me all the rest. Maybe this will all fade away once I help them find her body."

"Okay," Paul interrupted, "this is getting too weird. If you think we've got a hard time convincing the court that you can read minds, you introduce a ghost story into all this and we'll get tossed out on our butts. We need to stick to what we know. Something the detectives, whoever they're going to be, can prove. You can tell the rest of that story to your grandchildren some night when you're deep in the woods around a campfire."

* * * * *

Life at home got a lot better once Mary was partially on board with Scott's story. She still went for walks when she needed her privacy, but otherwise, she pretended not to know he knew what she was thinking. They talked. They laughed. They strategized about the kids. She carefully avoided any significant thoughts about Alan. Scott suspected that part of her periodic walks included a cell phone conversation with his partner, but overall, life at home was almost pleasant. He began to see and feel some of the love Mary still had for him.

Paul dropped by that Saturday night. He had news: The forensics team in Lincoln had finished their analysis of the roommate's body, and the judge had ordered it preserved at an "undivulged location."

Then came the bad news: The trial date had not slipped. The court had completed their analysis of Scott's car and sealed it in a shipping container somewhere. The prosecution wouldn't divulge the findings of that investigation. That had Paul worried.

* * * * *

Scott mostly laid around and let his body heal. Mary had to call the court every time he had to leave home for medical appointments. His knee was doing well. His ribs were knitting. The scalp over the metal plate in his head had begun to grow hair, and the headaches had become tolerable. Better yet, he had stopped having seizures. The dream hadn't gone away, but now the only time he saw it was when he reached out and invited it in.

The cops dropped in from time to time—without any notice, of course—to be sure he and his GPS ankle bracelet were both still at home. When they did, Scott was very careful to carry on a cordial conversation without telling them what they were thinking.

A month passed without any news. Scott was feeling a lot better physically. He was walking well with his new knee, and his pain was under control. Alan brought him a laptop that held all the drawings and specifications for the building Scott had been working on in Lincoln in hopes it might help jog his memory.

Scott's training kicked in, and while he could understand what he was looking at, he didn't remember a single thing about the job itself. It helped him pass the time and made him feel better about eventually going back to work. He was frustrated, though, knowing he'd signed off on all the work he was reviewing and yet couldn't remember a single thing about the job.

Another week passed without any news. Then, early on a Thursday morning, Paul knocked on the door. The kids hadn't left for school yet, and even though Mary was still dressed in her pajamas, she opened the door for Paul and then hurried off to the bedroom to get dressed.

"What brings you around here so early?" Scott asked.

"I'd rather not talk until your kids leave," Paul said quietly. "I trust you're healing nicely?"

Scott read Paul's thoughts. When he did, his blood ran cold.

"You're carrying a handgun?" Scott whispered.

Paul looked around. "Things are bad. They arrested Ableman last night on capital murder charges. The evidence they found in and on the roommate's body was just what you told them it would be. When they started grilling his accomplice, Dean, he agreed to testify against Ableman. Ableman lawyered up and somehow got out on bail. I heard the judge imposed bail at half a million dollars. Even though he only had to come up with a paltry ten percent, that still equates to fifty grand in cash. Ordinarily, detectives aren't known to have that kind of money lying around. That confirms Ableman must have wealthy friends in low places."

Mary walked into the room, glanced at them, and went into the kitchen to hurry the kids along.

"Maybe you'd better wait for Mary," Scott said. "I'm not keeping secrets anymore."

"Under the circumstances, that's probably a good thing. I called the prosecuting attorney at seven this morning, and he has a few ideas I need to run past you both."

Scott became even more alarmed as he read Paul's thoughts, but he didn't press the man for answers. Time seemed to drag. By the time Mary had ushered the two boys out the front door, Scott was nearly frantic. Mary could sense something when she joined them in the living room.

"What's wrong now?" she asked.

"They arrested Ableman last night," Paul told her. "I was just telling Scott that he's already out on bail. I think it's safe to assume he has a lot of wealthy friends." He looked at Scott. "Ableman undoubtedly knows you're the reason he was arrested. That means he knows you read his mind to get that information. He knows you're dangerous not only to him and his case but also to those he is trying to protect. He and his dark friends need you to go away. I talked with the prosecuting attorney in Lincoln early this morning. We think it would be in your best interest to put you in state custody until Ableman goes to trial."

"What makes you think I'd be safe in jail?" Scott asked. "We made a case with the judge for home confinement based on my medical condition. My head isn't any less vulnerable than it was then."

"This wouldn't be county jail," Paul said, "this would be solitary confinement in the state penitentiary."

"I've heard all kinds of horror stories about prison life," Mary said. "They kill people in prison every day."

"It's not as bad as the press would have you think it is," Paul told her. "He'd go in under a fake name and set of charges. Nobody inside will know who he really is."

"And what if the other inmates find out what I can do?" Scott said. "Don't you think there's a lot of people in there who would be uncomfortable having a snitch living next door?"

"If you keep your mouth shut," Paul said, "nobody will know what you can do. Your only other option is the Witness Protection Program. That takes time and resources that the state won't commit without getting something in return, and right now you don't have anything significant to offer them. It's not like you're fingering a big crime boss or something like that."

"What about my family? Who's going to protect them if you throw me in the slammer?"

"Ableman isn't afraid of your family. He's afraid of *you*. He knows what you're capable of. You're his enemy, not your family."

"I suppose you've already worked this all out with the prosecuting attorney?"

"Actually, I spoke with Floyd Carter and the judge this morning. After what happened in the Ableman case, they believe you. And they're convinced that for the immediate future, solitary is your best option."

Paul looked at Scott and Nancy before he continued.

"I know that putting you behind bars may seem a little rash, and I apologize for that, but I have even better news. Floyd and his team went over the sworn testimony of the victim's dead roomie. Better yet, they interviewed her ex-boss and kicked around her apartment complex. They found three witnesses who saw her leave the apartment around seven thirty the day of the murder. The prosecution is ready to offer you a deal."

"What kind of deal?"

"It's in everybody's best interest that they put Nancy Bennion's murder to bed. They told me they are willing to drop the charges against you if you will help them with their investigation. I sort of threw them a bone when they made that offer. We had a bit of a verbal arm wrestle until Floyd came through for you."

"You didn't tell them about the car and the grave, did you?" Scott gasped.

"I did."

"And?"

Paul paused to let the fact sink in before he continued. "Once I did that, Floyd rolled over and told me your car came out clean, and that their forensics lab had concluded Nancy's blood had been *smeared* on your shoe, not dripped—they indicated it was hours if not days old when it was planted—far beyond the time when you got in your crash. Better yet, they found cotton fibers in the blood, just like you told them they would."

"Will miracles never cease!" Scott exclaimed sarcastically.

"I need to tell you, though, that he still has a hard time swallowing the dream scenario. But he did admit that by using the drawing, the description, the license plate number of the car, and the location of the grave, they might be able to find the real perp."

"And?" Scott prodded.

"Okay, so I should know I can't hide anything from you. The 'and' is, I've already worked out all the arrangements with Floyd and the judge. I've got everything in writing."

"What have you got in writing?"

"The termination of charges against you."

Scott wanted to shout for joy. He turned to Mary. "What do you think?"

"Why ask me?" she said. "You already know what I'm thinking."

"Oh yeah, I suppose I do. But I need to hear you say it."

"I'm afraid," she said, "not *of* you anymore, but *for* you." She hesitated. "But I think we need to trust them."

"Okay," Scott said as he looked back at Paul. "How does this work, then?"

"I'll call the judge and tell him you've agreed. He'll have his people work out the details."

"So why are you carrying a handgun?"

"Ableman doesn't much like me, either. When you disappear, he'll know we've stashed you somewhere. I don't feel like answering any of his or his buddy's questions. Especially under duress."

"I'm sorry," Scott said. "I didn't mean to put you at risk."

"This thing with the detective is none of your doing. But you're going to owe me big time."

"I'll do everything I can to pay you back," Scott said.

Paul smiled. "Actually, in the twenty-five years I've been practicing law, this is the most excitement I've ever had on a case. When this finally hits the news, I'll be famous!" Paul turned away, punched a few buttons on his cell phone, and held it up to his ear. "We're ready," he said into the phone. "Tell me the details."

After listening for a minute, he closed his phone and turned to Mary. "Call the court and get permission to take Scott in for his routine doctor's exam. Then load him up and haul him to the hospital, like always. Take him to the appointment desk. A couple of guys in doctor's scrubs will come down and pick him up. Wait for about a half hour and then go home. I'll call you when I know more."

Scott got to his feet and held out his arms. Mary wrapped herself in his arms and pulled him close until it felt like she was going to crush his broken ribs.

"Careful," Scott said softly, "I'm still pretty sore."

She kissed him like she had back when they were first dating—long, wet, and passionate.

"Hey, you two," Paul teased, "you don't have time for that. We need to get going. They'll be waiting for you."

Chapter 19
Prison

Scott felt warm nearly all the way to the hospital. Mary was conflicted. Her lips still burned from the whiskery kiss. She'd felt Scott's love. She needed him; she wanted him—and yet her own guilt hung over her like a huge wave, ready to crush her at any minute.

"Hey," Scott said softly from the back seat. "I forgive you, Mary. Don't beat yourself up. This was all my fault, not yours. If you decide you can't live with me anymore, I'll understand. I think we can work this all out, but it's your choice. If you decide you can't, I'll understand."

He could see tears streaking down her cheeks in the rearview mirror.

"No," Scott added, "I don't know how long I'll be gone. I'll call you before I come home."

"Quit that!" Mary ordered. "You could at least have the decency to let me ask my own questions before you blurt out the answer. I'm trying to pretend I still actually have private thoughts."

They rode in silence the rest of the way. Scott tried to turn his thoughts inward so he could give Mary her privacy. He invited the vision back and walked through the haunting memories again for what seemed like the thousandth time. He was watching the dirt rain down on Nancy's body when Mary interrupted his thoughts.

"We're here, Scott. Are you okay?"

"Just living the dream," he said sarcastically. "I wonder if it will ever leave me alone?"

Everything went like Paul said it would. Two men with rather large and course hands—obviously not doctors—met him at the front desk and walked him down the hall to an elevator. Inside, one of them pressed the B button, and the elevator descended to the basement. When the door opened, they ushered him into an underground parking complex to a dark, windowless van. They unlocked his GPS shackle and opened the sliding door for him.

"There's a set of prison duds back there," one of the men said as he climbed in and closed the door. "Everything comes off, including the underwear. When you're done, settle down and fasten your seatbelt. We've got about an hour's drive ahead of us. Do you need to use the facilities before we leave?"

"No, I believe I'm okay," Scott said.

"Those are nasty-looking scars you've got on your head. I wish we could cover them up, but you can't have any wigs or headgear of any kind in the joint. You should probably have a story ready if anybody should ask you how that happened."

"What is my story?" Scott asked. "I mean, what am I supposed to be in prison for?"

"Your paperwork says your name is Dennis Peterson. You're a mental patient accused of multiple murders. You're too dangerous to incarcerate at a mental institution. You come with a pharmacy of medication they're supposed to give you until you calm down enough to be evaluated for mental competency."

The man turned around in his seat to look at Scott.

"The warden will meet us when we get there. He already knows about your meds, so there won't be any reason to talk to him. He may try to ask you a few questions. It says in your paperwork that you won't respond, so don't."

"Wow, I don't feel real good about this," Scott said. "I can just imagine him torturing me or something to try to get me to talk."

"Don't let your imagination run away with you. He knows you're a high-profile inmate. He won't risk messing you up. We'll have to shackle you up before you go in. That's just procedure. Just remember, you need to maintain a low profile. You'll be in solitary confinement with no exercise release. You'll have everything you need in your cell—shower, clothes, all that. You'll get no music, no books, nothing. Any questions?"

"Nope," Scott said, "I guess not. Do they really treat solitary inmates like that?"

"Depends on the offense. Some are in solitary to protect them from the rest of the inmates. Some are in there to protect the inmates from people like you. Your papers say it's the latter. Without knowing you, that's usually enough to ward off the dudes who might want to whoop you just to prove they can."

"You make it sound like a real picnic."

"It isn't, believe me. You better hope that whatever's going on in the legal system happens fast. A person could go nuts in a place like that."

"I already am nuts. Haven't you read my paperwork?"

Chapter 20
<u>Solitary</u>

Everything happened just like his quasi-captors had said it would. Almost. They stopped alongside the road about five minutes away from the prison and shackled him. A team of four men met them at the gates and took possession of their prisoner, along with his paperwork and the bag of drugs they'd sent with him.

"Hey, asshole," one of the uniformed guards said as soon as he saw Scott, "what's up with your head? It looks like you tried to stop a truck."

Scott just stared at him, despite the fact he was scared to death the man was going to touch his head—or worse yet, smack him.

"You don't talk much, do you?" another guard asked.

One of his drivers addressed the bunch. "You better read his paperwork before you start messing with him," he said. "He's a freak. They couldn't keep him in a mental lockup."

"What the hell happened to his head?"

"He put it through a windshield during a high-speed chase. He's got a plate in his head. He took out his knee in the process. They replaced that, too."

"What's he doing here?"

"Waiting trial for murder. The shrinks are all afraid of him. The state is trying to prove he's mentally competent to stand trial, but he won't talk. He punched a lady shrink in the face when she tried to talk pretty to him. The judge hopes that a couple of months in the box will give him enough time to wind down so he'll feel like talking."

"Oh, we'll soften him up," one of the guards said.

"I don't recommend that. If he gets messed up, I guarantee someone will lose their job over it. We think he may have killed something like eight people. The judge really wants him to talk, and with that plate in his head, a little knock might kill him. Then the state will have paid out a lot of money, all for nothing. You get my drift?"

"We'll go introduce him to the warden and let him decide what to do with him."

"Good luck, guys. I know we're damn glad to be rid of him."

Scott shuffled along behind two of the guards while the other two walked a pace behind.

"You don't look like you're all that tough," one of the guards behind him scoffed. "Hell, we've got guys in here who'd eat you for breakfast."

Scott believed him. He was grateful for the send-off his chauffeurs had given him, but he wished they'd simply let his paperwork do the talking. He had a bad feeling that all they'd done was thrown him to the wolves. These guys were used to dealing with the scum of the earth. He was sure they knew how to make him talk—or kill him. He wanted neither.

The warden was a hard-looking man of about fifty with a Marine-style haircut and tattoos showing below the short sleeves of his white, open-collared shirt. He took the paperwork from the guards and glanced through it. His mind was not on the paperwork. He was worried about how he was going to keep his people away from the prisoner.

"My name is Bruce," the warden said, "but you'll call me Warden."

Scott stared at him and said nothing.

"I have to assume you can talk. Things might go a lot easier for you in here if you would. Maybe if you won't talk, you could write notes."

Scott didn't respond.

"Alrighty then, a few days in the hole without anything to eat and maybe you'll change your mind."

Scott simply stared. Warden Bruce picked up the phone on his desk and barked a couple of orders. In seconds, two more men dressed in uniform crowded into the room.

Bruce reread Scott's paperwork. "I see you crushed a knee in a car crash when you busted up your head. It says here that they replaced your knee a little over a month ago. That's got to be smarting a little. I'm guessing those meds they sent you with have something in there for pain."

Scott said nothing.

"Friendly cuss, aren't you? Well, they told me you wouldn't talk. I assume you can understand the King's English, though. I'll tell you what, Dennis. If you play ball, we'll feed you, and you'll get your meds. If you don't . . . well, let me just say you might not like it here very much."

Four uniformed guards led Scott down two sets of stairs and along a stark corridor lighted by bare bulbs hanging from the cement ceiling. The hallway was lined with steel doors. They all looked the same. The only sounds in the corridor came from Scott's clinking chains. Nobody talked, at least not verbally. All four men had thoughts running through their minds ranging from belligerence to apathy. Scott didn't much care for any of their thoughts. None of them were friendly thoughts.

The lead guard stopped in front of a door that had the number seventy-eight stenciled just below a small wire-reinforced glass window. He pulled out a heavy key, opened the door, and motioned Scott inside. Once Scott was inside, the guard produced another key and stripped off his shackles and handcuffs. The other three guards stood outside the cell watching.

Inside the stark cell, a cement slab about four inches thick, six feet long, and a couple of feet wide had been anchored to the wall. It stood about a foot-and-a-half off the floor. In one corner sat a stainless-steel commode and sink. A circular drain in the floor lay next to the commode below a stainless-steel shower head. A single handle protruded from the wall that Scott presumed controlled both the hot and cold water for the shower—if, of course, both were available. A single lightbulb glared down from the ceiling some ten feet off the floor. There was no switch to turn it on or off. Scott figured it stayed lit until the bulb burned out.

One of the guards in the hallway leaned in and handed Scott two large plastic sacks. "Make yourself comfortable," he said. "It looks like you're going to be here a while." With that, they closed the cell door and locked it.

Scott looked inside the sacks. One contained a thin foam mattress, two coarse wool blankets, and a lumpy pillow. The other contained a washcloth, towel, bar of soap, toothbrush, and a medium-sized tube of toothpaste. At the bottom of the sack lay a single roll of toilet paper and two sheets of typewritten paper containing the rules for his cell.

He pulled the eggshell-type mattress out of the sack and spread it across the polished concrete bunk. When he looked around, he realized there was no place to put anything on the sink or commode. Everything but the bedding had to stay in the sacks. He stuffed the plastic sacks beneath his bunk and lay back on his thin pad. That's when he spotted the surveillance camera protruding from the concrete, high above the door.

So, this is life in solitary confinement, he thought.

There was no comfort, no privacy, and—for someone incarcerated here for life—no hope. To pass the time, he closed his eyes and invited the all-too-familiar vision to roll through his mind.

At some point, he dozed off. When the door lock crunched under the thrust of a key, he sat up, disoriented. The door swung open and three men stood in the doorway. Two were in uniform. One wore a white lab coat.

The white-haired man in the lab coat handed Scott a small plastic cup containing several pills. "I'm the medic," he said. "The warden told me to bring you your meds. He said your paperwork says they're psycho drugs of some sort and you'll go nuts without them. We can't have you hurting yourself. You'll need to take them while we watch so we know they're going down. If they don't, well, we have other ways of getting them into your body. I guarantee you won't like that."

The men waited. Scott put the pills in his mouth and drew water out of the sink in his hand to swallow them.

"Open your mouth and show me your hands," the medic ordered.

Scott did as he was told. When the medic was satisfied that Scott had swallowed the pills, they all turned around and left.

Three guards brought dinner a few minutes later. Two held him while the other slapped him around with open palms to avoid bruising. He avoided Scott's head, but his half-knitted ribs took a pounding.

"We have ways of making people talk," one of the guards growled as they filed out. "We took it easy on you this time. If you want to avoid that, I suggest you remember how to talk."

Scott remembered every name. Somehow, he'd get even.

That chance came at suppertime. This time, three men appeared at his door again. One of them was the warden.

"Hey, Dennis," Warden Bruce said as he walked in with a small food tray. "They tell me they brought you your meds. I hope you're feeling a little better."

"I was feeling pretty good, thank you," Scott answered, "until I got a visit from Fred, Clayton, and Gary. They roughed me up pretty good. I guess nobody told them I've got busted ribs. Check your surveillance footage if you don't believe me. They offered to leave me crawling next time."

A thin smile spread across Bruce's lips. "It looks like our methods are effective. It didn't take you long to remember how to talk. I'll have a look at the surveillance tapes, but I'm pretty sure I won't see anything. Last time I looked, that camera wasn't working."

Without saying it in so many words, the warden had left him a distinct message: Scott was on his own and was expected to play by some set of unwritten rules.

"So what do I have to do to get my next favor?" Scott asked.

Bruce's smile broadened. "Now, that's better. You're learning really quick."

Scott didn't say a word.

"Nobody told you the names of those guards," Bruce said. Then he offered an evil grin. "Rumor has it that the paperwork they gave me on you is a bunch of bullshit. I happen to know you're some sort of mental freak who can read minds. I also know that you fingered a certain detective. Now, I won't verbalize anything else, because these men here don't have the need to know."

Scott's blood ran cold. Warden Bruce obviously had ties to Ableman—maybe even to whoever it was he was trying to protect. His life was suddenly worthless.

"I'm thinking that I could use a guy with your obvious talents," Bruce said.

Again, Scott didn't answer.

"You know, Dennis, I'm sure by now you've figured out that I could make your stay with us tolerable or really miserable. So, tell me, which way do you want it?"

"What do you want me to do?" Scott said.

Bruce's smile faded. From his thoughts, Scott could tell he was almost afraid of him.

"How close do you need to be to a person to find out what he's thinking?" Bruce asked.

"A few feet."

"I need a little favor. We have this guy . . . I guess you'd call him a guy . . . He likes to molest little girls. Nobody around here likes him much, but he's a masochist. He gets off on pain. The more we beat him up, the better he likes it. He got convicted on five counts, but everybody knows there's probably more. We've been trying to get him to tell us about the others. Maybe if we get you close enough, you could spend a few hours picking his brain."

"What exactly are you looking for?"

"Anything he has to say."

"I suppose that means coming out of solitary?"

"Nope. He lives just three doors down. We had to put him in the box so the rest of the guys wouldn't kill him. Nobody in here likes child molesters. There's an empty cell right next to his."

"I don't know if I can."

Bruce's sickly smile returned. "Give it the old college try. I'd put you two together, but I think he'd tear you up."

"You want it written down, or memorized?"

"I suppose I could get you a pencil and a few sheets of paper. To show you I have a heart, I won't send Fred and his buddies down to move you to that new cell."

With that, they were gone. But true to the warden's word, a half hour later a single guard opened Scott's cell door, handed him a pencil and a sheet of paper, and locked him in a new cell two doors down.

At first, Scott felt nothing. But knowing Warden Bruce wouldn't accept failure, he moved closer to the door and concentrated. When he was just about ready to give up, the man next door woke up and his thoughts flowed.

The man was daydreaming, using his tiny victims to fuel his fantasies. The memories Scott saw disgusted him, but he scribbled furiously for a while before the man's mind moved to other things and he got up to take a shower.

Scott sat down on the bare concrete bunk to rest while the man cleaned up. The inmate eventually laid down on his bunk and began daydreaming again. This time, Scott saw graves—dozens of them—but he didn't recognize anything around them. There were trees. Willowy, tangled trees; nothing large or noteworthy. The trees seemed to stretch on for miles. There was a road—an old, rutted two-track, and a rusty abandoned car. Scott didn't recognize the car. It had to be a thirties or forties vintage. Both doors were missing. The top was caved in. There were bullet holes in the trunk.

In Scott's vision, the man walked past the car and down the brush-choked road. Then, suddenly, the brush parted and there was a pickup truck—a blue Ford pickup with Kansas plates. Scott scrawled down the plate number. Then the memory stopped and the door to the pedophile's cell opened.

"Chow time, pervert," he heard someone say.

Scott waited. Then he heard a key in his lock and the door swung open. Warden Bruce stood in the door with two of his deputies.

"Well?" he asked. When Scott handed him the papers, Bruce's face lit up. "You've done very well for a first try!"

"There's more," Scott said. "I saw where he buries his victims."

Bruce looked stunned. "He's in here for child sex abuse. We didn't know he'd killed anybody."

"I saw a bunch of graves," Scott said. "The problem is, they were all in a small forest of short, spindly trees along an old overgrown two-track road. There was an old rusty car, but I didn't recognize the make or model. I did see his truck, though, when he walked back to the main road. I wrote the license plate number down on the last page. It was a blue Ford Ranger. I don't know what year."

"I hope you're not making this all up," Bruce said as he flipped to the last page and looked at the plate number. "I'm going to get this information to the court. We'll run the numbers. If this pans out, I'll see to it that your life here is more tolerable."

"I'd appreciate it if this stays between the two of us," Scott said. "Your guards don't like me much, and at the end of the day, a snitch is a snitch."

"I'll see what I can do," Bruce said as they put him back in his own cell and locked the door.

Scott ate the cold food they left him and then stretched out on the hard slab. The thin mattress helped but did little to ease his aching body. Eventually, he spread the two blankets on top of the pad. They helped, but sleep was slow in coming.

When the door opened sometime later, he assumed it had to be morning. Without clocks or windows, it was impossible to tell what time it was. The least they could do, he thought, was turn off the light at night so he could sleep.

"Here's your breakfast," a guard said. "Eat and get showered up. The warden wants to see you."

The rubbery hard-fried eggs and single cold sausage patty coated the roof of his mouth with grease. The dry toast helped scrape the tallow out of his mouth. He stripped down and turned on the shower. There was no hot water. Worse yet, the water got colder the longer it ran. His body shook convulsively as he toweled off and climbed back into his boxers and orange jumpsuit. There was nothing to hang his wet towel on, so he draped it over the sink after he brushed his teeth.

Two men joined him in his cell a few minutes later. One watched while the other cuffed and shackled him.

There were five men waiting in the warden's office. The guards left and closed the door behind them.

"I trust you slept well," Bruce said.

Scott quickly scanned Bruce's thoughts before he answered. The warden expected a positive response.

"I did, Warden. Thanks for the blankets. They really helped."

Scott had said the right thing. Bruce was pleased.

"I made a few phone calls last night, and it seems the state is very interested in the story you told me yesterday. These men drove all the way up here this morning to test the validity of what you told me, so I hope it wasn't bullshit."

Scott looked from man to man and quickly picked out the one in charge.

"Brent," Scott said as he singled out one of the men. "I assume you're the one I need to talk to?"

"That's very impressive," Brent said. "Can I assume you know the other men, as well?"

"I know their names, but I haven't had time to learn anything else."

"Your warden tells me you can read minds. Or something like that."

"I watched a guy in the room next to me rattle through some memories."

"We spent some time last night, and again on the way up here this morning, validating your story. The license plate numbers you gave the warden matched the prisoner's truck. We know where he was living, so we spent some time with Google Earth, looking over the countryside within twenty miles of his house. We think we've got a couple of possibilities, but we need your help." Brent turned to Warden Bruce. "Warden, could you take of his cuffs? He needs to be able to run a trackpad."

Bruce picked up the phone, and a few seconds later a guard knocked and strode into the office.

"Unlock him," Bruce said. "He needs his hands."

Brent pulled a chair up next to the warden's desk so Scott could sit down. Then he set an open laptop in front of him. As Scott watched, Brent pulled up an application and zoned in on the first area.

"Based on your description," Brent said, "we started looking at areas within twenty miles of the perp's house. See if anything looks familiar."

Using his index finger to manipulate the trackpad, Scott carefully scanned along a paved road, watching for any tracks leading off into the woods. A couple of long moments later, he realized the futility of what they'd asked him to do.

"Can I make a suggestion?" Scott asked, looking up at the warden.

Bruce nodded.

"Why don't you bring him up here and then show him some of these areas on the computer? He might not say anything, but if he recognizes something you show him, I'll know it."

"That's not a good idea," Bruce said. "He's not a popular inmate, and I don't want anyone connecting the dots between him and you. That might not be good for your health, if you get my meaning."

"Then take the laptop down there. I could either be in the cell with him or just outside."

"There's no Wi-Fi access."

"We won't need it," Brent said. "This application can do stand-alone. We updated all the maps on the way up here."

"Okay, let's make it happen," Bruce said.

They re-shackled Scott, and a couple of guards led the group down to solitary. Brent turned to Scott as they got to the abuser's door. "How do you suggest we do this?"

"I'll leave that up to you. Somehow, you've got to ask him a question that will make him think about where he buried the kids. You might start by letting him look at the areas on the map you've already highlighted."

Brent didn't look hopeful, but he nodded at the guard, who unlocked the door. The guard stayed in the hallway with Scott as the rest of them filed inside the cell.

"Hey, Ralphie," Warden Bruce said, "we've got something we want you to look at. I suppose you've seen satellite pictures of the earth before, haven't you?"

Ralph was instantly on guard. "Sure," he said. "What's that got to do with me?"

"Word on the street is you may have a little graveyard somewhere out in the trees by your farm, and we'd like you to show us where it is."

"That's bullshit!" Ralph stammered. "I never killed nobody."

"But if you had, I bet you'd know a good place to bury the bodies, wouldn't you? I hear tell they're in a bunch of scrub not far from a major road. We looked all around your house and haven't seen anything like that. Did you drive very far from your house? Do you remember seeing an old rusty shot-up car back in there?"

Ralph was on the verge of panic. Scott concentrated on his

thoughts. Then, in an instant, he saw the spot. He touched the guard on the sleeve and whispered, "Bring me the computer."

The guard opened the door a crack and nodded at the warden.

"What's up?" Bruce said as he stepped into the hallway and closed the door.

"I think I know where it is," Scott said. "Bring me the laptop. I'll see if I can spot it, then you can take it back in and show it to him. I'll know if I was right."

Bruce walked quickly back into the cell and returned with the laptop. Brent followed. Scott zoomed out on the map displayed on the screen, then followed the main road with his finger until it curved sharply to the left. Then he zoomed back in several times. There, barely visible, a faint, two-track trail meandered through the woods to the left, away from a pull-out along the blacktop highway. He scrolled along the track until a brown dot appeared. He zoomed in even further. The old car was clearly visible.

"That's it," Scott said, pointing to the car. "That's the car I saw in his thoughts. The grove and the graves are a few yards down that two-track on the left."

Brent put a waypoint on the old car and zoomed back out several times. "That's nearly twenty miles from his house. Are you sure?"

"Show him the map, then zoom in a few times until he can see the car. I'll know if that's the right place," Scott said.

Brent looked at the warden. Bruce shrugged, and they walked back inside the cell.

Scott listened to Ralph's thoughts as Brent showed him the map. When he zeroed in on the old car, Ralph freaked out. The guard left Scott standing by the door and charged inside to help subdue the inmate.

* * * * *

Three cycles later (or days, Scott thought, if he marked the passage of time based on his meals), the cell door swung open and four guards pushed their way inside.

"Grab your shit," one of them said roughly, "you're getting out of here."

They shackled him and took him upstairs to the warden's office. Bruce offered Scott a seat and nodded at the guards. They unchained Scott and left the room.

"It seems I owe you an apology," Bruce said. "I got a couple of telephone calls late yesterday. First, some detective from the state told me to thank you for what you did a few days ago."

"That was all your doing," Scott said. "They should be thanking you, not me."

"They came and got Ralphie yesterday and took him out into the woods," Bruce continued, ignoring Scott's comment. "He's not talking. He lawyered up, and his attorney is making all this noise about him being interrogated without being represented by counsel. They've already found eleven graves, and they have dogs and diggers looking for more. Now they're trying to sort out who all those kids are. I don't suppose you'd want to help with that, would you?"

"I don't see how I could," Scott said, "especially if he's lawyered up."

"I don't understand all the legal ramifications either. With your special abilities, they were thinking that if they got you and Ralphie in a room together and started showing him pictures of all the missing kids within a three-state area, you might be able to tell them when they got a hit. Then Legal got in the middle of it and said that probably wouldn't stand up in court unless he confessed to each crime. You just saying so would be judged by the court to be hearsay."

"I think the parents of all those missing kids would want to know where their kids are, even if he can't be convicted," Scott said.

"That's what I'm thinking. He's already serving a hefty prison sentence for molesting five little girls. I'd think prison time is prison time, regardless of why you're doing it. Would it even matter if they added another couple hundred years to his sentence? All that would accomplish is getting him held without the possibility of parole."

"So what do you want from me?"

Bruce stared at Scott for a few seconds before he spoke. "I had an interesting chat with a prosecuting attorney from Lincoln late yesterday afternoon. He confirmed that the paperwork I've got on you is little more than a pack of lies. You're here so that certain other parties don't take you out."

Scott didn't answer.

"I've got a little problem," Bruce continued. "The word has got out in here that I've got a snitch in a cell, and like you told me yourself, snitches aren't very popular in prison. I can't guarantee your safety, and I sure as hell can't have you killed on my watch."

Scott held his peace.

"Some boys are coming up here to move you to a safe house," Bruce said. "Tell me, Scott—that is your name, right? What are you going to do when this all blows over?"

"Start over."

"How?"

"Go someplace where nobody knows me and keep a low profile. Nobody needs to know what I can do. I'm an architect by trade."

"That's a pity, really. You could be invaluable in a place like this. This place is full of liars. It'd be a lot of fun to make some of them squirm. I bet we could solve all sorts of crimes."

"They'd just write a law that made it a crime for me to read minds."

The phone rang. "Your ride is here," Bruce said, hanging up. "Think about what I just told you. With the right people protecting you, you could make a lot of money."

Chapter 21
<u>The Killer</u>

Outside the prison, two men—one named Blake, the other Milt—put Scott in the back of a windowless van and unlocked his shackles.

"Word on the street is you're a hero," Blake said as they pulled away. "I hear they've found eleven kids so far. They haven't identified any of them yet, but they're getting DNA from all the parents who've lost kids."

"That's got to be such a heartbreaking task," Scott said. "If they find a match, it'll finalize somebody's search, and they'll cry. When it's all done, those who don't get a match will cry knowing their kids are still out there somewhere."

"I guess I never thought of it that way," Blake said, "but you're right. I hear they pulled the perp out of prison. They can't guarantee his safety there anymore, even in solitary."

"I'm here to tell you that solitary isn't safe. I got slapped around for basically doing nothing."

"I hear you can read minds, and that's how they got the information from that pervert in prison."

Scott didn't answer.

"In case you're wondering," Blake said, "that's why we're taking you to a safe house in Lincoln. Like you said, prison isn't safe. I hear they're going to set you up in the Witness Protection Program. This house in Lincoln is just something temporary until the trials are over."

"Why the Witness Protection Program?" Scott said. "Last I heard, I just needed to stay out of sight until they put a certain detective behind bars. That hardly warrants the cost of the program. I'd think as long as I was safe until after the trial, that would be the end of it."

"Let's just say that the detective we're talking about has a lot of ties to some influential people who would rather remain anonymous. If they find out about you, they won't want you to have access to Ableman for fear you'll find out who they are."

"So what you're telling me is the detective could just be the tip of the iceberg?"

"You've got it."

Scott wondered what kind of ties Ableman had to the killer and how much more involvement he personally would have before it was all over. He didn't like it. That could take years.

"What about my family?" he asked.

"We don't know. I heard the state has moved them to an undisclosed location."

"Before or after I got that kid-killer busted?"

"Before, actually. There was a lot of talk about whether or not you qualified for the program, but I hear your attorney got that all pushed through."

Scott was wary. Blake and Milt were obviously more than taxi drivers. He tried to sort out some of the things they were thinking, but their thoughts weren't taking him very far.

"I'm going to owe that man a lot of money," Scott said, trying to get their thoughts leading elsewhere.

"Actually, you won't," Blake said. "That's one of the perks. The state paid all your legal bills, because when you make the break it has to be clean. You can't leave behind any loose ends. If you felt morally obligated to pay your legal bills after you disappeared, somebody could pick up the money trail and find you."

"This is going to be tough. My kids all have friends. We *all* have friends. And extended family."

"That's the ugly part of the program. Everybody has to start over. In a way, it'll be like you all died. None of you can come back from the dead."

"My daughter's in love. She'll never stand for that."

"They can't force you to do anything, but if you don't sever all ties, it won't take long for somebody to find you."

"Speaking of leaving things behind," Scott said, "what about my house and all our personal property?"

"Like I said, it's like you all died. The state will probably confiscate your home and bank accounts to compensate them for what it's going to cost to set you up in a new life. At the end of the day, everything else is just property. It can all be replaced."

"My wife will have a problem with that," Scott said. "She has little things—keepsakes—that she'll never leave behind. I might be losing a lot more than just my house and business. I guess I don't understand why this is all necessary. It's not like the mafia is after me."

"I can't answer that question. I don't make the decisions. Clearly, somebody knows a lot more about what's going on than either one of us does." Blake handed Scott a cell phone. "This is yours, by the way. Your wife has a new one too. Her number is on your contacts list. In fact, it's the only number on your list. If you remember any others, don't put them on your list and don't call them from your new phone."

Scott looked the phone over. It was a little different than the one he'd lost in the wreck, but everything was pretty standard.

"You may want to call your wife," Blake said.

Scott fidgeted. "I really need some privacy to do that."

"You don't have to call her right now. We'll have you in the safe house in about an hour."

"Man, I'm going nuts back here. What do I do for money? For clothes? For a car?"

"You'll have to trust us to do some clothes shopping for you for now. You won't need anything else for a while." Blake handed him a small notepad and a pen. "Write down your sizes. I imagine you'll be wanting to get out of that prison garb."

"The trial could take months. What do I do in the meantime?"

"Pretend you're in prison. In solitary, I suppose. But it will have its perks. You'll have a nice place to stay, plenty to eat, a TV, and a phone. And you won't have to worry about getting beat up by the guards."

"What about my family?"

"They'll be safe. You can talk to them on the phone. You can FaceTime with them, but you can't visit them."

"This sucks!"

"It could be worse. You could be dead."

A prior thought crossed Scott's mind and he asked, "How much do you guys know about my case?"

"Not much," Blake said. "For the sake of confidentiality, we're not told any more than we need to know." Blake turned around in his seat and looked at Scott. "I heard you dreamed about a murder and said you could identify the real killer. I'm thinking that detective must have known who the killer was and had some dealings with him. I have to assume they were keeping you in prison to keep you alive until they caught the real perp."

Blake waited for Scott to answer. When he didn't, he continued. "I also have to assume you found out all of that stuff the same way you got that kid-killer busted."

Scott could tell Blake was fishing for information. He didn't know whether to be nervous about that or not. He knew from digging a little deeper into Blake's thoughts that the man was a badged employee of the state. Scott decided to test him a little.

"I don't know who your sources are, but did they mention anything about the charges against me being dropped?"

"Yes, we heard that. We heard that after you ratted out those detectives, they checked out your alibi and decided you couldn't have killed that woman. I guess that's when they started believing the rest of your story."

"Did my lawyer turn over an audio tape?"

"No, why?"

"Because if I'm no longer a person of interest in the murder, I have other information that may help catch the real killer. My attorney has the audio tape."

Blake looked at the driver. "What do you think, Milt?"

"That's above our pay grade. You better call the boss."

Blake picked up his cell phone and dialed a number. Scott listened to his side of the conversation. By the time the call was over, Scott was worried.

"Who was that?" he asked.

"Our boss," Blake said simply. "He wants to talk to you. He'll meet us at the safe house. He may bring a few people with him."

* * * * *

Scott's temporary new home was in the old part of Lincoln. It wasn't much to look at. The yard was overgrown with unkempt bushes and tall weeds. Large half-dead trees lined the street and dwarfed the tiny house. There was a little white paint here and there on the clapboard siding, but what was there was peeling. A ramshackle single-car garage stood behind the house down a long two-track driveway.

Milt pulled the van down the side of the house. As the van approached the garage, the door swung up so they could drive inside. The van barely fit.

"It may not look like much," Blake said, "but most of what you see is camouflage. It's actually pretty nice inside. We need it to look like the rest of the neighborhood, so we don't do much with the outside."

A small screened-in back porch stood just off the garage. There was no doorknob on the old wooden screen door; just a rusted metal handle. A return spring groaned as Blake grabbed the handle and pulled the door open. Old, dusty linoleum covered the floor. Blake waited until they were all inside the porch and held the screen door as it swung shut so it wouldn't bang.

Blake smiled. "Don't let first impressions fool you," he said. "I think you'll like it."

He was right. From the moment Blake keyed the back door and ushered him inside, Scott could not only see but smell the difference. Every surface was clean and either new or well kempt. The sweet scent of a plug-in air freshener permeated the air.

"There's two little bedrooms, a kitchen, a living room, and a couple of closets, but not much else," Blake said. "It serves its purpose. Nobody stays here very long. The fridge and cupboards are well stocked. If you don't like what's there, you're just a phone call away from a grocery store that delivers. The market's phone number is on the wall above the phone. We have an account there, so you don't have to pay anybody. Whatever kid they send with the groceries gets his tips from the account, so you don't need to feel obligated. They'll open the screen door and leave the stuff on the porch. Nobody will see you unless you're stupid enough to walk outside."

Scott followed him through the tiny kitchen into a modest living room. A big-screen TV hung on one wall over a short entertainment center.

"There's cable TV, a DVD player, and a fair selection of movies. If you get bored, there's an online movie subscription. There's no Wi-Fi or computer, though. You've got a smartphone, but don't visit any of your social media accounts, especially Facebook. This place is only as safe as you make it. The doors lock from the inside, so there's nothing keeping you from wandering the streets, but I wouldn't recommend that. Every place has eyes, and we don't own the neighborhood, so you never know who might see you walking about."

Milt pulled an edge of the front curtain back and peered out. "It looks like Eric came alone."

"That's just as well," Blake said. "The fewer who know the details, the better."

Milt unlocked the front door and let a man inside.

"Scott," Blake said, "this is Eric Sponbeck. He's the Lincoln City District Attorney. Eric, this is Scott Corbridge."

Eric held out a pudgy hand. "Happy to make your acquaintance," he said. "I saw you in court, but we were on opposing sides, so I didn't make the effort to meet you."

Scott shook Eric's soft, warm hand. He didn't remember seeing the man in court. His statement bothered him a little. The courtroom had been packed, but it wasn't that large. He tried to remember what Blake had said about first impressions. Eric didn't make a good one. The man was at least sixty pounds overweight, balding, and his wrinkled suit hung on him like an old dishrag. He was surprised he hadn't noticed him before. From what Eric was thinking, though, Scott could tell he was no dummy. There was something about him he didn't like.

"I took the luxury of speaking with your attorney before I came here," Eric said. "We had a brief but frank discussion about the evidence he withheld, but I think we're still friends. He agreed it's in both of our interests that you help the state find the person or persons who committed that murder."

"Did you ask him about the tape recording?" Scott asked.

"I did, but he claims that with your *gift*, I shouldn't need it. Can we talk just a minute about that? I've heard some random talk, but nobody I spoke with seems to know exactly what you can do."

Scott was instantly on guard. He'd felt a flash of emotion from Eric when he asked about the tape recording. He didn't know if Eric was lying, but something wasn't right.

"I could go into a long explanation," Scott said, "but I don't think you want to know all the details. In short, I had a bad car wreck. When I came out of a coma, I was terrorized night and day by a dream, or a vision . . . whatever you want to call it . . . where I witnessed a woman's murder."

"I know all of that," Eric answered quickly. "What I'm more interested in right now is the other stuff. Apparently, you can read minds?"

Scott didn't answer right away. Instead, he tried to see what Eric's expectations were. The man obviously knew what had happened in prison, so Scott knew he couldn't blatantly lie to him, but he didn't want to say any more than he needed to know.

"I can see things," Scott offered. "At first, I thought I was just in tune with people's emotions. But then I realized that sometimes I could tell what they were thinking."

"So what am I thinking?" Eric said. A sly smile slid over his fleshy lips.

"I can tell you don't believe me," Scott said. "Beyond that, I really don't know."

Eric stared at him for a few moments. "Let's talk about the guy you say killed that woman. Her name was Nancy, if you didn't already know. It may be bad luck to talk about the dead, but I'd rather use her first name than refer to her as 'the victim' or 'that woman.' Can we sit? I have a few things to show you."

Eric motioned to the sofa and set a small briefcase on the nearby coffee table. They sat, and Eric pulled out a copy of the police drawing Scott had helped the cops put together.

"I believe you might recognize this," Eric said, handing Scott the black-and-white sketch.

"I do."

"What else can you tell me about this person?"

"Nothing, really," Scott said. "I wasn't there, so I can't tell you who he is or what his motives were. All I can tell you is I watched him stab her to death."

"Could you tell us about the actual crime, then?" Eric asked. "Maybe we can use something from that to help us catch this guy."

Scott searched Eric's thoughts. He seemed overly interested in what Scott had to say. Scott didn't want to tell him everything he'd already told Paul, but there was something just beyond the fat man's thoughts—something sinister—that told him things might get physical if he refused to talk.

Scott hesitated at first, but then he figured since Paul already knew everything it wouldn't matter if he repeated the story to Eric. "I know he dragged Nancy's body out of the bathroom after he stabbed her to death. Then he wrapped her up in a fitted bottom sheet he pulled off her bed. There was so much blood coming through the first sheet, though, that he wrapped her in the top sheet too. Then he carried her body out to the trunk of his car. I don't know what color his car was. It was either white or some other lighter color. But it was an Infinity. It had Nebraska license plates. If you have a pen and pencil, I'll tell you the plate number."

Scott's words took Eric by surprise. "You saw that much detail in your dream?"

"Not at first," Scott said. "The first time, I was so freaked out by what I saw that I didn't remember any of the finer details. All I knew was this guy had stabbed a woman to death and buried her in the woods by the old stone well. You've got to realize that this dream has plagued me night and day ever since I came out of the coma. I've literally seen it hundreds of times."

Scott paused to let the building emotion dwindle before he continued. "After I got over the shock of what I'd seen, I started noticing things. Like the license plate number."

"Why didn't you tell the cops all that from the start?"

"Because nobody believed me. My attorney wisely counseled me to keep the details to myself, because the more I told them, the more the prosecution would be convinced I'd killed her. Who else but the actual murderer would know all those facts?"

"What made you change your mind?"

"I didn't, really. Not at first. Then I eventually became convinced Nancy's ghost wasn't going to give me any peace until I told somebody. You probably don't believe in ghosts either, but now I do."

Eric was thinking the part about Nancy's ghost was mostly bullshit.

"I decided I needed to tell the whole story in case something happened to me, so I called Paul and had him record all the details I could remember. It wasn't until then that Nancy finally left me alone and the dream quit coming into my mind when I didn't want it to."

Eric's sly smile was gone.

"When the prosecution finally verified my alibi and dropped the charges against me," Scott continued, "that's when I finally felt I could tell the rest of the story."

Eric pulled a pen and a yellow pad of paper out of his briefcase and wrote down the numbers of the Nebraska plate as Scott read them off to him.

"After he loaded her in the trunk," Scott continued, "he drove to the freeway."

Eric took notes as Scott narrated the rest. When he finished, the room was deathly silent.

"Wow," Eric finally said. "I wish we'd known all this weeks ago. We might have found the perp. We might have found blood evidence on him, or we might have found his bloody clothes. We might even have found the murder weapon. Now I'm not sure what, if anything, we're going to find. Whoever this is has had weeks to get rid of any physical evidence. Without that, all we've got is a tall tale by a mind reader. And an amazingly detailed drawing of the perp. But unfortunately, your story won't convince a jury unless there's some physical evidence to support it."

Eric was talking a good story, but his thoughts were shouting something entirely different. He knew who the perp was too, and now that he knew what Scott had told his attorney, he had to move fast to cover Vince's tracks. Scott was suddenly sick to his stomach.

Eric looked first at Milt and then at Blake. "What we just heard stays in this room. Do I make myself perfectly clear? I've got a bad feeling about this. We need to be very careful who knows Scott's story until we can start gathering up some physical evidence."

But what Eric was really thinking was, *Until we can get rid of the physical evidence.*

Scott needed to call Paul, and sooner rather than later. The good side had to act immediately or it would be too late.

Eric looked at Scott. "I don't know what you plan to do with the rest of your life, but you should consider working for law enforcement." He closed his briefcase and got to his feet. "I believe I have your new phone number. If we need anything else, I'll call."

"I'd like to know what you find out," Scott said.

"I'll call you," Eric promised, "but you need to keep anything I tell you in the strictest confidence. I'm going to piecemeal this information out. Nobody but me and the prosecuting attorney will know the whole story."

"I assume you're talking about Floyd Carter?"

"You've met, then?"

"We have."

"And what do you think about him?"

Scott smiled. "I think I'll keep my opinion to myself. We didn't exactly get off on the right foot. He was trying to put me in jail."

"Fair enough. I'll keep in touch."

Blake saw Eric to the front door and locked it behind him. "We need to be going," he said, motioning to Milt. "We'll do a little shopping for you this afternoon and bring you some new clothes in the morning."

"Why don't you just go back to my house and pick up my clothes?" Scott said.

"Bad idea. First, I don't want to drive all the way to Omaha. And second, if Ableman has somebody watching the house, they'd just follow us back here. What are your colors? Do you like blues, greens?"

"Blues are good."

"Levi's it is, then, and anything to match. We'll get you a pair of walking shoes. That way, if they're a little off-sized, they won't be uncomfortable the way a pair of leathers would be."

The second Milt and Blake left, Scott hurried to the house phone and called Paul. Something seemed off. He didn't want to use his cell phone for obvious reasons. He knew he shouldn't call anybody, but he trusted Paul.

"I'm not supposed to call you," Scott said when Paul answered, "but I've got a bad feeling."

"Where the hell are you?" Paul exclaimed.

"In a safe house."

"Where?"

"I'm not supposed to say."

"Fair enough, I suppose, but why did you call me?"

"I just saw the Lincoln City District Attorney. He's—"

"Who?"

"His told me his name was Eric. He said he was the Lincoln City District Attorney."

"I don't know anybody by that name," Paul said, "and I pretty much know them all."

"They moved me from the prison to a safe house in Lincoln today. The two guys who drove me down here called him before we got to the house."

"Had you been talking to the guys who drove you? I mean, do they know what you can do?"

"They know some of what I'm capable of, yes. I know their names."

"And you just couldn't resist telling them something about themselves, could you? Tell me about this Eric."

"He's a big guy. Overweight, balding. He kept probing me about what I could do, but I played dumb. Except for Nancy's murder. I figured there was no harm in talking about that. He had a copy of the police drawing. He seemed to know all about the case. He said he'd had a conversation with you today about withholding evidence."

"Nobody talked to me. What did you tell him?" A sense of urgency clouded Paul's voice.

"I pretty much told him everything I'd told you about the car, the license plate number, and where the body was buried."

"Shit!" Paul nearly shouted. "I don't like this. I need to make a few phone calls. I think we need to either get the county or the feds involved, if we can, and get them out to that burial site before whoever Eric works for beats us to it. I'll call you back."

Scott wandered into the living room and collapsed on the sofa. He felt stupid; duped; used. With his "gift," he should have never fallen for that. He thought about Milt and Blake. He wondered how much they knew. Based on what he'd seen in their thoughts, he didn't think they had any ulterior motives. They were probably nothing more than what they said they were—somebody's drivers. Eric's thoughts, though, were another matter. He'd felt ill at ease the whole time. Now Scott knew why.

Paul said he would call back, but Scott realized the only number Paul had was the house phone—the one he was supposed to use to call the market. Rather than call Paul and risk interrupting his conversation with whomever he was calling, he sent a simple text message with his new cell phone number.

He sat stewing in his feelings for a half hour before he decided to call Mary. She answered his phone call on the fourth ring.

"Hello," she said hesitantly.

"It's me. I'm out."

"Where?"

"I can't say. Or I shouldn't say. We don't know who may be listening."

"I hate this," Mary said. "They put us in a house with a couple of guys watching outside. We can't go anywhere. We're not supposed to call anybody we know. Trish wants to drop out and run away with Brandon."

"It won't last forever."

"Paul told me today that Ableman's defense lawyer has already filed for an extension. This could go on for months."

"I didn't think you were supposed to talk to Paul."

"I'm not, but I was going crazy not knowing what's going on. He told me he doesn't know where you are. He told me he figured you were in the Witness Protection Program because the state paid your legal bills."

"Not yet," Scott said, "but I think it's just a matter of time."

"I heard something on the news last night," she continued after a long pause. "It said the authorities, acting on an anonymous tip, found the bodies of a bunch of kids in Kansas. Did you have anything to do with that?"

After Scott told her the whole story, Mary sighed heavily. "They're going to use you, Scott. You know that, don't you?"

"They can't force me to do anything I don't want to do."

"That's the point. This whole damn thing has come up because you can't say no. If you'd just kept your mouth shut from the first, none of this would have happened."

He didn't want to argue. She was right, in a way, but she didn't know Nancy's ghost the way he did. The entity would have eventually driven him crazy if he hadn't talked.

"I can't do this, Scott," she said. "I can't walk away from my family and friends. Worse yet, I can't live with a man who knows my every thought. I've tried to work it all out in my mind, but I just can't."

"You have to stay hidden until after the trial. If you don't, they will try to use you or the kids to get to me. I don't think you have a choice at the moment."

"This could go on for months! No, I won't wait. When I talked to Paul today, I asked him if they'd leave me alone if I divorced you."

Scott's heart sank at her words. "They might leave *you* alone, but what about the kids?"

"It's over, Scott. I can't live with you. I'm sorry, but I can't."

He wanted to bring Alan into the conversation but decided not to be cruel. He couldn't blame her. If the tables were turned, he would probably do the same thing.

"I won't beg," he said softly. "I'm sorry. I think I understand how you feel. Have you told the kids about me?"

"No. I won't do that to them. Right now, because you've been able to use your so-called gift to figure out how to talk to them, they think you walk on water. We'll just leave things that way for a while. Maybe by then, all this will have blown over and you can come back into their lives. In the meantime, I'll have Paul file the paperwork."

More silent moments passed between them.

"I'm sorry, Scott," Mary said. "I'm sorry for all of it. For Alan, and . . ."

"Stop it," Scott said. "I told you before that wasn't your fault. None of it was. Just don't destroy his marriage if you can help it. He's a good guy. I put you in a bad place. There's already been enough hurt. Just break it off. Let him go. When you're single, you can find somebody and start over without hurting anybody else."

Mary didn't talk for a long time. Scott wished he knew what she was thinking, but he felt nothing over the phone.

"In spite of what you might think," he finally managed, "I still love you, Mary. I wish it could work, but I know it can't. Give the kids my love."

He pressed the disconnect button on the phone and walked

down the hall to one of the small bedrooms. He hadn't slept well in weeks. Now that he'd done all he could for Nancy, maybe she would leave him alone.

He felt he should be screaming, or crying, or something. Instead, he felt totally numb.

Chapter 22
<u>Retribution</u>

Scott's cell phone rang early the next morning while he was frying bacon. He lunged for the phone. Paul hadn't called him back yet.

It was Eric Sponbeck, the Lincoln City DA. "We need to talk," he told Scott, "but I don't want do it over the phone. Do you mind if I drop by?"

"I'm not going anywhere," Scott said, "but maybe I should throw the hookers out before you get here."

"Very funny," Eric said. "I wanted to be sure you were up. I didn't want to knock. I thought it might scare you. I'll come to the back door."

"Sounds pretty ominous."

"Not really. I'll be there in about ten minutes."

Scott pulled the frying pan off the stove and quickly dialed Paul's number.

"Is this Scott?" Paul answered.

"It is. What's going on? You didn't call back. I'm sort of going crazy here."

"Sorry. I've been working a lot of loose ends. To make a long story short, the county decided to involve the feds. They found and secured the burial site last night. They're supposed to start digging this morning."

"Eric just called a couple of minutes ago," Scott said. "He said he needed to talk to me but didn't want to do it over the phone. He said he'd be here in about ten minutes."

"Listen to me very carefully, Scott," Paul said. "You need to tell me where you are, and then you need to get out of that house until I can come and pick you up."

"I don't know where I am. All I know is I'm in the old part of Lincoln in a safe house somewhere. I don't know the address. It's an old house. It looks pretty run down from the outside, but it's really nice inside. They told me they use it as a safe house all the time."

"Okay," Paul said hesitantly. "That really doesn't tell me much.

Lincoln is a big town. Get out of the house. Go hide somewhere. See if you can get to an intersection and find a street name or something so I'll know how to find you. In the meantime, I'll see if I can get someone to talk to me about where you are."

"I'm wearing an orange prison jumpsuit, for hell's sake," Scott said. "I can't just go strolling down the sidewalk. I'll stick out like a sore thumb."

"Go," Paul said. "Right now! If someone sees you and calls the real cops, it might save your life."

"Should I go pound on somebody's door?"

"No, but try to put some distance between you and that house. Whoever is coming to talk to you will probably pull out all the stops to find you when they realize you're missing. The first place they'll look is in that immediate neighborhood."

"In case you don't remember," Scott said, "I'm stumping around on a sore knee."

"Suck it up. You may not get another chance. Call me when you get your bearings. Now go!"

Scott pulled on his prison shoes and unlocked the back door. He paused on the screened-in porch to look out. The driveway was empty. He slipped out and turned toward the street. Then he stopped. He didn't know how long it would be before he—or they, if Eric brought somebody with him—would be there. Walking down the street would be like waving a flag. Instead, he turned and walked around the back of the house. Maybe he could travel through the back yards.

The lot behind the house was a tangled mass of tall weeds and untrimmed brush. It was bracketed by an old wooden-slat fence that marked the property boundaries. He frantically looked for an opening in the fence. There didn't seem to be one, and he couldn't climb over it with his knee the way it was.

He limped around the house to the side yard, looking for a break in the fence. There, the house only stood six feet from the property line. Thick brush blocked his way down the side of the house. He was just turning around to go back when he heard a car slowing down on the street out front.

He was out of time. He turned down the side of the house and stooped down to try to force his way under the brush. That was when he saw the small opening to a crawlspace under the house. It was blocked by a rusted metal lattice. He knelt on his good knee, put his fingers through the holes in the lattice, and pulled. It resisted a little but finally pulled away. He flopped onto his belly and tried the opening. It was small, but if he turned his shoulders diagonally, he could just push through it.

He wriggled through, arms first, and then pulled the rest of his body through the impossibly small opening. His hips barely squeaked through. As soon as his legs hit the dirt floor, he turned around, grabbed the lattice, and pulled it back in place behind him.

He peered through the holes in the lattice at the ground outside the opening. The hard dry dirt appeared to be undisturbed. The stale air in the crawlspace stank of old building materials, dust, and mildew. Luckily, he was only mildly claustrophobic.

Scott lay still, trying to control his breathing as his heartrate slowed. Then he realized if they came looking for him and saw the lattice, they would probably shine a light inside. He had to get away from the opening.

He started to spin himself around and then realized that if he disturbed the dry dirt beneath him, they'd probably notice the marks.

In the inky blackness under the house, he had no idea where he was going. Rather than crawl, he began to roll over and over, away from the opening. After he had traveled a few feet, the dirt floor suddenly dropped away. He reached out and touched the bottom of what appeared to be a shallow depression. Cautiously, he eased his body into the trench. He pulled himself up into a sitting position, his head just inches from the floor joists.

Now that his eyes had grown somewhat accustomed to the darkness, he glanced back toward the hole in the foundation. What little light flowed through the lattice barely illuminated the bottoms of the rough-sawn floor joists.

He crab-walked to the center of the house. His ribs didn't like the exercise. He stopped often to rest, reaching above him to feel for anything that might be hanging down in his way. He couldn't risk the possibility of bumping his head.

Then he heard the muffled bang of the screen door on the back porch. The old floorboards on the porch above him squeaked as someone walked across it and toward the back door.

Scott held his breath and waited. Then he heard muffled voices. He mentally reached out across the distance, searching for thoughts.

There were two of them. It was Blake and Milt. He breathed a sigh of relief. They'd probably brought him some clothes. Then he heard their thoughts. Eric had sent them.

Scott nearly panicked. They were there to move him before the authorities figured out where he was. Eric and Warden Bruce were working together; the safe house was only temporary until they could move him out of state.

Their footsteps pounded on the floor as they ran through the house, looking for Scott in every closet, nook, and cranny. Eventually, the screen door banged again. They had moved outside. Scott lay prone so that if they found the lattice and shined a light inside, they wouldn't see him.

In seconds, they'd moved beyond where he could hear their thoughts. He thought about his cell phone. They'd screwed up there! They probably hadn't expected him to call somebody for help. He silenced the ringer, then quickly realized the phone probably had a GPS tracking device in it. He flipped on the tiny internal light and looked for the battery cover. The battery was built in. Although it was his only contact with the outside world, he knew he had to destroy it.

He felt around for something hard to smash the phone against, then stopped. He needed to tell Paul where he was and what was going on, but he didn't dare call for fear they'd hear his voice. He texted him instead.

After sending the message, Scott began to slither his way along the trench. He didn't know how long it would be before they started trying to trace the location of the phone, but he knew it wouldn't be long. Just then, the phone buzzed in his pocket. He looked at the incoming number. It wasn't Paul. He stuffed it back in his pocket and let it vibrate.

Not far from where he'd started crawling, the trench split off in two directions. He remembered the bathroom being off to the right. The old house probably had cast-iron plumbing. If that was the case, he thought there should be a four-inch soil pipe below the toilet heavy enough to crush the phone against without telescoping much noise back into the house. He turned the corner and crawled on. He didn't have to go very far before he found the plumbing under the bathroom.

The phone vibrated in his hand again as he took aim at the pipe. He glanced at the lighted dial. It was a message from Paul: *Stay where you are. I've called the judge. We're going to find out where that house is. I'll come and get you.*

Scott answered with a simple *Okay*, then swung the phone

against the pipe. The screen shattered with the first blow, sounding off with little more than a dull thud. He slammed it down again until it came apart in his hands. Then he tore at the remains until he found the built-in battery and ripped it away. He had no idea how a GPS unit worked, but it made sense to him that it had to have power to transmit a signal.

He took deep, slow breaths to calm his heart and mind. He reached out mentally, feeling for any stray thoughts from the people who were looking for him. There weren't any. All he could do now was wait.

As he waited in silence, it occurred to him that something didn't fit. Why would they go to the lengths of stashing him in a safe house only to haul him away and do . . . whatever it was they had planned for him? He wondered if it was even a safe house at all and how the good guys would find him if it wasn't. How would the warden explain his disappearance? They could have just had him killed in prison—but that would have implicated Bruce.

The whole affair stank of a combination of both legal and illegal players. Maybe that's why he was still alive. The legal side had started the process to get him out of prison and into a safe house, but now it seemed the bad side would finish it. Somebody was desperate. His disappearance would undoubtedly bring all kinds of heat to bear on the connection between the sides.

His guts wrenched. Because of the phone conversation he'd had with Eric the night before, they knew Paul had the rest of the information. That meant Paul was probably in danger. They probably also knew where Mary and the kids were. Scott kicked himself. Maybe he'd acted prematurely in killing the phone.

Anguish cascaded over him as he lay there in the dirt, helpless and trapped. Paul said he'd called the judge, whatever good that would do. Scott hoped Paul was smart enough to figure out everything that had just raced through his mind. This had to be big. The thing with Ableman had to be small by comparison.

Suddenly, the floorboards above him squeaked again and the heavy footsteps of more than one man thudded across the kitchen. Scott tuned in. There were three of them now: Blake, Milt, and Eric. Blake and Milt were listening to what Eric was saying into a phone.

"I think he's the only one besides the mind freak who knows about the car and the grave," Eric was saying. "You need to stop him before the whole world finds out. I don't care how you do it. You're a smart man, you figure it out. Do I need to remind you that this whole damn house of cards will come crashing down if you don't?"

Blake and Milt were freaking out. They needed to do something but didn't dare act on their own. If Eric was willing to take out a high-profile attorney, the situation was bordering on insanity.

"We're going to find him," Eric shouted into the phone. "I don't know how. We just will!"

The scene in the kitchen echoed strangely in Scott's mind. He could read the men's thoughts, but their voices were muffled. The more agitated they got, the more intertwined their thoughts became. Try as he might, Scott couldn't sort out their thoughts fast enough to make sense of what was going on. Then the footsteps moved away in the direction of the back porch. They left, their thoughts passing out of range again.

Scott lay breathlessly in the dark, waiting, searching every sense he had. He heard nothing. He felt nothing but fear and anxiety. He had to do something. But what? He was trapped under an old house in an old neighborhood where at least three men were looking for him. He was wearing a blaze-orange jumpsuit. His bald, horribly-scarred head made things even worse. It was the first thing people saw when they looked at him. He couldn't run. He couldn't climb over the fence and hide in another yard. Meanwhile, Paul—his only hope for rescue—was in imminent danger himself, not to mention Mary and the kids.

Then, strangely, Scott felt Nancy's presence. Did she know what was going on? If she didn't, could he somehow convey his thoughts to her? Could she help in any way?

He concentrated. He couldn't read her thoughts, but he knew she was there all the same. There was no emotion, nothing besides a strange feeling that betrayed her presence. Why was she there? If she'd come to torment him, it was working.

I can't do anything to help you! Scott fumed in his mind.

Then, he felt strangely peaceful.

Emotions! he thought. *That's how we can communicate.*

He concentrated his thoughts as hard as he could and sent them to Nancy.

You need to protect Paul! he mentally shouted.

Then she was gone. Had she understood? Could she really do anything to help? God only knew he'd done his best to help her.

As Scott lay alone with his tortured thoughts for what seemed like hours, a thought came to him. It only made sense that they would search the house and the immediate neighborhood first.

They'd probably be gone by now. He was having trouble breathing. It was dusty. He tried to swallow. He needed water. He considered the irony of it all. Even though he lay within inches of the water pipes, without a tool of some sort to cut them or loosen the joints, they might as well have been a thousand miles away. Mild claustrophobia began to choke him. He couldn't stay under the house much longer.

He struggled back down the trench toward the small hole in the foundation and found the opening. Despite the pain, he rotated his body a half turn, put his arms over his head, and struggled out through the hole.

He sat up and looked around him. There was no evidence that anyone had trampled the weeds alongside the house. He wanted to crawl, but the pain in his right knee made that impossible. Instead, he got to his feet and used the wall for support, moving around the back of the house. There wasn't a car—at least none that he could see. He walked to the corner of the house nearest the garage and peered around the edge of the old wooden siding. The driveway was empty.

He looked at the cloudless sky overhead. There was only a slight shadow there on the north side of the house. It had to be noon or a little after. He watched the street for a few minutes. A couple of cars drove by, but there was nobody walking on the sidewalks.

He needed water and something to eat. He also needed a change of clothes but knew that was out of the question. He hurried to the screen door on the porch. If they'd left the back door open, he could at least eat something and get a drink of water. His heart sank when he touched the door handle. It was locked.

He looked around for something to pound on the door with but found nothing. He wished he'd stayed under the house. At least nobody had found him there . . . yet. But on the porch, he was completely vulnerable.

He looked down at his clothes. His jumpsuit was horribly orange, and filthy from rolling around in the dirt under the house. There was no way he could walk down the street looking like he did.

He looked out at the old garage. He needed to get off the porch, but was the garage any better? If they didn't come back to drop someone off, they might not open the garage door.

There was no handle or lock on the garage door, but there was a four-pane window on the side of the garage about four feet off the ground. The window was split horizontally in the middle to allow the top or the bottom half to slide up or down, probably for ventilation. Scott could barely see the window latch through the dirty window, but it was in the unlocked position.

He pushed on the bottom half. It moved a little, but it obviously hadn't been opened in a long time. Dirt, and probably paint, were blocking the window channel. He forced it up and down a few times until it finally slid far enough that he could squeeze through. He wriggled in headfirst and dropped to the floor, but not without a chorus of complaints from his battered body.

A black van with dark-tinted windows sat inside the garage. It looked like the same one Blake and Milt had picked him up in at the prison the day before. Scott pulled the van door open and looked inside. The ignition slot was empty. He didn't think they'd be dumb enough to leave the keys, but he'd had to look. He climbed into the driver's seat and looked into the back of the van. A plastic shopping bag lay near the side door. He grabbed it and looked inside. It was full of men's clothes. The boys had gone shopping for him after all.

It only took him a couple of minutes to shuck off his orange garb and slip into his new wardrobe: a pair of Levi's, a knit pullover, socks, shoes, a belt, and even a hat. He stuffed his prison clothes back into the sack and dropped it back on the floor where he'd found it. Now, with any kind of luck, he'd be able to walk down the street without drawing a lot of attention to himself.

He opened the sliding door on the side of the van, stepped out, and glanced at himself in the sideview mirror. That's when he noticed the small personnel door at the back of the garage. It was locked from the inside, but that was hardly a problem. He stepped out into the hot sunshine and looked around.

He needed to find out where he was, and he needed to call Paul, if it wasn't already too late. He walked boldly along the fence to the sidewalk and instinctively turned left. He didn't know why; turning left just felt *right*. He found he was only three houses from the corner.

When he got to the intersection, he took note of the street marker. Now he had to find a telephone. The through street was a lot busier. Cars whizzed by in both directions. Rather than walk across the busy street, he turned left again, thrust his hands in his pockets, and limped along.

He'd only walked about fifty yards when he came upon a lawn sprinkler wetting down the sidewalk. He reached down and picked up the hose.

"Hey!" a lady's voice called out from the nearby house. "That's secondary water. You'll get sick drinking that."

Scott looked up. A plump, white-haired old woman was sitting in a porch swing.

"If you're thirsty," she told him, "come on up here. I'll get you a cold drink out of the fridge."

"You're so kind," Scott said. "It's powerful hot out here, and I've been walking a while."

She watched him closely from her perch as he limped down the driveway toward the house. "You hurt your leg or something?" she asked.

"I got in a car wreck and had to have a knee replaced."

"Then what are you doing out walking around on a hot day like this?"

Scott thought fast. "The physical therapist told me I'm supposed to walk on it. It's supposed to strengthen the muscles or something."

"You're pale as a sheet," the old lady said. "I think you've overdone it. Why don't you sit down on this swing here while I go get you a pitcher of water?"

Scott sat, amazed by the woman's thoughts. Although he was a total stranger, she had no fear of him at all.

"I can't drive anymore," she said a few moments later when she rejoined him on the porch. She was carrying a pitcher of ice water in one hand and a glass in the other. "I can't give you a ride home. I'm old, and I get a little confused, so my kids took my car away. They're really good to come around once a week and take me to the grocery store, though."

"You must have good kids," Scott said as she poured him a tall glass of water and handed it to him. He could tell from her thoughts that she had three kids—two boys and a girl. The boys lived in town; the girl lived in Pittsburg.

She sat down in the swing beside him and watched as he drank a full glass of water in one gulp. "I do," she said. "My two boys and their wives take turns running me around. I know they're busy, but I can depend on a visit from one or the other every Saturday morning. Do you have kids?"

"Not here in Lincoln. I got divorced a little over a year ago, and my wife and kids live on the outskirts of Omaha."

"That's too bad. Why do you live here in Lincoln, then?"

"I'm an architect. I designed a building here, and I rented a place in town so I could oversee the construction. When it's done, I'll find another apartment close to my next job."

"Did you design that new big steel-and-glass thing down by the freeway on seventy-seventh?" she asked.

Scott quickly read her thoughts. She wasn't testing him.

"Why, yes," he lied. "Do you like it?"

"It's nice, I suppose. Looks like a lot of glass to keep clean. Isn't it hot in the summer with the sun glaring down on it?"

Scott suddenly had a flashback. He could clearly see an eight-story building in his mind: a gray-and-white building with dark windows. It frightened him. If he regained his memory, would his other abilities go away?

He noticed she was staring at him.

"Are you okay?" she asked.

"I'm feeling a little dizzy," he lied again. "Maybe I've been out in the sun too long."

"You should call somebody to come get you."

Scott smiled inside. That's what he was hoping she'd say. He needed to get hold of Paul. "My cell phone got messed up in the car crash," he said. "I haven't had the time to get a new one yet."

"You're welcome to use my phone if you'd like," she offered.

"You're an angel. Are you sure that's okay?"

She got up. "You sit right there. My kids got me one of those new-fangled phones with a portable hand thingy, kind of like a TV remote. I'll go get it. You can wait right here on the porch and rest 'til somebody comes after you."

Scott hadn't been paying much attention to traffic. Now he felt vulnerable. He was sure Eric and his boys were still frantically looking for him, and this lady was living on what appeared to be a fairly busy street.

She bustled back out onto the porch, gave him the handset, and sat down beside him.

"What's your address here?" Scott asked as he dialed Paul's number.

She began to tell him when Paul answered the phone. Scott held up his hand to stop her while he talked to Paul.

"Hey, Paul. Can you come pick me up? I've been walking too long in the heat, and a nice lady let me sit on her porch. She's feeding me ice water."

It only took Paul an instant to answer. "Where's your cell phone?"

"I crushed it."

"Good man. I was on my way to Lincoln when it suddenly dawned on me that if they gave you a new phone, they'd know how to track you. Can I assume you can't talk openly?"

"Yes, you can assume that."

"Where are you, exactly?"

"Here," Scott said, "I'll let her tell you the address."

He held the phone out to the old woman. She rattled off her address, listened for a second, and slowly repeated the address. When she was done, she handed the phone back to Scott.

"You get that, then?" Scott asked.

"I'm about twenty minutes out," Paul said. "I got the address of the safe house, but I've been waiting around for you to call."

"Be careful," Scott warned him. "The traffic can be really bad this time of day, if you know what I mean."

"I assume you're talking about Eric?"

"Yes, I believe so."

"I figured as much. I got a really bad feeling a couple of hours ago like someone was trying to warn me away or something. I stopped at the airport and rented a car. They're probably looking for mine. I know you probably can't talk, so I'll let you go. Watch for a white Ford Taurus four-door."

"Okay, I'll be sitting on the porch in a porch swing."

"Based on the address she just gave me, you're pretty close to the safe house. You may want to see if she'll let you go inside out of sight."

"Have they called *your* cell phone yet?" Scott hinted, hoping his host wouldn't get suspicious.

"I read you," Paul said. "I'll remove the battery. If anyone else pulls up, lock the doors and call 911."

"Okay," Scott said. "Hey, thanks for coming after me. I owe you one, buddy." He switched off the phone and handed it back to the woman.

"Is there a problem?" she asked.

"No," he said. "Traffic is pretty heavy. He might be twenty minutes or so."

"I heard you tell him that you crushed it. What did you crush?"

Scott stretched out his right leg and pointed at his knee. "My right knee. When I got in that car wreck. That's why I had to have it replaced."

"You're awful pale," she said. "Are you sure you're feeling okay?"

"Just a little faint. I'll be okay now that I'm out of the sun and have some cold water."

"Would you like to put your leg up?" she asked. "I've got a bum foot, and I know it helps a lot to get it up off the floor."

"I hate to put you out," Scott said. "If you've got a bucket or something, I could sit right here and do that."

"You seem like a nice enough man. My name is Rita. What's yours?"

"I'm Scott Corbridge," he said, holding out his hand.

She shook his hand, got up, and held the front door open for him. "Come on in, Scott. I'll get you a couple of pillows. You can prop that leg up on the coffee table. I don't have air conditioning, but I've got a big old fan I'll aim down on you. I don't want you passing out on me before your friend gets here."

"Are you sure? I really don't want to be any trouble."

"You're no trouble at all. Besides, it gets pretty lonely here by myself. It'll be nice to have some company for a change."

Chapter 23
<u>Rescue</u>

Rita had a lot to say. She talked about her kids and grandkids. She talked about her dead husband, Carl, who she missed dearly—she'd been a widow for eight years. She and Scott talked about their respective health issues. At one point, Scott even took off his hat and showed her the scars on his head. He kept her talking about herself by tuning into her thoughts.

There wasn't a clock visible anywhere, so Scott lost track of time. He began to fidget. It seemed like it had been a lot longer than twenty minutes.

"Are you uncomfortable?" Rita asked.

"What time is it?" Scott said. "I haven't had any pain medication since breakfast."

"I've got some aspirin if that'll help."

"That would be very kind of you."

The phone rang when Rita got up. She answered, then handed the phone to Scott.

"I couldn't figure out how to pull the battery out of my phone, so I'm a little worried," Paul told him. "I drove around the block a few times looking for anything suspicious. I think we're in the clear, but you're on a busy road. I don't want to draw any more attention to us than I need to, so be watching for me. Rather than stop on the road, I'll pull into the driveway."

"Okay, thanks," Scott said.

He handed Rita the phone and struggled to his feet. "He said he'll pull into your driveway so it'll be easier for me to get into the car. Thank you so much. You're an angel."

"Not yet I'm not," Rita laughed. "But I think Carl may come and get me any day now."

She held the door open for him, and Scott offered her a handshake. She put an arm around his waist instead and gave him a quick hug.

"You take care of yourself now," Rita said, "and next time you want to go for a walk, you might want to wait until it's cooler in the day. If you happen to get down this way again, stop in. I'd love to chat with you some more."

Scott smiled and returned her hug. "Thanks again, Rita. You're a good woman."

Her countenance broke for a brief instant. "That's what my Carl used to tell me. Are you sure he didn't send you here?"

"He may have," Scott said softly. "I believe the dead can help us."

Rita's eyes watered. "So do I, Scott. Thanks so much for saying that."

A white Taurus pulled into the driveway. Scott hurried down the porch steps. Rita waved as they drove away.

"I see you have a new friend," Paul said.

"I'd like to think so. You can never have too many friends."

"Do me a favor and hunch down in the seat a little. We don't know who we're dealing with. I'm going to do a little creative driving to be sure we're not being followed."

They rode in silence as Paul drove aimlessly through several of the older neighborhoods. Scott tried to follow his thoughts, but Paul was thinking more about what he was seeing as he drove and less about why Scott was hunched down in his front seat in the first place.

Finally, Paul took a freeway entrance and settled into the heavy afternoon traffic. "I think it's safe to sit up now," he said after a few minutes. "Speaking of friends, we've got a few working for us now. The feds are at that old farmhouse as we speak, exhuming Nancy Bennion's body. She was right where you said she'd be. They haven't found the car yet, but they know who it belongs to. It's registered to one of the many businesses that a local multimillionaire owns. I don't like him much. He's one of those men who exudes power, if you know what I mean. He's got his fingers in more pies than Little Jack Horner."

"I'm glad you got the feds on the case," Scott said. "Until I told Eric the details about my vision, you and I were the only ones who knew where the killer had buried the body. I feel better about our chances of survival now."

Paul stared at him disbelievingly. "Do you think it would have come down to that?"

"I don't know who Blake, Milt, and Eric are. But from what I gathered from their thoughts this morning, somebody they know is very afraid of me, and it isn't necessarily Ableman. Because you know about the car and the body, they're afraid of you, too. I heard

Eric tell somebody to take you out."

Paul didn't answer.

"Tell me again why you rented this car," Scott said.

Paul turned his head to look at him for an instant and then looked back at the road. "I don't think you'd believe me if I told you."

"Oh, please!" Scott exclaimed. "You must not have been listening when I told you about Nancy."

"What's she got to do with me renting a car?"

"I was hoping you'd tell me," Scott said.

"Well, I didn't have a manifestation from the dead, if that's what you're getting at."

"Are you sure?"

"Yes, I'm sure," Paul said angrily.

"She visited me this morning while I was hiding in the crawlspace," Scott said. "I sent her to warn you."

Paul glared at him.

"Well?"

"I won't deny that I felt something," Paul said. "But I didn't see an apparition."

"Neither did I. That's the way it works. I could feel her, but I couldn't tell what she was thinking like I can with . . . real people."

"So why ask me the question if you already know the answer?"

Scott smiled. "Maybe I just wanted to introduce you to my world. Making you admit it makes it real."

"Okay, Houdini," Paul said, "tell me where we should go from here?"

"I can't see the future."

"Why do you suppose Nancy is so wrapped up in your life?"

"I wish I knew," Scott said. "I have no idea why she picked me. Unless, of course, she knows what I can do. But if that's the case, why aren't I haunted by everybody else who's been brutally murdered? There has to be some sort of a connection somewhere."

"Do you think you might get some sort of closure if you went out to the site where she's buried?"

"Isn't that a little risky? I'm the only one who has been formally charged with her murder, and even though they've dropped those charges, I'm clearly the only one who knows all the facts surrounding her death. The last thing I need is to be slammed back in Bruce's prison. I'm pretty sure I wouldn't come out of it alive the next time."

"Why do you think he'd want to hurt you? You just made him a hero in the state's eyes. As far as they know, he was the one who got that pervert to confess to where he'd buried all those kids."

Scott thought for a moment before he spoke. "Somehow, the warden found out that my credentials were crap. He's got to be tangled up in this mess somehow. I'd love to know who arranged to have me pulled out of solitary and taken to that so-called safe house."

Paul glanced quickly across the seat at Scott. "Maybe you scared the warden when he found out what you could do. Maybe he's got something to hide and had to distance himself from you before you found out what that was."

"Why didn't he just have a couple of his inmates take care of business, then, instead of having somebody haul me to a safe house?"

"He probably didn't want you to die on his watch. That might have drawn too much attention to him. He's clearly playing both sides of the street, though. I wish I knew who Eric is."

"Whoever he is, he's got to have connections," Scott said, "because he seemed to know a lot about my preliminary hearing and about you. He knew enough about the case to suggest you were withholding evidence. He knows Floyd Carter, the prosecuting attorney. When we were introduced, he said something about being on the other side of the table—meaning he was working with the prosecution."

"This is making my head hurt," Paul said. "First things first. We need to find someplace to hide you until I can nose around a little."

"You could take me to Mary's new place," Scott suggested.

"That wouldn't be a good idea. If Eric, whoever he is, knew about your safe house, he probably knows where Mary is too."

"You're probably right. He knows her new cell phone number. It was the only one they'd programed into my new phone."

"Scott," Paul said, "I hate to seem cold, but she's not a threat to anybody. She can't put them in prison."

Scott looked out the window but didn't say anything. After a while, he looked back at Paul. "I thought once we got past all this dream crap that I'd be able to go back to my old life."

"Are you kidding me? Think about it. By the time this is done, you'll be a celebrity. Even if the judge puts a gag order on the evidence presented in court, the news will get out. The good guys will want you to come and work for them, but they'll be afraid of you. The bad guys will want you dead. You're a threat to anybody who has a secret. And I'm sorry to say that pretty much includes the entire population."

"I should have kept my mouth shut," Scott said, "but I couldn't. Nancy wouldn't leave me alone. I didn't know it was her, at first. I couldn't sleep. I couldn't even daydream without that damned vision replaying in my head. When I finally surrendered and decided to look at every element of that vision, or dream, or whatever it was, I finally felt peace. It was as if she knew what I was thinking. Once she got her message across, she backed off."

"Maybe you could have been more selective," Paul said. "You didn't have to get wrapped up in that thing at the hospital with Talbot. Once you did that, you picked up another mortal enemy."

Scott looked down at his hands. "I guess I just couldn't let it go," he said. "My daughter is only seventeen. If she'd been seeing a shrink and he took advantage of her, then murdered her to keep from losing his business, I'd want him in prison, or worse. I just couldn't let it go."

"I hate to say this, Scott, but you can't fix everybody's problems. You're not an immortal superhero. You may have a gift, but you need to be very careful how you use it or you're going to be dead. Believe me, in my line of work I've dealt with some real slimeballs. I've seen people shot for a lot less."

"Okay, Counselor," Scott said. "What do you suggest I do now?"

"Hide, watch, and wait for now. If the good guys can do their job and come up with enough physical evidence, there's a good possibility you'll never have to see the inside of another courtroom. Then you can slink off into the sunset and start over. Hopefully, next time you'll be a lot wiser and not stick your nose where it doesn't belong—even if you think you need to right the world's wrongs."

"What about you? Now I've got you wrapped up in the middle of this."

"I was just your legal counsel. Now that the state has dropped the charges and the feds have found the body, I no longer have a dog in the fight. The last I officially knew, they'd carted you off to a safe house somewhere. Nobody knows I rescued you."

"Eric knows my new phone number," Scott said. "He's probably in law enforcement or has connections. I'll bet he can come up with a list of phone numbers I called from that new phone. I'll bet he can even come up with a copy of the text message I sent you and the one you sent back. Eventually, he'll know you rented a car at the airport. If this car has GPS on it, they'll know where you went. You can't drop me off anywhere without them finding a surveillance video with me in it. Then they'll be able to come around and just scoop me up."

Scott listened to Paul's thoughts as he tried to work the problem out in his head.

"I thought we decided a few minutes ago that going up to the burial site would be a bad idea," Scott said.

"Quit that," Paul grumbled. "That's just one of the many options I'm mulling around in my mind."

"But to you, it's the only one that makes sense right now, and I don't agree. We may have been able to convince the judge of my innocence, but once you called the feds, you opened a whole new can of worms."

"The same facts apply," Paul argued. "You've got an established alibi. We've got three witnesses who saw Nancy's roommate leave her apartment after you'd already been in your wreck, and we've got sworn testimony from his partner that Ableman murdered her roommate, probably to invalidate her testimony."

Paul braked hard to avoid slamming into a sudden backup of heavy traffic. Scott was impressed. Paul's adrenaline shot up, but he didn't utter a single curse word. Moments later, he picked right up where he'd left off.

"I frankly don't think the feds will push the issue even if there happens to be a clairvoyant in the mix," he said. "I'm sure they've dealt with stranger things. And if you think about it, they're the only ones with the resources to guarantee your safety. In my opinion, you need to get out of this city—maybe even out of this state—until this all settles out."

Scott struggled with his emotions. He was sure that, given a little time, Mary would work things out in her mind and agree to let him come home. He'd felt her love. She was afraid of his abilities, but she'd seen the good he could do. The high emotions surrounding the murder and the near misses in the hospital had to be a factor in her wanting a divorce. She didn't necessarily want to get away from *him*. She just wanted to get away from everything else.

"Maybe you should call the feds before you just show up out there," Scott said.

"I'll call the judge. He's the one who called in the feds when he found out about the warden's involvement."

Paul picked up his cell phone and dialed a number. Scott listened to Paul's side of the conversation as he talked the situation through with the judge. When the conversation was over, Paul dropped his phone into his shirt pocket.

"The judge is going to make a few telephone calls and get back to me," Paul said. "He's in agreement that we need to tread lightly. He can't bias himself in the event this all comes through his court, but in my opinion, he already has. He told me himself that he's afraid there's a lot more to the connection between the detective, the warden, and whoever Eric is than we know about."

"What about me? Is he willing to try to explain me to the feds?"

"He already has. At issue is whether or not there's sufficient reason to put you in federal protective custody."

"Sorry, Paul. This is putting you and your firm out on a limb."

"Officially, I'm no longer involved," Paul said. "I cashed the state's check yesterday. We've been paid in full for services rendered. I'm no longer on retainer."

"If that's the case, what do you call this?"

Paul grinned. "Curiosity. That, and maybe I'd like to see if the shirt you're wearing with a big red S on the front might fit me."

Chapter 24
Protective Custody

Paul's phone rang again. He picked it up, listened for a few minutes without saying much, then merged into the freeway exit lane.

"We're probably about a half hour out," he said into the phone. "I'll meet you at the site."

"Are we going out to the burial site?" Scott asked.

"No, that was Agent LuAnn Amberson with the Federal Bureau of Investigation. We're going to meet her at a rest stop a few miles from here. She's coming from Omaha."

"A rest stop," Scott said. "Isn't that a strange place for a meeting? Are you sure she's who she says she is?"

Paul laughed. "Settle down. I was just one of four people on a conference call. The judge initiated the call. The other two were feds. Nobody's going to arrest you. They've got this covered. Amberson will whisk you off to a federal safe house that only they know about. I doubt they'll let you call anybody once you get there. I don't know how this will work with your family, but I'm sure the Bureau has had a lot of experience with this sort of thing."

"Can I call Mary before we get there?"

"Are you daft, man? You told me yourself that they know her new phone number. Whoever *they* are may be listening for any incoming chatter on that number."

Paul crossed under the freeway and took an eastbound entrance back toward Omaha. "I was going to go to the airport and change cars first," he explained, "but we won't have time for that. I'll have to do it after our meeting with LuAnn."

"What are you going to do next?" Scott asked. "Are you worried?"

"Not now. I'm not dangerous anymore. The feds know everything you told me. If the criminals don't know that by now, they soon will, and I'm not the one who can read minds."

Scott began to grow worried. "What about my wife and kids? They don't know about any of this, but I'm sure Eric knows where they are. He could use them to get to me."

"The feds know that their location has been compromised. I'm sure they'll know how to deal with that."

"What if Mary refuses to go into the system?"

"They'll probably assign a few agents to watch them until the trial is over. But after that, who knows? They can't force her into hiding. Maybe with you out of the picture, it'll no longer be an issue."

"I still can't wrap my mind around all this urgency," Scott said. "When Ableman goes away—"

"Wake up, Scott!" Paul snapped. "Think about what you've just gone through in the past few days. We both know Ableman is protecting somebody. That somebody probably came up with the bail money. That wasn't chump change. I can't believe the state let him out on bail in the first place. If I were a betting man, I'd bet he never makes it to trial. And if they feel threatened enough to eliminate him, what does that mean for you? This doesn't mean just hiding out for a few weeks or months. This is for all the marbles. This is permanent."

Scott stared silently out of the passenger window at the trees and houses and farms as they passed by. This stupid dream was taking over his world. He had to forget everything: family, friends, business, church. He suddenly hated his so-called gift. He hated Nancy. He hated her killer. He hated his gift more than anything else. It had taken over his life.

Why had he been given this ability? Had a higher power actually given him this gift, or was it nothing more than the byproduct of an accident? He thought about the two men in the documentary about clairvoyants from years earlier. Their gifts had come to them as the result of an accident. Were his abilities any different? Had they also grown up having precognitive dreams too, only to have their abilities intensified by an accident? Could they do more than the public knew about?

He wondered where they were now and what they were doing with their lives. Had they been able to hide their abilities from the world, or were they, like him, being used by somebody?

* * * * *

Paul made another call when they were still about five miles from their destination. Neither party said much. When they pulled off the freeway, Paul slowed to a snail's pace as he drove past a long string of cars angle-parked alongside the rest stop.

"That's them," Paul said, nodding toward two dark SUVs parked near the end of the row of parked cars. There was a single parking space between them. When he began to pull in, a stocky man in a coat and tie stepped out of the first car and stood in the opening so he couldn't park.

"This is where we part company," Paul said, offering his hand. "Good luck, Scott."

"Thanks for everything," Scott said.

"I'll look out for your family," Paul told him. "I don't know how this all works, but I'll try to keep in touch."

"Thanks. That means a lot."

The man in the coat and tie walked up to Paul's window and presented a badge. Paul rolled down his window.

"Paul Rodriguez, I presume?" the man asked.

"I was told to meet LuAnn."

The man turned and nodded toward the dark-tinted windows of the other vehicle. The front passenger door opened, and a middle-aged woman carrying a sturdy-looking handbag stepped out of the car. She wore a modest dark skirt, black flats, and a white blouse. She approached Paul's window and presented a badge.

Scott quickly searched their thoughts. He put his hand on Paul's arm. "They're legit."

"I wasn't too worried," Paul said, "but thanks for verifying that."

Scott got out and the woman stepped forward, offering her hand. "I'm LuAnn Amberson," she said. "You'll be riding with me."

She was tall for a woman—nearly six feet. Her medium-brown hair was pinned back alongside her head, covering about half of her ear. Scott noticed a pair of modest ear studs. She wasn't bad to look at, but not a beauty. He shook her hand. Her grip was feminine but firm.

Scott glanced sideways at the man in the coat and tie. "I assume Agent Charlie is going to follow us?" he asked.

"If it makes any difference," the man said, "my name is Charles."

"But your friends call you Chuck, am I right?" Scott said.

A slight smile curled the corners of Charlie's full lips. "They told us about you. You're the real deal, aren't you?"

"I'm afraid so."

"We need to go," LuAnn said. "Agent Charlie and his partner are going to make sure we're not followed."

"Do I ride up front, or hide in the back?" Scott asked.

LuAnn nodded at the rear passenger door. "In the back, unless you want to sit on my lap. You probably didn't notice, but I have a driver."

There were two other agents in the car with them. Both were nervous until they got back on the freeway. Scott reached out to them but found their thoughts focused only on the moment at hand.

The driver, a slight man in his thirties with a light complexion, was watching the other SUV behind them in his sideview mirror. His thoughts switched rapidly from the following SUV to the cars around him, then back to the road. He hadn't had lunch; he was hungry.

LuAnn's thoughts were similar as she carefully watched the traffic around them. Eventually, she turned around in her seat to look at Scott. "That's funny about Agent Charlie," she said. "Everybody calls him Chuck. His last name is Norris—I think he likes the association with the movie star. I believe you unnerved him a little when you called him Charlie. That's what his mom calls him. Not many people know that."

"Sorry," Scott said. "That's the name that was rattling around in his brain."

"How do people react when they find out you know what they're thinking?"

"Most are uncomfortable. Some freak out. My wife hasn't been able to come to terms with it."

"I won't ask you to demonstrate," LuAnn said. "I'm going to pretend I'm immune."

"I won't invade your privacy."

"We got a briefing on the way up here, so we know what's going on," she said. "I won't bother asking. Let me explain a little about what happens from here. I imagine you'd like to know that?"

"I've got a few questions."

"I'll bet you do," she said. "First, let me start by explaining the logistics. We need to keep you close to Lincoln so you'll be available until the trial winds down. You'll be staying in another safe house in the Omaha area. Unlike the one that just got compromised, this one is strictly confidential. Nobody but the agency knows about it, and it's under twenty-four-hour guard. You probably won't notice anything unusual. If you do, we're not doing our job. Once the trial is over, we'll reassess your situation. If it warrants a full relocation, we'll give you a new name and a set of credentials. You'll be relocated somewhere in the continental United States as far away from friends and family as possible—and nowhere near a major theme park. You don't want to accidentally bump into someone you know."

She paused for a few seconds to gather her thoughts.

"Now for the hard part," she continued. "There are rules. First, your relocation is only as airtight as you make it. You have to voluntarily walk away from everything. One telephone call, one letter, or a post on the internet can ruin everything. If *you* compromise your identity, you don't get a second chance. If your adversaries find you through no fault of your own, that's different. Any questions yet?"

"No."

"We've been told about your marital and family status. You have my condolences. That's going to be really tough on you, in more ways than one. I hate to seem heartless, but you not having a family makes our job a lot easier. It's not hard for us to hide a single guy. A whole family can be a real challenge. But if they don't want to play, we can't force them to."

"I suppose that means I can't even call or FaceTime with them?"

"No. Smartphones are great, but they're not secure by any stretch of the imagination."

Scott had been trying to steel himself in anticipation of this conversation, but now that the reality of it came crashing down on him, his hatred for his gift and Nancy's killer only deepened.

"I still have a hard time believing that this is necessary," he said.

"That's why I told you that after the trial, we'll reassess your needs. We haven't been told everything about your case by any stretch of the imagination, but for now, we're treating this very seriously."

Scott didn't say anything. He was so busy running scenarios in his head that he wasn't paying any attention to her thoughts.

"I don't think I need to tell you that we'd love to have you work for us," LuAnn said. "What you did to expose that mess in Kansas is a great example of how valuable you could be."

"I could have done more."

"We figured that much, but under the circumstances, we didn't want to take any chances. We're going to have our hands full protecting you in the murder case. We didn't want to expose you to that too. I'm sure you realize that the more exposure you get, the harder it's going to be to keep you safe."

"I found that out the hard way," Scott said. "I should have just kept my mouth shut from the beginning."

"I think that would be good counsel, especially after we relocate you. A reputation like yours spreads like wildfire. You can be invaluable in so many different ways."

"I've been wondering what I would do for a job. I'm a licensed architect."

"Not anymore you aren't. At least not under your own name. Your license dies with that name."

"What the hell do I do then?" Scott protested. "Set up a fortune telling booth in New Orleans?"

LuAnn didn't smile. "If you're accepted into the witness program, you'll be funded until you can either cross-train or establish a license in your new name."

"Maybe I should work for the Bureau. How much do you think that would pay?"

She held his gaze for a few seconds. "You don't have to decide that right away. But after things settle down, if you're serious, you need to get in touch. You won't get rich, but it'll pay the bills."

Scott looked away. He'd only been half serious. There were too many unknowns. Then something Mary had said crossed his mind. "They'll just use you, Scott."

He wondered what the difference was between being used and being needed and/or appreciated. If he decided to work for law enforcement, he would have something to do for the rest of his life, however long that lasted. Taking down bad guys had its appeal, but it had its consequences as well. He had a lot of thinking to do.

* * * * *

Scott's new home was a two-bedroom apartment just across the river from Omaha in Council Bluffs, Iowa. Like the other safe house, it came with all sorts of indoor amenities including a treadmill and weight set. He used the treadmill a bit to strengthen his knee, but the weight set went untouched. He was still too sore for that.

He couldn't leave his apartment to go shopping—even if he had money, which he didn't—or even to use the jacuzzi or swimming pool downstairs. There was no telephone and no computer, but there was a big-screen TV complete with cable and several movie channels.

One of his guards, Jack Paitland, introduced himself the first day and then brought him a new wardrobe. Barbara, a CNA on retainer to the agency, checked in on him every day. She helped him with his physical therapy and brought him pain meds, the first he'd had in days. She was pleasant enough but was obviously uncomfortable anytime she was around him. It didn't take Scott long to learn her history, but he wisely kept everything he learned about her to himself.

Jack wasn't nearly as squeamish. He knew about Scott's abilities but never asked for a demonstration, and Scott didn't offer one. When Jack was on duty, he often stopped in for a game of chess. Scott even let him win most of the time. Sometimes they'd just watch a game on cable. It was good having someone to talk to. The loneliness and isolation were the worst.

Scott watched every news channels religiously. The episode in Kansas had slipped to the back burner; whatever was going on down there in that wooded graveyard was no longer newsworthy. He'd heard nothing from Lincoln for two weeks. It was as if he'd imagined the whole thing. There was no mention of finding Nancy's body. There was no news about Ableman or Eric.

LuAnn came to see him on a Friday.

"I thought I'd drop by and fill you in on what's going on up north," she said after they exchanged pleasantries. "We know who Eric and his two accomplices are, but all three have gone missing."

"What?" Scott exclaimed. "What exactly do you mean they've gone missing?"

"All of their respective wives have filed missing person reports on them," she said. "We haven't found bodies, so we have to assume they're probably hiding out together. We've been watching for credit card use and all that, but so far nothing has surfaced. We're beginning to think somebody is sponsoring them."

"Meaning what?"

"Meaning this whole mess is bigger than we thought," LuAnn said. "We picked up Detective Ableman the other day and leaned on him a little, but he refused to talk. After what you told your attorney, we've been digging into the warden's background as well. We think that all of this might be connected, but we haven't turned up anything significant yet."

"Okay," Scott said, "I'm going to ask the obvious. How does this affect me and my status here?"

"Until further notice, you're pretty high priority. The boss wanted to get you in the same room with Ableman, but Legal has told us to back off."

"I don't have to be in the same room."

"We know that, but his attorney knows about you and has

warned us off. We couldn't use anything against him that we got that way anyway."

"What if I could find out who he works for—besides the Omaha Police Department?"

"Believe me, Scott, we've been working all those angles. It looks like the only time we're going to be able to question him is in court. And we don't know if it would even be wise to have you there."

"When is that going to happen?"

"He got a ninety-day continuance. Right now, his trial date is set for the twelfth of November."

"In view of the disappearance of those other three, I'd think he's a flight risk," Scott suggested. "Can't you pull his bail and put him in custody?"

"We thought about doing that, but we can't get a judge on board. We tried to find out who came up with the fifty-grand cash for his bail but drew a blank. The money was wired to him from an offshore account that we can't touch."

LuAnn's thoughts ran rampant for a while. Scott didn't interrupt her. When she realized he wasn't talking, she blushed.

"You're listening to me, aren't you?"

"Guilty as charged."

"I hate that."

"Sorry, I was just following your train of thought. Speaking of that, what's going on with Ralph and that case in Kansas?"

"Oh, thanks. I meant to talk to you about that. I think I already told you that we've exhumed a lot of bodies."

"The last I'd heard, there were eleven."

"It's up to eighteen now, and we're coming up with some really bizarre findings. As near as we can tell, none of those graves are more than four years old, but one of the kids we've identified went missing from Grand Island, Nebraska, around eight years ago. That means that weirdo must have had her stashed away somewhere for years before he murdered her. We're going over his farmhouse with a fine-toothed comb as we speak."

Scott shuddered. "How many of the bodies have you identified?"

"Only two, and that in itself is really strange. You'd think with all the missing kids reports we've got from a three-state area that we'd have more hits than that."

Suddenly, Scott felt Nancy's presence. It unnerved him. Why now? They weren't talking about her murder. Was she connected in some way to the graves in Kansas?

A strange thought formed in his mind—a thought that was not his own. "Maybe you're not looking far enough away," Scott said.

LuAnn's heart skipped a beat. "I was thinking the same thing. Ralph was a loner. He's only got an old truck that he's had for the last five years, and from his credit card receipts, we know he hasn't traveled much."

"The warden said he was in prison for child molestation. Bruce said something about him liking little girls. Where did he pick up his victims?"

"All of them were local girls," LuAnn said. "There was never any physical evidence of forcible rape, but they told their parents and the authorities that he took all of their clothes off. The best part—if there could be one in a case like this—is he didn't physically assault or murder them. He'd expose himself, do his thing, and drop them off on a country road somewhere. They were so young and traumatized that it took a while to get a good description of him. The local cops caught him on a fluke. An officer stopped him for speeding and noticed a pair of little girl's panties on the floor of his truck. It turned out they belonged to his latest victim. Once they had his DNA profile, they linked him to all five girls."

Nancy wouldn't leave him alone. Another thought came into his mind. "Maybe he was being used as somebody else's dump site."

His comment struck a nerve with LuAnn. Her thoughts lit up, and for a moment they moved so quickly Scott couldn't follow them.

"That thing in Kansas isn't even my case," LuAnn said as she began to refocus, "but what you just said suddenly makes perfect sense. If you'll excuse me, I need to go make a confidential phone call."

Chapter 25
<u>Ralph</u>

Jack knocked on Scott's door about an hour later. "Your protective services officer would like to talk to you," he said and handed Scott a cell phone.

"It's me," LuAnn said. "How would you feel about helping the Bureau with the case we were talking about earlier today?"

"I offered before, but nobody would take me seriously," Scott said. "I heard that he'd lawyered up. Can we even question him?"

"We offered him a deal. Kansas is a death penalty state. He's agreed to talk if we take the death penalty off the table."

"Why do you need me, then? I would think you guys know all the right questions."

"The boss wants you there to validate what he tells us and maybe ask some guided questions that we won't think or even know to ask him. In his own words, this is pretty high-stakes. We may not get another chance."

"Okay," Scott said. "I'm willing, so what's the next step?"

"We catch a plane for Topeka, Kansas, at five thirty this afternoon. The site is just a few miles north, near a little town called Elmont. Ralph lived in an old farmhouse a few miles north of Holton, which is another twenty-five miles or so north."

"I think you lost me at Topeka."

"I thought you told the warden where to find the place."

"I saw the burial site, but I had no idea where it was on the map. All I saw was a bird's-eye view from Google Earth. That's when Ralph started freaking out."

"It'll be too late for us to go out to the site by the time we get there tonight," LuAnn said, "so we'll stay in Topeka and drive up in the morning."

"Are you my security, then, or is Jack coming with us?"

"I'll be your muscle. We've got a single room with two double beds for as long as we need it."

Scott didn't know why, but he smiled.

"I can almost see you grinning," LuAnn said. "Don't get any

ideas, though, because I'm armed."

"Is the Bureau too cheap to spring for two rooms?" Scott joked.

"No, but I can't ensure your safety if I'm staying in the room next door."

"Where are they holding Ralph?"

"In jail in Topeka. A couple of officers will drive him and his legal counsel up to the site in the morning."

"I just love field trips," Scott said and laughed.

After the call, Jack left to make arrangements and Scott stood at the window watching the foot traffic three floors below.

He wondered why Nancy had visited him when they were talking about Ralph. She had to be connected in some way, but how? Scott replayed the vision in his head. It left him feeling anxious and hollow. He couldn't imagine why she was still bothering him. They'd found her body. Both she and her parents would have closure.

Maybe she won't have closure until they catch the guy who killed her, he thought.

Was that it? Was Ralph somehow connected to her killer? If Ralph was running the dump site for the murdered children, maybe Vince was his contact. Was that the connection?

Jack's knock at the door interrupted his thoughts. He held out a backpack for Scott. "We need to get on the road in about ten minutes," he said.

"I'm ready now," Scott said. "It doesn't take me long to pack a pair of pants."

"Saddle up, then," Jack said. "I think maybe you should wear your hat."

Scott grabbed his hat off the end table. He hadn't been in public for a while and had nearly forgotten what a sideshow his head had become.

* * * * *

LuAnn picked up their tickets at the airport kiosk and easily got them through security. Of course, it meant handcuffing Scott and showing her Bureau identification at the checkpoint. Because she was an armed agent and he was wearing handcuffs, security led them both around the metal detectors and sent them on their way.

As soon as they were through the checkpoint, and because they were an hour early for their flight, LuAnn took off his handcuffs and treated him to a burger and fries while they waited.

212

"Do you want to talk shop?" Scott asked after they got their food and sat down in a booth near the wall.

She looked around discreetly. "What's on your mind? And keep your voice down. I don't want any eavesdropping going on."

"When we were talking about the site," Scott said, "you said things were strange. If I remember right, you said that one of the victims you'd found was probably missing for several years before she was buried."

"So?"

"So I saw a TV documentary a year or so ago about sex trafficking," he said. "They said some kids were either kidnapped or sold into the system as young as four or five. They said some of those pedophiles would pick up a little girl and keep her until she reached puberty. Then they'd get rid of them. Do you think that Ralph was running one of the dump sites for those kids?"

"We're looking into that," LuAnn said. "I got a briefing early today so I wouldn't be going in blind. Keep in mind that what I tell you can't go beyond us."

"Who would I tell?" Scott said.

"Just so we're clear on that issue."

"We are."

"Okay, then. First, I need to tell you that the Bureau is way ahead of us on this. This certainly isn't the first time they've seen this sort of thing. The victims we've found so far range in age and sex. We're pretty certain that Ralph was providing a service. We think he was being used to dispose of kids that had been all used up. What we're really looking for from him are the names or descriptions or telephone numbers of his contacts."

LuAnn stopped speaking as a couple sat down at the table across the aisle from them. She nodded at a table on the far side of the room. After they had relocated, she picked up where she'd left off.

"We believe that some organizations are big enough to cater to all sorts of customers," she said. "Some of the kids, especially the little ones, eventually break mentally and don't have street value anymore. We think what we've found in Kansas is just one of the landfills for those kids."

Scott shuddered at the thought. "What are the demographics of these pedophiles? Are they married, single, rich, poor?"

"Most of the ones we've caught are single males, either bachelors or divorced. But beyond that, they can be about anyone and anywhere on the economic scale. If that's your only hobby, you can afford to spend a lot of money on it. Nobody we've busted to date can tell us anything about what happens to the kids who fall out of the system."

She paused to take a long drink on her soda.

"We busted one guy who took a road trip to Seattle and spent three weeks finding his victim," she continued. "She was only five years old. He locked her in the trunk of his car and was headed for a little town outside of Lincoln when he was pulled over for erratic driving. He'd been trying to drive straight through by living on energy drinks and caffeine tabs. That was one of the few happy endings we've seen . . . if you can call that a happy ending."

"The parents got their kid back," Scott said.

"Yes, but she was probably so mentally damaged by that affair that she'll never be the same."

"That ought to warrant the death penalty," Scott hissed.

"You've got a lot of folks who think the same," LuAnn said. She offered him a strange smile and nodded discreetly at a table behind him.

"What's up?" Scott asked, not wanting to turn around.

"We've got listeners," she said. "We should go. We can continue this discussion in our hotel room."

The rest of the trip was uneventful. When they finally got to the hotel, LuAnn spent about a half hour on the phone making arrangements. Ralph and his entourage would be at the site by nine in the morning.

Scott watched what news he could catch on TV while LuAnn used the shower. He felt anxious and awkward. He'd never been in a hotel room with anyone but Mary, and even though he knew there would be no tryst between them, he still wasn't comfortable with their sleeping arrangements.

LuAnn was dressed in pajamas when she stepped out of the bathroom. She had a towel wrapped around her wet hair.

"Your turn," she said. "There's plenty of towels."

Scott took his time, soaking up as much hot water as his aching body could stand. He didn't have any pajamas, so he pulled his Levi's on and put on a t-shirt.

"I've never seen you without a hat," LuAnn said, looking at the scars on his head. "Do you think your hair will eventually cover those scars?"

He was instantly self-conscious. "I really don't know. I know there's no hair growing on the scars, and it hurts to comb what little hair I have. I may have to wear a hat the rest of my life."

"Does it bother you much?"

"The scars, or the pain?"

"The scars, I guess. I hadn't considered the fact that they're probably still painful."

"I don't have many headaches," Scott said, "but if I'm not wearing a hat, the scars are the first thing people see."

She smiled. "It's like a train wreck. You just can't look away."

"Gee, thanks!"

LuAnn laughed, and in an instant Scott caught a glimpse of her thoughts. She was happily married, with three daughters ages ten, twelve, and sixteen. He looked away.

"Okay," she said. "What did you see?"

"Your girls. I'm sorry. It's just become second nature."

"I can see why your wife can't live with you," she said. "Not being able to have your own private thoughts is really uncomfortable."

"You asked."

"I was curious. I could tell by the expression on your face that you knew something."

"Am I that transparent?"

"Not to somebody who doesn't know what you can do, I suppose."

"Let's talk shop," Scott suggested to change the subject. "That would help."

"Okay, what would you like to talk about?"

"You're going to think I'm nuts," Scott said, "but I'm going to tell you anyway. You know the case about the woman who was murdered? Her name was Nancy."

"The one you see visions about?"

"Yes. Anyway, I feel her spirit from time to time. In fact, until I started looking for details in the vision I was having, she wouldn't leave me alone. She forced that dream on me night and day until I thought I was going to lose my mind. When I finally looked past the horror of her murder and noticed the little things and told my attorney about them, she left me alone. That's when I first realized she'd been hanging around. Because when she wasn't there anymore, I knew it."

LuAnn looked skeptical but swallowed hard. "And?"

"She puts thoughts in my mind from time to time, even now. Like when you told me about what was going on with Ralph's case. I'm convinced Nancy's murder is somehow tied to all the rest: to

Warden Bruce, to the disappearance of the three guys who hauled me to that first safe house, to Ableman's obsession with my case and his actions to try to protect someone by the name of Vince. And finally, to Ralph's case. I had the distinct thought on the plane that I needed to get a photo of Nancy and show it to Ralph when we see him tomorrow."

"When do you see this ghost?" LuAnn asked timidly.

"I never see her, I just feel her. Like when I was hiding under the safe house in Lincoln. She basically told me that I needed to crush my phone so they couldn't track it. When she comes around, I feel anxious. I can't stop thinking about her. When I finally realize why she's bugging me and do what she wants, she leaves me alone, and I feel total peace."

"That's so weird," LuAnn said. "Did you bring a picture of her?"

"I don't have anything but my clothes. You've got a laptop. I was hoping you could conjure up a photo."

"Interesting choice of words," LuAnn said, reaching for her laptop. A few minutes later, she found a newspaper article with Nancy's photo and saved it to her laptop. "I'll print a copy downstairs before we leave in the morning," she said, then looked at Scott. "Okay, I'm curious. What can you tell me about my girls?"

"Whatever you can tell me about them," Scott said. "In your mind."

"Okay, what's Susie's favorite color?"

"You don't have a Susie. You have a Richelle, a Karen, and a Janice. Richelle is the oldest. She's sixteen and driving you crazy because she has a steady boyfriend."

"Either you're for real, or you have access to my dossier and have a photographic memory."

"Are you done testing me?"

"I think so. I really don't want to know what else you're sucking out of my brain."

"That's a horrible way of putting it."

"Probably, but that's the way I feel. I feel like you're sitting there violating me and I can't do a thing to stop you."

Scott looked away. "I'm really sorry," he said after a few seconds, "I didn't want to go there. You told me to."

"I'm sorry too. You're right. I asked for it. Don't feel bad. In fact, I'm really pretty impressed by you."

"How's that?"

"Most of the men I know would be totally taking advantage of that gift if they had it. You're different. You have a heart."

"That's sort of what my attorney, Paul, told me. You can't imagine how many times I wished I'd have just shut my mouth and kept all of this to myself. I'd still be at home with my wife, and by now I'd be back on the job, doing what I trained most of my adult life to do."

"I thought you just told me that Nancy wouldn't leave you alone."

"That's the issue, isn't it? I don't know how she found out about me. I'm afraid to know, actually, because I'm afraid if I ever solve her problem, I may have a lineup of others waiting to haunt me."

LuAnn rubbed her elbows absently and stared down at the carpet. "I read in the court documents that she was killed about the same time you had your accident. Maybe that's the connection. Heaven only knows if there's some sort of psychic dimension you enter when you die . . . or nearly so, in your case."

"I can only hope so," Scott said. "I don't know if I can handle another mess like this one."

Scott glanced up at the TV just in time to see a photo of Detective Ableman on the screen. He hurried to the set and cranked up the volume. The newscast was reporting that Detective Patrick Ableman had been found dead in his home of an apparent self-inflicted gunshot wound. There was no note or explanation left. The police were investigating.

"Well, so much for that trial," LuAnn said, sighing.

"The trial isn't the issue," Scott said. "I know he's tied to all of this somehow. I'm afraid that whoever is calling the shots is systematically clearing the slate. If I was Warden Bruce, I'd be catching a plane to Hidesville, USA."

"You really think Ableman was murdered?"

"I'd bet on it," Scott said. "If I were the feds, I'd be going over that crime scene with a fine-toothed comb. I'd find his accomplice, Dean, and put him in protective custody along with the prison warden until all of this can be sorted out."

LuAnn picked up her phone and made a call. She walked into the bathroom and shut the door behind her while she talked. Scott felt he probably didn't have the need to know, so he tuned his mind away and didn't listen in.

Instead, he moved closer to the TV and flipped through every news channel he could find, looking for anything else about the story. When he found nothing, he clicked back to the local news channel. He was watching the weather report when the bathroom door opened.

Before he could stop himself, he zoned in on LuAnn's thoughts: Ableman's accomplice, Dean, had been found dead in his car only an hour ago. He had rigged up a hose from the exhaust pipe and died of carbon monoxide poisoning.

"Is the agency going after the warden now that Dean's dead?" Scott asked.

"I suppose that means you heard me talking?" LuAnn said.

"No. I didn't *hear* you talking to anybody."

"You know, Scott, I'm going to suggest that the Bureau immediately does a background check on you and gets you a top-level security clearance. It's obvious to me there's no way we can keep sensitive information away from you."

"There's another way, you know," Scott said solemnly.

"What's that?"

"Either distance yourself from me or kill me."

A shocked look crossed LuAnn's face.

"You may think I say that in jest," Scott said, "but it's true. What if one of your superiors decides I'm a security risk? I'm not saying the FBI goes around killing people, but what better way of stopping an unstoppable leak?"

"Are you a security risk?" she asked.

"Not to the good guys," Scott said. "I still have morals."

"Yes, you do, and I'm a witness to that."

"So where do we go from here?"

"We try to get some sleep and see what happens tomorrow. But can I give you a piece of advice?"

"Of course."

"Get used to keeping information to yourself until somebody asks for it. And only give them what you think they want to hear."

"I've actually done that with my kids," Scott said, forcing a smile.

"Just pretend I'm one of your kids, then. I'll pretend I don't know what you can do."

* * * * *

They were on the road by eight. Scott pretended to be engrossed with the passing landscape so LuAnn wouldn't guess he was finding out more about her. He practiced what they'd talked about the night before. He let her tell him whatever she thought he should know, and then he only acknowledged what they talked about. When they were a few miles away from the little town of Elmont, she got on her phone and asked someone called Howard for directions.

Even before she began to slow down, Scott recognized the turnoff from the satellite image he'd seen in prison. He kept his thoughts to himself until she blew past the intersection. Then, using his best acting skills, he whipped his head around and looked behind them.

"Hey," he said, "I think I recognize that turn from what I saw on Google Earth. Are you sure you didn't just miss the turn?"

LuAnn lifted her foot off the accelerator and picked up her smartphone. "They dropped a pin on my GPS map. I thought I'd . . . damn, you're right. It's a good thing you've got a great memory, or we'd be in Holton before I realized I missed the turn. Did you rob my brain again, or did you really recognize the turn?"

"I recognized the turn," he lied. "From what I remember, you turn off on a dirt road for less than a quarter mile, and then there's a pull-off. There's an old overgrown two-track road beyond that on the left, then there's an old car off to the side. The site is just a little way beyond that."

"Okay, I believe you, Scott. Nobody told me all that."

She made a U-turn in the road and headed back the way they'd come. Scott pointed out the intersection, and she slowed to turn off. A couple of minutes later, they saw a small armada of vehicles choking both sides of the narrow dirt road.

"I think we've found it," LuAnn said sarcastically. "It looks like Barnum & Bailey is out here."

She parked behind the nearest vehicle—a pickup truck with a sheriff's insignia on the tailgate—and they began the long walk down the dirt road.

"It's a good thing I brought my sneakers," she complained. "I had no idea I'd have to take a five-mile hike."

A four-man team stepped out to intercept them when they reached the turnout. LuAnn already had her badge in her hand so she wouldn't freak anybody out by reaching into her purse. The officer in charge gave them a few brief directions and let them pass.

Someone had cleared the brush and graded the road, turning the two-track into a sixteen-foot-wide rutted dirt track through the scrubby trees. A motorhome-sized crime lab and a coroner's van were parked in the road just past a rusted old car with no doors and bullet holes in the trunk.

A man stepped out of the crime lab and held up his right hand in welcome.

"Hi, LuAnn," he said. "I assume this is Scott."

Chapter 26
<u>Confessions of the Damned</u>

LuAnn stepped forward and shook the man's hand. "Scott, this is Howard McIntosh. He's the Bureau's point man on this case. Howard, this is Scott Corbridge. I don't think he needs an introduction."

Howard shook Scott's hand. "Pleased to make your acquaintance," he said.

Howard had that confident air about him that had obviously come from years of experience with the agency. His full dark-brown mustache was sprinkled with gray, as was his full head of hair. His broad shoulders and firm handshake spoke of a man who spent time in the gym.

"Thanks," Scott said. "I hope I can help. This has got to be a heartbreaking assignment."

Howard sighed. "You're right. I was just thinking that. It's never easy when there's kids involved."

Scott knew Howard's thoughts were genuine; the man had kids of his own. His training was in forensics, and he'd seen a lot of bad things, but this was the worst assignment he'd ever had. His eyes searched Scott's, and Scott instantly liked him. Despite his years of expertise, Howard wasn't full of himself.

"Do you have kids?" Howard asked.

"I have three," Scott said.

A look of concern flashed across Howard's face. "This may be hard for you, then. Most of the victims are just kids."

"That's what LuAnn told me. I talked to a highway patrolman once about car wrecks. He told me it was always hardest when there were kids involved."

"He's right," Howard said, his face grim. He motioned them toward the open door of the mobile crime lab. He introduced them to the two forensic scientists working near the rear of the van, then offered them a seat at a table cluttered with photos and paperwork. They sat down, and Howard drew a deep breath.

"I'm sorry for the smell," he said. "Between the chemicals and, well, the obvious . . . it's not very pleasant in here." He ran his fingers through his hair and leaned back in his seat. "So, Scott, what can I tell you that you don't already know?"

"Despite what you may have been told," Scott said, "I don't really know a lot. I can tell you that I've seen this site from a satellite view, but other than that, it's all new to me. Ralph started freaking out in prison when the cops told him what we knew, so I didn't really get much from him. LuAnn told me yesterday that you've found something like eighteen bodies."

Howard looked at LuAnn briefly and then back at Scott. "We just found number nineteen yesterday. We've got cadaver dogs and a host of other experts out here looking. The bodies are buried so close together that there's scent everywhere, so the dogs are becoming less effective. We've started using a host of electronic tools to try to see beneath the surface. The woods look like a war zone."

He looked down at the spread of photos on the table. "Even though digging them up is a slow, tedious process, my forensics team can't keep up. When we find a new victim, we mark the site on a GPS grid and assign them a number. The perp made it sort of easy for us, though. All of the bodies we've found so far were in body bags. We've been looking for a connection between Ralph and the military, or law enforcement, or someone who might have access to body bags, but so far, we've drawn a blank. We take the usual photographs and take tissue samples for the lab before we exhume the remains and put everything in a fresh bag. The local lab in Topeka is swamped, so we've been sending the bodies to every available lab in a two-state area for detailed analysis."

"Any obvious causes of death?" Scott asked.

"We were hoping you could help us with that once Ralph gets out here. There's nothing obvious. No bullet holes, no skull trauma, no broken necks or anything of that nature. It'll take time to get the chemical analysis back to see if they were drugged."

"I think somebody told me that Ralph has been in prison for a while, so I imagine most of the graves are pretty old?"

"The further out we go, the graves are older, more scattered, and they're deeper. The newer graves are a lot closer together and only a couple of feet deep. Those are pretty easy to find because of the settling that occurs as the body decomposes. Sometimes, we've found them so close together that we have to be careful not to compromise one site while we're digging in another. We don't know if he just got lazy, or busier."

Scott didn't want to see what was in Howard's mind. He turned his head and stared out the window.

"In case you're wondering," LuAnn interjected, "Scott does that when he doesn't want to know what you're thinking."

"I'm sorry," Scott said. "This is pretty brutal."

"You have no idea," Howard said. "I'm going to need some therapy when I'm done here. Having said that, would you like a tour?"

"I'd rather wait to do that until Ralph gets here," Scott said. "I'm thinking that if I can walk through the woods with him it might aid in your search."

"Do you think he'll remember where he buried them all?" Howard said.

"Maybe. I won't know until he's here. I never know if the thoughts I'm seeing are active or subconscious. I once heard a man say that his memory was excellent, it was just his retrieval process that was flawed. I don't really know if I can go beyond Ralph's short-term memory. This is all new to me. I don't know what I'll find."

The loud barking of several dogs interrupted their conversation.

"Sounds like the K9 crew is here," Howard said. "I need to go coordinate their team. You're welcome to stay here and have some coffee or step out and get some fresh air. Be careful where you walk, though. I'd prefer it if you stuck to the beaten path."

"I'd like some air," LuAnn said when Howard left.

Scott led the way outside. He paused to look around. Mounds of fresh earth lay heaped at irregular intervals on both sides of the faint two-track road leading off through the woods. The forest of scrubby trees had been cordoned off in a grid pattern of heavy white twine tied to orange stakes driven into the ground at regular intervals. The grid ended alongside the winding track. It appeared that whoever had made the track had simply wound through the woods, turning here and there to avoid the larger trees.

Scott turned to follow the track deeper into the heavy growth, and LuAnn followed.

He thought about Nancy and wondered if these kids were waiting in the trees for someone to find them. He reached out but thankfully felt nothing. He'd had quite enough of that.

Eventually, the woods thinned and the grid ended. Even though it wasn't yet nine in the morning, the day was already hot and muggy. He walked on. They eventually crested a short hill. The trees ended abruptly at the top, and a grain field stretched out before them. The heads on the wheat waved heavy and full under a slight breeze. The stalks had turned yellow; harvest wasn't far away.

Scott took a deep breath of the heavy air. He couldn't imagine what it might be like to have to dig in that heat.

"What's on your mind?" LuAnn asked.

"Just wondering what my kids are doing," he said. "That, and wondering how awful it would be to lose them and not know where they are."

"I'd rather know they were dead. I can't walk through here without thinking about my girls. They're the same ages as a lot of the ones here. I can only guess at the horrors these kids had to endure before . . ."

Scott turned to face her. She had tears in her eyes.

"We should get back," LuAnn said.

A small entourage of people were standing alongside the motorhome when they got back. Ralph was there, dressed in a bright-orange jumpsuit, his hands and feet shackled with short chains. Everyone stopped talking and turned their heads to gawk as they approached.

Scott concentrated on Ralph. He was shorter than he remembered, probably less than five-and-a-half feet tall. Scott could feel Ralph's terror. He didn't want to be there. He didn't want to face what he'd done.

"Good morning, Ralph," Scott said as he approached. "I'm Scott."

"I know who you are," Ralph said, "and I don't have nothin' to say to you."

"I'm not here to harass you. This has got to be really hard for you. Do you need a drink or anything? It's really hot."

Ralph's thoughts softened. "I could use some water."

"Could somebody get Ralph a bottle of water?" Scott said. "And, if possible, could you take off his shackles? I don't think he's going to go missing in that bright garb he's wearing, and he doesn't seem very dangerous to me."

Howard nodded at the deputies flanking Ralph, and the men moved to unlock his chains. Scott waited for Ralph to drain the plastic bottle of water someone handed him. Then, after listening to his thoughts again, he turned to a man dressed in a suit and tie standing behind him.

"Are you his counsel?" Scott asked.

"Yes," the man said, stepping forward. "I'm Stan Williams."

"If it's okay with you," Scott said, "I'd like just the three of us to take a little walk." He looked at Howard. "Would that be okay?"

"I suppose so," Howard said. "I don't want you out of sight, though."

"No problem there," Scott said. "I'd just like to let Ralph relax a little." He turned to Stan. "Are you okay with this? I realize you're here to protect Ralph's interests. I'm not here to get a confession. I'd like this to be a voyage of discovery. I don't know if Ralph told you or not, but we're here because I'm a clairvoyant. I met Ralph in prison and—"

"He told me all that," Stan interrupted. "And we're going to move to have your testimony ruled inadmissible in court. If you can really do what you say you can do, what you did in prison was nothing short of questioning my client without his consent or without his legal counsel being present."

"I'm not an attorney or a detective," Scott said. "In fact, I don't even work for the feds. I'm here because it's obvious there are a lot of kids buried out here, and there's got to be a lot of parents wanting to find out where their kids are. I'm hoping Ralph can help with that. He's free to decline, of course, but I would think that any help he might provide would weigh heavily in his favor in court."

Stan wasn't convinced.

"Let's face the issue, shall we?" Scott suggested. "Ralph has already been convicted of several charges that will keep him in prison for a good number of years. In addition to that, he's already admitted to burying at least one of these kids. I don't think anything he can tell me will make or break your case." He looked past Stan at the audience that was listening to everything they said.

"Let's walk down the road a little way where we can be alone," Scott continued. "I'd just like to chat without all these other guys hanging around. Would that be okay with you, Ralph?"

Ralph looked at his attorney and nodded.

"Do you need another drink?"

"No, I'm fine. But you should know that this ain't gonna get you nowhere."

Scott led the way down the path a few yards and then stopped to face Ralph. "Look," he said, "I'm not here to bust your balls. We all know what's going on here. You've got your deal. They've taken the death penalty off the table. It can't get any worse. Do you have kids of your own?"

The question caught Ralph off guard. "Ah, no," he stammered. "I never married."

"That's got to be tough," Scott said. "Being alone sucks. This thing I can do with my mind drove my wife away. I really miss her. I have three kids. They don't know what I can do, and my wife has agreed not to tell them. I'm going to be totally honest with you, Ralph. I don't know why I can do what I can, but I pretty well know what you're thinking. Can I show you something?"

Ralph nodded suspiciously.

Scott took the printout of Nancy's picture out of his back pocket and handed it to Ralph.

"Do you know this woman?" he asked.

"I met her once. She was with Vince."

"Is that who brought you the girls?"

"He always brought a woman with him. But it wasn't always the same one. I think he did it to . . . well, you know . . . to calm the kids down."

Scott reached inside his front pocket and took out another folded piece of paper. "Is this Vince?" he asked as he unfolded the police sketch and held it up.

"Yup, that's him," Ralph said. "He never looked that mean, but that's him."

Scott put the sketch and photo of Nancy back into his pocket. "Ralph," he said, "will you help me? They've already found a lot of kids out here, but I'm wondering if there are any more. If I lost one of my kids, I'd want to find them, even if they were here. I think I know why you did this, but I don't want to know any of that right now. I just want to help some heartbroken parents find their kids."

Ralph looked up at Scott. The fear in his eyes was gone. "What do you want me to do?"

"Do you know how many are out here?"

"Maybe, but it's been a long time for some. The woods change. Sometimes I came in summer, sometimes in the spring or fall. I don't do winters. It's too hard to dig."

"Did you have any in the winter?"

"A few."

"What did you do with them?"

"The river's close. I have some cinderblocks. I didn't like doin' that, though. It just didn't seem right. A person needs a proper burial."

"Did you say words over the ones you buried?"

226

"Most of the time. You probably think that's stupid, but just 'cause I'm bad don't mean they were. They can't help it if somebody just took 'em. After what they lived through, it only seemed proper."

"Do you remember where you went on the river?"

"There's a big bend not far from here. There's a boat dock. Nobody uses the ramp in the winter. There's too much floating ice."

"Will you show me?"

Ralph looked out through the trees for a few long moments. "I used to go to church," he said. "The preacher said confession was good for the soul. I don't think I've got much of a soul left, but I suppose these kids do. I guess it wouldn't hurt to come clean."

"Thank you, Ralph. You're going to bring closure to a lot of devastated parents."

"What do you want me to do?" Ralph asked.

"Just walk with me. Look around. See if you can remember where they are."

"Maybe you ought to get a few of them orange stakes," Ralph suggested.

Scott turned to Stan, who was standing a few feet away and listening quietly. "Would you mind?" Scott asked.

"No, not at all," Stan replied. "I'll be right back."

"How much did you tell the warden after I found out where these kids were buried?" Scott asked when he and Ralph were alone.

Rage flashed through Ralph's mind. "I hate that bastard! He was always sending his boys down to rough me up. I hardly ever got a moment's peace."

"Would it make you feel better to know that the feds are on to him?" Scott said. "Now, that's just between you and me, okay? You can't tell anybody."

A sly grin spread across Ralph's face. "I can keep a secret. I'd love to have a cell next to his."

Stan returned carrying a small bag of orange stakes.

Scott winked at Ralph. "I'll see if we can make that happen," he said.

"Make what happen?" Stan said angrily. "I'm supposed to be present any time you're interrogating my client."

"I wasn't interrogating him," Scott said. "We were just chatting."

The three of them walked slowly down the lane past the upturned earth. A half-dozen men followed at a discreet distance behind them.

"I think they found 'bout everybody here in the new part," Ralph

227

said as the graves thinned out. "There's more off that way."

Scott followed as Ralph turned off the track and walked past the last of the grids. Ralph carefully scanned the thicket as they walked. Eventually, he took a stake from Stan and stuck it in the ground.

"They're mostly between the trees," Ralph said as he stood back up. "There's too many roots up by the tree trunks." He walked a few steps and planted another stake, and then another, forming a circular pattern.

"These graves aren't random, are they?" Scott said.

"Nope," Ralph answered. "I'd find the first good place, then use my compass. They're every ten degrees from the center point, and then ten paces out. If it wasn't good digging there, I'd sometimes go another ten paces, or go back and go to the next mark."

"Did you always do it this way?"

"Only early on. When I started running out of room, like back by the trucks, I'd just dig where there was room."

"Are these graves deep?"

"Most out here are shovel deep," Ralph said. "It'd take me all day to dig a proper grave."

"Did you ever get interrupted?"

"Nope, I never did. At least not by men. There was a few deer and a lot of turkeys. I ate some of both. Never did build a fire here. Didn't want to draw attention to the place. I'd haul the deer home in a bag. Most times, I'd just chuck the birds behind the seat 'til I got home."

"Did you shoot them?" Scott asked.

"The deer, or the kids?"

"I was thinking about the game animals."

"I'm a fair shot with a bow," Ralph said, "and I keep my broadheads razor sharp. If you get my drift."

In an instant, Scott did get his drift. Ralph kept the victims tied up but alive in a body bag until he got their grave dug, then a quick thrust with the broadhead through the carotid artery put them out of their misery. He couldn't bring himself to bury them alive.

"Are they all girls?" Scott asked after recovering from the horror he'd just seen.

"Not all. But the boys was the hardest. They reminded me of when I was a kid."

"Did you molest the girls?" Scott asked. He knew he was treading on thin ice, but decided to broach the subject anyway.

Ralph stared at him for a few seconds before he answered. "No, I never did. By the time I got 'em, they'd already been all used up in that way. They didn't need no more misery."

"So you didn't ever kidnap any kids yourself?"

"Nope. Folks probably don't believe that, but I didn't."

"You were in prison for molesting little girls."

"I never raped nobody. Those other kids, we'd just play games. Sometimes I'd touch 'em, but I never . . . you know . . . did nothin' to them with my parts. We was just havin' fun. Then they told their moms, and it got ugly after that." He stopped and turned around in a slow circle. "That's all in here."

"Are there more?" Scott asked.

"Just one more circle, then maybe some back by the cars. I don't know how many they found back there."

"They said they'd found nineteen."

Ralph searched his thoughts. "I lost count a long time ago. That might be right, but I just need to look around. I'll know if they've missed some."

"The ones by the cars aren't shovel deep. Is there any reason why?"

"Rocks," Ralph said simply. "I couldn't go no deeper without using a pick and a bar. That's way too much work."

"Is there another place?"

"Nope. I was gonna go lookin' but got sent to jail before I could."

"Where's the other circle?"

"About fifty yards or so, off to the right of the old car."

Scott glanced up at the sun bearing down. "It's getting hot. Do you want to wait 'til it's cooler?"

"No sense in that. We're here now. The heat don't bother me much, 'less I'm diggin'. In the summer, I used to dig at night by lantern light. Some folks might think that's spooky, all out here in the woods by myself with all these dead kids, but to me, it was like home. These kids is sort of like my family."

Scott fought back a violent shudder at Ralph's words. "You know," he said, "they brought you the kids when they were still alive. You could have just turned them over to the cops."

"Vince woulda cut my heart out. Him and that fancy stiletto he packed around. He showed it to me a few times, probably just to scare hell out of me."

"How did you get hooked up with Vince in the first place?"

"He pulled into the yard one day in this fancy car. I was up to my elbows in grease. My tractor broke down. Anyway, he came out there all lookin' like a pimp or somethin'. He said he was lookin' to buy a piece of property. He wanted to know if I was interested in sellin'. I told him I figured every man had his price, then he pulls out a wad of bills that would choke a horse. He came right out and told me he needed a place to plant a little weed, and if I was interested, he'd make it worth my while. I was about to lose the place anyway 'cause it was too small to compete with the big spreads. I figured what the hell, I'd give it a try."

Ralph cleared his throat and spat on the ground. "He brought me the seeds, and about harvest time, he shows up with this dude in a uniform and tells me he's gonna send me up the river unless I did him a favor. He said he needed a place to bury a body. He'd pay me five grand to do it and keep my mouth shut. I figured I was already in deep, so I agreed. I needed the cash bad. The bank was about to take everything."

Ralph scuffed his feet on the ground and took a deep breath. He was nearly in tears.

"The first one was dead. I buried her in the woods out back of my house. Course I shoulda known there'd be more. Once Vince had me over a barrel, he started showin' up with live ones. He told me this story about how they'd been all used up and just needed a place to die. Course he came with that dude in a uniform the first few times just to show me he meant business. After a while, he started comin' with a woman, and instead of the kids bein' in a body bag, they was just sittin' by the lady in the back seat. She'd give 'em a shot to calm 'em down, and then I'd put 'em in the bag."

A thought suddenly fought its way into Scott's brain. "Ralph," he asked, "do you think you'd recognize the guy in uniform if I showed you a picture?"

"Probably. It's been a few years, but I suppose I would."

"If you don't mind, I'd like to have the lady I came with see if she can find a picture of the guy I'm thinking about. While she's doing that, you can show me the other circle."

"No, I don't mind," Ralph said. "You're a right kind sort of guy, not all scary like I'd think a soothsayer would be."

They turned and headed back in the direction of the mobile crime lab. Scott beckoned to LuAnn as they approached.

"Do you think you could find a recent photo of Detective Ableman?" Scott asked her. "Maybe on your laptop?"

"I left my computer back in the car," she said. "I'll be right back."

"We're going for another walk in the woods while you're looking," Scott told her. "We'll be back in a while."

Ralph led the way back down the track to the old car, then turned left and walked out into the trees. Scott didn't notice at first, but Ralph was counting his paces. He stopped at a hundred and looked around. Then he walked in a slow circle, carefully watching the trees as he moved.

It took Ralph a couple of minutes to orient himself. Then he reached into the bag of stakes and began laying them out at rough ten-degree increments. When he finished, he looked up and slowly began walking in a circle around the array of stakes.

"Yup," Ralph said, "this is the spot. If you walk about ten paces out in the woods from each one of them stakes, you should find what you're lookin' for."

"Ralph," Scott said, "are there really that many graves out here?"

"I ain't proud of what I done," Ralph said. "I thought you wanted to know where they was."

"I just had no idea there were so many."

"Been doing this for five years or more. I usually got one or two a month. It don't take long to add up."

"This breaks my heart," Scott said. "That means there's over a hundred kids out here."

"Don't forget the ones in the river," Ralph said. "There's probably twenty or more down there."

LuAnn was waiting with her laptop when Scott, Ralph, and Stan walked back out of the woods.

"That's him!" Ralph said as soon as he saw Ableman's picture. "Course he had a little more hair when I saw him last."

They spent another half hour wandering among the freshly dug graves and the grid lines. Ralph dropped three more spikes before he turned back to Scott.

"It's hard to tell with everything bein' dug up like this, but that's all I remember."

"Ralph," Scott said. "You told me Vince always brought a woman with him to calm the kids down. Do you think you might be able to identify some of those women? The cops would like to find out who they are. If they can catch them, they might be able to put a stop to this. You remember that sketch of Vince I showed you? A police artist drew that just from my memory. Do you think you might be able to do that?"

"I can try, but I don't know how much good I'll be. Most of 'em I only saw once or twice. That one girl, the one you showed me a picture of, as I recall she only came out once. She didn't look very happy."

"Somebody murdered her," Scott said. "It might have been Vince. She was stabbed to death with a switchblade."

"I'm not surprised," Ralph said. "That idiot was always flashin' that thing around. The blade popped straight out of the handle. He thought it was really cool."

"If we find him, do you think you could identify him in a lineup?" Scott asked.

"Long as I don't have to look him in the face, I'm good with that. I don't never want to see him again."

Chapter 27
The Bureau

After everyone got back from the river and the deputies headed back to Topeka with Ralph, Howard gathered the rest of the group around the mobile crime lab.

"I've been on the phone with my supervisors," he said, "briefing them and pleading for more resources. This site is going to get very busy in the next couple of weeks. Now that Ralph has named and positively identified Vince, a lot of pieces of the puzzle have fallen into place. This site is probably only the small tip of a very filthy iceberg. Unfortunately, the media knows about this site, and I'm sure it's no secret that the bigger players in this mess will know we've found it too."

Howard looked from face to face. "I usually wouldn't tell you something that doesn't directly involve you, but I want you to know how important this site is and how important what you're doing out here is. The police in Omaha just found the bodies of a police detective and an accomplice. To make a long story short, they were involved in evidence tampering in the homicide of a young woman in Lincoln who Ralph has connected to this site. Cause of death in both cases was apparent suicide. I'm pretty sure we're going to find out that the alleged suicides were actually homicides. The Bureau will be taking over the investigation of those deaths effective immediately."

Scott was happy to hear the feds hadn't been fooled by their apparent suicides. It was all too obvious that Ableman hadn't taken his own life. For one, the bail money someone had paid to get him out of jail spoke of wealthy backers. Scott was sure that if those people felt threatened by what Ableman knew, they wouldn't have hesitated to take him out of the picture. Getting him out on bail had simply facilitated their move.

"I want you to know," Howard continued, "how important it is that we find and identify all of these kids. When we know who they are and where they're from, we hope to be able to understand how big this organization is, which in turn will help us shut it down. I know it's hot, gritty work, but it's important. That's all I can tell you for now. Thanks again for what you're doing."

Scott and LuAnn waited as the crowd dispersed. Howard stepped inside the mobile crime lab and beckoned to them. They went inside and sat down around the table.

"It's obvious to me," Howard said, "that whoever is at the head of this mess is getting reckless, and that could prove to be their undoing. We need to move quickly before they can cover their tracks."

He paused for a moment and ran his hand through his damp hair as he gathered his thoughts. "As I see it, we have several immediate challenges. We need to find Vince, and we need to find the car he was driving. The Bureau told me this morning that the car we identified from the plate number Scott gave us was reported stolen. But the owner didn't report it missing until after Scott produced that drawing of Vince and after Ableman mentally identified the guy. In my mind, that implicates the car's owner. We need to find that car, even if it's in pieces."

What Howard said made perfect sense to Scott. When Ableman tipped off Vince—or whoever Vince worked for—it would only be natural for the owner to report it stolen to distance himself from the crime. Still, it seemed like a foolhardy move. Had it been reported stolen before the police artist's rendition hit the streets, one might have believed the claim. Reporting it after the fact only turned the spotlight directly on the owner.

Scott wondered if he was missing something. He looked for LuAnn's thoughts and saw they were nearly identical to his own. But her worries ran deeper. Cars used in crimes were known to disappear. Howard's comment that the car might possibly be in pieces was especially on point. More than once, the agency had discovered pieces of bodies in cars that had been sent to the salvage yard and shredded before being sent to a steel smelter to be melted down. If the perps were able to get that accomplished, any evidence in Vince's car would disappear forever.

Howard leaned back in his chair and stared at Scott for an instant. Then he focused on LuAnn. "It seems all of the bad guys who had anything at all to do with this case are going missing. Keeping Ralph safe until he can testify against Vince is a priority, so I'm going to have him pulled out of jail and sequestered someplace with the agency. Hopefully, his sessions with our artists will help identify some more of Vince's accomplices. The more people we can identify, the more chances we'll have of pinning down the big guys."

Howard collected his thoughts again and went on. "After what we learned from Ralph today, I'm sure that Nancy Bennion was also a co-conspirator. For now, we can only guess why Vince decided to take her out and why he decided to do it in such a messy manner. We know the car was registered to one of the companies held by a wealthy businessman, so we'll put that man and his various organizations under surveillance. A lot of times, people get away with things because nobody had a reason to put them under the microscope. We're going to see what we can find out about him."

Howard picked up a sheaf of papers off his desk and fanned his face. "The problem is, when you start messing with big money, things can get very interesting. I don't have to tell you that there's big money in sex trafficking. It's getting bigger than the illegal drug trade. It seems you can buy about anything in this world. Not the least of which is sex with children."

The gravity of Howard's words weighed heavily on Scott. He couldn't bear the thought of one of his own children vanishing without a trace. He looked at LuAnn. The rosy glow of her overheated face had paled when she considered Howard's statement. She had tried to distance herself from the reality that lay all around them—the bodies of sons and daughters stolen from someone else's home—but when she thought about her own children and how vulnerable they might be to the same fate, the tragedy of the situation became very personal.

"I need you to get Scott on a plane tonight," Howard said. "You should have tickets waiting for you for the late-afternoon flight back to Omaha. I want him under guard for the time being. I realize his direct testimony probably won't be allowed in a court of law, but he's proving to be invaluable to the agency on this case. The hard evidence he helps us discover will be admissible, even if his direct testimony may not be."

* * * * *

LuAnn didn't say much until they got in the car and began the drive back to Topeka. Once they were on the road, she had plenty to say.

"Okay, Scott," she said as soon as they hit the main road. "I want to know how you got Ralph to talk."

"I didn't make him do anything he didn't already want to do,"

Scott said. "The man was writhing in agony. He knew what he'd done was horrible. He wanted to talk about it. He just needed to feel we were interested in him as a person and weren't just using him."

"All you did was offer him a drink."

"He was thirsty."

"So was I, and you didn't offer me a drink."

"He needed to feel safe. He's afraid of dying. He may not appear to be, but he's a religious man of sorts. He's convinced he's going to Hell for what he's done, but he doesn't want to go there right away. He rightly believes Vince and his co-conspirators forced him to do what he did. At the back of his mind, he thinks Christ may show him some mercy. He honestly believes those kids were 'used up,' as he put it. They had been mentally broken by people like Vince and his customers. Ralph honestly believed he was simply putting them out of their misery. And that, in his mind, was good."

"What a crock," LuAnn said angrily.

"I'm not saying he isn't warped, but what he believes has some merit. What nobody knows is that he feels deeply about those kids and their deaths. He said words over the graves of all his victims, including the ones he dumped in the river."

"Sounds like the wild imaginings of a lunatic to me."

"I can't argue that," Scott said. "I'm just telling you what he believes. His attorney had already told him they would pull the death penalty off the table if he testified, but it took an independent third party, like me, to make him really believe it. Another thing nobody knows about Ralph is that he never sexually abused any of the kids he killed and buried. He felt like they'd gone through so much at the hands of others that he couldn't hurt them himself. He even told me that although he touched the little girls he was sent to prison for, he never used any of *his parts*, and in his perverted mind, he didn't think that was wrong."

"And you believed him?"

"That begs an interesting question," Scott said. "From what I saw in his thoughts, he was telling the truth. At least that's how he views it. I haven't seen the evidence that put him in prison, but can a person tell himself that something isn't a lie so often that he eventually begins to believe it himself? I can hear thoughts, but I can't play back a person's memory."

"What Howard said really bothers me," LuAnn said, changing the subject. "He's not one to exaggerate. I think he's seriously worried that this is way over his head. I overheard part of his conversation with the lieutenant. I think if Howard had his way, he'd call in the National Guard. If he thought it would do any good, that is."

"It's a murder case, for Pete's sake."

"No, it's way bigger than that," LuAnn said. "Howard was worried when he found out who that car was registered to because he's been up against big money before. But when Ralph got done out here today, he knew he was dealing with a lot more than some sicko with a kid fetish. Ralph didn't travel halfway across the nation to snatch those kids. That site back there is little more than a landfill for a lot of other people's garbage."

"I wonder what Vince's motives were in killing Nancy," Scott said, staring out the window. "Was he afraid she'd go to the authorities? Was she blackmailing him, or maybe whoever Vince works for?"

"We'll probably never know," LuAnn said.

"Oh, I think we will. You've never met her, but Nancy is a very persistent being. She'll never let me rest until this is resolved. Or until I'm dead."

* * * * *

Jack arrived at Scott's secure apartment early the following Monday morning. He knocked on the door before using a key to let himself in. "It's moving day," he said when Scott walked out of the bedroom in his underwear. "Don't ask where. I can't say it out loud. The walls may have ears."

They were in the lobby fifteen minutes later. A man Scott had never seen flanked them as they exited the rear of the building to the underground parking plaza. Jack didn't introduce him.

Scott reached out to the other man's thoughts. The guy was agitated. He normally got off at seven in the morning. He didn't know what the big deal was—Jack was plenty qualified to babysit a witness. Court didn't start until ten. They had plenty of time to drive to Lincoln by then. This guy wasn't dressed for court, anyway. Maybe they had to run him by his house to change on the way.

Scott worried. Why would they be going to Lincoln? Nobody had told him anything about court. Then it hit him. The court thing was a ruse to make the new guy think they were taking him to Lincoln. But why was the agency going to this extreme?

Jack turned to Scott and motioned toward an SUV—a Chevy

Tahoe with dark-tinted windows parked beside another just like it. "You're riding in that vehicle. We'll be following."

Scott climbed in. There were two men in the front. One held a finger to his lips for silence and motioned to the opposite passenger door, which was slightly ajar. Scott shut the driver's-side door and then slid across the seat and pushed the other door open.

A third car—a gray sedan with dark-tinted windows—was parked alongside the Tahoe. The driver's-side window was rolled down just far enough for Scott to see LuAnn in the driver's seat. She gave Scott a quick hand signal to climb into her car and rolled up the window. Scott was confused but played along, exiting the Tahoe and sliding into the rear passenger seat of LuAnn's car.

"Don't shut the door until they start their engine," she told him in a low voice.

When Scott heard the SUV's engine start, he closed the door.

"What's with all the stealth?" he asked with a soft laugh.

"Sit still and be quiet until they leave," LuAnn said.

Scott watched through the dark-tinted window as the first Tahoe backed out of the parking stall and headed for the exit. The second Tahoe waited until the first was out of the way, and then it followed.

LuAnn was alone in the front seat. "Stay in the back," she said. "I'll explain as we drive."

Scott reached for her thoughts. There was no explanation, only caution and observation. Then, finally, her thoughts and her speech became one.

"We're moving you into the formal Witness Protection Program," she explained as she put the car into gear and headed for the parking plaza exit. "We've found out a lot in three days. You were wise to suggest we put Ralph into protective custody. A couple of guards were in the process of beating the crap out of him when our people swooped in and rescued him. They probably would have killed him if we hadn't intervened. Both of those guards were arrested."

She stopped before moving from the parking lot into the street and carefully watched the traffic. After a minute, she drove into the street and made an immediate right turn at the next corner. She accelerated through the next block and took another right. As LuAnn watched behind and all around, Scott listened to her thoughts.

At the next intersection, rather than waiting for the light, she took another right and drove past the apartment building they'd left

238

only a couple of minutes before. As she approached the next intersection, she got in the left-hand turn lane and slowed until the light turned yellow. When there was no chance for the car behind her to make the light, she sped through.

"That was impressive," Scott laughed. "I'll have to remember that one."

"Sorry for all the secrecy," she said. "We had to let Jack in on our little shell game back there, but we needed the other guy to think you were being taken to Lincoln for a court hearing. The agency has identified him as a leak and needed him to throw his contacts off to make this happen."

"If you know he's dirty, why not arrest him?"

"He won't be with us for every long, but sometimes we need someone like him so we can feed information to certain third parties."

LuAnn gunned the engine and took the freeway onramp.

"What's really going on?" Scott asked.

"The agency decided to get you under deep cover as soon as they can. With Ableman and his accomplice dead, you don't have to appear in court, so it's time. We can't take the chance of them finding you, whoever they are. We haven't figured that out yet, but we're working on it."

"Where am I going?"

"I'll tell you in a few minutes. Meanwhile, I think you should know what else is going on. They found Eric, Blake, and Milt—at least what was left of them—in a burned-up car in the country. They had to identify the bodies by their dental records. So far, there's no conclusive cause of death. That and Ralph's beating convinced the agency to send us a lot more resources."

"At the site in Kansas, or with this whole investigation?"

"Both, really. They also found the alleged stolen car Vince had been driving. The agency did some stellar work there. The car had already been shredded and loaded onto a train car bound for a steel smelter. I don't know what strings they pulled to find all that out, but they impounded the entire rail car and dumped the contents to pore over it. They actually found the remains of the license plate you told us about, but more importantly, they've already identified enough parts of the car to know there was blood on the seats and in the trunk. They're cross-matching that blood to Nancy's, but we don't have any doubt we'll find a perfect match. They're isolating all the other parts and pieces of the car from the rest of the junk. Once they've done that, they're going to be looking for anything that might have Vince's fingerprints on them."

"What about the car's owner?" Scott asked.

"I was getting to that," LuAnn said. "They know who Nancy's alleged killer is. His proper name is Vincente DeLuca, otherwise known by his associates as Vince."

"Okay," Scott interjected, "that would make him of Italian descent. And that might explain the switchblade I identified as the murder weapon. The cops said it was of Italian make and fairly rare. Ralph said he was always waving it around. I'm guessing it's an heirloom, maybe handed down from father to son."

LuAnn glanced at him in the rearview. "That's good, for a civilian. I'll pass that along. I'm not sure the agency knows that. Anyway, he's listed as an employee of a national auto parts subsidiary that operates in the greater Omaha and Council Bluffs area. As you can imagine, there are a lot of players in that game. Vince hasn't been at work ever since the company car he was entrusted with was reported stolen. Nobody we've talked to has heard from him, and the cell phone registered in his name hasn't been used either. The agency has subpoenaed his phone records and are running all of those traplines. For all we know, he may have gone the way of Detective Ableman. My boss thinks that as big as this may be, he's either dead or on the run."

"I'd say the big boys are working hard to do away with anything or anyone who might be able to point a finger at them," Scott said.

"That's what we're thinking. He's been married and divorced several times, and was currently living in a lavish downtown penthouse in Omaha. Based on the wages he was being paid by his employer, we know his lifestyle cost significantly more than what he was earning. I suppose when they find him, if they find him alive, they can put him in prison for income tax evasion, if nothing else."

"What are they doing to try to connect all this to big money?" Scott asked.

"That's a much bigger problem," LuAnn said. "The agency is looking at stock holdings and financial records of not only the major players in the subsidiary but also of the major money men in the mother firm. At the same time, the street agents are looking for anything that looks, tastes, or smells like sex trafficking in the three-city area. The biggest challenge we have is, based on what we already know and what Ralph told us, these people probably deal mostly in cash. So we probably won't find any incriminating financial records."

"Cash from the sex trade, or from the drug trade?"

"Both, actually. They're often closely related. The older girls and women they 'recruit' are generally already addicts, or else they're held and injected until they are. That makes it a lot easier to control them. Unfortunately, we don't believe what you and Ralph stumbled on is related to that trade. Like what we've already discussed, we think that involves a whole different category of perverts—those who like little girls, or little boys."

"Both make me sick," Scott said.

"No argument there. But the thing with the little kids is so much more abhorrent to me. Don't get me wrong here—a lot of older girls in the sex trafficking business may have been kidnapped, but . . . well . . ."

"I get you," Scott said. "It's all sick, but in my mind, anybody found guilty of kidnapping innocent little girls or boys before they even have a chance to grow up, and then submitting them to all of those horrors, should be summarily executed."

"I could give you a list of other adjectives besides 'summarily,'" LuAnn said.

They drove in silence for a few miles. Scott watched the landscape rolling past and thought of how far from home his misadventures had taken him.

"You said the agency was moving me into the formal Witness Protection Program," Scott said. "Where exactly would that be?"

"New Jersey," LuAnn said. "You and I are going on a little road trip."

Chapter 28
New Jersey

"Why New Jersey?" Scott said. "I don't know a thing about New Jersey."

"That's the point," LuAnn said. "We're trying to hedge our bets. New Jersey has a big population, mostly urban, so it'll be easy to be invisible. The Bureau owns a home near a little town by the name of Woodstown. I think you'll like it. I've seen pictures. They tell me it has a rural flavor without being backwoodsy, but it's still close enough to metropolis so there should be plenty of good job opportunities without having to commute forever."

"What do you mean the Bureau owns a home there? Is it a drug bust seizure or something?"

"I don't know the particulars. I didn't pick the place. The system did. Suffice it to say if you keep your nose clean, it's yours free and clear. As far as the local real estate firms and the banks know, you sold a home in Connecticut and paid cash."

"Why a road trip? That's going to take forever. Can't we just fly?"

"We haven't had time to establish your new credentials yet, so we can't fly, and this case has gotten hot enough that we can't afford to wait around until we have. It's an eighteen-hour drive if we drive straight through, but they won't have things set up for a few days, so we'll take our time. If we spend about three short driving days on the road, that'll give them time to finish up. Once we get there, it'll probably take another two or three days to get you established."

"How does this work, exactly?"

"Aren't you're full of questions," LuAnn said. "Settle down, already. You may not think so, but we're on your side."

"You can't fault me for being skeptical," Scott said. "This is a life-changing event for me, and it's not like I've had a few months to think it over."

"Sorry, Scott. I know it's a lot to throw at you all at once, but we're doing the best we can. To answer your question, besides a place to live, you'll get a new name and identity, including a credit rating, Social Security number, bank account, credit card, a phone, and educational references."

"Am I still an architect? Can I still work in my trained field, or does that go away too?"

"We're working that angle. You're going to want to keep a low profile, though. I think you can still work as an architect, but you won't be able to work for a major firm. We'll establish your credentials and get you a few interviews. Until something works out, you'll get regular deposits into your new bank account to keep you going."

"What about my family?"

"We've already talked about that. For the time being, we'll tell them you're safe, but for security reasons, they won't know where you are and you won't be able to make contact. If things work out so you don't have to stay in hiding anymore, you can decide then whether you want to come back to Omaha or stay in New Jersey. Under the circumstances, I'd think it would be wise to move your family to Jersey."

Scott shook his head. He had hoped it wouldn't come to this. "Be honest with me. Do you think this is a rest-of-my-life thing, or will this blow over at some point?"

"I can't tell you that yet. You're only dangerous to the bad guys as long as they know you can put them in jail. If and when that happens, we'll have a better feel for the underpinnings. I won't lie to you, though. You've got one factor in your disfavor that may never go away. People on both sides of the table know what you can do, and you've already found out how unsettling that can be. In my humble opinion, you should plan on starting over. Hopefully, you've learned your lesson and know how to be quiet."

"That's easy for you to say," Scott said.

"No, actually, it isn't. I'm not heartless. I think I know what you're going through. I have a family, but you have a decision to make. You can slink off into obscurity, keep your gift to yourself, and start a new life. Or you can throw this all away and put both you and your family in jeopardy. It's your choice."

LuAnn was staring at him in the rearview again.

"We'll be on the road for three days," she said as she looked back at the road. "You've got at least that long to decide, but soon after we hit New Jersey, you'll have to make a decision. We're working on your credentials first, but we can't pull all of the other levers until we know you're committed."

Scott sat still and looked out the window for a few minutes. He had a lot to consider.

"So," he asked after a while, "do I have a new name yet?"

She smiled. "How does Matthew Rollins strike you?"

"That sounds like a good, common name. I suppose I could go by Matt."

He recited his new name over in his mind a few times.

"May I make a suggestion?" LuAnn said. "How would you feel about wearing a toupee?"

"I've never really thought about it. I'm not in love with the idea. I've seen some horrible rugs in my time."

"I think we could set you up with something that people would have a hard time telling from the real thing. You're at a good age for it. You don't have any gray hair yet, so they could match your natural hair color pretty well. I don't want to make you feel bad, but your head is a mess. It looks like something out of a Frankenstein movie. You don't have any identifying tattoos that we need to worry about, but that cranium. Wow. I'm sorry, but when I see you without a hat, that's the first thing I see."

Scott pulled his hat off and leaned forward so he could look at himself in the rearview. He wiped his hand cautiously across his head. "The hair's growing back pretty good," he said. "Are you sure I'll need one?"

"You might change your mind after it gets longer, but we can't risk it right now. It may have to be permanent. Those scars will never have hair on them. You might be able to do a combover, depending on how your hair lays after it grows in, but for now, you really need to consider a wig. You can't wear a hat everywhere."

"I suppose the Bureau can set me up with that?"

"I'll make a couple of calls when we stop for the night. I'm sure somebody will know somebody. That's what we're good at."

"Speaking of stopping for the night," Scott said, "I assume we'll have the same sleeping arrangements as we did in Topeka?"

"I think that worked out okay, don't you?" she said. "Besides, I told Jack to get you a pair of pajamas. That should make things a little less awkward. The Bureau gave me a different credit card and I.D. We'll be staying as Mr. and Mrs. Peyton."

"Speaking of a credit card trail," Scott said, "you said you had a leak. Aren't you worried that might go deeper than you think? What if somebody already knows about your new false identity? Do you have enough money to get us there?"

"No," she said, "but that's not a bad thought. I'll stop and get some cash."

Scott listened as a few thoughts rattled around in her head.

"We've got enough gas to get us to Des Moines," she said. "I'll stop at a bank and pick up a couple of thousand in cash. I don't have to worry about the return trip. I had planned on flying out of Wilmington, Delaware. I'll check in with the agency when we get you settled. I'll have them get me a boarding pass with somebody else's name on it."

"What'll you do with the car?"

"It's yours. We'll have it registered in your new name."

"That's cool. I've always wanted a Lexus, but I could never afford one."

"This one is a little special," LuAnn said. "The GPS system has been disabled, so even if we have a leak, they won't be able to track you. It has a clean title. There's nothing that might lead back to a drug seizure or anything like that, so nobody will be able to trace it back to the Bureau."

"Sounds like you've covered everything."

"We've done this a few times," LuAnn said.

Scott shifted uncomfortably. "Hey, do you think I might get to ride up front like a first-class citizen when we stop in the city?"

"I think we can do that," LuAnn said, "but you can't drive. The last thing we need is for you to get stopped for speeding or something stupid like that. I have to assume that you've still got your wallet with your real driver's license in it?"

"I do."

"I think we need to get rid of that as soon as we stop. You're no longer Scott Corbridge from Omaha."

* * * * *

They stopped for the night in Marseilles, Illinois, a few miles outside of Joliet. Knowing they couldn't stay in a major hotel chain without using her credit card, Scott used LuAnn's smartphone to find a room at a one-star travel lodge for under eighty bucks a night. The twenty-something clerk didn't bat an eye when they offered cash instead of a credit card.

"I'm really afraid of what we're going to find inside," LuAnn said as they carried their luggage up to their second-floor room. "We're checking for bedbugs first thing."

"I'm sure that guy is wondering why we're driving a Lexus and paying cash for a low-rent room," Scott said.

"Oh, I don't know about that," LuAnn said with a sly smile. "I'm sure at these prices, they're used to renting that room several times a night. They probably won't think twice about the car. Rich guys cheat too. They might wonder about the luggage, though. I doubt many couples renting a room by the hour carry in much luggage."

"I worry about the car," Scott said. "That'd be a fine howdy-doo if somebody swiped it during the night."

LuAnn held up a device that looked like an electronic chip. "Without this, it's not going anywhere," she said. "This is an add-on provided by the Bureau. It's not a stock Lexus thing, so even if somebody breaks in and messes with the ignition, it'll never start."

Scott keyed the motel room lock and pushed the door open. The room stank of stale tobacco and old coffee grounds.

"Oh, lovely," LuAnn said. "I'll bet there's buckets of tiny livestock living in those mattresses."

"You mean *the* mattress, I assume," Scott said as he glanced quickly around the room.

"You didn't get a double?" she fumed. "It looks like you'll be sleeping on the couch."

"There isn't one."

"Then I hope the carpet isn't crawling with vermin, because you'll be sleeping on the floor."

Scott picked up the room phone and dialed the office. When he hung up, he started studying the floor for the least-traveled part of the carpet.

"What are you doing?" LuAnn asked.

"Picking out a place to sleep. They only have a dozen doubles, and they're all booked."

Without saying another word, LuAnn dropped her luggage by the side of the bed and ripped all the sheets off the bed.

"What are you doing?" Scott asked.

"Looking for bedbugs. I was dead serious when I mentioned them earlier. You can find them in the best motels. I'm not taking any chances here."

Together, they searched the edges of the mattress and along the headboard. Then they slid the mattress off to one side and checked around all of the edges of the box springs.

"That's amazing!" LuAnn said. "I don't see anything."

"Maybe nobody stays here long enough to feed them."

"You've got a point there."

She tossed the blanket and comforter onto the floor in the corner. "I wouldn't touch those if I were you. They might wash the sheets after each use, but I'm betting those haven't been touched in weeks. If you looked at them under a blacklight, you'd probably puke."

"I'll fold them up and use them for a mattress," Scott said. "They can't be dirtier than the carpet."

"You can pick your dirt, I suppose, but I'd pick roach droppings over human filth any day."

"I'll shower before we leave."

"Speaking of showers," LuAnn said, "it's muggy in here. See if the air conditioner works."

Scott flipped the switch, but nothing happened.

"Oh, great," LuAnn said. "I guess that's a good thing, though. You won't have to pull one of those filthy blankets over you."

"You're really on one," he teased.

"Sorry. It's just nerves. This isn't going exactly as planned."

Scott's mind caught on a thought. "About your cell phone. If that has a GPS device in it, isn't it traceable?"

"It's not my phone."

"I suppose it's a company loaner, like the credit card?" he said to make a point. "They could follow that phone right to this room. Are you sure it's secure?"

LuAnn tossed her suitcase onto the bed, unzipped it, and pulled out a small makeup bag. Scott watched as she used a nail file and a small eyeglass screwdriver to take her phone apart. Then she stuffed her disabled phone and its separate battery into her makeup bag.

"Grab your bag," she said. "You're right about the trace. Ordinarily, I wouldn't worry about it. But we still don't know how much our leak knows. It looks like we'll be sleeping in a rest stop."

"Isn't that a little risky in a big town?"

"We'll sleep in shifts."

"Then we'll essentially be driving straight through. Maybe we could crash in my new house until they've got my credentials all worked out."

"We've already been on the road over seven hours. I'm beat."

"Then we'll drive until we find a place, and I'll keep watch while you sleep."

She tugged the zipper closed on her suitcase. "That might work. We'll need to pick up a road atlas at our next gas stop. I'd planned on using my phone to navigate."

"What if your boss needs to get ahold of you?"

She looked at her watch. "It's probably too late today, but we'll stop somewhere tomorrow and buy a burner phone. Then we'll find a landline somewhere and I'll call in my new number. That way, he'll have my number if he needs to reach me, but I won't compromise the phone by using it to call in. What makes me sick is, if they're tracking us, they already know we're just outside of Joliet."

"Chicago's a big town," Scott said. "Now that you've gone dark, they won't know if we're staying here or going on to Wisconsin, or Michigan, or someplace else. There's a lot of country between here and New Jersey."

"Look at you, standing there and being all optimistic," LuAnn said. "I'm beginning to think that letting our known leak think we were going to Lincoln was a really bad idea. That only served to draw attention to ourselves. When that guy figures out we hoodwinked him on purpose, he'll put the word out and somebody might do some serious looking."

"Look on the bright side," Scott said. "At least we figured all of this out before you pulled up at my new house in Jersey."

He noticed the hotel clerk watching them as they loaded their luggage back in the trunk. Scott smiled. LuAnn had been right about their bags. They'd been in the room less than an hour. That part fit; the luggage didn't. The maid, or whoever went into the room to ready it for its next hourly occupants, would probably wonder what had happened when they found the mattress stripped.

LuAnn stopped at a local gas station and filled up before they made their way back to the freeway.

"Next time we stop for gas," she said, "we'll pull off the freeway. We can't risk stopping at a major truck stop. If somebody decides to use surveillance videos to track us, now that we've gone dark, that's the first place they'll look."

"What about rest stops? Don't they have cameras there?"

"Not very often, and when they do, they're generally set up to watch the vending machines. You better try to get a little sleep. I'll wake you when I need to stop."

Scott laid the seat back and closed his eyes, but he couldn't sleep. He entertained himself by listening to LuAnn's thoughts as she drove. Until they got through the major Chicago metropolitan area and took an interchange headed for South Bend, Illinois, her thoughts mostly dealt with traffic and direction finding. Occasionally, they switched to other things: her family, Scott, the bodies they'd found in Kansas.

He sat up when he felt the car slow. "Where are we?" he asked as he adjusted his seat and looked around.

"Porter, Indiana, wherever that is. I need a coffee and a bathroom. That hotel room was so disgusting, I couldn't go while we were there, and I was too keyed up when we got gas. I'm about to explode. We might as well get gas while we're here. I'll stop at the desk and get the pump activated. If you'll be so kind as to fill it up, when I'm done, I'll watch while you go."

When Scott came out of the restroom, LuAnn was standing at the checkout counter, arms filled with munchies. Scott picked up a road atlas from a nearby display case.

"They've got some hot dogs and chicken," she said when he joined her, "but they looked disgusting. Maybe we can find something better before we stop for the night."

"I'd think you would want to stop pretty soon. Aren't you tired?"

"I'm going to be buzzed on coffee pretty soon. I'll let you know when it's time."

When they got back in the car, Scott settled back in his seat, flipped on the overhead map light, and found Illinois in the atlas. "I assume we'll be sticking to I-80?" he asked.

"That's the most direct route. As I recall, it will take us all the way to New York City, but somewhere before then, we need to dip south. It might be smart to drop south earlier and get away from I-80. That might not be the fastest way, but we're not pressed for time."

Scott studied the atlas. "From what I'm seeing on the map, you could take I-75 south near Toledo and then catch I-70 east from there. I-70 hits I-76 somewhere in Pennsylvania. I don't know where that little town is you were talking about in New Jersey, but I-76 goes all the way to Atlantic City."

"I see your lips moving," she laughed, "but I didn't understand a thing you just said. You navigate, I'll drive."

"Just look for the I-75 south as we're getting close to Toledo."

"Okay," she said. "I just saw a road sign that says it's two hundred miles to Toledo. Two hundred miles is what, about three hours? I'll probably need to stop before then. Look for a rest stop."

Scott studied the map for a couple of minutes. "I see gas stops, but no rest stops, per se. It looks pretty populated. We may not find one."

"We'll play it by ear, then. Maybe they're just not listed on the map. If nothing else, I suppose we'll have to dive off the freeway and see if we can find another roach motel somewhere now that we're not being tracked. It's already been a long day. I don't know how much longer I can drive."

"There's a lot of little towns along the way. Why don't we pick one now and not take the risk of you falling asleep at the wheel?" Scott suggested.

"Okay, I see there's an exit coming up for Chesterton. How brave do you feel?"

"You're the one with the gun. I'm not afraid."

"You know what I mean."

Before he could answer, she'd taken the exit. A few minutes later, they spotted the sign for an Econo Lodge. The neon vacancy sign glowed a welcome as they drove up in front.

Much to their delight, there was a double available. The clerk gladly accepted cash, and a half hour later they were both tucked away between the apparently bedbug-less sheets.

* * * * *

When Scott woke up in the morning, he could hear the shower running. He was tempted to get up, but he'd need to use the john if he did, and he was sure the bathroom door was locked.

"Matt Rollins," he said aloud. "That's not a bad name. It rolls easily off the tongue."

The name itself wouldn't draw any undue attention to him. He worried about the educational credentials they were working on. He wondered how the feds did that. Maybe they had the ability to hack into a school's computer system and create records.

LuAnn walked out of the bathroom wearing a towel.

"Turn your head," she said. "I forgot my undies."

"Then get dressed out here," he said. "I'm about to explode."

"Sorry. These sleeping arrangements are really awkward. Maybe we'll just stop at a rest stop tonight."

"You said yourself we had three easy days to get there," Scott said. "I think being in an awkward position once a day trumps sleeping in the car alongside the road. I'm not a pervert, and I know you're happily married. I can respect your privacy."

He closed the bathroom door behind him, and when he was finished, he took a quick shower. He got dressed before he opened the door. When he stepped back out into the room, he could smell food.

"The motel has a little breakfast bar. I got you a breakfast burrito and a coffee. I hope that's alright."

"The burrito is fine," he said, "but I shouldn't drink the coffee. Since my wreck, I even have a problem with the caffeine in soft drinks. I get the jitters, and my messed-up head doesn't like that. I don't want to have a seizure."

"Sorry, I didn't know that. If you'll load up the suitcases, I'll get you a juice."

She tossed him the keys.

It was raining when they hit the freeway. The dismal day weighed heavily on Scott. He tried to carry on a conversation but after a while, he could tell LuAnn had a lot of private things on her mind, so he turned inward. He worried about his family. He wondered if they were still in hiding, or if Trish had talked Mary into going back home. He worried about Vince and his organization.

Suddenly, a random thought popped into his mind. Then he realized it was more than a thought. It was almost like the murder scene he'd seen—and the trip out to the well, and the gravesite. He saw a shovel—a short-handled shovel with a loop handle. It was in a garden shed in the back yard of a mansion. There was a car parked in the driveway. He could see the Nebraska plate and the number. He felt Nancy in the car with him . . . or at least her thoughts.

"I need a pen and something to write on," Scott said.

"You making a grocery list?" LuAnn laughed.

"Don't ask, I need to remember something."

"There's one in my purse."

He found a pen, but instead of searching for something to write on, he scrawled the plate number on the palm of his hand while it was still fresh on his mind.

"What are you doing?" LuAnn said.

"Nancy was here. I know where the shovel is that Vince used to bury her."

LuAnn stared at him for a few seconds and then looked back at the road. "And what—you wrote the address on your hand?"

"No, it's a license plate number. You need to call your boss."

"I disabled my phone."

"Then we need to find a landline. This wasn't a casual visit. Every time she haunts me, something important has happened or needs to happen. She showed me a shovel in a garden shed in the back yard of a mansion. This plate number is on a car parked in the driveway. I think if your boss can find that shovel, he can link her murder to Vince's boss."

"I swear, if I hadn't seen you in action, I'd drop you off at a psych ward. Are you sure about this? Because if the agency gets a warrant, there better be something there or your credibility is shot."

"All I can tell you is if I ignore her, I won't be able to sleep. In fact, she'll just drive me nuts until I do something. I wasn't asleep, but I saw that shovel, the shed, the mansion, and the car as clearly as if she'd hauled me there in spirit and walked me around the yard."

LuAnn glanced in the rearview, signaled, and took the next exit. There was a truck stop off to the right of the exit a hundred yards down the road. She pulled in.

"I thought we couldn't risk the security cameras," Scott said.

"You're the one who's all spun up over this. I figured this was urgent. The cameras are generally on the fuel island. We might not draw any attention just walking into the lounge."

They asked at the fuel desk if there was a landline they could use. The clerk directed them to the trucker's lounge, where a short row of pay phones hung on one wall.

LuAnn made the call and then handed Scott the phone. Howard listened patiently as Scott recited what he'd seen.

"I know better than to question you," Howard said when Scott finished, "but where are you?"

"I shouldn't say. On the road somewhere."

"I tried to call LuAnn's phone a while ago. The call wouldn't go through."

"She pulled the battery. She's afraid somebody might be able to track her."

"Let me talk to her," Howard said.

Scott handed the phone back to LuAnn and listened as she explained why they were being so secretive. When she finished, Scott followed her to the car without asking any questions.

"You were right," she said when they closed the car doors. "He was trying to call me to tell me that I may have been compromised. He was pretty happy when he found out I wasn't using my phone or credit cards. The leak is evidently a lot bigger than Howard thought it was. He's worried now how much the bad guys know about the case. He told me to call again in a couple of hours, but to keep it short like this time."

"What about my new house?" Scott asked as they headed back for the freeway. "Will Guido and his happy band of thugs be waiting for me in the closet?"

"For now, we have to assume not. But we should know more in a couple of hours."

They took the I-75 exit out of Toledo a little while later and pulled off the freeway near Bowling Green for gas. Their two hours weren't up yet, so they ate lunch in a small café. There was a pay phone in the back near the restrooms. LuAnn made a few quick notes as she listened, then hung up.

"He wants me to call back in a half hour," she said. "He has more to tell us, but he's worried about getting our call traced. He gave me another number to call. I think that's a headquarters number. It should be secure."

"Do we head down the road for another half hour, or just kill some more time here?"

"I need to buy a burner phone, but I don't think we'll have time to go shopping before we need to call him back."

"When we stopped at that last truck stop, I noticed a display at the front counter that had phones. I thought you'd seen them."

"Sorry, I didn't. Maybe we could risk stopping at another truck stop. It would save time. I suppose we could have dessert and just relax. We've been on the road what—three and a half hours already? I don't know if there's a place like this further south. Pay phones are nice, but you don't find them on every street corner anymore."

A half hour later, LuAnn called Howard back. Scott leaned close to the receiver so he could hear what was being said.

"I won't even ask how you knew about that shovel," Howard said, "but we served a warrant after you called. We found the shovel right where you said it'd be. If I didn't know better, I'd think Scott had planted it there."

He paused to let Scott offer an explanation. When he offered none, Howard continued. "At first blush, it looked like the handle had been wiped clean, but when we sprayed some luminol on the wooden loop handle, it lit up like a Christmas tree. The handle is made out of oak. Oak is an open-grain wood. Fortunately for us, simply wiping it clean doesn't clean the grain. Not only did it check positive for blood, but we got a partial fingerprint on the lower handle. Thanks to you two, the shovel is on its way to the lab and Legal is working with the judge to get a warrant for Vince's penthouse apartment. The subsidiary has a long-term lease on it and pays the lease, utilities, and maintenance. Evidently, Vince lived there gratis. We've pulled his financial records and have found no indication he was making any rent payments to the company on either the apartment or the car he was driving, so that implicates his boss. There's a private elevator that goes from the underground parking terrace to the penthouse. We find that very convenient, if you know what I mean. We're betting we'll find a wealth of DNA evidence in that penthouse. With any kind of luck, we may find a match to one of those kids in Kansas."

Howard paused for a few seconds. They could hear a muffled conversation with someone else in the room.

"I'm assuming the blood we found on the shovel will be Nancy's," he said when he came back on the line. "We're hoping the partial print belongs to Vince. The important thing now is we've got a hard link between Vince and his boss. I'm a little disappointed, though, that we haven't been able to establish a link yet between him and any other significant players. Maybe there is no connection. The good thing for now is we have probable cause to continue our investigation further up his management chain."

"What's next?" LuAnn asked after a short pause.

"Same plan as before. When we start pointing fingers, people are going to squirm. The opposition already knows about Scott. Word on the street is there's a significant reward being offered for his whereabouts. I think the rats know if they have to sit anywhere near Scott, he'll find out all their dirty secrets. Keeping him safe is a major priority."

"For how long?" Scott asked.

"I wish I knew the answer to that question. I've just been given a lot more resources. We're also teaming up with some other organizations that work with the sexual exploitation of minors. We're getting a lot of help, but I can't tell you this won't be a lengthy investigation."

"I don't suppose you've found Vince yet, have you?" LuAnn asked.

"No, and we may never find him. Unless he's tightly connected, he may be at the bottom of the river for all we know. The DeLuca name is not unknown among the major crime syndicates, though, so for all we know he may already be out of the country."

"Should we maintain radio silence, so to speak?" LuAnn asked. "Or should we check in from time to time?"

"Call when you pick up a phone so I'll know your new number. Then I can call you if I need something. It's better that you get on with the original plan as soon as you can."

"See you soon, then," LuAnn said as she hung up the phone.

They hurried back outside to the car. "Well," LuAnn said when she started the car, "let's hit one more truck stop and buy a phone, and then spend another four hours or so on the road. I think your recommendation to go south to I-70 sooner rather than later is a good plan. If they're brazen enough to offer a reward for you, they must be getting pretty desperate. It shouldn't take much probing by the feds to find out who's offering the rewards. That might help them connect a few more dots."

"What are the chances that someone knows what we're driving?" Scott asked. "If I were crime king for the day and knew what the guy I was looking for was driving, I'd put the word out on the major interstates. There's several million trucker's eyes at any one time on the freeways. A gray Lexus with black-tinted windows isn't a real common vehicle."

"I guess that could happen," she said. "We can't trade cars, but maybe we should switch routes."

"You told me we've got the time. That might be a smart thing to do."

"Look at the road atlas, then, and find me an alternate route."

"Look for State Road 30," Scott said after scanning the atlas. "It goes straight across the middle of the state from I-75 all the way into Pennsylvania. It looks like it gets curvy in places and probably won't have a very high speed limit, but it'll probably be scenic. When it gets dark, we may want to find a small-town hotel somewhere so we have less of a chance of nailing a deer or something."

"The only problem I have with little roads like that is they're fraught with small-town cops and speed traps," LuAnn said.

"All the more reason to take our time and not travel after dark."

They stopped twice for gas and found a small hotel when she got too tired to drive. The next morning, they lost Highway 30 in Pittsburg and ended up on I-70, but by then there was so much congestion and traffic that they decided to stay on the freeway. I-70 eventually became I-76, and they followed that into New Jersey. They arrived right on schedule. Although they'd kept their pre-paid phone plugged in and active, they hadn't heard a word from Howard.

LuAnn called the agency when they hit Jersey and got directions to Scott's house. Two agents met them at the house with the keys and the rest of Scott's documentation. At that point, they destroyed Scott's driver's license and he officially became Matthew Rollins.

LuAnn spent another day there, working out the kinks—one of which included a fine new hairpiece for "Matt."

They left him alone on a hot, late-August morning with the Lexus, a couple of emergency contacts, a new smartphone, and a lot of specific instructions about what it meant to be in the Witness Protection Program.

Chapter 29
<u>Vince</u>

Scott did his best to navigate around his new neighborhood using his new smartphone, but after getting lost repeatedly, he found himself at a Lexus dealer having his navigational system fixed. After that, his new ride talked him flawlessly to each of a half-dozen job interviews. He got a callback on two and was finally offered a job with a medium-sized architectural firm in Millville.

By late September, Scott had settled into his new identity as Matt Rollins, and the newness of the job had worn off. He was well liked because he was self-motivated and willing to do the crap jobs nobody else wanted to do. He judiciously guarded his secret "gift," knowing he'd ruin everything if anybody figured him out this time. He found the same frustrations haunting him on the job that had encouraged him to split off and start his own firm in Omaha, but the thing that kept him going to work every day in spite of the stress on the job was the realization he was financially secure and reasonably safe.

Thoughts of his family haunted him night and day. He watched Facebook religiously, looking for any indication that his family had stepped away from the system. He heard nothing until he got a piece of mail from Paul, forwarded to him from the agency, informing him that his divorce to Mary had been finalized. LuAnn had added a personal note that until further notice, the agency would cover the financial obligations awarded by the court to Mary and the kids. They didn't want anyone to be able to follow the money trail.

Scott's new home was pleasant enough; large and homey, but very quiet and empty. When he got the notice from Paul about the divorce, he spent all day Saturday just driving.

Nancy came to him that night as he lay awake trying to deal with the loss of his family and trying to decide what he should do with the rest of his life. There were no lights, no apparition, no voices. He just had a profound feeling that he needed to go to Atlantic City and play poker.

He smiled at the thought. He loved to play poker, but he hadn't sat in on a game since he and Alan had started up their business. Then he realized he had a decided advantage. He'd know what the other players in the game were thinking. It was cheating in its worst form, but he was intrigued. If he was cautious, he could lose just often enough to make it appear he was simply incredibly lucky.

LuAnn had left him nearly a thousand dollars of the cash she'd withdrawn from the bank to cover their travel expenses, which would give him enough seed money to get rolling. The thought of going to Atlantic City kept him awake most of the night. It was just before eight in the morning when his phone rang.

"Matt Rollins?" a woman asked.

"Hi, LuAnn," he replied. "Long time no hear. What's going on in your world?"

"Howard called me late last night," she said. "He doesn't know how to get in touch with you, so I told him I'd pass along what the agency has turned up." She hesitated before continuing.

"Is it that bad?" he asked.

"No, no. I'm just trying to decide where to begin. Okay, first the thing with Ralph. He's in FBI protective custody and doing well. He's worked with a police sketch artist and has identified eight female accomplices. The agency knows where three of them are and have them under surveillance. They found a total of a hundred and twenty-seven bodies, including eleven in the river. They found a lot more cement blocks than that, but he'd used bailing wire to tie the bodies to the blocks. When the wire rusted through, the current during the spring runoff probably carried away what was left. They've only identified seventeen of the bodies they found in his graveyard through DNA analysis. All of those were young girls. Some had been missing for seven or eight years, others for only two or three."

"What about Vince's penthouse?"

"I was getting to that. They didn't find a lot at first until they opened up the shower and sink drains. They found a lot of hair, but there's no DNA matches to any of the girls they found in Kansas. They're thinking the hair may have belonged to some of Vince's girlfriends, or his accomplices, or possibly some other victims, but until they get a positive match, they really don't have a lot. Vince must have left in a hurry. He had an extensive wardrobe. They said he had very expensive tastes, whatever that means, but they found an expensive leather belt that had stains on it. The stains were found in the stitching. They were able to get a positive DNA match to

Nancy."

LuAnn abruptly changed the subject. "Oh, yeah," she said, "the blood on the shovel was Nancy's, and the partial print was a perfect match to a print they took from Vince's hairbrush. They're leaning on his boss, but nothing has come of that yet. He probably feels pretty safe as long as Vince stays missing. DeLuca has been put on the FBI's Ten Most Wanted list, but they haven't had any hits yet."

"Is there still a reward on my head?"

"No, that's died down. The agent who leaked the information that you were being put in the Witness Protection Program has been caught and incarcerated. I think they knew who he was before he ratted you out, so it was easy to catch him."

"What about my family?"

"That's where things get a little sticky. Once your divorce was final, Mary chose to move back into your house. The agency still has them all under surveillance, and they will be until they break this case. But I've got to tell you, that isn't easy. Our agents have had to turn to clandestine surveillance. Mary thinks we're overreacting. She refuses bodyguards or any visible surveillance."

"Is she seeing Alan?"

"Who?"

"My ex-partner, Alan Stiver. They were having an affair."

"I didn't know that. Do you want me to find out?"

"No," he said. "The only reason I wonder is that I asked her to break it off so she wouldn't ruin his marriage."

"She got a protective order issued against you when the judge granted the divorce. I think her attorney suggested that as a ploy to show the bad guys you were no longer in her life."

"I guess if I were in her shoes, I might feel the same way. I'm a pretty scary person, when you think about it."

"I don't think so, and I spent almost a week with you in various bedrooms. I don't think you're a threat at all."

"Not as long as you know that you can't keep any secrets from me."

"You've learned to hide that well. I wasn't intimidated by you at all."

"I was on my best behavior when I was with you. I didn't want to screw up anybody else's life."

"You wouldn't have. I'm secure in my marriage."

"Are you sure?" Scott asked. "I know what you were feeling that day on the site."

"What I was feeling was empathy for all those poor little girls," LuAnn snapped. "If you got something else from that, you were wrong."

"I'm sorry. You're right."

"How's the job going? I hear you got one."

"It's okay, but it reminds me of all the reasons why I started my own business. Sometimes it's hard to work with a bunch of other architects. Everybody has their own ideas about what is productive and what isn't."

"What are you doing to stay out of trouble?"

"Nothing much. I'm going to Atlantic City today, though, to do a little gambling. I had a visit from a very persistent spirit last night."

"Nancy?"

"Who else?"

"What happened?"

"She more or less told me to go to Atlantic City today and play poker at some casino. I didn't catch the name, but I'm sure I'll know it when I see it."

"Why would she tell you that?"

"She probably knows I can make a killing at the poker table if I'm careful. Maybe she's feeling guilty about ruining my life and wants to make amends."

"I really don't like the sounds of that," she said. "You and Nancy don't exactly have a history of being good for one another."

"Probably not," Scott agreed, "but she won't leave me alone until I do what she tells me."

"I'll tell you what," LuAnn said, "put me on speed dial. If something happens, ring me up and just tell me to send in the cavalry. In case you've forgotten, I have contacts there."

"To tell you the truth, I haven't felt very good about doing this, but I figured it's because somebody will catch me cheating and shoot me or something."

"This isn't the old wild west," she laughed. "They don't string up gamblers anymore, and I doubt firearms are allowed on the premises."

"Aren't you late for church or something?" he asked.

"Actually, I need to leave pretty soon. I'll call you tonight."

Scott thought about his family after he got off the phone. Church was the one place they'd always been together ever since the kids were little. Even Trish didn't mind going. He wondered what they'd do if he just appeared in services one day.

* * * * *

Atlantic City was bustling. It was afternoon before Scott got there. Nancy appeared to be riding along, because when he saw the casino he identified it immediately. The drive had left him hungry, so he took advantage of the smorgasbord and ate a good meal before he went looking for the poker tables.

Not ever having played poker in a casino, he stood and watched for about an hour before a player decided he'd had enough and left the game. Nobody else jumped in to fill his vacancy, so Scott offered a fistful of money and was given a stack of chips and a seat at the table.

There was so much going on around the table that it was hard for him to concentrate at first, but after several hands, he began to get the hang of the game. It was challenging, to say the least. Even though he might know what the other players were holding, the cards often didn't treat him well. When his hand sucked, he'd minimize his bet. When the cards were there, he'd pile it on. It didn't take long for the others in the game to figure him out, so when he did win a hand, there wasn't much in the pot.

Recognizing his mistake, he started playing on their thoughts. He won three out of five hands on crap cards before the game shifted again. From there on, he simply played wise. He could pick and choose his hands. When he finally got up to take a break, he was up nearly a thousand dollars.

On his way to the john, he passed a table where the chips were all a different color. He paused to watch and was politely asked by a rugged-looking man in a casino sports jacket to move along. It was a high-stakes game, and the players didn't like "looky-loos" watching the table.

He stopped by the roulette wheel on the way back to the poker tables and watched for a while. Finally realizing there was nothing he could do there, he began sauntering through the mass of bodies on the casino floor. This time, when he reached the high-stakes table, there were three men in jackets placed strategically around it to keep the crowd back a few paces. He could read the thoughts of a nearby guard. There was big money on the table. He tried to keep moving but was blocked for a few seconds while a small, snakelike movement of people in single file moved past the guards.

Scott glanced to his right and his breath caught in his throat.

261

Vince was seated at the table. His broad, hairy fingers were clutching a couple of cards. A long, white, hairless scar stretched the length of one of his fingers.

As soon as he was able to move past the table, Scott reached instinctively for his phone. LuAnn answered on the second ring.

"Send in the cavalry," he said quietly. "Vince is at the high-stakes poker table."

"Are you sure?"

"I'm positive. Unless he has a twin, he looks just like that composite drawing I gave the cops."

"Keep him in sight," she said. "Somebody will call you."

Scott held his phone in his hand so he wouldn't miss the buzz when it rang. Time screeched to a halt. His head pounded. Sweat trickled down between his shoulder blades. He wanted to stare at the men at the table, but he couldn't. He didn't know if Vince even knew who he was, but he didn't dare take the chance.

Then a thought occurred to him. How had the bad guys put a bounty on him in Omaha without knowing what he looked like? Somebody somewhere had to have pictures of him. Then it dawned on him: If they knew he had an architectural firm, they most certainly had his photo. Photos of him and Alan were plastered across the yellow pages, as well as on placards on the door of their business. There were probably countless other ways they could have got a picture of him. The real question was: Had Vince actually seen any of those photos?

Scott nearly dropped his phone when it buzzed. "Hello," he answered.

"Is this Matt Rollins?" a man asked.

"It is."

"Can you still see the suspect?"

"There's a few guards around the high-stakes poker game," Scott said, just loud enough for the man to hear him over the din of the crowd. "They're keeping people back, so I'm standing a few yards away. It's crowded in here. I haven't seen him for a few minutes, but I haven't seen anyone leave the table."

"I will be one of four officers who will be on scene within about ten minutes. We will need you to identify the man for us. We have requested a photo download from headquarters, but we haven't seen one yet."

"Where should I meet you?"

"Stay where you can see the man. If he moves, try to stay with him. We'll call again when we get to the main lobby. We'll be in plain clothes, but we'll all be wearing light-blue blazers with a gold pin on the lapel that looks like a golf ball. How can we identify you?"

"I don't know," Scott said, "let me think. I'm wearing Levi's and a dark-blue shirt. I have medium-brown hair and am wearing a hairpiece. It's a good one, though, so you may not know it's a rug. I'll hang out by the high-stakes table unless he moves, and then I'll call this number and try to keep you on the phone. Meanwhile, I'll try to keep an eye on him, but it isn't going to be easy."

"We're en route," the man said.

"He's on the FBI's top-ten fugitives list," Scott said. "As a last resort, can't you just have the casino security catch and hold him until you can get here?"

"Is he armed?"

"I don't know that. I do know he ordinarily carries a switchblade. If they've got metal detectors here, he may not have it on him, though."

"We'll see what we can do. Please let us know if he moves."

Scott moved back toward the table. This time, in contrast to the rest of the crowd in the casino, those who could see the table had grown silent, mesmerized by what was going on.

One of the casino guards intercepted him as he crowded his way closer to the table. "Hey," the guard said roughly, "I thought I told you to move along."

"Sorry," Scott said, "I . . . well, never mind. I'll leave."

He tried to see Vince's face through the crowd as he slowly moved a few paces away, but all he could see was a wall of heads—all sizes, shapes, and colors, all turned to watch the spectacle at the table. Instead of standing near the crowd, he spaced himself off a few paces and watched the crowd. If anyone from the table left, he figured the crowd would shift.

Agonizingly long minutes slipped away. He looked down at the phone in his hand a dozen times. Each time, only one or two minutes had passed. When it finally buzzed, he eagerly held it to his ear.

"Matt?" a man asked.

"Speaking."

"We're here. Casino security has been alerted. We did get a photo of the suspect off the net, and the pit boss has that photo. We'll try to be as unobtrusive as possible, but I'd like you to positively identify him when we move in."

"The table has three casino guards around it," Scott said. "One of them told me to shove off twice. I don't want to cause a scene. I'm standing about thirty feet to the right of the table. I'll watch for you."

"We'll move on the table from different directions, hopefully to keep him from feeling threatened. We want to avoid a hostage situation at all costs. Leave your phone open. I'm wearing an earbud so we can talk."

Scott tried not to act nervous, but it wasn't easy. He wanted to whip his head back and forth watching for the agents but instead kept his head forward and moved his eyes from side to side. He spotted the bullish guard watching him. He almost turned to leave. The last thing he needed was a blow to the head.

Then, suddenly, the crowd around the table erupted in cheers. Somebody must have won big. After the cheer, a number of the crowd began to move away from the table. The guard held his hand to his ear as if he were trying to hear something that was coming through his earpiece.

Someone touched Scott on the elbow. He wheeled around to see a man in a light-blue jacket standing behind him. A golden pin looking like a miniature golf ball stood out from his right lapel.

"Matt?" he asked.

"Yes."

"Come with me," he said as he moved toward the bullish guard. Matt followed the agent as closely as he could without walking on the backs of the man's shoes. Out of the corner of his eye, Scott could see another similarly attired man moving in from the right. As they approached him, the guard reached for a sap that was hanging on his belt.

Scott stepped back. The agent leading the way held up something for the guard to see, and the guard turned and pushed his way toward the table with the agent in tow. Seconds later, the sounds of a scuffle broke out and the crowd around the table scattered.

Vince was on his feet, facing seven men standing at various angles and distances from him. He held a knife in his right hand. A millisecond later, the officer who had touched him on the elbow drew a Taser from his belt and shot Vince in the chest. Vince went stiff and tipped over backwards.

The second he hit the floor, all seven men rushed him. A long minute later, they bodily pulled Vince to his feet. His eyes were darting wildly around in their sockets.

An agent looked at the crowd, then spotted Scott and motioned him forward. "Is this the suspect?" he asked as Scott walked within six feet of the man he'd seen a thousand times in his dreams.

"That's him," Scott said. "Please be careful with that knife. If it's a double-edged switchblade where the blade retracts into the handle, it's a murder weapon and may have evidence in it or on it that will link him to a murder he committed in Omaha."

The agent held up the knife. The blade looked right.

"Pull the slide back on the handle," Scott said.

The agent did what he said, and the silvery blade disappeared slowly into the handle.

"That's the knife," Scott said.

The agent reached in his back pocket and pulled out a rubber glove. He dropped the knife in the glove and tied the open end of the glove shut over the handle. A large crowd of spectators stood watching.

"I'm sure I don't need to tell you that he's a flight risk," Scott said. "He's been a fugitive for a little over two months. I'm sure your agency in Omaha would love to fly out and pick him up."

The casino guard stepped toward Scott. "Hey, I'm sorry," he said, "I had no idea—"

"Forget it," Scott said, offering a handshake. "I'm just glad you didn't hit me with that sap. It probably would have killed me. I've got a plate in my head the size of a dessert plate."

Vince's eyes bored into Scott. The hatred that flowed out of him instantly matched the vision Scott had seen standing behind Nancy in his dream.

Scott turned to the agent. "I need to get out of here before somebody takes my picture, if you know what I mean."

"It's too late for that," the agent said. "I'm sure the pit boss has everything on video. I understand where you're coming from, though. I'll see what I can do."

"By the way," Scott asked the casino guard as he turned to leave, "who won?"

The casino guard grinned. "I think the house did. There was over fifty grand in the pot, but if that guy is a felon, it'll all be confiscated by the house."

"Lucky house," Scott muttered as he turned to make his way through the crowd. He'd nearly made it to the front entrance when two other men in casino jackets stopped him.

"Could we have a word with you?" one of the men asked.

"I should really be going."

"I think you'll like what we have to say."

"You want to talk here?" Scott asked.

"We'd rather do it in private."

"Do I need to have one of my agents with me?"

"No, it's not like that," the man said. "I'm sorry, we didn't mean to seem aggressive. The pit boss would just like a word with you."

One man led the way to an elevator door. The other followed closely behind. The first flashed a card across a reader on the door frame and the door pulled open. They stepped inside, and Scott felt a floating sensation as the elevator rose a couple of floors. When the door rolled open, half a dozen men were waiting. One stepped forward and offered his hand.

"Hi," he said. "They call me Jasper to my face. I don't really care what they call me behind my back. Who might you be?"

"My name is Matthew," Scott said, "but my friends call me Matt."

"I'd like you to look at something with me if you don't mind," Jasper said and motioned to a bank of computer screens. "We like to watch our poker players. We couldn't help but notice you. It was obvious to us that you aren't a regular. You looked nervous. We watched you for a while. We could tell you were cheating, but for the life of us, we couldn't tell how you were doing it. I believe you came out about a grand up after an hour or so. That's pretty good wages for an hour's work."

Jasper regarded Scott with a curious eye and lit a cigarette. Scott studied him carefully.

"Now, don't get me wrong," Jasper continued. "I really appreciate what you did down on that high-stakes table. That guy you got busted is a regular. He rolls a lot of money through here. Sometimes he loses big, sometimes he wins. The house liked him because, over the last month, he probably dropped twenty grand here. We know he wasn't cheating because he mostly lost. He was winning big tonight, then your friends busted him. And, well, house rules say that if he's proven to be a felon, he forfeits his winnings. So there's nothing I can do because we don't know how you were cheating. We see a lot of cheats, and we thought we'd seen them all, but you're different. If you'd like to enlighten us so we can add your method to our database, I'll let you keep your winnings. But of course, you're not welcome at our tables again."

"I can read minds," Scott said.

Jasper laughed out loud. "Now that's a new one, for sure."

"I can demonstrate."

266

"Please do."

"Do you have a deck of cards?"

Jasper grinned. "What about it, boys, do you think we could find a deck of cards for the man?"

A man standing behind Jasper reached in an open case and pulled out a sealed deck of cards.

"I just love card tricks," Jasper joked. "Don't you?"

Scott didn't answer.

"Okay," Jasper said, "what do you want me to do?"

"Open the deck and pick a card," Scott said. "Look at it, then shove it back in the deck."

Jasper broke the cellophane seal on the new deck, pulled the box open, then turned away so Scott couldn't see what he was doing. Scott instantly saw the man's thoughts.

Jasper turned back and held up the deck. "Okay, now I suppose you need to shuffle the deck or something?"

"No. You pulled the queen of hearts."

Jasper's jaw tightened. "What kind of parlor trick are you trying to pull here?"

"To be fair, have all your guys pull out a card, look at it, and put it in their pocket."

Jasper passed the deck. Each man turned his back, took a card, put it in his pocket, and passed the box. Jasper was the last to take a card.

Scott faced each man in turn and told him what card he'd pulled. The fifth man had pulled two; Scott told him what both cards were. Jasper pulled the last card out of his pocket and dropped it face down on the table in front of him.

"Ace of clubs," Scott said.

Jasper stared at him for a few long seconds and then turned over the card: an ace of clubs. "Okay, then, Matt," he said. "It seems like you've got quite a gift. I'm afraid I can't have you back, though, because the games here are supposed to be games of chance. Does your gift work at the blackjack table too?"

"No, that's truly a game of chance. You never know what cards are going to come out of the shoe. I have no advantage."

"What you're telling me is you can stand here and know everything I'm thinking."

"Yes."

"So what am I thinking?"

"Do you want me to censor the embarrassing stuff, or just blurt it out to all your employees?"

"Maybe we should step into the elevator where we can be alone," Jasper said.

"After you," Scott said.

They entered the elevator. The door closed, but Jasper didn't press a button.

"You're fifty-one years old," Scott said. "Divorced twice. You've got a mistress who is one of your employees. Your casino makes a lot of money, but it's financially stressed because the owners made an investment last year that hasn't been paying off well. You spend a lot of time in the casino, but you never drink, and you never play the games. You think everything I showed you tonight is a gimmick. You have an ingrown toenail on your right foot that is killing you, and you need to piss like a race horse."

Jasper smiled nervously. "I suppose you're going to tell everyone you know about all that stuff?"

"No. That's not my style. You accused me of cheating. I told you the truth. What I didn't tell you is I came here tonight because I had a feeling Vince was going to be here, and he's wanted in the murder of a woman I know. This was very personal for me. I didn't come here to cause trouble. You were right when you said I was nervous, because this is the first time I've played poker in a casino."

Jasper stared at him for a few seconds and pressed an elevator button. "If you don't mind, I'm going to tell my boys that you're bullshit."

"I'd really appreciate that," Scott said. "I didn't come here to make trouble, and I can't afford to have anybody know what I can do. I answered your questions the best I could because I knew if I didn't, you were going to have two of your boys rough me up. I got in a bad car wreck a few months ago and have a plate in my head. A knock on the head would probably kill me."

"Is that why you wear a rug?"

"Yes. I'm trying to cover the scars."

Jasper offered his hand. "Thanks, Matt. It's been a pleasure meeting you, but please don't come back. I'm going to have to tell my boys to watch for you."

"I understand," Scott said. "No offense, but I hate casinos. They're way too crowded for me."

The elevator doors opened on the main level. Jasper watched Scott walk out the front doors. He still didn't believe the guy—but damned if he didn't need to piss, and the big toe on his right foot was killing him.

Chapter 30
The Phone Call

Scott went to work on Monday as usual. And, as usual, by the end of the day, he wished he hadn't. His heart just wasn't in it anymore. He wondered if he could make a living doing something else. More than one person had told him he could have a bright future in law enforcement, but he wasn't in love with the drama.

He wanted to call LuAnn to ask about Vince but decided not to. She'd done her job. The contact numbers she'd left him bore local New Jersey area codes. They were there to help if he needed them. But what he wanted was information, and they couldn't give him that. He needed to know, after all he'd gone through, that there would be some resolution.

He wondered if Nancy would leave him alone now. He'd done all he could. He'd led the authorities to her grave, to her killer, and to the evidence that should convict Vince. What more could he do? No sooner had the thought entered his mind than another popped in: What about the kids—what about the ones still trapped in the system?

Scott instantly dismissed the thought. He didn't have any knowledge that could help with that, and after living through the first vision, he didn't want another one.

He spent one of his endless hours alone, grilling a steak and making a dinner to go with it: a baked potato, steamed veggies, and a couple of slices of garlic bread. He had beer in the fridge, but he chose cold water instead. He didn't like the way he felt after he drank alcohol. Rather than dine inside, he carried his plate onto the back deck, dusted off the glass-topped table and single chair, and sat down to enjoy his meal.

The loneliness that enveloped him was palpable. The marinated steak seemed flavorless, the mixed vegetables bland, the baked potato hot but grainy. After a couple of bites of each, he pushed his plate away, leaned back in his chair, and closed his eyes.

He shivered in the late-September breeze. It had been cool enough the past few mornings that his furnace had kicked on. The weatherman claimed it was just a freak early-fall cold front that had come down out of Canada and that soon, the weather would warm back to normal.

He thought about Rita. He wondered if her children were taking good care of her. He thought of her warmth and selflessness and smiled. Then, in a flash, he saw his family. He wondered how they were dealing with life without him. He wondered what Mary had told the kids. He wondered if Alan was in their life, or if Mary had taken Scott's advice and broken off the relationship so she wouldn't ruin Alan's marriage. Those thoughts were so painful that he set them aside.

He thought about Ralph. He wondered where he was and if he was being treated well. He knew once the trials were over, Ralph would go back to prison. He wondered how long he'd last in there with the inmates knowing what he'd done.

He recalled the scene in the woods in Kansas. He imagined all those kids standing by their open graves, waiting to be identified and sent home to the parents who had lost them. He pictured a group of others standing on a cold boat dock, knowing they'd never be recovered. It was suddenly more than he could bear. Cold tears trickled down his cheeks. What had happened to those innocent kids was so sick, and so wrong. He silently hoped that God in his mercy would comfort them and their parents and send their abductors to the deepest pits of Hell.

Then he thought of the hundreds, perhaps thousands of others who were still being brutalized in a system that it seemed nobody could touch.

Before he could help himself, he remembered Vince, standing there in the casino, captured, disheveled, yet defiant—seemingly confident he'd never be convicted. The sorrow and loss that had choked Scott only seconds before was replaced by loathing and rage. Where did Vince fit in all this ugliness? Why had he murdered Nancy? Had there been others besides the children?

If they convicted Vince, what would the man's life be like in prison? He thought about Warden Bruce. Would Vince do time in a place like that—pampered and showered with special privileges, maybe even released early for good behavior—as attested to by a corrupt jailer? After all, what was a single murder? Without being convicted as an accessory to the murders of hundreds of children, there was no call for "life without parole." Would his defense attorney argue that Nancy's murder was a crime of passion deserving a lighter sentence after rehabilitation? There were so many unanswered questions.

Then it hit him. If he could be in the room with Vince and the prosecuting attorney when he was asked those questions, even if Vince said nothing in answer to each question, Scott would know the answers. That exercise probably wouldn't get Vince any more time behind bars, but the man's thoughts might lead to other involved parties—and to the evidence that could convict them, as well.

Scott knew what he had to do. Even if it ended badly for him, he needed to get Vince to answer all of those questions.

He pushed himself away from the table, picked up his cold plate and glass, and walked back inside.

His phone was ringing, but it stopped before he could answer. He looked at the missed call phone number. It was LuAnn. He quickly punched the redial button and waited impatiently as the call clicked through.

"Matt?" she answered.

"Yes," Scott said. "I was just thinking about you. What's up?"

"I have some bad news. Maybe you'd better sit down."

"What," Scott said angrily, "did they let that bastard go?"

"It's worse," LuAnn said quietly. She fell silent for a moment, as if struggling for words. "They found your family this morning in their house. Scott . . . they're all dead."

Scott dropped onto a kitchen chair. He could hardly breathe. What little he'd just eaten suddenly wanted to come back up. He leaned forward as his mouth watered, expecting at any moment to throw up. His breath came in short gasps. He needed to run to the bathroom, but he couldn't stand. His hands were shaking so badly he could barely hold the phone.

Long moments passed as he fought for control. He knew LuAnn was expecting a response, but the only thing that raced through his head were expletives. There was no sentence structure, no thought process—only a hail of endless, vile, ugly words. He wanted to scream. He needed to scream. He opened his mouth, but only a guttural groan escaped.

"Scott?" LuAnn asked. "Are you okay?"

He forced out a single word. "No!"

"Talk to me," she demanded. "Do I need to call someone?"

"No," he said, softer this time. Then a thought crossed his mind. "Were they murdered?"

"They're still investigating," LuAnn said quietly, "but it looks like possible carbon monoxide poisoning. They were all still in their beds. There were no signs of trauma. The doors and windows were all locked from the inside."

"But how?" Scott croaked.

"It's been cold here the last few days. They're thinking the furnace malfunctioned."

"That's bullshit!" Scott suddenly raged. "We replaced that furnace two years ago! It's practically new!"

"We have a theory," LuAnn said after a few seconds.

"Who's we?"

"The agency."

"What sort of theory?"

"It may not occur to you for a while, until you've had time to come to grips with this, but do you remember when we got word that there was a bounty on your head?"

"Yes, so what?"

"Vince saw you in New Jersey. He probably told somebody you were there. They were worried about what you could do to them even before we captured him. We're thinking they're at a fever's pitch about now. Using Vince, you could rat them all out. Vince is in custody at the U.S. Marshals' office in Omaha. His people can't get to him, so that leaves you. They probably know by now that you're in New Jersey, but as you know, Jersey's a big place. They needed to draw you out."

"So they murdered my family . . . knowing I'd come home for the services."

"That's just a theory."

"Oh, I'll come home, alright!" he yelled into the phone. "And when I do, I'm going to find the filthy slimeballs who killed my kids. Before I'm done, I'll see every damned one of them in jail—or dead."

LuAnn didn't answer for a while. When she did, her voice was barely audible. Scott could tell she was on the verge of tears. "I'm so very sorry, Scott," she managed. "You can't believe how badly we feel. We never dreamed it would come to this."

Scott didn't answer. He knew he couldn't say anything without opening the floodgates.

"How can we help?" LuAnn finally asked after a long silence.

Even though he hadn't been able to answer, his mind had been running rampant. "I want to get in a room with Vince," Scott said angrily. "And have somebody ask him a lot of embarrassing questions. You need to ask him who he works for, how their operation works, where they keep the kids—all of that. Even if he doesn't talk, I'll know the answers."

"I can talk to my boss, but I think you coming back here is too risky."

"But isn't it risky staying here, too? If they don't find me, their only other recourse is to shut up Vince. If they can do that, then we have nothing. I need to talk to him before that happens."

"I can't promise that we can guarantee your safety."

"Because of this lousy 'gift,' I have nothing left anyway. So, what if they do kill me? If I can get something out of Vince before they do, I'm perfectly willing to take the chance."

"I'll talk to my boss and get back to you," LuAnn said. "In the meantime, you should probably pack your bags. I don't think it's safe for you there anymore. In fact, as soon as you get packed, lock up, leave the key under the matt on the rear deck, and get out of there. Someone will call you and give you instructions. No . . . on second thought, I will call and give you directions. Don't listen to anyone else."

An hour later, Scott was packed and ready. LuAnn hadn't called, but he knew what he had to do. He studied the street for a few minutes, watching for any suspicious cars, moving or parked. Finally convinced there was nobody waiting, he pulled the Lexus out of the garage and left in one fluid movement.

Remembering the ploy LuAnn had used the day she whisked him out of Omaha, Scott drove randomly around several city blocks, watching all the while for any sign he was being followed. Having not seen anything suspicious, he stopped at a local gas station to top off his gas tank. He didn't know what the feds had in mind, but he knew he needed to be in Omaha. He knew he couldn't attend the funeral services, but just being in the same city seemed the proper thing to do.

Scott was just leaving the gas station when his phone rang. He looked at the number before he answered.

"This is LuAnn," she said. "My boss doesn't think it's smart to come here. He believes, like you do, that they took out your family to get you back in town. That means they'll have a lot of eyes on the street watching for you."

"I'm already on my way," Scott said, "so you'd better think of something."

"You're getting ahead of me. I didn't say to not come to Omaha, we just don't want you to show up at the Bureau. The boss likes the idea of questioning Vince, but when I told him what you said, he wants to bring him to you. He thinks he can convince the U.S. Marshals that Vince is in danger from his own people and should be moved to a secret location. When we decide where that is, I'll call and give you instructions. In the meantime, do you remember how we got to Jersey?"

"Of course."

"Don't fly. They'll be watching the airports. Do a reverse repeat of what we did on the way out there. This time, though, you can use your credit card, because as far as we know, your new identity hasn't been compromised. All they know at this point is your general location, meaning they'll be watching for you."

After he hung up, Scott had another idea. They might be watching for the Lexus, but what if he traded cars? Or, better yet, what if he took the bus? Everything he owned was in two suitcases in the trunk. If he was on the bus, he wouldn't have to worry about hotel rooms or falling asleep at the wheel.

He pulled over and, using his smart phone, found the nearest bus terminal. The bus to Omaha was scheduled to leave in three hours.

LuAnn called a while later. "I've got news, and then I've got news," she said. "They have determined the cause of death was definitely carbon monoxide poisoning, and you were right about your furnace. It checked out. The gas came from an internal combustion engine, not the furnace, and not the engine in Mary's car. Even though her car was parked in the garage, the carbon signature was different. They're still checking, but they think the gas was containerized somewhere else and injected into your home. Probably through the furnace exhaust."

The dull rage that had been lying just beneath the surface all day nearly reached fever pitch. Scott could hardly breathe.

"Are you still there?" LuAnn asked.

"Yes."

"Have you left your house?"

"I'm headed for the bus terminal," he said. "I decided I didn't want to worry about the drive. I didn't think they'd be looking for me on the bus."

"That's brilliant," she said. "I assume you're coming to Omaha, then?"

"Yes, but I don't know what to do once I'm there. I'm leaving the Lexus here in the bus station parking lot."

"Leave your keys on top of a rear tire. I'll have the agency pick it up. We'll pick you up when you get here. When will you be in?"

"They told me over the phone that the trip would take about twenty-four hours, so probably about this time tomorrow, unless I get delayed."

"Call when you're an hour or so out so we can make arrangements."

"You better send somebody I know," Scott warned her, "or I won't get in the car."

"I was going to send a marshal. I worry about one of us meeting you. They might be watching us."

"How about Paul?"

"Your attorney?"

"My wife's divorce attorney," he corrected her.

"That might work. I'll call him."

"No, don't. Let me call him. I'll make my own arrangements. When you decide where the meet with Vince will be, call and let me know."

Scott drove to the bus terminal, bought a ticket, and parked his car in a small lot behind the terminal. Rather than wait inside for the bus, he stayed in the car. Now that he had his ticket and knew his projected arrival time, he dialed Paul's number.

"Paul Rodriguez, attorney at law," Paul answered.

"Hello, Paul," Scott said.

"Scott, where are you?"

"This is Matthew Rollins," Scott said. "I hear Scott Corbridge is dead."

"Sorry," Paul said. "I obviously didn't know that."

"I've been talking to the feds. Did you hear about Mary and the kids?"

"Yes, I got a call. Damn, I'm so very sorry about your family. I heard it was a faulty furnace."

"That's what Vince's buddies want us to believe," Scott said. "But I just talked to the feds. They're treating it as a homicide. Did you know they caught Vince?"

"No, I hadn't heard that," Paul said.

"That's probably good. Maybe his arrest isn't common knowledge, but if it isn't yet, it soon will be. I spotted him in a casino and called the feds. He wasn't happy when they took him down. Now the feds are telling me they think that one of us, either me or Vince, probably needs to get dead to protect the guilty. The feds think they murdered my family to get me to come out of hiding to attend the services. They went to great lengths to make the deaths appear accidental."

"What are you going to do? Nothing stupid, I hope."

"I want to attend the memorial services, but I can't. That's exactly what whoever murdered my family is expecting me to do. The bad guys put a bounty on me before I left. I'm sure they're no less anxious to find me now. They know I have certain abilities and if I gain access to Vince, I'll be able to find out what he knows. The U.S. Marshals' office has Vince in custody, hoping they can keep him alive. That leaves me as one of two people who has to be taken care of. I'm sure the bad guys don't want to blatantly mess with the Marshals. That means if they can find me, they'll take me down instead."

"Okay," Paul said hesitantly. "Why are you telling me all this?"

"I need your help. I'm on my way home, but the feds who put me in the Witness Protection Program are worried they may have a leak. They don't want to risk picking me up. I was hoping you might do that."

"I'd be glad to. When's your flight?"

"I didn't dare use the airlines. That's too obvious. I'm coming by bus. I'll be there tomorrow about this time. Can you meet me at the bus terminal?"

"Sure," Paul said. "Where are you going to stay?"

"They haven't told me yet. I'll let you know when you pick me up."

"If you're not planning on attending the services, why are you coming in?"

"The feds think I may have blown my cover when I ratted out Vince, so I had to get out of town anyway. Then I got to thinking. I need to do as much damage to Vince's organization as I can before they drop either me or Vince. To do that, I need to be in the room with Vince when they question him."

"He won't answer your questions."

"He won't have to. All he has to do is think about the answers when they ask the questions."

"Don't they have to have his attorney present when they do that?"

"I'm leaving that to the feds," Scott said. "I don't know how they'll work that out and frankly, I don't care. Just as long as I have access to Vince."

"You're going to call me, then—when you need a ride?"

"I'll call you about an hour before I get in so you'll have time to find the place. I don't want to be sitting on the curb with two suitcases in front of God and everybody, if you get my drift."

"Okay," Paul said. "I'll be glad to help."

"One more thing," Scott added. "Bring my handgun and the box of ammunition I gave you. I may be ready to quack, but I won't be a sitting duck."

* * * * *

The bus left on time, but it didn't take long for Scott to get totally frustrated. The supposedly straight-through bus would cruise on the freeway for a little while, then take an exit to a little town in nowhere, USA, pick up or drop off a passenger or two, and then head back to the freeway.

He kicked back in his seat and tried to relax. Sleeping was out of the question. There was too much noise and too many random thoughts filling the air around him. He pulled inward to try to shield himself. That was a mistake. Instantly, he felt Nancy's presence, and a new vision filled his head. At first, he tried to push it away. But remembering the anxiety he'd felt when he refused to listen the last time, he relaxed and studied every detail as it flowed through his mind.

He saw the mansion with the storage shed out back where they'd found the shovel. Then he noticed a side door not far from the shed. A small keypad hung on the door under the deadbolt. The numbers 6-3-6-3 lit up in sequence. Then the door opened, and to his left was another panel. This one had a number grid rather than a ten-digit pad. He tried to remember the numbers as they glowed yellow but was prompted to remember the light pattern instead. A red light at the top of the panel turned green as the last number lit up.

Then, almost as if he was watching through the lens of a video camera, he moved to a stairway on his right and climbed the stairs. There was a short hallway at the top. The first door on the right opened, and he found himself in a lavishly finished bedroom. A huge four-poster bed stood in the center of the room and a big-screen TV hung on the wall near the foot of the bed. There was a door leading to a walk-in closet. In the closet, there was a large gun safe with an electronic keypad. This time, the numbers were random, but he remembered them all.

When the safe door swung open, he expected to see rows of guns. Instead, the whole interior, including the backs of both doors, had been modified with shelves. The shelves were filled with row after row of DVDs several layers deep. Just as he started to wonder why someone would go to that much effort to lock up movies, he realized what they were. These were movies taken of the victims, many of whom may have been laid to rest in a scrubby patch of trees in Kansas.

The vision vanished. Scott was left feeling sick to his stomach. There had to be over a thousand DVDs in that safe.

He opened his eyes and looked out the window. It was dark. The lights of dozens of passing cars reflected off the wet pavement. He pulled out his phone to look at the time. It was nearly ten. The vision, which had seemed to take only a few seconds, had lasted over an hour. It was no wonder he could remember nearly every detail. He thought about writing down the numbers he'd seen before he forgot them but stopped when he realized he would likely see the dream many more times before it came time to act.

He eventually dozed. When he awoke, the bus had stopped. It was still dark, but it had stopped raining. The aisles were filled with people filing toward the front of the bus.

"We've got a half-hour rest stop," a redheaded woman across the aisle said with a slight smile, answering his unasked question. "You were out cold."

Scott forced the cobwebs out of his mind and returned her smile. She looked forty, but when he looked closer he noticed she was probably younger. Heavy worry lines furrowed her forehead, and puffy purplish bags hung under her eyes. They had taken a toll on her beauty.

"Thanks," Scott said. "I could use a bite to eat."

The damp, crisp night air forced an involuntary shiver as he stepped out of the bus. He hurried into the terminal and waited in line at a glassed-in display case of various kinds of fast foods. He settled for a cardboard boat of hot wings and potato wedges. When he looked around, there wasn't an empty table in sight. As he headed back out the door toward the bus, the redheaded woman hailed him.

"We've got room here," she offered. She was sitting in a booth with two other women.

"You're very kind," Scott said and sat down. He was in no mood for small talk with strangers, but he forced himself. "Are you ladies going all the way to Omaha?" he asked.

"We're actually changing buses in Omaha," one of the women, an older brunette in glasses, said. "We're headed to Topeka."

Scott winced at the mention of Topeka.

"What about you?" she asked.

"I'm going to see family," Scott said, not wanting to offer details. His throat constricted at the thought. He wanted to see them before they were buried—to gain closure and to see where they were buried. They didn't have a cemetery plot. They'd never discussed it before. He had thought it would be a long time before any of them would need one.

"You're from the Omaha area?" the brunette asked.

Scott choked down a potato wedge. When he noticed they were staring, he knew he had to say something. "I was, until a while ago. My wife and I divorced. I took a job in New Jersey." He considered saying more but decided to change the subject. "Are you ladies from Kansas?"

"No, we're all from New Jersey," the brunette said. "I'm Roberta. This is Janice, and that's Fran," she said, pointing to the redhead.

"Why Topeka?" Scott asked.

Roberta stared at Fran for a few seconds. "Do you want to tell him, or should I?"

"I really can't talk about it," Fran said.

"Her ten-year-old daughter went missing a couple of years ago," Roberta said. "She got a call a month ago asking if she had pictures and maybe a DNA sample. I guess the FBI found some graves. They matched the DNA from some hair Fran sent them to one of the bodies. We're on our way out there to bring her home."

Scott was having a hard time breathing. He wanted to blurt out what he knew but couldn't. The last thing this poor woman needed was a description of where her child had been found and why she had been there.

"That's awful," he managed. "I'm so sorry."

Fran looked down at her hands for a few seconds. "I knew in my heart that I'd never see her again," she said, choking on the words. "But I always had hope. At least now I know where she is."

"Are you alone?" Scott asked, already knowing that she was.

"Divorced," Fran said. "This thing with Marci . . . that's my daughter's name . . . destroyed our marriage. I tried to get him to come with me, but he's moved on. I never could."

"I hear that happens a lot," Scott said. "I mean when something bad happens to one of your kids."

"He didn't want to deal with it," Roberta said, "but a momma never gives up."

Scott thought about all of those graves. He thought of all of the mothers who either knew and were facing the finality of it all, like Fran, or who were still waiting, hoping and praying they'd see their children again. Suddenly, the inconvenience of his visions and his personal loss seemed like a small thing. At least he knew where his family was. He knew indirectly who had killed them and why. He also knew he had to do everything he could to bring their killers down.

"I can't even begin to understand what you've been through," he said. "I'm glad to see that you've got friends with you."

Tears were streaking down Fran's face as she reached across the table and held hands with the two other women.

Scott wasn't hungry anymore, and he felt awkward sitting there as the three women cried. He picked up his food and dropped the containers in the garbage as he walked back out to find his seat on the bus.

He slumped down in his aisle seat, leaned back, and closed his eyes. He opened his mind to the new vision, but nothing came. Maybe he'd seen all there was to see—or maybe Nancy was sitting with the three women now. He still couldn't connect the dots between Nancy, Vince, and the man who lived in the mansion, whoever he was. Ralph had seen Nancy with Vince at least once. That made her guilty by association. But if she was with the criminals, what had sent her to Scott? Was it profound guilt over what she'd done, or something else?

Fran touched him on the shoulder as she took her seat across the aisle. "I'm sorry about all that," she said. "It's embarrassing. I didn't mean to get you wrapped up in my problems."

Scott opened his eyes and sat up straight in his seat. "That's okay. I've seen news articles from time to time. That's got to be awful."

"It is, but at the same time, it's cleansing. Maybe now I can get on with my life. The last two years have been ugly."

"I don't mean to pry, but are you going to take her back to New Jersey or bury her in Topeka?"

"I can't afford much," Fran said. "I called some mortuaries in Topeka. They're going to cremate the remains. The police said there wasn't much left anyway. I'll take her home in an urn and then decide what to do. I may just set her on the coffee table for a while, in the middle of her pictures. I guess it's better to remember how she was rather than see her . . . well, you know."

"That's got to be so hard," Scott said. Then he saw her thoughts. She had photos. "I don't mean to pry," he added, "but do you have pictures of your girl?"

Fran smiled and reached for her carry-on bag. "That's probably the only good thing about this whole nasty affair," she said as she handed him a short stack of five-by-seven photos. "She was our only child. We took lots of pictures. People think I'm obsessed. I have them sitting everywhere in my apartment. I've rearranged them dozens of times. It gives me something to do when I don't think I can live another day. A lot of my Facebook friends have blocked me. They're sick of hearing about it."

"Other people don't understand unless they've lost someone themselves," Scott said. "Most parents never have to deal with the trauma of burying a child, and those who have at least have a chance to kiss them goodbye."

Fran quickly turned away and reached into her purse for a tissue. Scott turned his attention to the pictures. Even under the bus's dim aisle lights, the photos seemed to glow with warmth as he slowly thumbed through them. He was on his second time through the stack when Fran discreetly blew her nose and looked over at him.

"From what you just said, you must know what that's like," she said.

"I just lost three at the same time," Scott said sadly. "That's why I'm going to Omaha."

"Oh, my!" Fran exclaimed softly. "What happened?"

He wanted to tell her the awful truth, but he saw her thoughts. She had enough to deal with.

"They say it was an accident. Carbon monoxide from the furnace. They all died in their sleep."

"And their mom?"

"Her too."

Fran's tears flowed again. For the first time since LuAnn's telephone call, Scott's did too. She handed him a tissue.

"What are you going to do?" she said after a while.

"Same as you. I'll just take it one day at a time."

Chapter 31
The Mansion

The weather had cleared by the time Scott called Paul.

"LuAnn called me," Paul told him.

"What did she have to say?" Scott asked.

"She wondered if I was picking you up. When I told her I was, she gave me a set of directions but no actual location. I've got a phone number that I'm supposed to call, and then they'll give me final instructions. Do you still want your pistol?"

"Yes. I have a permit, or at least I had one under Scott Corbridge. I suppose the feds can whip me up another, unless they decide they don't want me to carry a gun. But under the circumstances, I don't think there will be a problem. Did you tell her you were bringing me a firearm?"

"I didn't tell her much of anything. She didn't act like she had time to make small talk."

"Did she tell you anything about Vince?"

"No," Paul said. "I didn't think to ask."

"Will you do me another huge favor?"

Paul hesitated, then cautiously agreed.

"I'd like final photos of my family," Scott said. "Maybe even a video of the funeral. Can you do that?"

"That's not a problem. There's also the matters of the life insurance, and your house and furnishings."

"I'll talk to the feds about that. They think I may have compromised the other place I was living in when I ratted out Vince. They've got a lot of money invested. They may seize everything to help defray my costs. I don't know how this all works. I know they may be interested in the furniture and all that. It can be sold or used to set up someone else in the program. But I'd like to get all the rest. You know, photos, mementos, knickknacks, all that."

Then it occurred to Scott that Paul was only his attorney—or had been. He certainly wasn't family. He didn't have a dog in the fight anymore.

"Hey, you know what, never mind," Scott said. "I'll have LuAnn do it. She may have someone else do it for her. I don't want to expose you any more than I already have."

Paul didn't argue.

"Thanks for picking me up," Scott said. "I didn't know who else I could trust."

"No problem," Paul said, but Scott could tell by the tone of his voice that he was wearing out his welcome.

Paul picked him up at the bus terminal and they headed back across the bridge into Council Bluffs. He pointed to the glove box without saying anything. Scott's pistol was there, along with the ammunition he'd asked for.

Scott pulled the empty magazine out of the handgun, loaded it, then snapped it back in place and racked the slide, putting a live round in the chamber. Then he leaned forward and tucked the weapon into the waistband of his pants in the small of his back. He dropped the box of ammunition in his backpack and settled back in his seat.

Paul didn't say much. He seemed nervous. Scott was worried until he read his thoughts. Paul was concerned because of the direction that Scott's case had taken. If Vince's organization was willing to take out his family to try to get to him, who else would they be willing to use?

Paul stopped at an intersection and picked up his cell phone. "I'm at the intersection," he said, then dropped the phone back in his shirt pocket without saying another word.

Two minutes later, they pulled into a Walmart parking lot and approached a blacked-out Chevy Tahoe. In Scott's opinion, it wasn't the best place to meet. The hand-off, including his luggage, was completed in seconds. Scott barely had time to thank Paul for his help before they whisked him away.

LuAnn sat in the back with Scott. "Sorry for the location," she said as they sped away. "We knew the rendezvous point would be easy for Paul to find, and we don't want anyone, including him, to know where we're taking you."

Scott nodded but said nothing. The driver went through all the typical evasive turns, then pulled into an underground parking garage where they traded cars yet another time. The two male agents left in the Tahoe almost immediately, while Scott and LuAnn waited for ten minutes in a tricked-out Mustang.

"Why the shell game?" he asked.

"Diversionary tactics only work with ground traffic. They don't do a thing for drones," she said.

"I'd never thought about that. Did you take this car away from a gang banger?"

LuAnn smiled. "Actually, yes. It was seized in a drug bust, but it came from California in the back of an enclosed semi-trailer. Don't get a big head, though. We didn't do this just for you. Let's just say that from time to time we need something that doesn't look so 'federal,' if you know what I mean."

"Where are we headed?" Scott asked.

"We're going to take a little road trip."

"Correct me if I'm wrong, but didn't we just do that about a month ago?"

LuAnn smiled. "I love Highway 30, don't you?" When Scott didn't answer, she explained. "We're headed for Fremont, Nebraska, just north and a little west of Omaha. Have you heard of it?"

"I think I may have, but why Fremont?"

"We have a place there. If things go well, you might even get to talk to Vince while you're there. We're still working with Legal on the arrangements. They're not convinced that what we have in mind is actually legal, at least not the interrogation part. They're afraid that if we learn something significant, we won't be able to use it against him in court, and we really want to nail this sucker."

"May I make a suggestion?" Scott said.

"Of course."

"Do it anyway. Then, when we've milked him for all we can, move him to minimum-security somewhere and let the bad guys know where he is. Be sure they also know that you're setting up a little chat between me, him, and his attorney. If you give them a couple of days, I'm betting he mysteriously dies in his sleep or something. Problem solved. Nobody has to pay to keep him in prison, and the bad guys relax, thinking they're safe because I didn't get a chance to interrogate him. At the end of the day, we've got everything you need to know, and all that really happened was one slimeball killed another."

"You're seriously evil," LuAnn said. "But I like the way you think. Legal, of course, can't know any of what you just said. Nor can anyone beyond a very tight circle of people."

"And, I might add," Scott said, "if you play your cards right, you might even be able to bust the slimeball who murders him. Two problems solved."

Scott's thoughts turned to his family again and his stomach tightened. After a few minutes of silence, he turned to LuAnn. "I wonder if you might be willing to do something for me?"

"Maybe. It depends."

"You don't have to kill anybody. Just have someone take pictures and maybe make a video of the funeral for me. I don't suppose you'll let me attend."

"You already know the answer to your second question. The answer to the first is yes. I can't afford to be seen there, but we have connections. I'm sure we can set that up." LuAnn's face darkened. "I really am sorry, Scott. We tried to keep her undercover, but she fought us. Had I known it would come to this, we'd have put them all in mandatory protective custody until after Vince's trial. It takes a court order to do that, though, and it's not often easy because it's like being in prison—no phones, no friends, no jobs, no light of day."

"The name is Matt," he said. "I have a driver's license to prove it."

"Sorry. You're right. I need to be more careful."

"Mary and Trish would have hated me if you had done that to them," Scott said, "but at least they'd still be breathing."

"We feel awful. If it makes you feel any better, we're leaving no stone unturned. We will find out who did it."

"And then what?" Scott interrupted angrily. "You'll send them where? To Warden Bruce's holiday hotel for a little pat on the back? I'll tell you what. Find out who did it, put them in handcuffs, and leave them in a room with me for a few minutes. Then afterwards I can go visit Bruce. He'll tell his buddies in the hole about me, and that'll be that. Another problem solved. No more weirdo who knows what you're thinking."

LuAnn let him steep in his rage for a few minutes before she responded. "You probably don't believe me, but we are truly sorry. I know it's premature to tell you this, but our people have put together what I think is a very attractive proposal. We were going to fly out last week and talk to you about it, but now with all this, it's been put on the back burner."

"I suppose you want me to become a *federale*, is that it?"

"In a nutshell, yes, but it has some amazing perks."

"I don't think so. I'd have to be looking over my shoulder the rest of my life."

"You probably will anyway. What did you plan to do with your life once Vince went to jail?"

"Drop off the map, keep my mouth shut about what I can do, try to start over. I was even thinking that I'd eventually be able to convince Mary and the kids to come back. She knew I could control it. I think I did a pretty good job of convincing her the last week I lived with her."

"And yet she chose to divorce you anyway."

"The damn case drove her to that. If I was freaking out over it, what do you think was going on in her mind? She just wanted to be left alone to live a normal life."

"Even if that meant sleeping with your business partner."

Scott flinched. "That was my fault."

"Was it, really? This may sound insensitive, but don't put her up on a pedestal. If you do, you'll never be able to start over."

"I had another dream," Scott said after they'd both had time to cool down.

"So whose body are we looking for now?" LuAnn asked sarcastically.

"Maybe we can find a few victims before they become bodies."

"Okay, I'm interested. We need to change the subject anyway."

"How much do you know about what Howard is working on?"

"Some, but obviously not everything. Why?"

"Did you hear about the shovel they found?"

"Yes, they found it in a shed at the back of Vince's boss's mansion. The boss, of course, completely disavowed any knowledge of it. He claims Vince did some work for him around the house. That's why he was driving a company car."

"And staying in a six-figure penthouse apartment," Scott grumbled. "I think that's a little hard to swallow. How many gardeners do you know who make that kind of money?"

"Okay, so we agree on something. You were about to tell me something about the shovel?"

"No, actually, I was going to tell you something about the mansion. I believe I've told you about the relationship I've developed with Nancy, haven't I?"

"If you want to call that a relationship."

"She visited me on the bus ride from Newark. She showed me how to get in the side door of his mansion, how to disable the alarm, and where to find a gun safe full of child porn. I had the distinct impression that some of the images on the DVDs in there came from the victims we found in Kansas."

"Okay, I'm having a hard time swallowing this," LuAnn said.

"How would your dead woman know all of that?"

"Only one reason that I can think of. She's been there. Maybe that's why she had a huge black eye the night she was murdered. I didn't see Vince hit her. She was standing in front of her mirror, crying, trying to do something with her eye, when Vince came up behind her. When she spun around, he started stabbing her. Maybe she was doing things for the boss. Maybe she and the boss got in a little tiff. She may have said something that caused him to smack her, and he sent Vince home after her to shut her up before she could go to the authorities."

"That makes some sense, but we know she was in Kansas with Vince on at least one occasion. Ralph told us that. If she was doing that, why was she messing around with the boss?"

"Did you see her picture?" Scott said. "She was young and beautiful. Maybe the boss got tired of little girls and 'invited' her to spend some time in his mansion while his wife wasn't home."

Now Scott had LuAnn's full attention.

"Suppose the boss is so warped by what he's into that he decides to show her a little kiddie porn to get her in the mood," Scott continued. "She's so disgusted by that, after hauling kids to Kansas with Vince, that she freaks out and says stuff he doesn't like. He smacks her around. She says a few more things, maybe threatens to rat him out to his wife—or worse yet, to the authorities. He simply sends Vince after her before she can do either."

LuAnn looked over at Scott and then back at the road. Her mind was going a mile a minute. "Are those your thoughts, or am I indirectly talking to Nancy?" she said.

"I don't know anymore. I've been trying to come up with a motive. Maybe that's it. If that's what really happened, she hasn't actually shown me that."

"But she showed you how to get into his mansion?"

"That, and exactly where the evidence is and the combination to the safe they're locked up in."

"In view of everything that's happened, don't you think he'd be trying to get rid of that evidence in case we were able to get a warrant to search inside his house rather than just a shed in his back yard?"

"Didn't you tell me you were watching him?"

"He's one of several."

"Then don't you think he knows that? How would that look if all of a sudden a moving crew shows up at his house and hauls away a gun safe?"

"And how would it look if we got a warrant and found guns in that safe instead of a bunch of DVDs?" LuAnn said. "The last time she would have been in that house was months ago, and now that we have Vince in custody he's even got more of a motive to move the evidence."

"Maybe I should go in and check before you get a warrant."

"That's probably the stupidest thing I've ever heard you say. Hello, is there anybody at home in there, or is all this sneaking around to keep you safe just a figment of my imagination?"

"If you could connect those tapes to one or more of the bodies in Kansas, wouldn't it be worth the risk?" Scott said.

"We need to change the subject. You going in that house is off the table. Right now, buddy, you're probably the most valuable material witness we have."

"Okay," Scott said. "What else would you like to talk about?"

LuAnn hesitated for a few moments. Scott knew what she was thinking but decided to keep quiet and let her bring up the questions the agency wanted to ask Vince.

"Do you actually have to be in the room with him when we ask the questions?" she asked.

"That depends on the size of the room and how many other people will be in there with him. For instance, when I was in the courtroom with Detective Ableman, I had to concentrate to zero in on what he was thinking. It wasn't easy, but having him in sight helped. What have you got in mind?"

"Legal doesn't want us to interrogate him without having his lawyer present, and for obvious reasons, we don't want to take a parade of people to our safe house."

"Take me to him, then."

"We've thought about doing that, but it'll take a little time to work the logistics so we know we can protect you. If you could be in an adjacent room, we could control the number of people who know you're back in town."

"You may not have heard, but the cops hauled me into an interrogation room down at the jail so a high-powered shrink could see if I was competent to stand trial. There were several people in the room behind the one-way glass. I could hear what they were thinking. Are you in a big hurry to question Vince, or do we have some time?"

"You already know the answer to that question," LuAnn said.

"You know we have leaks. We don't know who we're dealing with. Before Vince was in custody, the bad guys didn't seem to be too worried. Now that he's here and they don't know where you are, they've got to be nervous. He may have been a good soldier, but they'll protect the king, if you know what I mean. What you told me earlier about putting him in minimum-security was closer to the truth than you imagined. But what we may think is maximum-security may not be. I'm not sure we could sneak you into jail without someone spotting you."

"You're good at hiding people. Put me in disguise. Hey, maybe I'd look good in nylons with a long curly wig."

"You'd make an ugly woman."

"Gee, thanks!" Scott remarked.

"But you may be onto something. You wouldn't have to be a woman. I wonder what you'd look like in a black wig with a little darker makeup and wearing a U.S. Marshals uniform? I wouldn't dare use a county sheriff or a local police uniform. The people in the lockup pretty much all know each other. When we called in the U.S. Marshals, we introduced a bunch of new faces."

"Are they holding him in Omaha, or in Lincoln?"

"In Lincoln. That's who has jurisdiction over Nancy's murder. I'll get you settled in and then go talk to my people. I think Legal would go for that because we'd have his attorney in the room with him."

"Can't you just call them?"

"I can't take the chance that somebody might be listening to my phone calls. That's why we took the precautions we did in Omaha today. Anybody can fly a drone. It's pretty easy to track a car from the air."

* * * * *

Highway 30 took them to the outskirts of Fremont. Scott tried to remember street names as LuAnn turned south off of 30 onto Bells Street and followed it, eventually turning west into what appeared to be the old part of town. The narrow streets were lined with trees, but instead of seeing just old homes, there was a combination of narrow wood-sided homes interspersed with newer brick homes. They eventually pulled up in front of a narrow old home. There was no driveway between it and the homes on either side, and no garage at the back of the lot like there had been in Lincoln.

"What's with you guys and old homes?" Scott asked.

"We get them cheap, and most of the time the neighborhood is transient, so we don't draw a lot of attention to ourselves."

"I don't think this Mustang is exactly a low-profile machine," he said. "I'll bet every eye in the neighborhood watched you drive up."

"There's a tiny university here in town. Doesn't this look like what a college stud might drive?"

"Maybe, but when two old coots climb out of it, that sort of defeats the purpose."

"Speak for yourself. I think I look pretty good driving this, and you're not so old yourself. You grab one bag, I'll get the other. That'll make it look like we're either married or roomies."

LuAnn unlocked the front door and handed Scott the key fob. "It's not much," she said, "but it's clean. There's a TV, and the fridge and pantry should be well stocked. Make yourself at home, keep the doors locked, and don't open the door to anyone but me unless I call you first and tell you somebody else is coming."

"Love 'em, and leave 'em," Scott said as he looked out the front window at the dry grass in the yard.

"I do have a life," LuAnn said as she turned to go. "If I hurry, I'll be home in time to eat dinner with my family."

"Lucky you," Scott said. "It must be nice to have a life."

"Hey, I'm sorry. That was cruel. I was just—"

"Making small talk," he finished for her.

"I hate that."

"Fifteen feet down that walk, you'll be free of me."

She paused in the doorway and turned to look back at him. "I'd tell you I know how you feel, but I don't."

"Don't worry about it. It's not like you could do anything to keep this from happening. I really appreciate everything you've done and are doing to keep me safe."

"When I call you, don't talk about where you are, okay?"

"I know," he said. "I never know who may be listening."

LuAnn closed the door and Scott locked it behind her. He watched until the Mustang disappeared down the street, then he lugged his bags into the larger of the two small bedrooms at the back of the house and set them on the bed. He checked out the bathroom before he unzipped either of them. It had been a long bus ride. He could use a shower, something to eat, and a little rest.

* * * * *

It seemed Scott had only been asleep a few minutes when the dream of the mansion came again. This time, he woke up before the safe opened. He could feel Nancy's presence. There was an urgency about her visit. He reached for his cell phone to see the time. It was nearly one in the morning. He felt like he should call LuAnn, but didn't. What could she do in the middle of the night, anyway? She was going home to her family after she left him. He doubted she'd had any time to talk to her people. He didn't have any transportation, and for that matter, he didn't know where the mansion was.

He rolled over, pulled the covers up under his chin, and tried to sleep. But Nancy wouldn't leave him alone.

"What do you want me to do?" Scott raged in the dark. "I don't even know where he lives!"

Nancy flooded him with thought. In an instant, he knew where the home was. But he still didn't have a car.

"I can't just float there like you can," he yelled. "Leave me the hell alone!"

Sleep, at that point, was impossible. Scott angrily got out of bed and pulled his pants on. Maybe there was something on TV that would take his mind off the dream. He stopped at the fridge on the way to the living room and pulled out a can of Coke. He was just sitting down on the sofa when he heard his phone ringing. He raced to the bedroom and caught the call just before it went voicemail.

It was LuAnn. "I just got off the phone with one of our agents," she said. "There's a bunch of activity going on at the mansion. I told him about the safe. They're going to arrest a few people out there and shut down the house until we can get a judge to issue a warrant. I hope to hell what you've told us isn't a bunch of crap. This could be for all the marbles. If there's nothing there, we'll get sued."

"What do you want me to do?"

"I need the combination to that safe you were telling me about, and I need you tell me again exactly where it is in the house."

Scott told her where the safe was and gave her the sequence, then had her read the numbers back to him.

"I've got to go," LuAnn said. "I've got an incoming. I'll call you as soon as I know any more."

As soon as he hung up, Scott got dressed. He didn't know why. There was nothing he could do, but if nothing else, he had a waistband to stuff his pistol in and a shirttail to pull down over it. For some reason, that just felt right. He hadn't shot the gun in years.

He used to be a fair shot. He hoped shooting was like riding a bicycle. He thought he might have to use the gun, and he didn't have the luxury of getting in any practice.

He flipped through the late-night TV offerings while he waited. An hour passed, and then another. He was exhausted. He'd had less than four hours sleep in the last twenty-four, yet he didn't dare close his eyes.

His phone rang at three thirty.

"It's me again," LuAnn said. "We hit the jackpot. The judge was pretty cranky, but he signed the order. We had twenty officers on scene. The perps had a pickup with an enclosed trailer hooked behind it. They had some sort of apparatus to move the safe and already had it loaded in the trailer by the time our agents shut them down. From what I hear, there was a lot of yelling and threats made. Two men tried to sneak out the back, but our men had the site contained. They arrested them both when they found out they had outstanding warrants. The homeowner was livid. His attorney showed up with a couple of deputies in tow before we got the order from the judge. I guess in the end, things got really tense. Guns were drawn, but luckily there was no gunplay."

"Did they open the safe, then?" Scott was on the edge of his seat.

LuAnn laughed. "Yes, and I would love to have been there to see the look on that bastard's face when they did. They tell me his attorney started yelling crap about illegal search and seizure, but our Legal boys tell us they have no leg to stand on. It's a good thing the agency was covering their tracks. Everything they did was by the book. They tell me it was a good bust. They're still taking photos and tagging all of the evidence as we speak."

Scott breathed a deep sigh of relief.

"Now here's the good part," LuAnn continued. "Whereas we already had a warrant to search the house, a few agents did just that while the others were busy with the arrests and the evidence in the safe. Apparently, the boss forgot to pull a very graphic DVD out of the player in his bedroom. That one DVD alone will bust the owner big time—and the rest is all gravy."

"Okay," Scott said. "Where does that leave us with Vince?"

"I've been talking to my people while all this was going down. They want you in Lincoln at the jail at one tomorrow afternoon. They're going to work up a list of damning questions to ask Vince in front of his attorney. Now that we've busted his boss, we're going to 'mention' that his boss might be willing to rat Vince out on Nancy's murder. We hope that might loosen his tongue. If it does or doesn't, we hope to have you sitting there behind the mirror telling us if he's lying."

"Don't you already have enough evidence to convict Vince? I heard you had pulled evidence from the car to place him at the wheel, and you found Nancy's blood in the trunk."

"Better yet," LuAnn said, "our people pulled his fancy knife all apart. It's a little hard to clean inside a handle like that. They found traces of Nancy's blood, along with three others that they're running DNA on. From the measurements of the blade and the evidence they took from her body, they've determined the knife wounds match the blade. I think he's toast."

"What else do you expect to get from him when you interrogate him tomorrow?"

"I'm leaving all those questions up to people smarter than me," LuAnn said. "We don't know how much Vince knows about the rest of the organization, but it would be nice if we could find some victims . . . who aren't already in the ground."

Chapter 32
The Monster

Scott's phone rang again at seven, dragging him out of a fitful sleep.

"Sorry to call you so early," LuAnn said, "but you'll have visitors at eight. Two U.S. Marshals are coming to pick you up. We've got the boss in custody, and my management wants you to interview him before you talk to Vince. We want to have you in Lincoln early. It might be interesting to hear what the big boy *doesn't* have to say. I'm sure he'll either have his attorney with him or he'll refuse to answer any questions until he's present. That's where you come in. At any rate, I think it's going to be a fun morning."

"I'll be ready," Scott said. "But you've got a strange sense of fun."

"Gotta go," LuAnn said.

"What about the funeral?" he asked.

"It's tomorrow. We've got that covered. See you about nine."

Thoughts of his family rained down on him as he lay in bed. He shifted his mind from face to face, determined to remember them the way he last saw them. Then he felt Nancy. There was no vision; no extemporary thoughts. Just a familiar feeling that she was there.

"I hope you got what you wanted," Scott said. "Look what you cost me!"

With that, he rolled out of bed. She was gone. He wanted to feel remorse for sending her away, but there was none. She'd put herself in harm's way and paid dearly for it. Then she'd put her illness on him and his family, trying to make amends for what she'd done. He was sick of the whole sordid affair. He hoped Nancy was done with him. He needed to be done with her and all the rest of the anguish.

As the hot water cascaded over his body, he remembered LuAnn's words from the day before. The feds wanted him to work for them. They were working up a proposal. At first, in view of everything else, the thought ran cold. But as the water warmed his body, the thoughts grew warmer, too. He remembered how the magic had gone out of his job in New Jersey. Without family, working a tedious nine-to-five seemed without purpose. He thought of Fran, the lady on the bus, and the bittersweet thoughts that had filled her mind knowing she was finally going to get closure. If nothing else, maybe he could use his gift to bless the lives of others who had lost so much.

Scott was fussing with his toupee when a knock came at the door. He pulled off the hairpiece in disgust, tossed it on the bed, and pulled a hat out of his suitcase. As the second knock came—more insistent this time—he stuffed his pistol in the small of his back, pulled his shirttail down over it, and headed for the door.

He pulled back the window curtains a little and peered out. Two men in uniform stood at his door. He hoped they'd been sent by the agency. He reached out for their thoughts. They were impatient but legitimate. He steeled himself and opened the door.

"Matt Rollins?" a tall muscular man asked.

"That's me."

The agent showed his badge. "I'm Officer Fredricks with the U.S. Marshals' office. We have orders to transport you to Lincoln."

Scott stepped out and locked the door behind him. The marshals flanked him as they walked to a dark-blue four-door Ford pickup with a U.S. Marshals insignia stenciled on the door. Fredricks' partner, Officer Hancey, held open the rear door and waited while Scott climbed in and buckled up.

Neither spoke as they drove through the narrow streets. Fredricks was agitated. It had taken them a while to find the address. They were running behind schedule. He pushed the speed limit whenever he felt he could.

"Take 27," Hancey pointed as they came to an intersection.

"Damn backroads," Fredricks grumbled. "There'll probably be a bunch of sodbusters on the road with their farm equipment. They wanted us there fifteen minutes early so we wouldn't attract a bunch of attention."

"Didn't they tell you the interview doesn't start 'til ten?" Scott said.

Fredricks looked in the rearview. "They told us they wanted us there by nine."

"That's because they don't want anybody to see me. Isn't it only about sixty miles or so to Lincoln? I'd think we'll be fine."

"You don't know our boss."

"Tell her you had to wait for me to do my hair," Scott said as he pulled off his ball cap.

The marshal looked in the rearview. The sight of Scott's scarred head rattled Fredericks at first, then he saw the humor in what Scott had said and grinned. "That's funny. What happened to your head?"

Scott put his cap back on his head before he answered. "I was in a car wreck. They had to give me a titanium plate."

"Just curious," Fredericks said, "but how did you know my boss was a woman?"

"Lucky guess."

"You're that guy, aren't you?" Hancey said. "Word on the street is the feds have somebody who can read minds. Is that you?"

Scott looked out the window. He thought everybody knew. Here again, he'd screwed up. He wasn't learning that lesson very well. "If I tell you yes, will you freak out on me and get all worried that I'll know your deepest, darkest secrets?"

"That could be a little disturbing," Hancey said.

"I promise that what's in your head stays there. Unless, of course, you're lying to the law to cover up a crime."

"Damn," Fredricks muttered. "That's heavy."

"You have no idea," Scott said. "And no, I don't do demonstrations. That usually just gets me in trouble."

Neither one of his new companions wanted to test him. They drove in silence the rest of the way to Lincoln.

Howard and two of his agents met them in the underground parking garage and escorted Scott upstairs to a small, dimly lit theater-style room. When they stepped into the room, Scott recognized the back side of a one-way mirror that kept the small room of people hidden from view of the interrogation room. Even though they were forty-five minutes early for the "event," the viewing room was nearly full. It grew quiet as Scott entered, and every eye turned to him.

He quickly turned to Howard. "Can we talk in the hallway?"

Howard nodded, and they stepped out and closed the door. A deputy in uniform was posted at the door.

"I can't work this way," Scott said quietly. "You may not realize it, but for me, being in that crowded room is like being in a room full of screaming children. Even though everybody quit talking when we walked in, they're all projecting their thoughts at me. It's going to be tough to concentrate on what Vince's boss has to say."

"We may have a problem, then," Howard said. "That's my team in there. Everybody wants to know what this guy has to say."

"Then brief them afterwards. If they're expecting me to shout out every thought the guy has, they're going to be disappointed. I can't talk and listen at the same time." He looked sideways at the deputy standing near them in the hallway. "Besides, I really don't want everybody knowing who I am. LuAnn told me you have a leak."

"I trust all the people in that room," Howard said, "but I can see your point. Nobody expected a play-by-play, but this case is very personal. Most of them have kids."

"I did too, until a couple of days ago. Believe me, I understand. That's why I want to be at my best. I'd rather be sitting in the room with that jerk, asking him the questions, than be sitting in that glassed-in room with an audience."

Howard considered him for a few long seconds, then a slim smile curled the corners of his mouth. "You know, that might be a great idea. We've got a typewritten list of questions we want to ask him, but if you know what he's thinking, what better way of tailoring the questions as you go? We didn't want him to know who you are, but at this point, it probably doesn't matter much anyway. Wait here while I run this past my team."

Howard left Scott standing in the hallway with the deputy and slipped back into the room.

They didn't run me through a metal detector on the way in here, Scott thought. *I'm still carrying my weapon. If I find out that this pervert ordered the murders of my family, can I keep from shooting him in the face? Maybe a dose of cowboy justice is just what this situation calls for. At the very least, I'll be saving the courts untold time and money by just dropping the jerk.*

Then he felt Nancy, and a calmness settled over him. He didn't want another vision. She didn't offer one, but just her being there helped settle his nerves.

Howard returned a few minutes later. "I explained things to my team," he said. "They're good with you asking the questions. You'll have a bailiff in the room with you, and the prisoner will be shackled. That's protocol. We've got a few minutes before they bring him in. I want to go over the questions with you, but once you're in there with him, I suppose you'll be winging it."

A half hour later, they all watched from behind the mirror as a bailiff led Vince's boss into the interrogation room. They were accompanied by a man wearing a business suit that Scott assumed was the suspect's attorney. The bailiff seated them at a metal table and snapped the prisoner's shackles to a steel loop in the table.

Howard nodded at Scott. "It's showtime. Good luck."

The deputy in the hallway escorted Scott to a gray steel door with the words *Interrogation Room 1* stenciled conspicuously at eye level. He produced a ring of keys, unlocked the deadbolt, and held the door open.

A wave of contempt swept over the attorney's face as Scott walked boldly to an empty chair and sat down at the table. Scott could tell the lawyer was going to try to intimidate him.

"Who are you?" the attorney asked. "I know everybody on the prosecution team, and you're not one of them."

"Good morning," Scott said, glancing at the stapled sheets of paper he laid on the table in front of him. "My name is Matthew Rollins. I represent the Federal Bureau of Investigation. Whereas this is now a federal case and not subject to local or state jurisdiction, it is my assignment to interview your client. May I continue?"

He could tell the attorney was skeptical, but at the same time, he had never dealt with the feds before.

"I apologize for my appearance," Scott added. "Ordinarily, I'd be in a suit and tie, but I've been working with a forensics team in Kansas and didn't have time to fly home for better clothes before this meeting."

The mention of Kansas immediately got the attorney and his client's attention.

"Go ahead," the attorney said, "but I reserve the right to interrupt your line of questioning if I can see that my client may incriminate himself by answering."

"Fair enough," Scott said. "For the sake of formality, may I ask your name and what business you have with this man?"

"My name is Peter Dorius. I am Mr. Critchlow's attorney."

"Thank you, Mr. Dorius. If it's okay with you, I'd like to direct my questions to your client."

Scott turned to the man shackled to the table and began. "It says here that your given name is Lyle Critchlow, and that you've been read your Miranda rights. Is that statement accurate?"

Critchlow nodded.

"I'm sorry, Mr. Critchlow," Scott said, "but these proceedings are being recorded. I need an audible response. Is your name Lyle Critchlow?"

"Yes."

"And is Mr. Dorius representing you as counsel?"

"Yes."

"And have you been informed of your rights in these proceedings?"

"Yes."

"I believe we both know where you live," Scott said, "so I won't bother asking you that. Let's get down to the important stuff, shall we?"

Critchlow said nothing.

"Are you aware of the charges against you?" Scott said.

"My client is well aware of why he's here," Dorius answered.

"I'm sorry," Scott said pointedly. "I'm here to interview your client, not you. I believe we've already agreed that he will not be required to answer any question that will incriminate him unless he chooses to. I have a list of questions that my people would like to ask him, so let's do this. For the sake of fairness, after I ask each question, Mr. Critchlow can look at you. If you don't want him to answer the question, simply shake your head. I don't want you to keep interrupting. Is that clear?"

Dorius wasn't comfortable with being told to shut up, but after all, these were the feds. "I suppose that's fair enough," he said.

"I'll get right to it, then," Scott said, making eye contact with the boss. "The Bureau has recovered over a thousand recorded DVDs that were in your possession, Mr. Critchlow. We obviously haven't had the time to review all of them, but the ones we have looked at, including the one in the DVD player in your bedroom, all contain explicit examples of child pornography. In addition, we have discovered multiple copies of many of the movies, which would indicate that you may be charged with the crime of distributing those materials."

Scott paused to give Critchlow time to think.

"After a subsequent search of your premises," Scott continued, "we did not discover any recording devices that would be capable of making the movies in your collection."

Scott lifted his eyes from the typewritten pages and looked Critchlow directly in the eyes. Critchlow was freaking out. They obviously had enough evidence to convict him of possession and distribution. He was wondering if they would be satisfied and not go looking for his studios if he offered up some of his customers.

"So here's my first question," Scott said after an idea popped into his mind. "Do you have any information that might lead our investigators to the source of those movies, either to the recording studios or to the victims themselves?"

Critchlow's mind squirmed as he fought for something to say that wouldn't incriminate him. Scott saw a multi-story building in his thoughts. He couldn't see any victims, but he knew there were a number of them being held there.

"Take your time," Scott said, "but carefully consider your answer. If these people simply supply you the materials that were found in your possession, that's one thing. If, on the other hand, they receive direction or funding from you to produce those movies, that is quite another."

In Critchlow's thoughts, Scott saw bank transfers and adult faces. Some were actors in the films, others had more significant roles. He saw victims. He saw acts. He found himself struggling to hold back the nausea. He felt the bulk of the pistol in his waistband and was tempted to end this all now. Instead, he waited.

Critchlow turned to Dorius, who shook his head.

"I see that your attorney has advised you not to answer," Scott said. "Is that correct?"

"Yes," Critchlow answered.

"Yes, you do have the information I asked for? Or yes, you're refusing to answer at the direction of your counsel?"

"No, I don't have any information like you're looking for."

"That's unfortunate," Scott said. "I won't push you at this time, but I think you should think about that as our conversation continues. I'll come back to that question before we finish and give you another opportunity."

Scott looked down at the papers on the table and then made eye contact with Critchlow again.

"We understand you had one Vincente DeLuca in your employ. Is that correct?"

"Yes," Critchlow answered quickly, "but I didn't have anything to do with the things he's accused of doing. After he stole my car and disappeared, I terminated him."

"One question at a time, please. What exactly was the nature of Mr. DeLuca's employ? To ask it another way, what was he possibly doing for you to warrant the use of a luxury company automobile and the apparently free use of an upscale penthouse apartment that your company pays the lease on?"

"We maintain the penthouse for company business. Vince was the caretaker of that apartment, and he acted as my personal driver. I like fine cars."

"What sort of business is carried out in a luxury four-bedroom penthouse? Could it be that you entertained guests there using underage individuals?"

"Stop right there!" Dorius demanded. "You're badgering my client. This line of questioning is way out of line."

Despite the lawyer's outburst, Scott had already seen Critchlow's thoughts. In them, he saw more adult faces. This time, he also saw a veritable parade of young victims being brought up that private elevator to perform for Critchlow's customers. Scott could barely look at Critchlow, afraid that at any moment he might lose control and splatter the man's brains all over the walls. He took a deep breath and looked at Dorius.

"Let me re-phrase that question. Keep in mind, this same question will be asked in open court, and the judge will more than likely demand an answer. Mr. Critchlow, I understand that the nature of your business is automobile replacement parts. What is the nature of the business you conduct in that penthouse apartment? I have to assume there must be some business purpose, because you write off that lease on your company's corporate income taxes every year."

Dorius nodded his head, and Critchlow explained. It was obvious they had already rehearsed the answer. Much of what Scott heard coming from Critchlow's mouth he had already read in his memorized thoughts. Between the rhetoric about confidential business strategy meetings and attempts to persuade certain large distributors to use their auto parts, Scott caught glimpses of the other activities—none of which had anything to do with auto parts.

Scott waited for him to finish. After a slight pause, he asked the next question. "Mr. Critchlow, we have discovered enough evidence to convict your ex-employee, Vincent DeLuca, of the murder of Nancy Bennion. I won't take the time to enumerate all of that evidence at this time, but among other things, it involves your company car and a shovel we found in a shed on your property that we believe was used to bury the victim's body. Did you know Miss Bennion?"

"No," Critchlow answered emphatically. "I never met her. She may have been Vince's girlfriend, for all I know. I didn't get involved in his personal life."

With that question, Scott finally had his motive. As Critchlow's lying lips were saying the words, his thoughts were painting a much more vivid picture.

Scott's premonitions, no doubt provided by Nancy, had been right. Nancy had been "invited" to Critchlow's house. The video he had shown her to get her in the mood had so disgusted her that she'd pitched a fit, despite the thousand dollars he had offered to pay her. When she threatened to expose Critchlow to the authorities, he hit her and knocked her unconscious. When she didn't regain consciousness, he carried her to his Mercedes and drove her home. Nancy had been conscious by the time they got there and walked into her apartment under her own power. Critchlow called Vince and gave him explicit instructions. The woman simply knew too much.

"Mr. Critchlow," Scott said, moving on to the next question, "when we review all of those videos, will we find any connection between the victims in those movies and the hundred or so bodies we found in a forest in Kansas?"

Critchlow blurted out his reply before Dorius could stop him. "I have no idea! Like I've already told you, I don't know who makes those movies or where they find their actors. I just buy them. And yes, I distribute a few."

"Do you have a list of customers that you might be willing to offer up in return for a possible plea deal?"

Dorius nodded, and Critchlow said, "I do. But you need to keep my name out of it. Some of my customers are powerful individuals. If they're exposed, my life may be in jeopardy."

The thoughts that came to Scott with Critchlow's verbal reply identified a lot of faces—faces Scott had never seen before. He didn't bother pondering over what he saw. He suspected that once the feds found Critchlow's building and followed the money trail to the production facility and the people his money paid, his list of customers would be the least of the FBI's concerns.

Scott dutifully read through the remaining questions Howard had given him, but mentally he couldn't get past what he'd learned about Nancy and the little victims. Critchlow refused to answer most of the questions anyway. When he was finished, Scott returned to one of the first and most disturbing questions he'd asked.

"Mr. Critchlow," he said, "I'm going to ask you one last time, are you certain that if the federal government subpoenas your financial records we won't find any connection in either your personal or business finances that might lead us to production facilities where those pornographic movies are made and distributed?"

"Yes," Critchlow said angrily, "I'm sure."

His anger was only outdistanced by his panic. In seconds, Scott saw account names, one of which was an offshore account. Critchlow needed to call people, or have people call people to warn them. He knew on the surface that the accounts looked legitimate, but his people needed to somehow destroy the links to the houses and facilities or everything would go up in flames.

"Okay, Mr. Critchlow," Scott said as he stood to leave. "The government will consider your answers and decide whether or not you have anything to offer us in return for a plea deal."

"And what would that deal involve, exactly?" Dorius asked.

"I'm not at liberty to say at this point."

"I've already told you," Critchlow said, "I had nothing to do with the production of those movies. I just buy and sell. I'm sure I don't need to tell you that there's big money in that."

"Do you use your company to launder the money you get from those sales?" Scott asked. "Or do you maybe have another subsidiary we need to look at that makes its money from the distribution of more legitimate movies?"

Dorius vehemently shook his head. Critchlow had nothing more to say.

Chapter 33
Building a Case

Howard had a huge grin on his face when the deputy escorted Scott back into the hidden portion of the interrogation room. "That was awesome!" he said. "We had no intention whatsoever of offering him a plea deal, but I think that helped soften him up."

"I told you I might have to wing it," Scott said. "I trust I covered all the questions you wanted me to ask?"

"Yes. But right now, we're all dying to find out what you heard that we didn't."

"The hottest thing right now," Scott said, "is finding his movie production facility before they shut it down and move the victims."

As Scott expected, there was an immediate reaction from the people in the room.

"I saw a multi-story building in his thoughts where some of the underage victims are being held," Scott continued, "and where the movies are being produced. I didn't see an address, or even a reference to a city or state, so that might be tough. I'd follow the money trail if I were you. I know I touched a major nerve when I mentioned the money. You might be able to find a list of the buildings he owns or leases. The building I saw looked more like an apartment complex than a business building."

Howard pointed at a member of his team. The woman nodded and hurried out of the room.

"I'd also try to monitor his attorney's phone if you can," Scott said. "Critchlow can't call and warn the rest of his organization from jail, so he'll have to have somebody else do it. You're probably going to find out that his attorney has been with him for a good long time. For all we know, he may be personally involved. They're going to want to call a few people and tell them to start hiding stuff. You may want to keep track of his auto parts trucks, especially semi-trucks. He very well may be using them to transport the equipment and the victims. The next thing you need to do is get a search warrant for Critchlow's Mercedes. He ordered the murder of Nancy Bennion."

Scott recounted the details of Nancy's murder as he'd seen them in Critchlow's thoughts. "From the bruising and the cut I saw over her eye," he continued, "she may have left some blood evidence in his car. I don't know if you've got any evidence out of his penthouse apartment or not, but I know he was using the private elevator to take the kids up to the penthouse, where he used them to entertain his 'guests.' I don't know if the men he invited were business associates or simply people he was trying to sell his movies to, but there were a lot of them. If I have a little time and access to a good sketch artist, I can probably come up with drawings of around eight or more adults. The ones I saw in his thoughts were probably regular customers."

Scott paused to collect his thoughts and then went on. "When I mentioned the money laundering, I thought he was going to start screaming obscenities. I think I hit the nail on the head when I accused him of laundering the video revenue through his car parts business. It must be big money, or he wouldn't have freaked out about it. I think a good financial audit will probably find that money trail—not only from the customer sales but also to the people he was paying to keep track of the victims and produce the movies."

"We never discussed a plea deal," Howard said. "How did you think to offer that up?"

"I picked that up from his attorney, actually," Scott said. "I don't know if you noticed or not, but they were well rehearsed when I asked about what auto parts business they could possibly be carrying on in a penthouse."

"I think I'm going to have a follow-on chat with Critchlow's attorney," Howard said. "Under the circumstances, we might actually consider offering him some sort of deal if we could get a list of his movie customers. I'm thinking those customers weren't dealing in a few DVDs at a time. I'm betting the ones that came to the penthouse were buying them by the case."

"He got really nervous when I asked about those names," Scott said. "When he indicated that some of them were powerful individuals, I had the feeling he wasn't talking so much about politicians or big businessmen as he was organized crime people. Why else would he be worried for his life?"

"Speaking of that," Howard said, "I wish you hadn't used your new name when you introduced yourself. Nobody was going to ask you for I.D., and quite frankly, that identity cost the Bureau a lot of money. I don't think it'll take them long, once we start moving on everything else you've told us today, to figure out that you weren't who you were masquerading to be."

"I feel bad about that," Scott said. "But I assumed that because I was involved in the identification and arrest of Vince, my identity was probably compromised anyway."

"You may be right. We'll talk more about that later."

Howard turned to the rest of his team and spent about ten minutes brainstorming with them. Scott took a seat and listened quietly, responding only when asked a specific question. During the session, Howard handed out several assignments.

After the last agent left the room, Howard turned to Scott. "On another matter, when I spoke to LuAnn earlier today, she said she'd already told you we're putting together a proposal to recruit you to work for us. Have you given that any thought?"

"Some," Scott said, "but my whole life just got dumped in the gutter. I can't make a decision like that right now. I'm having a hard time believing they murdered my whole family just so I'd come back to Omaha. I was secretly hoping I'd find out that Critchlow had ordered the hit."

"And if you had?"

Scott hesitated. He almost showed his weapon to Howard but chose at the last second to keep that a secret. "I'd have probably used that metal chair I was sitting on to bash his brains out."

Howard smiled. "Those are big words coming from a man with a glass cranium, but I honestly know how you feel. After digging up victims in Kansas and meeting a few of their parents, I don't think I could sit across the table from that creep and hear what he was thinking without strangling the life out of him."

"Speaking of Kansas," Scott said after a moment, "what happens if you can link one of those kids to the videos you found in his house?"

"Nothing, unless we can find his production facilities and prove he's been paying the production studio. If we can make that link, we may be able to charge him as an accessory to murder—in Kansas, no less—and possibly give him the death penalty that we took off the table to get Ralph to talk."

"Has anybody questioned Vince yet?"

"No, not yet," Howard said. "Until now, we didn't have a reason to. We found enough evidence in the remains of that car—the shovel, Nancy's body, and his knife—to convict him. That's an interesting thought, though. He clearly did the deed, but we might be able to offer him something in return for his sworn testimony against Critchlow."

"If he lives that long," Scott said. "I've had the distinct feeling ever since I got him busted in Jersey that somebody needs to eliminate either him or me. And after talking to Critchlow, I'm almost sure it was him."

Now he had Howard's undivided attention. "I believe Critchlow is the one who ordered the hits on Detective Ableman and his accomplice," Scott said. "As well as on Eric, Blake, and Milt. I think all of them were involved in some way or another in his trafficking and porn business. When he heard about me, he couldn't risk having me talk to any of them. It's a good thing he doesn't know who I am. What he doesn't know is that his own thoughts fingered him in Nancy's death. I'm sure he still thinks that if I get to Vince before he does, DeLuca will give him up."

"We've been working under that same premise," Howard said. "That's why we've got Vince in the custody of the U.S. Marshals. It's aggravating as hell having a leak in our Omaha office right now. If whoever that is gets wind of what we're doing, there's going to be a lot of evidence disappearing at the blinding speed of light. And it could very well compromise your safety."

"I thought you already knew who your leak was, and that's why LuAnn did that evasive thing in the parking garage when you sent me to New Jersey."

"We've busted one guy, but we think he may have had accomplices. We've got Internal Affairs looking into it. They told us to butt out and let them do their thing. I did my best to let them know how important it is that we stop that leak immediately, but I think my pleas fell on deaf ears."

"So what's next for me?"

"You'll be going back to the safe house in Fremont. I think you need some down time. LuAnn will be in touch."

"I wish I could dress up in a clever disguise and attend my family's funeral tomorrow," Scott said hopefully.

"There's not a chance in hell of you doing that," Howard said. "Nobody on my team knows this, but we've got a little something up our sleeves in that regard."

"Why would you keep something like that from your team? Don't you trust them?"

"Because they don't have the need to know," Howard said. "When LuAnn told you we've got the funeral covered, that was a big understatement. If things go the way I think they might, we'll not only get your funeral videos, but we might also get another one of Critchlow's players."

"Do you think when you do, you might find out he's the one who poisoned my wife and kids?"

"I simply don't know that. We'll be using a decoy to stand in as you. If there's an attempt made, we may not even catch the perp. I seriously doubt they'll have someone come at you out of the procession. We're watching for snipers. Critchlow can't afford to have us tag another one of his people."

* * * * *

Scott got a ride back to Fremont in a certain hopped-up Mustang. When he told LuAnn about the funeral decoy, she seemed surprised.

"Sometimes I hate being the go-to girl in personal protection," she said. "I miss out on everything else."

"Sorry," Scott said. "I just assumed that when Howard told me you had the funeral covered, you knew about the decoy."

"He asked me to arrange for pictures and video. I assumed that was all for you. I didn't know he had a plant. I'm not on his immediate staff. I'm a resource. What I get is on a need-to-know basis, as it should be. That's how you reduce your exposure."

She was quiet for a few moments before she continued. "Take this thing with the funeral tomorrow, for example. The fewer people who know we're sending in a decoy, the more probability it has of success. If our leak finds out there's a plant, the bad guys won't show up. If, on the other hand, our potential leak is fed just enough information to know that you might be there, the decoy thing might work."

She nervously watched the rearview mirror as they wound their way around on the narrow back streets of Fremont.

"I thought this was a safe house," Scott said after watching her for a few minutes.

"It is, and we want to keep it that way."

"Yet you had a couple of marshals pick me up. Wasn't that a little foolish?"

"We have to trust someone. I can't be your personal chauffer. It may not seem like it, but I have a life."

"I heard one of your daughters when we were talking on the phone this morning."

"Sorry, that was probably cruel. I should have stepped outside."

"I've got to deal with it sooner or later."

"I'm sorry anyway."

"I'm so pissed off that I'm having a hard time seeing the remorse."

"You need to grieve and let us deal with the vengeance," LuAnn said.

"I can't do that. I'm too wrapped up in all this. I never wanted to kill anybody before, but I think I could now."

"If you do, you'll end up in Warden Bruce's prison. The law pardons self-defense. It frowns on revenge."

* * * * *

After LuAnn dropped him off at the safe house, Scott tried his best to simply sit in front of the television and relax, but there were too many things rumbling around in his mind. He decided to investigate the tiny old house. There was no cellar. Then he remembered crossing the Platte River on the way out of town and wondered if they often had floods here.

There were two tiny bedrooms at the back of the house that barely had room for double beds. The room with the armoire for his clothes was an even tighter fit. There were no closets. There was an ancient clawfoot tub in the bathroom with a shower curtain that circled it. Everything in the house was ancient. Nothing was antique—it was just old, musty, grimy, and heavily used. It was a far cry from the other safe house, but then it probably didn't get much use. He wondered if anyone besides the people who lived in town even knew where Fremont, Nebraska, was.

As darkness closed in around him, the house seemed to shrink even more. Except for the living room, every other light fixture in the house consisted of a bare bulb hanging from a fiber-covered cord. A dusty five-bulb chandelier hung in the center of the living room. Two lamps, set on tiny battered lamp tables, stood against the wall on opposite sides of the front door. Heavy beige curtains hung over the two tall windows that flanked the door. The only modern feature in the house seemed to be the shiny door handle and deadbolt lock on the solid six-panel front door.

Although he still walked with a limp from his new knee, Scott decided he needed a walk and some fresh air. Not knowing what sort of neighborhood they'd plunked him down in, he decided to slip out the back door instead of making a spectacle of himself under the front yard light. The crisp night air sent him back inside for his jacket. As an afterthought, he grabbed his handgun.

There were no fences defining the property lines between the cramped houses, so he walked through several back yards, finally finding himself on the narrow sidewalk of a side street. He turned down the walkway and poked along. He was certainly in no hurry, and for the first time in weeks, he felt somewhat at ease.

He winced when he thought about his family's funeral, now only a few hours away. There would be extended family there, and they'd undoubtedly wonder where he was. Mary's mother knew they'd divorced, but she would think he was a jerk for not showing up. He knew nobody would explain why he hadn't.

Scott knew Alan would be there, and that didn't bring him any pleasure either. He'd meant it when he told Mary the affair hadn't been her fault. She'd been vulnerable, but Alan . . . well, in simple terms, Alan had taken advantage of her. He doubted his partner had had any intent whatsoever of leaving his wife for Mary.

When the side street came to an intersection, there was more traffic. Scott turned to the right and followed the busy street for a few blocks. Then, suddenly, he could smell coffee. It seemed to be too strong to be coming from a house, so he stopped and looked around him. A small business district lined the far side of the street. The neon lights of Lavern's Bar and Grill welcomed him.

The place was busy. When Scott walked through the door, there were no empty tables. He claimed one of the two empty swivel seats at the bar near the door, and a bartender immediately materialized in front of him.

"What'll it be?" the bartender asked.

"I'd love a beer, but I'm a recovering alcoholic," Scott lied, "so if you don't mind, I'll just have a stiff cup of coffee and whatever Danish you might still have this late."

"The coffee I can do," the bartender said, "but the closest thing I've got to Danish is fresh peach pie."

"I'd love that," Scott said.

As the bartender walked away to fill his order, Scott looked over the patrons. They were all involved with their own little circles, and nobody was looking at him. A couple of young waitresses scurried among them. He remembered LuAnn telling him that there was a university in town. The waitresses were probably students. The rest of the customers were a motley bunch. There were a couple of cowboy hats, a few ball caps, a lot of bare heads, and a few bald ones. Scott felt at home here.

Then he felt Nancy. She wasn't calm. He instantly felt the tension. Maybe he'd missed something. He looked around the bar again. Nobody seemed to have noticed him.

His pie and coffee came. and even though he thoroughly enjoyed them both, he couldn't push off the tension. He felt like screaming at the ghost. Why wouldn't she just leave him alone? He'd done everything he could. What more did she want? Finished, he paid the tab and left.

Outside, the temperature seemed to have dropped ten degrees. He didn't know if it actually had, or if the body heat in the small bar had just made it seem that way. He zipped up his light jacket to his chin, thrust his hands in his pockets, and walked to the corner where he could cross the street on a green light. He could see his breath when he exhaled.

Scott had forgotten how many blocks he'd walked to get to the bar, but he knew the street name he was looking for, so he walked on. Nancy wouldn't leave him alone. He saw no visions. No thoughts popped into his mind. And yet she was still with him.

"Look, Nancy," Scott said aloud, "I don't know why you won't quit bothering me, but there's nothing more I can do for you. I don't know if you know what's going on in your little ghost world, but my life here is a wreck. My family is dead, thanks to you. I'm in hiding, thanks to you. I'm cold, and I'm lonely, and I don't need an apparition following me around. Why don't you go bug Vince or Critchlow? Scream at them in their sleep. Haunt them. Throw shit at them. Make their lives a living hell. But give me a break. I'm trying to help here, so why can't you just leave me the hell alone?"

She didn't leave. In fact, the tension he felt only escalated. He looked up and spotted the street sign. His safe house was only four doors away. Suddenly, he knew he couldn't walk down the sidewalk. He retraced his steps a hundred feet or so and then began walking through the back yards.

He paused near the back corner of the house just west of the safe house and peered around it into the street. There were several cars parked along one side of the narrow tree-lined road. He tried to remember which ones had been there when he left.

Just as he thought that was probably a futile exercise, he spotted the dark sedan. It was parked three houses away. It didn't blend into the neighborhood. It was too dark to see if there was anyone sitting inside. A car drove past, its lights illuminating the dark car, displaying its black-tinted windows.

An eerie feeling coursed down Scott's spine. He couldn't tell if what he was feeling was still Nancy, or if his own premonitions were acting up. He couldn't decide whether to turn around and leave or enter his house through the back door. Then, just as he made up his mind and took a step forward, the driver's-side door on the dark car opened and a large figure stepped out.

Scott quickly pulled his foot back and pressed himself against the house, peering around the edge. The dark figure walked briskly across the street and paused alongside a tree trunk a couple of houses down. Scott crouched low until his head was only a couple of feet off the ground. He slowly reached into his waistband and pulled his pistol free.

The figure moved briskly and approached the back door of the safe house. From his walk and his stature, Scott could see it was a large man, but nobody he could recognize in the dark.

The man looked around. Seeing no one, he reached into the pocket of his jacket. Scott heard the jingle of keys as the man lifted his hand to the lock on the back door. He only tried one key. It fit. He turned the lock and opened the door.

Scott knew he had found the agency's leak. Who else would know where the safe house was? Who else would have a key for the back door? Moving quickly, Scott stepped backwards out of sight, pulled his cell phone out of his shirt pocket, silenced the ringer, and sent LuAnn a text. Then he peeked back around the corner. The back door of the safe house was closed.

Scott couldn't see any lights on inside, then realized he probably wouldn't, even if the man flipped on every light in the house. The heavy draperies over the windows would effectively block any light coming from inside.

His phone vibrated. It was LuAnn. She told him to get away from the house and find someplace to go where she could pick him up.

Scott nearly turned to leave, then stopped when a thought came to him. It was not his own.

Obeying the thought as if it were a command, he hurried east across two more back yards until he could see the dark car parked at the curb out front. He scurried through the dark and stopped alongside a tree in the front yard. Then he nearly panicked. What if the stranger wasn't alone? What if there was someone else waiting in the car? With the windows being tinted the way they were, he had no way of telling.

At that moment, another strange thought entered his mind. He instantly obeyed, crossed the street, and stood behind the sedan. He read the license plate, typed it into a text message to LuAnn, and pressed "send." Instead of crossing back over the street again, he turned and walked back in the direction of Lavern's Bar and Grill.

LuAnn's next text was not brief. He needed to stay out of sight at all costs. The dark car the stranger was driving belonged to one of their agents. He answered with another brief text that simply gave the name and address of the bar. He sent one final message: "I'll be watching. You'd better be in the Mustang."

Scott waited on the curb outside of Lavern's for twenty minutes before deciding it would be safer inside. LuAnn would be coming from Omaha, and that was at least forty-five minutes away. When he walked back through the door of the tavern, a look of surprise crossed the bartender's face.

"Change your mind about the beer?" the bartender laughed.

"No, but now that I've had my dessert, maybe I'll have a burger."

"We've got a special going on our grilled pork chops. They're a lot better than the burger anyway."

Scott sat down at one of the empty barstools and smiled. "Make it happen."

The bartender poured Scott a cup of coffee and walked off, leaving him to study the crowd again. The mixture of hats and heads had changed, but the warm feeling inside the place hadn't. When his food arrived, the bartender poured him a fresh cup of coffee and left to take care of his other customers.

Scott was just chewing his last bite when his cell phone buzzed. This time it was a call.

"Where are you?" LuAnn said.

"In Lavern's. I'm just finishing up a great pork chop."

"I'm parked at the curb three buildings down. Pay up and get out here. Things are happening fast."

Scott hailed the bartender, dropped a twenty on the bar, and hurried out the door.

"You're early," Scott said as he climbed into the Mustang and buckled his seatbelt.

"I didn't spare the ponies," LuAnn said with a wry grin. "I had an escort with lights. It was pretty fun."

"What escort?"

"Four U.S. marshals in trucks. They should be at the safe house as we speak, and with any kind of luck, we just plugged our leak."

"Are we going there?"

"Nope. My orders are to get you back to Omaha posthaste. If we want to know what's happening, we can listen to the two-way."

"Why Omaha? Have you got another safe house?"

"We're running out of them. No, this is better. You'll be under twenty-four-hour guard for the time being."

"Why do I have to go to jail? I'm not the bad guy here."

"It's not jail. It's just a place we have. It'll be comfortable, you just won't be able to leave."

"I won't have a thing to wear," Scott said with a smile. "All my luggage is back at the house."

LuAnn grinned. "You know, you're beginning to sound like an old woman." She picked up her phone and made a call to have Scott's clothes picked up. When she hung up, she regarded Scott with a curious expression. "Why were you out of the house? Not saying it wasn't a stellar idea, but why?"

"It's a long story," Scott said evasively.

"We've got forty minutes. That should be enough time."

When he finished a brief version of his story, LuAnn stared at him, dumbstruck. "How much better can it get than that?" she said. "You can read minds, and now you've got a ghost on your side who seems to know everything."

"I had a little angry conversation with her on my walk back to the house. She may not be interested in helping me anymore."

"Please tell me it was a one-way conversation. If you tell me you're hearing her voice, I'm taking you straight to the psych ward."

"The hell you will. That's where this crap all started. And for the record, no, I don't hear her. I just know when she's there. Occasionally, a thought pops into my mind. She has the ability to do that."

"Either that, or because of your gift you can hear her, even if it's only random thoughts."

"I wouldn't call blazing visions random thoughts."

LuAnn considered what he'd said. "Wow. I wonder how all that works. Do you think if you accept our proposal that we can get her to sign up too?"

"That's not funny. This has ruined my life. I've lost everything, and I'm not happy."

LuAnn was quiet for a while. "Neither are the parents of all those kids," she finally said. "I'm not trying to downplay the horror you've had to live through, but maybe there's a little good news in all this after all."

"What are they going to do with your leak?" Scott asked.

"Haul him back to Omaha for questioning."

"Can I have first crack at him?"

"He's going to lawyer up. He probably knows who you are. He won't allow you to be anywhere near him. What did you have in mind?"

"Call your marshal buddies and have them take him back to the safe house. There should be enough muscle in the room to keep me safe. I, for one, would love to know who sent him. He might even be able to tell us who murdered my family and what they have planned for the funeral."

LuAnn pulled over to the side of the road and got on the phone. Five minutes later, they were on their way back to Fremont.

A man Scott had never seen was sitting on a chair in the kitchen of the safe house with his hands and feet handcuffed. Four men in U.S. Marshals jackets were standing around him. A short piece of chain connected two cuffs together in front of the man so even if he got out of the chair, he couldn't stand erect.

All eyes turned to Scott as LuAnn escorted him through the front door.

"We've never formally been introduced," Scott said as he approached the man. "I'm Scott Corbridge. You may know me by reputation, though. I thought it might be nice if we had a little chat. Do you mind?"

The man glared at him but said nothing.

"Okay, let's start with the simple stuff. What's your name, and what do you do for a living?"

Again, silence.

Scott looked back over his shoulder at LuAnn. "Is somebody going to take notes, or do I have to remember all of this shit?"

A marshal produced a notebook and pen from a flap pocket in his jacket.

"For the record," Scott said, "this is Craig Spackman. He works for the Bureau."

Scott could see the man was terrified.

"See," Scott said, "this is how it works. I ask you a question, then you can either say something, or I'll just talk for you. Either way, before we leave here, we're all going to know a lot about you. If you'd like to spare us the intimate details, you could tell us why you're here tonight, who sent you, and who your contacts are outside of the Bureau. If you do, I may not have to look so deep, and you'll still have a little privacy—at least from the other folks in this room."

Spackman said nothing.

"Okay, then. You found out where they were keeping me by overhearing a conversation about Fremont. You already knew where this safe house was. You made a telephone call." Scott turned to the marshal making notes. "If you check his phone, the last two numbers he dialed will tell you who his contacts are."

The marshal scribbled furiously as Scott turned back to Spackman. "Now, where was I? Oh, yeah. You were just about to tell me why you came here."

He gave Spackman a few seconds to collect his thoughts. The man was trying to think about a family vacation he'd gone on that summer, but in between those thoughts, Scott got what he needed.

"Mr. Spackman is playing mind games with me," Scott continued. "Apparently, he wants me to know all about what he did on his family vacation. Of course, he probably doesn't want us to know he went skinny dipping with his wife, Marjorie, at the lake after all the kids were asleep and made love to her on the beach."

Spackman's mind was squirming.

"I believe you guys found a syringe when you disarmed him," Scott said. "I think you'll find a fatal drug concoction in that syringe that he was supposed to inject me with. Oh yes, and if need be, I can tell you who gave him the drugs. Actually, that's a pretty slick way of killing a person, especially when you don't want a messy crime scene left behind in the safe house. If there weren't signs of a struggle, the agency might have thought I just wandered off. You planned to take my body back to Omaha and turn it over to one of your contacts who would make sure I was never found. Tell me, Craig, what do you know about a reception party your people had set up for me when I showed up at the funeral tomorrow?"

Spackman refused to make eye contact this time. He was hoping that would make a difference. It didn't.

"While we're talking about funerals," Scott said before he told the marshals what he'd found out, "who ordered the hit on my family?"

A name and face popped into Spackman's mind.

"Okay, thanks for that," Scott said. "Who does he work for, and where does he live?"

Scott mentally noted the answers before he turned to the marshal with the notepad.

"There are going to be two people at the funeral," Scott said. "A man and a woman masquerading as a couple. They have photos of me so they won't accidently stick the wrong guy."

He stopped to glare at Spackman. He wanted to shoot him in the top of his bowed head, but he restrained himself.

"Craig here found out something was in the works and gave them my photograph. Both will be armed with syringes like the one you took from him tonight. When they spot me in the crowd, they plan to get close and feign a little argument that will involve some shouting and shoving. Then one or the other will stick me, probably without my even knowing what happened. He doesn't know either of them. They were sent by none other than one of Lyle Critchlow's deputies. Even though Critchlow's in jail, his lawyer is calling the shots."

"You can't prove any of that!" Spackman yelled.

"Right now," Scott said, "proving things in a court of law is the last thing on my mind. I'm here to point people in the right direction. I'm assuming that once the agents know who and what to look for, they'll be able to come up with all the evidence they need. Oh, while I'm thinking about it, do you know where Critchlow's movie production facilities are?"

Scott gave him a few seconds to try to hide his thoughts. He did know where it was. He'd been there. In fact, he'd even starred in a couple of the movies. That's how Critchlow's team had recruited him.

Scott turned to LuAnn. "You'd better call Howard. I know where the building is, and I know why Craig here turned to the dark side. They need to hit that facility tonight. Thanks to Craig, they know the Bureau is looking for it. They're already moving the kids."

Spackman was staring at his feet.

"What is your wife going to say when she finds out what you've been up to?" Scott asked him.

The man was seething inside. Scott turned to LuAnn. "Tell Howard that when his people are reviewing those movies looking for lost children, they should watch for Craig. It seems he's a movie star."

Chapter 34
The Aftermath

Scott watched the funeral on a big-screen TV in a hotel room five stories above an Omaha street. The Bureau had arranged to stream it to him live. There were two heavily armed guards assigned to him—one inside his room, the other outside the door. From the moment the live views of the four open caskets reached him, he lost his composure and collapsed in a sobbing fetal position on the floor.

All the stress, anguish, loss, and vile hatred for the man who had murdered his family fueled his breakdown. He wanted to watch the screen. He *needed* to watch the screen. But he simply couldn't look up. He writhed on the floor, he cried, he groaned in agony. He was only vaguely aware that the guard inside his room had slipped out into the hallway to give him his privacy.

Scott eventually sat up and rested against the foot of the bed and watched as the two cameras scanned the proceedings. Mary's mom and dad were there, as were her two sisters. They sat on the front row in the chapel, holding handkerchiefs to their faces, listening as Scott's father delivered the eulogy.

As the cameras scanned the crowd, he saw others—family, friends, acquaintances. All had come to pay their respects. And all wondered, no doubt, why Scott wasn't there.

Then he heard his father say the words that had undoubtedly been planted by the feds. "I just received word this morning that my son, Scott, father and husband of this little family lying here before us, was found murdered last night."

Audible gasps erupted from the crowd.

"I don't know any of the details. I only know that soon we will lay his body alongside his loved ones. I believe that in spite of the tragedy of this day, Scott and his family are with God and holding each other in a joyful reunion."

Scott was livid. How dare they make that move without his permission! Then a calmness settled over him. What they had done was good. They told him that going into the Witness Protection Program was like dying. Now they had made that happen. Now he was dead to all of his family, friends, and acquaintances. The FBI snitch, the four marshals, and a few other feds were the only ones who knew the truth.

His thoughts ran rampant as the scene moved from the chapel to the cemetery. He knew who had killed them. He had never met the man, but he knew his name and his face. He knew where the man lived, and he knew who had sent him. He would kill them both, by himself. But not yet. He needed time to unlock their minds first. There was so much more to be learned from them both. All the feds needed to do was know what questions to ask the men—in Scott's presence, of course.

Scott Corbridge was dead. His own father believed that. Matthew Rollins, on the other hand, was still very much alive, and he was determined to get his revenge.

He considered the logistics of what he had decided to do. On the one hand, he wanted more than anything else to have the satisfaction of pulling the trigger. The problem was, he knew he would never have unguarded access to Critchlow like he had the first time. The man would probably never see the light of day again. Scott would never be allowed to carry a weapon when he saw him next. Scott hated the thought, but he would have to settle for only one of the two: the actual murderer. He would bide his time, waiting for the first opportunity to get away from the feds just long enough to make the drive.

Then he felt Nancy, and a few words drifted through his mind. *Vengeance is mine, sayeth the Lord God.*

He thought about that for a long time. He could think of little else as the video of his family's funeral played out before him. He had a gift. He'd had it all his life, in a lesser form. Had it come from God?

He thought of all the parents who had lost children to the acts of evil men. Had someone been preparing Scott for this mission all his life? He recalled his early prophetic dreams. They hadn't been the product of a car wreck.

The good book said *God acts in mysterious ways.* Had he simply become one of God's tools? He liked the thought. It didn't make up for the loss of his family, but what about the losses of others? He remembered Fran from the bus. She'd lost everything. Scott wasn't the first to lose everything, and he would not be the last. As long as there was greed, lust, and hatred, there would be victims.

The video ended. The TV screen went blank. His telephone

buzzed.

"Matt?" LuAnn asked.

"Speaking."

"Did you see the funeral?"

"I did," he said. "Thank you."

"Things are happening."

"I heard what my dad said. I have to assume that came from you?"

"Not me, personally, but yes. My boss took a chance and decided to act."

"I suppose I should be angry, but the words were true. Scott Corbridge really is dead. At least to the world as I once knew it."

"I'm sorry," LuAnn said softly.

"Yeah, me too. I'm sorry about a lot of things."

"We should meet. Like I told you, things are happening."

"I need some time. Maybe I don't have the need to know."

"I understand."

The words he'd just heard from Nancy drifted through his mind again, and he made a decision.

"I need to give you something. Do you think you could drop by?"

* * * * *

A short while later, a soft knock sounded on his door. He turned the handle on the deadbolt. LuAnn stood in the hallway, flanked by his personal bodyguards.

"If it's okay with you guys," Scott told them, "I'd like to have a few minutes alone with her."

They nodded, and LuAnn stepped into the room, closing the door behind her. She handed Scott an eight-by-ten manila envelope.

"That's your passport," she said, "a boarding pass, a credit card, a little cash, an itinerary, and a few brochures. We booked you for a couple of weeks in Mazatlán. Your flight leaves at six. We figured you might need some down time, and frankly, we need to get you out of here until we can process everything you've given us."

He took the envelope but didn't open it.

"There's also a copy of a proposal in there. We'd like to have you work for us. That's another reason we're giving you some down time. We don't want an answer right away. We want you to have a little time to think about it."

Scott wanted to read her thoughts, but he had too many of his own.

"You said you had something for me?" LuAnn asked.

Scott reached behind his back and drew the pistol out of his waistband. A look of alarm spread over LuAnn's face.

"Have you had that all this time?" she asked.

"Ever since I came back from New Jersey. I know who killed my family."

Along with the pistol, he handed her a sheet of hotel stationery with a name and address scrawled on it.

"Until a little while ago," Scott said, "I was convinced I was going to go find him myself."

LuAnn took the weapon, dropped the loaded magazine out, and racked the slide. A live round fell to the carpet.

She picked up the bullet and put the gun into her handbag. "What changed your mind?" she asked, reading what he'd written on the sheet of stationery.

"That's a story for another day. Maybe we'll talk when I get back from Mexico. Speaking of that, where *do* I go when I get back?"

"I'll call you before you come home," LuAnn said. "We need some time to figure out where we are. We may change your ticket to another location."

He was finally able to read her thoughts. He held out his arms, and she stepped forward. Their embrace was one of kinship, sorrow, and mutual respect.

"Thanks," Scott said as he released her and looked into her eyes. "I really needed that."

About the Author

Michel (Mike) Nelson was born and raised on a farm in Northern Utah. He enjoys most things out-of-doors. He served four years with the U.S. Air Force in the early 70s, where he spent most of his time overseas in communications intelligence. He is the father of six children and has been married to his wife Donnell for nearly fifty years.

Mike graduated from Weber State University in accounting and worked as a cost analyst for an aerospace firm for thirty-eight years before retiring in 2014. He started writing for "wintertime" entertainment and relaxation after being encouraged by an excellent English literature teacher in college.

Writing has always been one of Mike's many hobbies, but after the positive response to his first published novels, *Thorns of Avarice* and *Treehouse in the Hood*, writing has quickly become his favorite pastime. *Clairvoyant* is his third novel.

About the Publisher

Glass Spider Publishing is a hybrid publisher located in Ogden, Utah. The company was founded in 2016 by writer Vince Font to help authors get their works into shape, into print, and into distribution. Visit www.glassspiderpublishing.com to learn more.

 GLASS**SPIDER**PUBLISHING

92773914R00195

Made in the USA
Columbia, SC
01 April 2018